"We have challenges in front of us. I'd like to focus on them without...complications."

That part wasn't the whole truth, but it was certainly true enough.

It didn't matter. No more kissing. That was the rule and she was sticking to it.

"Caitlyn. You focus on your challenges your way, and I'll focus on my challenges my way."

"What's that supposed to mean?" she whispered, afraid she wasn't going to like the answer.

Antonio looked at her. "It means I'm going to kiss you again. You'd best think of another argument if you don't want me to."

* * *

Triplets Under the Tree is part of Harlequin Desire's #1 bestselling series, Billionaires and Babies: Powerful men... wrapped around their babies' little fingers.

Dear Reader,

This book holds a special place in my heart. I wanted to write a story about the fascinating world of mixed martial arts and my editor gave me the idea to write about triplets. But I had no idea when I started out that this book would turn into such an emotional and ultimately uplifting tale about finding your place in the world after horrific loss.

Antonio Cavallari is one of those guys who seemingly has it all until fate tests his mettle by taking away everything he knows about himself and where he belongs. Amnesia prevents him from remembering his late wife, his children, his mixed martial arts empire—even who he is at his core. Caitlyn Hopewell is his one ray of light in the darkness, which he desperately needs. But like a ticking time bomb, his memory holds secrets that will tear her from his arms.

I loved writing this Billionaires and Babies story about a man discovering he has kids, but as my readers know, I always do it with a twist. I hope you enjoy reading about Antonio and Caitlyn as they unwrap the most unexpected Christmas present—a new start with a new family.

Happy reading! Visit me online at katcantrell.com.

Kat Cantrell

TRIPLETS UNDER THE TREE

KAT CANTRELL

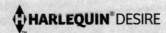

Recycling programs for this product may not exist in your area.

ISBN-13: 978-0-373-73427-6

Triplets Under the Tree

Copyright © 2015 by Kat Cantrell

This edition published by arrangement with Harlequin Books S.A.

For questions and comments about the quality of this book, please contact us at CustomerService@Harlequin.com.

Printed in U.S.A.

Kat Cantrell read her first Harlequin novel in third grade and has been scribbling in notebooks since she learned to spell. What else would she write but romance? She majored in literature, officially with the intent to teach, but somehow ended up buried in middle management in corporate America, until she became a stay-at-home mom and full-time writer.

Kat, her husband and their two boys live in north Texas. When she's not writing about characters on the journey to happily-ever-after, she can be found at a soccer game, watching the TV show *Friends* or listening to '80s music.

Kat was the 2011 Harlequin So You Think You Can Write contest winner and a 2012 RWA Golden Heart Award finalist for best unpublished series contemporary manuscript.

Books by Kat Cantrell

Harlequin Desire

Marriage with Benefits
The Things She Says
The Baby Deal
Pregnant by Morning
The Princess and the Player
Triplets Under the Tree

Happily Ever After, Inc.

Matched to a Billionaire
Matched to a Prince
Matched to Her Rival

Newlywed Games

From Ex to Eternity
From Fake to Forever

To Diane Spigonardo.
Thanks for the inspiration.

Prologue

Near Punggur Besar, Batam Island, Indonesia

Automatically, Falco swung his arm in an arc to block the punch. He hadn't seen it coming. But a sense he couldn't explain told him to expect his opponent's attack.

Counterpunch. His opponent's head snapped backward. *No mercy.* Flesh smacked flesh again and again, rhythmically.

The moves came to him fluidly, without thought. He'd been learning from Wilipo for only a few months, but Falco's muscles already sang with expertise, adopting the techniques easily.

His opponent, Ravi, attacked yet again. Falco ducked and spun to avoid the hit. His right leg ached with the effort, but he ignored it. It always ached where the bone had broken.

From his spot on the sidelines of the dirt-floored ring,

Wilipo grunted. The sound meant more footwork, less jabbing.

Wilipo spoke no English and Falco had learned but a handful of words in Bahasa since becoming a student of the sole martial arts master in southern Batam Island. Their communication during training sessions consisted of nods and gestures. A blessing, considering Falco had little to say.

The stench of old fish rent the air, more pungent today with the heat. Gazes locked, Falco and Ravi circled each other. The younger man from a neighboring village had become Falco's sparring partner a week ago after he'd run out of opponents in his own village. The locals whispered about him and he didn't need to speak Bahasa to understand they feared him.

He wanted to tell them not to be afraid. But he knew he was more than a strange Westerner in an Asian village full of simple people. More than a man with dangerous fists.

Nearly four seasons ago, a fisherman had found Falco floating in the water, unconscious, with horrific injuries. At least that was what he'd pieced together from the doctor's halting, limited English.

He should have died before he'd washed ashore in Indonesia and he certainly should have died at some point during the six-month coma his body had required to heal.

But he'd lived.

And when he finally awoke, it was to a nightmare of physical rehabilitation and confusion. His memories were fleeting. Insubstantial. Incomplete. He was the man with no past, no home, no idea who he was other than angry and lost.

The only clue to his identity lay inked across his left pectoral muscle—a fierce, bold falcon tattoo with a scarlet banner clutched in his talons, emblazoned with the word *Falco*.

That was what his saviors called him since he didn't remember his name, though it chafed to be addressed as such.

Why? It must be a part of his identity. But when he pushed his memory, it only resulted in his fists primed to punch something and a blinding headache. Every waking moment—and even some of those dedicated to sleep—he heard an urgent soul-deep cry to discover why he'd been snatched from the teeth of a cruel death. Surely he'd lived for a reason. Surely he'd remember something critical to set him on the path toward who he was. Every day thus far had ended in disappointment.

Only fighting allowed him moments of peace and clarity as he disciplined his mind to focus on something other than the struggle to remember.

Ravi and Wilipo spoke in rapid Bahasa, leaving the Westerner out of it, as always.

Wilipo grunted again.

That meant it was time to stop sparring. Nodding, Falco halted, breathing heavily. Ravi's reflexes were not as instantaneous and his fist clipped Falco.

Pain exploded in his head. *"Che diavolo!"*

The curse had spit from his mouth the moment Ravi struck, though Falco had no conscious knowledge of Italian. Or how he knew it was Italian. The intrigue saved Ravi from being pulverized.

Ravi bowed apologetically, dropping his hands to his sides. Rubbing his temples, Falco scowled over the late shot as a flash of memory spilled into his head.

White stucco. Glass. A house perched on a cliff, overlooking the ocean. *Malibu.* A warm breeze. A woman with red hair.

His house. He had a home, full of his things, his memories, his life.

The address scrolled through his mind as if it had always been there, along with images of street signs and impressions of direction, and he knew he could find it.

Home. He had to get there. Somehow.

One

At precisely 4:47 a.m., Caitlyn bolted awake, as she did every morning. The babies had started sleeping through the night, thank the good Lord, but despite that, their feeding time had ingrained itself into her body in some kind of whacked-out mommy alarm clock.

No one had warned her of that. Just as no one had warned her that triplets weren't three times the effort and nail-biting worry of one baby, but more like a zillion times.

But they also came with a zillion times the awe and adoration.

Caitlyn picked up the video monitor from her nightstand and watched her darlings sleep in their individual cribs. Antonio Junior sighed and flopped a fist back and forth as if he knew his mother was watching, but Leon and Annabelle slept like rocks. It was a genetic trait they shared with Vanessa, their biological mother, along with her red hair. Antonio had hair the color of a starless night, like his father.

And if he grew up to be half as hypnotically gorgeous as his father, she'd be beating the women off her son with a Louisville Slugger.

No matter how hard she tried, Caitlyn couldn't go back to sleep. Exhaustion was a condition she'd learned to live with and, maddeningly, it had nothing to do with how much sleep she got. Having fatherless eight-month-old triplets wreaked havoc on her sanity, and in the hours before dawn, all the questions and doubts and fears crowded into her mind.

Should she be doing more to meet an eligible man? Like what? Hang out in bars wearing a vomit-stained shirt, where she could chat up a few victims. "Hey, baby, have you ever fantasized about going all night long with triplets? Because I've got a proposition for you!"

No, the eligible men of Los Angeles were pretty safe from Caitlyn Hopewell, that was for sure. Even without the ready-made family, her relationship rules scared away most men: you didn't sleep with a man unless you were in love and there was a ring on your finger. Period. It was an absolute that had carried her through college and into adulthood, especially as she'd witnessed what passed for her sister Vanessa's criteria for getting naked with someone—he'd bought her jewelry or could get her further in her career. Caitlyn didn't want that for herself. And that pretty much guaranteed she'd stay single.

But how could she ever be enough for three children when, no matter how much she loved them, she wasn't supposed to be their mother? When she'd agreed to be Vanessa's surrogate, Caitlyn had planned on a nine-month commitment, not a lifetime. But fate had had different plans.

Caitlyn rolled from the king-size bed she still hadn't

grown used to despite sleeping in it for over a year. Might as well get started on the day at—she squinted at her phone—6:05 a.m. Threading her dark mess of curls through a ponytail holder, she threw on some yoga pants and a top, determined to get in at least twenty minutes of Pilates before Leon awoke.

She spread out her mat on the hardwood floor close to the glass wall overlooking the Malibu coastline, her favorite spot for tranquility. There was a full gym on the first floor of Antonio and Vanessa's mansion, but she couldn't bear to use it. Not yet. It had too much of Antonio stamped all over it, what with the mixed martial arts memorabilia hanging from the walls and the regulation ring in the center.

One day she'd clean it out, but as much as she hated the reminders of Antonio, she couldn't lose the priceless link to him. She hadn't removed any of Vanessa's things from the house, either, but had put a good bit away, where she couldn't see it every day.

Fifteen minutes later, her firstborn yowled through the monitor and Caitlyn dashed to the nursery across the hall from her bedroom before he woke up his brother and sister.

"There's my precious," she crooned and scooped up the gorgeous little bundle from his crib.

Like clockwork, he was always the first of the three to demand breakfast, and Caitlyn tried to spend alone time with each of her kids while feeding them. Brigitte, the babies' au pair, thought she was certifiable for breast-feeding triplets, but Caitlyn didn't mind. She loved bonding with the babies, and nobody ever saw her naked anyway; it was worth the potential hit to her figure to give the babies a leg up in the nutrition department.

The morning passed in a blur of babies and baths, and just as Caitlyn was about to return a phone call to her lawyer that she'd missed somewhere along the way, someone pounded on the front door.

Delivery guy, she hoped. She'd had to order a new car seat and it could not get here fast enough. Annabelle had christened hers in such a way that no bleach in existence could make it usable again and, honestly, Caitlyn had given up trying. There had to be some benefits to having custodial control of her children's billion-dollar inheritance.

"Brigitte? Can you get that?" Caitlyn called, but the girl didn't respond. Probably dealing with one of the kids, which was what she got paid well to do.

With a shrug, Caitlyn pocketed her phone and padded to the door, swinging it wide in full anticipation of a brown uniform–clad man.

It wasn't UPS. The unshaven man on her doorstep loomed over her, his dark gaze searching and familiar. There was something about the way he tilted his head—

"Antonio!" The strangled word barely made it past her throat as it seized up.

No! It couldn't be. Antonio had died in the same plane crash as Vanessa, over a year ago. Her brain fuzzed with disappointment, even as her heart latched on to the idea of her children's father standing before her in the flesh. Lack of sleep was catching up with her.

"Antonio," the man repeated and his eyes widened. "Do I know you?"

His raspy voice washed over her, turning inside her chest warmly, and tears pricked her eyelids. He even sounded like Antonio. She'd always loved his voice. "No, I don't think so. For a moment, I thought you were—"

A ghost. She choked it back.

His blank stare shouldn't have tripped her senses, but all at once, even with a full beard and weighing twenty pounds less, he looked so much like Antonio she couldn't stop greedily drinking him in.

"This is my house," he insisted firmly with a hint of wonderment as he glanced around the foyer beyond the open door. "I recognize it. But the Christmas tree is in the wrong place."

Automatically, she glanced behind her to note the location of the twelve-foot-high blue spruce she'd painstakingly arranged in the living room near the floor-to-ceiling glass wall facing the ocean.

"No, it's not," Caitlyn retorted.

Vanessa had always put the tree in the foyer so people could see it when they came in, but Caitlyn liked it by the sea. Then, every time you looked at the tree, you saw the water, too. Seemed logical to her, and this was her house now.

"I don't remember you." He cocked his head as if puzzled. "Did I sell you this house?"

She shook her head. "I…uh, live here with the owners."

The Malibu mansion was actually part of the babies' estate. She hadn't wanted to move them from their parents' house and, according to the terms of Vanessa's and Antonio's wills, Caitlyn got to make all the decisions for the children.

"I remember a red-haired woman. Beautiful." His expression turned hard and slightly desperate. "Who is she?"

"Vanessa," Caitlyn responded without thinking. She shouldn't be so free with information. "Who are *you*?" she demanded.

"I don't know," he said between clenched teeth. "I remember flashes, incomplete pictures, and none of it makes sense. Tell me who I am."

Oh, my God. "You don't know who you are?" People didn't really get amnesia the way they did in movies. Did they?

Hand to her mouth, she evaluated this dirty, disheveled

man wearing simple cotton pants rolled at the ankles and a torn cotton shirt. It couldn't be true. Antonio was dead.

If Antonio *wasn't* dead, where had he been since the plane crash? If he'd really lost his memory, it could explain why he'd been missing all this time.

But not why he'd suddenly shown up over a year later. Maybe he was one of those con men who preyed on grieving family members, and loss of memory was a convenient out to avoid incriminatory questions that would prove his identity, yet he couldn't answer.

But he'd known the Christmas tree was in the wrong place. What if he was telling the truth?

Her heart latched on to the idea and wouldn't let go.

Because— Oh, goodness. She'd always been half in love with her sister's husband and it all came rushing back. The guilt. The despondency at being passed over for the lush, gorgeous older Hopewell sister, the one who always got everything her heart desired. The covert sidelong glances at Antonio's profile during family dinners. Fantasies about what it would be like if he'd married her instead of Vanessa. The secret thrill at carrying Antonio's babies because Vanessa couldn't, and harboring secret dreams of Antonio falling at her feet, begging Caitlyn to be the mother of his children instead.

Okay, and she'd had a few secret dreams that involved some…carnal scenarios, like how Antonio's skin would feel against hers. What it would be like to kiss him. And love him in every sense of the word.

For the past six years, Caitlyn had lived with an almost biblical sense of shame, in a "thou shalt not covet thy sister's husband" kind of way. But she couldn't help it—Antonio had a wickedly sexy warrior's body and an enigmatic, watchful gaze that sliced through her when he turned it in her direction. Oh, she had it bad, and she'd never fully reconciled because it was intertwined with guilt—maybe she'd wished her sister ill and that was why the plane had crashed.

The guilt crushed down on her anew.

Tersely, he shook his head and that was when she noticed the scar bisecting his temple, which forked up into his dark, shaggy hair. On second thought, this man looked nothing like Antonio. With hard lines around his mouth, he was sharper, more angular, with shadows in his dark eyes that spoke of nightmares better left unexplained.

"I can't remem—you called me Antonio." Something vulnerable welled up in his gaze and then he winced. "Antonio Cavallari. Tell me. Is that my name?"

She hadn't mentioned Antonio's last name.

He could have learned the name of her children's father from anywhere. Los Angeles County tax records. From the millions of internet stories about the death of the former UFC champion and subsequent founder of the billion-dollar enterprise called Falco Fight Club after his career ended. Vanessa had had her own share of fame as an actress, playing the home-wrecking vixen everyone loved to hate on a popular nighttime drama. Her red hair had been part of her trademark look, and when she'd died, the internet had exploded with the news. Her sister's picture popped up now and again even a year later, so knowing about the color of Vanessa's hair wasn't terribly conclusive, either.

He could have pumped the next-door neighbor for information, for that matter.

Caitlyn refused to put her children in danger under any circumstances.

Sweeping him with a glance, she took as much of his measure as she could. But there was no calculation. No suggestion of shrewdness. Just confusion and a hint of the man who'd married her sister six years ago.

"Yes. Antonio Cavallari." Her eyelids fluttered closed for a beat. What if she was wrong? What if she just wanted him to be Antonio for all the wrong reasons and became the victim of an elaborate fraud? Or worse—the victim of assault?

All at once, he sagged against the door frame, babbling in a foreign language. Stricken, she stared at him. She'd never heard Antonio speak anything other than English.

Her stomach clenched. Blood tests. Dental records. Doctors' exams. There had to be a thousand ways to prove someone's identity. But what was she supposed to do? Tell him to come back with proof?

Then his face went white and he pitched to his knees with a feeble curse, landing heavily on the woven welcome mat.

It was a fitting condemnation. Welcoming, she was not.

Throat tight with concern, she blurted out, "Are you okay? What's wrong?"

"Tired. Hungry," he stated simply, eyes closed and head lolling to one side. "I walked from the docks."

"The docks?" Her eyes went wide. "The ones near *Long Beach*? That's, like, fifty miles!"

"No identification," he said hoarsely. "No money."

The man couldn't even stand and, good grief, Caitlyn had certainly spent enough time in the company of actors to spot one—his weakened state was real.

"Come inside," she told him before she thought better of it. "Rest. And drink some water. Then we can sort this out."

It wasn't as if she was alone. Brigitte and Rosa, the housekeeper, were both upstairs. He might be Antonio, but that didn't make him automatically harmless, and who knew what his mental state was? But if he couldn't stand, he couldn't threaten anyone, let alone three women armed with cell phones and easy access to Francesco's top-dollar chef's knives.

He didn't even seem to register that she'd spoken, let

alone acknowledge what he'd surely been after the whole time—an invitation inside. For a man who could be trying to scam her, he certainly wasn't chomping at the bit to gain entrance to her home.

Hesitating, she wondered if she should help him to his feet, but the thought of touching him had her hyperventilating. Either he was a strange man, or he was a most familiar one, and neither one gave her an ounce of comfort. Heat feathered across her cheeks as her chaste sensibilities warred with the practicality of helping someone in need.

He swayed and nearly toppled over, forcing her decision.

No way around it. She knelt and grabbed his arm, then slung it across her shoulders. The weight was strange and, oddly, a little exhilarating. The touch of a man was alien, though, no doubt—she hadn't gone on a date in over two years. Her mind went blank as he slumped against her.

Looping her own arm around his waist, she pushed up with her legs, grateful for the core strength she'd developed through rigorous Pilates, both before and after the babies were born.

Gracious. He smelled like three-day-old fish and other pungencies she hesitated to identify—and she'd have sworn babies produced the worst stench in the world.

The man hobbled along with her across the threshold, thankfully revived enough to do so under his own power. When she paused in front of the pristine eggshell-colored suede sofa in the formal living area, he immediately dropped vertically onto the cushions without hesitation. Groaning, he covered his eyes with his arm.

"Water," he murmured and lay still as death.

And now for the second dilemma. Leave him unattended while she fetched a glassful from the wet bar across the foyer in Antonio's study? It wasn't that far, and she was being silly worrying about a near comatose man posing some sort of threat. She dashed across the marble at breakneck pace, filled the glass at the small stainless-steel sink and dashed back without spilling it, thankfully.

"Here it is," she said to alert him she'd returned.

The arm over his eyes moved up, sweeping the long, shaggy mane away from his forehead. Blearily he peered at her through bloodshot eyes, and without the hair obscuring his face, he looked totally different. Exactly like Antonio, the man she'd secretly studied, pined over, fantasized about for years. She gasped.

"I won't hurt you," he muttered as he sat up, pain etching deeper lines into his face. "Just want water."

She handed it to him, unable to tear her gaze from his face, even as chunks of matted hair fell back over his forehead. Regardless of her immense guilt over his presumed identity, she couldn't go on arguing with herself over it. There was one way to settle this matter right now.

"Do you think you're Antonio?" she asked as he drank deeply from the glass.

"I…" He glanced up at her, his gaze full of emotions she couldn't name, but those dark, mysterious eyes held her captive. "I don't remember. That's why I'm here. I want to know."

"There's one way." Before she lost her courage, she pointed to her chest over her heart as her pulse raced at the promise. "Antonio has a rather elaborate tattoo. Right here. Do you?"

It wouldn't be impossible to replicate. But difficult, as the tattoo had been commissioned by a famous artist who had a unique tribal style.

Without breaking eye contact, he set his water glass on the side table and unbuttoned his shirt to midchest. *Unbuttoned his shirt*, as if they were intimate and she had every right to see him unclothed.

"It says Falco. What does it mean?" he asked.

The truth washed through her even before he drew his

shirt aside to reveal the red-and-black falcon screaming across his pectoral muscle. Her gaze locked on to the ink, registering the chiseled flesh beneath it, and it kicked at her way down low with a long, hot pull, exactly the way she'd always reacted to Antonio.

She blinked and refocused on his face. The sight of his cut, athletic torso—sun browned and more enthralling than she'd ever have expected—wouldn't fade from her mind.

That tattoo had always been an electrifying aspect of his dangerous appeal. And, oh, my—it still was.

"It means that's proof enough for me to know you're Antonio." She shut her eyes, unable to process the relief flooding through his gaze. Unable to process the sharp thrill in her midsection that was wholly erotic…and felt an awful lot like trouble. Stunning, resplendent, *forbidden* Antonio Cavallari was alive. "And we have a lot of hurdles in front of us."

Everything in her world had just slid off a cliff.

The long, legal nightmare of the past year as she'd fought for her right to the babies had been for nothing. Nearly two years ago, she'd signed a surrogacy agreement, but then a year ago Vanessa and Antonio had crashed into the South China Sea. After months of court appearances, a judge had finally overturned the rights she'd signed away and given her full custody of her children.

Oh, dear Lord. This was Antonio's home. It was his money. *Her children were his*. And he had every right to take them away from her.

Two

Antonio—he rolled the name around on his tongue, and it didn't feel wrong like Falco had. Before Indonesia, he'd been called both Antonio and Falco by blurry-faced people, some with cameras, some with serious expressions as they spoke to him about important matters. A crowd had chanted *Falco* like a tribal drum, bouncing off the ceiling of a huge, cavernous arena.

The headache nearly flattened him again, as it always did when he tried too hard to force open his mind.

Instead, he contemplated the blushing, dark-haired and very attractive woman who seemed vaguely familiar but not enough to place her. She didn't belong in his house. She shouldn't be living here, but he had no clue where that sense came from. "What is your name?"

"Caitlyn. Hopewell," she added in what appeared to be an afterthought. "Vanessa is—was—my sister." She eyed him. "You remember Vanessa but not me?"

"The redhead?" At Caitlyn's nod, he frowned.

No, he didn't remember Vanessa, not the way he remembered his house. A woman with flame-colored hair haunted his dreams. Bits and pieces floated through his mind. The images were laced with flashes of her flesh as if he'd often seen her naked, but her face wouldn't quite clarify, as though he'd created an impressionist painting of this woman whose name he couldn't recall.

Frustration rose again. Because how was it fair that he knew exactly what an impressionist painting was but not who *he* was?

After Ravi had knocked loose the memories of his house, Antonio had left Indonesia the next morning, hopping fishing boats and stowing away amidst heavy cargo containers for days and days, all to reach Los Angeles in hopes of regaining more precious links with his past.

This delicate, ethereally beautiful woman—Caitlyn—held a few of these keys, and he needed her to provide them. "Who is Vanessa to me?"

"Your wife," she announced softly. "You didn't know that?"

He shook his head. Married. He was *married* to Vanessa? It was an entire piece of his life, his persona, he'd had no idea existed. Had he been in love with her? Had his wife looked for him at all, distraught over his fate, or just written him off when he went missing?

Would he even recognize Vanessa if she stood before him?

Glancing around the living room for which he'd instantly and distinctly recalled purchasing the furnishings—without the help of anyone, let alone the red-haired woman teasing the edges of his memory—he asked, "Where is she?"

"She died." Grief welled up across her classical features. The sisters must have been close, which was probably why

Caitlyn seemed familiar. "You were both involved in the same plane crash shortly after leaving Thailand."

"Plane crash?" The wispy images of the red-haired woman vanished as he zeroed in on Caitlyn. "Is that what happened?"

Thailand. He'd visited Thailand—but never made it home. Until now.

Eyes bright with unshed tears, she nodded, dark pony-tail flipping over her shoulder. "Over a year ago."

All at once, he wanted to mourn for this wife he couldn't remember. Because it would mean he could still experience emotions that stayed maddeningly out of reach, emotions with clinical definitions—love, peace, happiness, fulfillment, the list went on and on—but which had no real context. He wanted to feel *something* other than discouraged and adrift.

His head ached, but he pressed on, determined to unearth more clues to how he'd started out on a plane from Thailand and ended up in a fishing village in Indonesia. Alone. "But I was on the plane. And I'm not dead. Maybe Vanessa is still alive, too."

Her name produced a small ping in his heart, but he couldn't be certain if the feeling lingered from before the crash or if he'd manufactured it out of his intense need to remember.

Hand to her mouth, Caitlyn bowed her head. "No. They recovered her...body," she murmured, her voice thick. "They found the majority of the fuselage in the water. Most of the forty-seven people on board were still in their seats."

Vivid, gory images spilled into his mind as he imagined the horrors his wife—and the rest of the passengers—must have gone through before succumbing to the death he'd escaped.

"Except me."

For the first time, his reality felt a bit like a miracle instead of a punishment. How had he escaped? Had he un-buckled himself in time to avoid drowning or had he been thrown free of the wreckage?

"Except you," she agreed, though apparently it had taken the revelation of his strange falcon tattoo to con-vince her. "And two other passengers, who were sitting across the aisle from you in first class. You were all in the first row, including Vanessa. They searched for survivors for a week, but there was no trace."

"They were looking in the wrong place," he growled. "I washed up on the beach in Indonesia. On the south side of Batam Island."

"I don't know my geography, but the plane crashed into the ocean near the coast of Malaysia. That's where they focused the search."

No wonder no one had found him. They'd been hun-dreds of miles off.

"After a month," she continued, "they declared all three of you dead."

But he wasn't dead.

The other two passengers might have survived, as well. *Look for them.* They might be suffering from memory loss or ghastly injuries. They might be frightened and alone, having clawed their way out of a watery crypt, only to face a fully awake nightmare. As he had.

He had to find them. But he had no money, no resources— not at this moment anyway. He must have money, or at least he must have had some once. The sum he'd paid for this house popped into his head out of nowhere: fifteen point eight million dollars. That had been eight years ago.

Groaning, he rubbed his temples as the headache grew uncontrollable.

"Are you okay?" Caitlyn asked.

Ensuring the comfort of others seemed to come naturally to this woman he'd found living in his house. His sister-in-law. Had she always been so nurturing?

"Fine," he said between clenched teeth. "Is this still my house?"

He could sell it and use the proceeds to live on while he combed the South China Sea.

Caitlyn chose that moment to sit next to him on the couch, overwhelming him with the light scent of coconut, which, strangely, made him want to bury his nose in her hair.

"Technically, no. When you were declared dead, it passed to your heirs."

"You mean Vanessa's?" Seemed as if his wife's sister had made out pretty well after the plane crash. "Are you the only heir? Because I'm not dead and I want my money back."

It was the only way he could launch a search for the other two missing passengers.

"Oh." She stared at him, her sea-glass-blue eyes wide with guilt and a myriad of other emotions he suddenly wished to understand.

Because looking into her eyes made him feel something. Something good and beautiful and he didn't want to stop drowning in her gaze.

"You don't remember, do you?" she asked. "Oh, my gosh. I've been rambling and you don't even know about the babies."

Blood rushed from his head so fast, his ears popped.

"Babies?" he croaked. Surely she didn't mean babies, plural, as in more than one? As in *his* babies?

"Triplets." She shot him a misty smile that heightened her ethereal beauty. Which he wished he could appreciate, but there was no way, not with the bomb she'd just dropped. "And by some miracle, they still have a father. You. Would you like to meet them?"

"I…" A father. He had children? Three of them, apparently. "They're really mine?" Stupid question, but this was beyond—he shook his head. "How old are they? Do they remember me?"

"Oh, no, they weren't born yet when you went to Thailand."

He frowned. "But you said Vanessa died in the plane crash. Is she not their mother?"

Had he cheated on his wife with another woman? Catholic-school lessons from his youth blasted through his mind instantly. Infidelity was wrong.

"She's not," Caitlyn refuted definitively. "I am."

Guilt and shame cramped his gut as he eyed Caitlyn. He'd cheated on his wife with his *sister-in-law*? The thought was reprehensible.

But it explained the instant visceral reaction he had to her.

Her delicate, refined beauty didn't match the obvious lushness of the redhead he'd married. Maybe that was the point. He really preferred a dark-haired, more classically attractive woman like Caitlyn if he'd fathered children with her.

"Were we having an affair?" he asked bluntly. And would he have a serious fight to regain control of his money now that his mistress had her hooks into it?

Pink spread across her cheeks in a gorgeous blush, and a foreign heaviness filled his chest, spreading to heat his lower half. Though he couldn't recall having made love to her before, he had no trouble recognizing the raw, carnal attraction to Caitlyn. Obviously, she was precisely the woman he preferred, judging by his body's unfiltered reaction.

"Of course not!" She wouldn't meet his gaze, and her blush deepened. "You were married to my sister and I would never—well, I mean, I did meet you first and, okay, maybe I thought about…but then I introduced you to Vanessa. That was that. You were hers. Not that I blame you—"

"Caitlyn."

Her name alone caused that strange fullness in his chest. He'd like to say it again. Whisper it to her as he learned what she tasted like.

She glanced up, finally silenced, and he would very much like to understand why her self-conscious babbling had caused the corners of his mouth to turn up. It was evident from the way she nervously twisted her fingers together that she had no concept of how to lie. They'd never been involved. He'd stake his life on it.

He cleared his raspy throat. "How did the children come to be, then?"

"Oh. I was your surrogate. Yours and Vanessa's. The children are a hundred percent your DNA, grown in my womb." She wrinkled her nose. "That sounds so scientific. Vanessa couldn't conceive, so I volunteered to carry the baby. Granted, I didn't know three eggs were going to take."

She laughed and he somehow found the energy to be charmed by her light spirit. "So Vanessa and I, we were happy?"

If only he could remember her. Remember if they'd laughed together as he vaguely sensed that lovers should. Had they dreamed together of the babies on the way, planning for their family? Had she cried out in her last moments, grief stricken that she'd never hold her children?

"Madly in love." Caitlyn sighed happily. "It was a grand story. Falco and the Vixen. The media adored you guys. I'll go ask Brigitte, the au pair, to bring down the babies."

Reality overwhelmed him.

"Wait." Panicked all of a sudden, he clamped down on her arm before she could rise. "I can't… They don't know me."

He was a father. But so far from a father, he couldn't

fathom the idea of three helpless infants under his care. What if he broke one? What if he scared them? How did you handle a baby? How did you handle *three*?

"Five minutes," she said calmly. "Say hello. See them and count their fingers and toes. Then I'll have Brigitte take them away. They'll get used to you, I promise."

But would he get used to them? "Five minutes. And then I'd like to clean up. Eat."

Breathe. Get his bearings. Figure out how to be Antonio Cavallari again before he had to figure out how to be Antonio Cavallari plus three.

"Of course. I'm sorry, I should have thought of that." Dismay curved her mouth downward.

"There is no protocol when the dead come back to life," he countered drily and smiled. Apparently he'd found a sense of humor along with his home.

His head spun as Caitlyn disappeared upstairs to retrieve the babies and Brigitte, whoever that was. A few minutes later, she returned, followed by a young blonde girl pushing a three-seated carriage. Everything faded away as he saw his children.

Three little heads rested against the cushions, with three sets of eyes and three mouths. Wonder and awe crushed his heart as he drank in the sight of these creatures he'd had a hand in creating.

"They're really mine?" he whispered.

"Really, really," Caitlyn confirmed at normal volume, her tone slightly amused.

She picked up the one from the first seat and held him in the crook of her arm, angling the baby to face him. The blue outfit meant this was his son, didn't it?

"This is Leon." Her mouth quirked. "He's named after my father. I guess it's too late to ask if that's okay, but I thought it was a nice tribute to Vanessa's role in his heritage."

"It's fine."

Antonio was still whispering, but his voice caught in his throat and he couldn't have uttered another sound as his son mewled like a hungry cat, his gaze sharp and bright as he cocked his head as if contemplating the secrets of the universe.

His son. Leon.

Such a simple concept, procreating. People did it every day in all corners of the world. Wilipo had fourteen children and as far as Antonio could tell, never thought it particularly miraculous.

But it *was*.

This little person with the short baby-fine red hair was his child.

"You can say hello," Caitlyn reminded him.

"Hello." His son didn't acknowledge that Antonio had spoken, preferring to bury his head in Caitlyn's shoulder. Had he said the wrong thing? Maybe his voice was too scratchy.

"He'll warm up, I promise." She slid Leon back into the baby seat and picked up the next one.

The pink outfit filled his vision and stung his eyes. He had a daughter. The heart he could have sworn was already full of his son grew so big, he was shocked it hadn't burst from his rib cage.

"This is Annabelle. I always wanted to have a daughter named Annabelle," Caitlyn informed him casually, as if they were discussing the weather instead of this little bundle of perfection.

"She has red hair, too," he murmured. "Like her brother."

Her beautiful face turned up at the sound of his voice and he got lost in her blue eyes.

He had a very bad feeling that the word *no* had just vanished from his vocabulary, and he looked forward to spoiling his daughter to the point of ridiculousness.

"Yes, she and Leon take after Vanessa. Which means Annabelle will be a knockout by the time she's fourteen. Be warned," she said wryly with a half laugh.

"I know martial arts," he muttered. "Any smarmy Romeo with illicit intentions will find himself minus a spleen if he touches my daughter."

Caitlyn smirked. "I don't think a male on the planet would come within fifty yards of Annabelle if they knew you were her father. I was warning you about *her*."

With that cryptic comment, she spirited away his daughter far too quickly and replaced her with the third baby, clad in blue.

"This is Antonio Junior," Caitlyn said quietly and moved closer to present his other son. "He looks just like you, don't you think?"

Dark hair capped a serious face with dark eyes. Antonio studied this third child and his gut lurched with an unnatural sense of recognition, as if the missing pieces of his soul had been snapped into place to form this tiny person.

"Yes," he whispered.

And suddenly, his new lease on life had a purpose.

When he'd set off from Indonesia to find his past, he'd never dreamed he'd instead find his future. A tragic plane crash had nearly robbed these three innocent lives of both their parents, but against all odds, Antonio had survived.

Now he knew why. So he could be a father.

As promised, Caitlyn rounded up the babies and sent them upstairs with Brigitte so Antonio could decompress. Brigitte, bless her, didn't ask any more questions about Antonio's presence, but Caitlyn could tell her hurried explanation that he'd been ill and unable to travel home hadn't satisfied the au pair. Neither would it be enough for the hordes of media and legal hounds who would be snapping at their heels soon enough.

The amazing return of Antonio Cavallari would make worldwide headlines, of that she was sure. But first, he needed to rest and then see a discreet doctor. The world didn't have to know right away. The household staff had signed nondisclosure agreements, and in Hollywood, that was taken so seriously, none of them would ever work again if they broke it. So Caitlyn felt fairly confident the few people who knew about the situation would keep quiet.

She showed him to the master suite, glad now that she'd never cleaned it out, though she'd have to get Rosa to pack up Vanessa's things. It was too morbid to expect him to use his former bedroom with his late wife's clothes still in the dresser.

"I'll send Rosa, the housekeeper, up with something to eat," she promised and left him to clean up.

She wandered to the sunroom and pretended to read a book about parenting multiples on her e-reader, but she couldn't clear the jagged emotion from her throat. Antonio's face when he'd met his children for the first time... It had been amazing to see that much love crowd into his expression instantly. She wished he could have been there in the delivery room, to hold her hand and smile at her like that. Tell her everything would be okay and he'd still think she was beautiful even with a C-section scar.

Except if he *had* been there, he'd have held Vanessa's hand, not hers, and the reality squelched Caitlyn's little daydream.

The babies were his. It wouldn't take long for a judge to overturn her custody rights, not when she'd signed a surrogacy agreement that stated she'd have no claim over the babies once they were born.

But the babies were hers, too. The hospital had listed her name on their birth certificates as their mother—who else would they have named? She'd been their sole parent for nearly eight months and before that, carried them in her womb for months, knowing they weren't going home with Vanessa and Antonio as planned, but with her.

It was a mess, and more than anything, she wanted to do what was best for the babies. Not for the first time, she wished her mother was still alive; Caitlyn could use some advice.

An hour later, Antonio reappeared.

He filled the doorway of the sunroom and the late-afternoon rays highlighted his form with an otherworldly glow that revealed the true nature of his return to this realm—as that of an angel.

She gasped, hand flying to her mouth.

Then he moved into the room and became flesh and blood once again. But no less beautiful.

He'd trimmed his full beard, revealing his deep cheekbones and allowing his arresting eyes to become the focal point of his face. He'd swept back his still long midnight-colored hair and dressed in his old clothes, which didn't fit nearly as well as they once had, but a man as devastatingly handsome as Antonio could make a bedsheet draped over his body work.

Heat swept along her cheeks as she imagined exactly that, and it did not resemble the toga she'd meant to envision. *Antonio, spread out on the bed, sheet barely covering his sinewy, drool-worthy fighter's physique, gaze dark and full of desire...for her...* She shook her head. That was the *last* thing she should be thinking about for a hundred reasons, but Antonio Junior, Leon and Annabelle were the top three and she needed to get a few things straight with their father. No naked masculine chests required for that conversation.

"You look...different," she squawked.

Nice. *Tip him off that you're thinking naughty thoughts.*

"You kept my clothes?" He pointed to the jeans slung low on his lean hips. "And my shaving equipment?"

All of which he apparently remembered just fine as he'd slipped back into his precrash look easily. Antonio had always been gorgeous as sin, built like a lost Michelangelo sculpture with a side of raw, masculine power. And she was still salivating over him. A year in Indonesia hadn't changed that, apparently.

She shrugged and tried to make herself stop staring at him, which didn't exactly work. "I kept meaning to go through that room, but I thought maybe there would be something the babies would want. So I left it."

"I'm glad you did. Thank you." His small smile tripped a long liquid pull inside and she tamped it down. Or she almost did. It was too delicious to fully let it go.

Serious. Talk. Now, she told herself sternly.

"I had a gym," he said before she could work up the courage to bring up item one on her long list of issues. "Did you leave it alone, too?"

"It's untouched."

"I need to see it. Will you come with me?"

Surprised, she nodded. "Of course."

Was it wrong to be thrilled he'd asked her to be with him as he delved into his past?

Well, if that was wrong, it was probably just as wrong to still have a thing for him all these years later. If only she hadn't given up so easily when she'd first met him— it was still one of her biggest regrets.

But then, her relationship rules didn't afford much hope unless a man was interested enough to hang around for the long haul. She'd thought maybe Antonio might have been, once upon a time. The way he'd flirted with her when they'd met, as though he thought she was beautiful, had floored her…and then Vanessa had entered stage left, which had dried up his interest in the chaste sister.

She followed him as he strolled directly to the gym, mystified how he remembered the way, and halted next to him as he quietly took in the posters advertising his many fights, his championship belts and publicity shots of himself clad in shorts and striking a fierce pose.

There was something wicked about staring at a photo of Antonio half clothed while standing next to the fully dressed version, knowing that falcon tattoo sat under his shirt, waiting to be discovered by a woman's fingers. *Her* fingers. What would it feel like?

Sometimes she dreamed about that.

"Do you remember any of this?" she asked as the silence stretched. She couldn't keep thinking about Antonio's naked chest. Which became more difficult the longer they stood there, his heat nearly palpable. He even smelled like sin.

"Bits and pieces," he finally said. "I didn't know I had martial arts training. I thought I was remembering a movie, because I wasn't always in the ring. Sometimes I was outside the ring, watching."

"Oh, like watching other fighters? Maybe you're remembering Falco," she offered. "The fight club."

He shook his head as if to clear it. "I feel as if I should know what that is."

He didn't remember Falco, either? Antonio had lived and breathed that place, much to Vanessa's dismay on many occasions. Her sister had hoped to see her husband more often once his time in the ring was up, but the opposite had proved true.

Caitlyn led him to a picture on the wall, the one of him standing with two fighters about to enter the ring. "Falco is your MMA promotional venue. You founded it once your career ended. That's where you made all your money."

"When did I stop fighting?"

"It wasn't long after you and Vanessa got married. You don't remember that, either?" When he shook his head, she told him what little she knew about his last fight. "Brian

Kerr nearly killed you. Illegal punch to the back of your head and you hit the floor at a bad angle. Knocked you out. You were in the hospital unconscious for two days. That's probably why your amnesia is so pronounced. Your brain has sustained quite a bit of trauma."

Really, he should have already been checked out by a competent doctor, but he'd refused when she'd mentioned it earlier. It wasn't as if she could make him. Caitlyn had no experience with amnesia *or* a powerful man who wouldn't admit to weakness.

Deep down, she had an undeniable desire to gain some experience, especially since it came wrapped in an Antonio package.

He stared at the picture for a moment. "Falco is the name of my company," he announced cautiously as if testing it out. "It's not *my* name."

Her heart ached over his obvious confusion. She wanted to help him, to erase that small bit of helplessness she would never have associated with confident, solid Antonio Cavallari if she hadn't seen it firsthand.

"Falco was your nickname when you were fighting. You transferred it to your promotional company because I guess it had some sentimental value." Not that he'd ever discussed it with her. It was an assumption everyone had made, regardless.

"What happened to my company while I was missing?"

Missing—was that how he'd thought of himself? She tried to put herself in his place, waking up with few memories, in a strange place, with strange people who spoke a different language, all while recuperating from a plane crash and near drowning. The picture was not pretty, which tugged at her heart anew.

"I, um, have control over it." And it had languished like the bedroom and his gym.

What did she know about running an MMA promotional company? But she couldn't have sold it or tried to step into his shoes. In many ways, his place in the world had been on accidental hold, as if a higher power had stilled her hand from dismantling Antonio's life. It had been here, waiting for him to slip back into it.

His expression hardened and the glimpse of vulnerability vanished. "I want control of my estate. And my company. Do whatever you have to do to make that happen."

The rasp in his voice, which hadn't been there before he got on that plane, laced his statement with a menacing undertone. He seemed more like a stranger in that moment than he had when he'd first appeared on her doorstep, unkempt and unrecognizable.

It was a brutal reminder that he wasn't the same man. He wasn't a safe fantasy come to life. And she wasn't her sister, a woman who could easily handle a man like Antonio—worse, she wasn't the woman he'd picked.

"It's a lot to process, I realize," she said slowly as her pulse skittered out of control. This harder, hooded Antonio was impossible to read, and she had no idea how to handle this unprecedented situation. "But you just got back to the States. You don't even remember Falco, let alone how to run it. Why don't you take a few days, get your bearings? I'll help you."

The offer was genuine. But it also kept her in his proximity so she could figure out his plans. If she got a hint that he was thinking about fighting her for custody of the triplets, she'd be ready. She was their mother, and this man—who was still very much a ghost of his former self—was not taking away her children.

Three

Antonio shifted his iron-hard gaze from the pictures on the wall to evaluate Caitlyn coolly, which did not help her pulse. Nothing in her limited experience had prepared her to face down a man like Antonio, but she had to make him agree to a few ground rules.

"You cannot fathom what I've been through over the past year," he stated firmly. "I want nothing more than to pick up the pieces of my life and begin the next chapter with these new cards I've been dealt. I need my identity back."

Which was a perfectly reasonable request, but executing it more closely resembled unsnarling a knotted skein of yarn than simply handing over a few account numbers. This was one time when she couldn't afford to back down.

Caitlyn nodded and took a deep breath. "I understand, and I'm not suggesting otherwise. The problem is that a lot of legalities are involved and I have to look out for the interests of the children."

His gaze softened, warming her, and she didn't know what to do with that, either.

"I'm thinking of the children, as well."

"Good. Then, it would be best to take things slowly. You've been gone for a long time and the babies have a routine. It would be catastrophic to disrupt them."

He pursed his lips. "If you're concerned that I might dismiss the nanny, I can assure you I have no intention of doing so. I couldn't care for one child by myself, let alone three."

Her stomach jolted and she swallowed, gearing up to lay it on the line. "You won't be by yourself. I'll still be here."

If only her voice hadn't squeaked, that might have come across more definitively. Besides, she was still breast-feeding and didn't plan to stop until the triplets were a year old. She was irreplaceable, as far as she was concerned.

"You're free to get back to your life," he said with a puzzled frown. "There's no reason for you to continue in your role as caretaker now that I've returned."

"Whoa." She threw up a palm as the back of her neck heated in a sweaty combination of anger and fear. "Where did you get the idea that I'm just a caretaker? The babies are *mine*. I'm their mother."

Nothing she'd said thus far had sunk in, obviously.

Antonio crossed his arms and contemplated her. "You said you were the surrogate. A huge sacrifice, to be sure, but the children would have been mine and Vanessa's. You've been forced to care for them much longer than anyone has a right to ask. I'm relieving you of the responsibility."

Her worst nightmare roared to life, pulsing and seething as it went for her jugular.

"No!" A tear rolled down her face before she could stop it as she tried to summon up a reasonable argument against the truth in his words. "That's not what happened. I care for them because I love them. They became mine in every sense when I thought you and Vanessa were both gone. I *need* them. And they need me. Don't take away my babies."

A sob choked off whatever else she'd been about to say. The one and only time she'd ever tried to fight for something, and instead of using logic and reason, she'd turned into an emotional mess.

Concern weighted Antonio's expression as he reached out to grasp her hand in a totally surprising move. His fingers found hers and squeezed tightly, shooting an unexpected thrill through her that she couldn't contain. Coupled with the emotional distress, it was almost overwhelming.

"Don't cry." The lines around his eyes deepened as he heaved a ragged sigh. "I don't know how to do this."

"But you don't have to know," she countered, clinging to his hand like a lifeline. "That's what I'm trying to tell you. Don't change anything. It's Christmastime and we're family, if nothing else. I'll stay here and continue to care for the babies, then we can spend this time figuring it out together. After the first of the year, maybe the path will seem clearer."

Please, God.

Relief coursed through her as he slowly nodded. "I want to be as fair as possible to everyone. If you don't have a life to get back to, then it makes sense for you to stay here. At least until January."

"This *is* my life."

Or at least it was now, since she'd given up her job as an accountant. She had no desire to be anything other than the mother she'd become over the past year. And now she had until the first of January to find a way to stay in that role. If Antonio decided his children would be better off in another arrangement, she had little to say about it.

What would she do without the family she'd formed?

"Caitlyn, I appreciate what you've done." His dark eyes

sought hers and held, his gratitude genuine. "You stepped into my place to care for my children. Thank you."

That he recognized her efforts meant the world to her. He was a good man, deep inside where brain trauma couldn't touch. As she'd always known.

She nodded, still too emotional to respond, but the sentiment gave her hope. He wasn't heartless, just trying to do the right thing.

Somehow, Antonio had to recognize that *she* was the right thing for the children and then the two of them could figure out how to be co-parents. After learning how to handle triplets, that should be a walk in the park.

The next two days passed in a blur. When Caitlyn had mentioned legalities, Antonio had half thought it was an excuse to avoid giving up control of his money. But she'd vastly understated the actuality. An avalanche of paperwork awaited him once the man who'd been his lawyer for a decade became convinced Antonio had really returned from the dead.

Funny how he'd instantly recognized Kyle Lowery the moment his lawyer's admin had ushered Antonio and Caitlyn into the man's office. His memory problems were inconsistent and frustrating, to say the least.

Antonio's headache persisted and grew worse the more documents Kyle's paralegal placed in front of him. The harsh lights glinting from the gold balls on the Christmas tree in the corner didn't help. Antonio wished he could enjoy the spirit of the season.

But Christmas and family and all of the joy others seemed to associate with this time of year meant little to him. Caitlyn had told him that his parents had died some time back, which probably explained why he remembered them with a sense of distance, as if the scenes had happened long ago.

After many more stops and an interminable number of hours, he had: a temporary driver's license, a temporary bank card, a promise of credit cards to come, a bank teller who'd fallen all over herself to give him access to his safe-deposit box…and a dark-haired enigma of a woman who'd stuck to his side like glue, determined to help him navigate the exhausting quagmire reentering his life had become.

Why was she still here?

Why did her presence make him so happy? She somehow made everything better just by being near him. And sometimes, she looked at him a certain way that burrowed under his skin with tingly warmth. Both had become necessary. Unexpectedly so.

He studied her covertly at lunch on the third day after he'd pounded on the door of his Malibu house, delirious and determined to find answers to the question marks in his mind.

What he'd found still hadn't fully registered. Caitlyn was an amazing woman and his kids were surprising, funny little people. Together, they were a potent package. But how did that make sense? She wasn't their biological mother.

While Antonio absently chewed on a thick sandwich designed to put back some of his lost weight, Caitlyn laughed at Leon as he shoved his food off his tray to the floor below.

She'd insisted on the triplets sitting at the table when the adults had meals, even though the babies ate little more than puree of something and bits of Cheerios. Antonio wouldn't have thought of having infants join them, but with the additions, eating became something more than a routine. It was a chance to spend time with his children without expectation since Brigitte and Caitlyn handled everything.

Secretly, he was grateful Caitlyn hadn't skipped through

the door the moment he'd given her the out. In the hazy reaches of his mind, he had the distinct impression most women would have run very fast in the other direction from triplets. He couldn't understand Caitlyn's motivation for staying unless she thought she'd get a chunk of his estate as a thank-you. Which he'd probably give her. She deserved something for her sacrifices.

"Your turn."

Antonio did a double take at the spoon in Caitlyn's outstretched hand and blinked. "My turn to what?"

"Feed your daughter. She won't bite you." Caitlyn raised her brows and nodded at the spoon. "Of the three, Annabelle is the most laid-back about eating, so start with her."

Since he couldn't see a graceful way to refuse, he accepted the spoon and scooted closer to the baby's high chair, eyeing the bowl of…whatever it was. Orange applesauce?

Scowling, he scooped some up and then squinted at the baby watching him with bright eyes. How was he supposed to feed her with her fingers stuck in her mouth?

"Come on, open," he commanded.

Annabelle fluttered her lashes and made an uncomplimentary noise, fingers firmly wedged where the spoon was supposed to go.

He tried again. "Please?"

Caitlyn giggled and he glanced at her askance, which only made her laugh harder. He rolled his shoulders, determined to pass this one small test, but getting his daughter to eat might top the list of the most difficult things he had to do today.

Antonio had learned to walk again on the poorly healed broken leg that the Indonesian doctor had promised would have to be amputated. He'd defied the odds and scarcely even had a limp now. If he could do that, one very small person could not break him.

He tapped the back of Annabelle's hand with the edge of the spoon, hoping that would act as an open sesame, but she picked that moment to yank her fingers free. She backhanded the spoon, flinging it free of Antonio's grip. It hit the wall with a *thunk*, leaving a splash of orange in a trail to the floor.

Frustration welled. He balled his fists automatically and then immediately shoved them into his lap as horror filtered through him. His first instinct was to fight, but he had to control that impulse, or else what kind of father was he going to be?

Breathing rhythmically, he willed back the frustration until his fists loosened. Better.

His first foray into caring for his kid and she elected to show him her best defensive moves. Annabelle blinked innocently as Antonio's scowl deepened. "Yeah, you work on that technique, and when you've got your spinning backhand down, we'll talk."

Spinning backhand. The phrase had leaped into his mind with no forethought. Instantly other techniques scrolled through his head. *Muay Thai.* That had been his specialty. His "training" with Wilipo had come so easily because Antonio should have been teaching the class as the master, not attending as the student.

Faster now, ingrained drills, disciplines and defense strategies exploded in his mind. Why now instead of in his gym, surrounded by the relics of his former status as a mixed martial arts champion?

The headache slammed him harder than ever before and the groan escaped before he could catch it.

"It's okay," Caitlyn said and jumped up to retrieve the spoon. "You don't have to feed her. I just thought you might like it."

"No problem," he said around the splitting pain in his temples. "Excuse me."

He mounted the stairs to his bedroom and shut himself away in the darkened room, but refused to lie on the bed like an invalid.

Instead, he sank into a chair and put his head in his hands. This couldn't go on, the rush of memories and the headaches and the inability to do simple tasks like stick a spoon in a baby's mouth without becoming irrational.

But how did he change it?

Coming to LA was supposed to solve everything, give him back his memories and his life. It had only highlighted how very far he had yet to go in his journey back to the land of the living.

An hour later, the pain was manageable enough to try being civilized again. Antonio tracked down Caitlyn in the sunroom, which seemed to be her favored spot when she wasn't hanging out with the babies. Her dark curls partially obscured the e-reader in her hands and she seemed absorbed in the words on the screen.

"I'll visit a doctor," he told her shortly and spun to leave before she asked any questions. She'd been after him to see one, but he'd thus far refused, having had enough of the medical profession during his months and months of rehabilitation in Indonesia.

No doctor could restore his memories, nor could one erase the scars he bore from the plane crash.

But if a Western doctor had a way to make his headaches go away, that would be stellar. He had to become a father, one way or another, and living in a crippling state of pain wasn't going to cut it.

"I'll drive you." She followed him into the hall. "Just because you have a driver's license doesn't mean you're ready to get behind the wheel. We'll take my—"

"Caitlyn." He whirled to face her, but she kept going, smacking into his chest.

His arms came up as they both nearly lost their balance

and somehow she ended up pinned to the wall, their bodies tangled and flush. His lower half sprang to attention and heat shot through his gut.

Caitlyn's wide-eyed gaze captured his and he couldn't have broken the connection if his life depended on it. Her chest heaved against his as if she was unable to catch her breath, and that excited him, too.

"Caitlyn," he murmured again, but that seemed to be the extent of his ability to speak as her lips parted, drawing his attention to her mouth. She caught her plump bottom lip between her teeth and—

"Um, you can let go now," she said and cleared her throat. "I'm okay."

He released her, stepping back to allow her the space she'd asked for, though it was far from what he wanted to do. "I'm curious about something."

Nervously, she rearranged her glossy hair, refusing to meet his eyes. "Sure."

"You said that you introduced me to Vanessa. How did you and I meet?" Because if he'd ever held Caitlyn in his arms before, he was an idiot if he'd willingly let her go.

"I was Rick's accountant." At his raised brows, she smiled. "Your former manager. He'd gone through several CPAs until he found me, and when I came by his house to do his quarterly taxes, you were there. You were wearing a pink shirt for a breast cancer fund-raiser you'd attended. We got to talking and somehow thirty minutes passed in a blur."

Nothing wrong with her memory, clearly, and it was more than a little flattering that she recalled his clothing from that day.

"And there was something about me that you didn't like?" Obviously, or she wouldn't have matched him up with her sister. Maybe she'd only thought of him as a friend.

"Oh, no! You were great. Gorgeous and gentlemanly." The blush that never seemed far from the surface of her skin bloomed again, heightening the blue in her eyes. "I mean, I might have been a little starstruck, which is silly, considering how many celebrities I've done taxes for."

That pleased him even more than her pink-shirt comment, and he wanted to learn more about this selfless woman who'd apparently been a part of his life for a long time. "You're an accountant, then?"

"Not anymore. I gave up all my clients when…Vanessa died." She laughed self-consciously. "It's hard to retrain my brain to no longer say 'when Antonio and Vanessa died'."

The mention of his wife sent an unexpected spike of sadness through his gut. "I don't remember being married to her. Did you think we'd be a good couple? Is that why you introduced us?"

All at once, a troubling sense of disloyalty effectively killed the discovery mode he'd fallen into with Caitlyn. He had no context for his relationship with Vanessa, but she'd been his wife and this woman was his sister-in-law. He shouldn't be thinking about Caitlyn as anything other than a temporary mother to his children. She'd probably be horrified at the direction of his thoughts.

"Oh. No, I mentioned that she was my sister and you asked to meet her. I don't think you even noticed me after that. Vanessa is—was—much more memorable than me."

"I beg to differ," he countered wryly, which pulled a smile out of her. "When I close my eyes, yours is the only face I can picture."

Apparently he couldn't help himself. Did he automatically flirt with beautiful women or just this one?

More blushing. But he wasn't going to apologize for the messed-up state of his mind or the distinct pleasure he'd discovered at baiting this delicate-skinned woman.

He'd needed something that made him feel good. Was that so wrong?

"Well, she was beautiful and famous. I didn't blame you for wanting an introduction. Most people did."

"Famous?" Somehow that didn't seem like valid criteria for wishing to meet a woman.

Caitlyn explained that Vanessa starred on *Beacon Street*, a TV show beloved by millions of fans, and then with a misty sigh, Caitlyn waxed poetic about their fairy-tale wedding. "Vanessa wanted a baby more than anything. She said it was the only thing missing from your perfect marriage."

He'd heard everything she'd said, but in a removed way, as if it had happened to someone else. And perhaps in many respects, it had. He didn't remember being in love with Vanessa, but he'd obviously put great stock in her as a partner, lover and future mother of his children.

Part of his journey apparently lay in reconciling his relationship with the woman he'd married—so he could know if it was something he might want to do again, with another woman, at some point in the future. He needed to grieve his lost love as best he could and move on.

Perhaps Caitlyn had a role in this part of his recovery, as well. "I'd like to know more about Vanessa. Will you tell me? Or is it too hard?"

She nodded with a small smile. "It's hard. But it's good for me, too, to remember her. I miss her every day."

Launching into an impassioned tribute to her sister, Caitlyn talked with her hands, her animated face clearly displaying her love for Vanessa. But Antonio couldn't stop thinking about that moment against the wall, when he'd almost reached out to see what Caitlyn's glossy hair felt like. What might have happened between them all those years ago if he hadn't asked Caitlyn to introduce him to Vanessa?

It was madness to wonder. He would do well to focus

on the present, where, thanks to Caitlyn, he'd forgotten about his headache. She'd begged him to allow her to stay under his roof and, frankly, it was easy to say yes because he needed her help. Incredible fortune had smiled on him since the plane crash, and he couldn't help feeling that Caitlyn was a large part of it.

Four

Instead of taking Antonio to the doctor, Caitlyn arranged for the doctor to come to the house the following afternoon. Antonio needed his space for as long as possible, at least until he got comfortable being in civilization again—or at least that was Caitlyn's opinion, and no one had to know that it fit her selfish desire to have him all to herself.

As a plus, Caitlyn wouldn't have to worry about wrestling Antonio into the car in case he changed his mind about seeing a doctor after all. Not that she could have. Nor did she do herself any favors imagining the tussle, which would likely end with Antonio's hard body pinning her against another wall.

Recalling yesterday's charged encounter had kept her quite warm last night and quite unable to sleep due to a restless ache she had no idea how to ease. Well, okay, she had *some* idea, but her sensibilities didn't extend to middle-of-the-night visits to the sexy man down the hall. One did not simply walk into Antonio's bedroom with the intent of hopping into bed with him, or at least *she* didn't. Risqué nighttime shenanigans were Vanessa's style, and her sister had had her heart broken time and time again as a result. Sex and love were so closely entwined that Caitlyn was willing to wait for the commitment she'd always wanted.

Nor did she imagine that Antonio was lying awake fantasizing about visiting Caitlyn anytime soon, either. They were two people thrown together by extraordinary circumstances and they both had enormous, daunting realities to deal with that didn't easily translate into any kind of relationship other than…what? Friends? Co-parents? Trying to figure it out was exhausting enough; adding romance to the mix was out of the question.

Especially since Antonio could—and likely would—have his pick of women soon enough. A virgin mother of triplets, former accountant sister-in-law didn't have the same appeal as a lush, redheaded actress-wife combo, that was for sure.

The doctor buzzed the gate entrance at precisely three o'clock. Antonio ushered the stately salt-and-pepper-haired physician into the foyer and thanked him for coming as the two men shook hands.

All morning, Antonio had been short-tempered and scowling, even after Caitlyn told him the doctor was coming to him. Caitlyn hovered just beyond the foyer, unsure if she was supposed to make herself scarce or insist on being present for the conversation in case the doctor had follow-up instructions for Antonio's care.

Vanessa would have been stuck to Antonio's side. As a wife should. Caitlyn was only the person who had made the appointment. And she'd done that just to make sure it happened.

"Caitlyn," Antonio called, his tone slightly amused, which was a plus, considering his black mood. "Come meet Dr. Barnett."

That she could do. She stood by Antonio, but not too close, and exchanged pleasantries with the doctor.

"I saw you fight Alondro in Vegas," the doctor remarked with an appreciative nod at Antonio. "Ringside. Good match."

Antonio accepted the praise with an inclined head, but his hands immediately clenched and his mouth tightened; clearly, the doctor's comments made him uncomfortable. Because he didn't remember? Or had he lost all context of what it meant to be famous? Either way, she didn't like anyone making Antonio uncomfortable, let alone someone who was supposed to be here to help.

"Can I show you to a private room where you can get started?" Caitlyn asked in a no-nonsense way.

"Of course." Dr. Barnett's face smoothed out and he followed Caitlyn and Antonio to the master bedroom, where Antonio had indicated he felt the most at home in the house.

Score one for Caitlyn. Or was it two since a medical professional was on the premises?

She started to duck out, but Antonio stopped her with a warm hand on her arm. "I'd like you to stay," he murmured. "So it will feel less formal."

"Oh." A bit flummoxed, she stared up into his dark eyes. "It won't be weird if the doctor wants you to…um… get undressed?"

On cue, her cheeks heated. She'd blushed more around this man in the past few days than she had in her whole life.

His lips quirked and she congratulated herself on removing that dark scowl he'd worn all day. Too bad his new expression had come about because he likely found her naïveté amusing.

"It will only be weird if you make it weird." His head tilted as he contemplated her. "What kind of doctor's appointment do you think this is?"

She scowled in return. "I'll stay. But only if you stop making fun of me."

He winked. *Winked.* "I solemnly swear. Provided you stop saying things that are funny."

"And," she continued as if he hadn't tried to be charming and slick, when, in truth, it fluttered her heart to be so firmly in the sights of Antonio's weapons of choice. "I'll stay if you'll be perfectly honest with the doctor. If you aren't, I will be."

At that, he smiled. "Then, you'll definitely have to see me undressed."

"For what reason?" she hissed with a glance at the doctor, who was pretending not to listen to their far-too-loud discussion. Did Antonio have zero sense of propriety?

"Otherwise, how will you know what to say about my badly healed broken leg?" Antonio responded innocently and laughed as Caitlyn smacked his arm. Over his shoulder, he called, "Dr. Barnett, can we start out dressed or shall I strip immediately?"

Dr. Barnett cleared his throat. "We'll talk first and then I'll take some vital signs. A more…ah…thorough examination will only become necessary pending the outcome of our discussion. Ms. Hopewell is free to excuse herself at that point."

Even the doctor sounded as if Caitlyn's lack of experience around naked men was cause for hilarity. She firmed her mouth and sank into the chair Antonio indicated in the sitting area, which was thankfully far from the bed, then crossed her arms. *Men.*

And speaking of pigheaded males—why was she just *now* finding out Antonio had suffered a broken leg? It probably needed to be reset and it must pain him something awful and…it wasn't her business. She'd gotten him in front of a doctor; now someone with a medical degree

could talk sense into the man, who apparently thought
he'd turned immortal.

Dr. Barnett settled into a wing-back chair with a clip-
board he'd pulled from his bag of tricks. After a quick
back-and-forth with the patient to determine Antonio's
age, approximate height and weight, the doctor took his
heart rate and peered into his throat.

"Now, then." The doctor contemplated Antonio. "Ms.
Hopewell indicated that you have trouble remembering
your past. Can you tell me more about that?"

"No," Antonio said smoothly, but Caitlyn heard the ob-
stinacy in his voice. "You're here because I have headaches. Make them go away."

Caitlyn frowned. *That* was the thing he was most worried about?

The doctor asked a few pointed questions about the
nature of Antonio's pain, which he refused to answer. Dr.
Barnett pursed his lips. "I can write you a prescription for
some heavy-duty painkillers, but I'd like to do a CT scan
first. I'm concerned about your purported memory loss
coupled with headaches. I'd prefer to know what we're
dealing with before treating the symptoms."

"No tests. Write the prescription," Antonio ordered and
stood, clearly indicating the appointment was over whether
the doctor wished it to be or not. "Ms. Hopewell misrep-
resented the nature of the medical care I need."

Caitlyn didn't move from her chair. "How long will the
CT scan take? Will you get results immediately or will it
only lead to more tests? Will you also look at his leg?"

Someone had to be the voice of reason here.

"It doesn't matter, because that's not the problem," Antonio cut in with a scowl. "I'm not sick. I'm not an invalid,
and my leg is fine. I just need something to make my headaches manageable."

Dr. Barnett nodded. "Fine. I'll write you a prescription for a painkiller, but only for enough pills to get you through the next few days. If you go to the radiology lab and get the CT scan, I'll give you more."

"Blackmail?" Antonio's lips quirked, but no one would mistake it for amusement. "I'll just find another doctor."

"Perhaps." Dr. Barnett shrugged. "Hollywood is certainly full of dishonest medical practitioners who will write prescriptions for just about anything if someone is willing to pay enough. Just keep in mind that many of those someones wind up in the morgue. I will never be a party to putting one of my patients there."

That was enough to convince Caitlyn she'd selected the right doctor, and she wasn't going to stand by and let Antonio destroy an opportunity to get the help he needed, not when he had three very good reasons to get better the medically approved way. "Dr. Barnett, please write the prescription for the amount of pills you think is appropriate and leave me the information about the radiology lab. We'll discuss it and get back to you."

Antonio crossed his arms, his expression the blackest it had been all day, but thankfully he kept his mouth closed instead of blasting her for interfering.

The doctor hastily scrawled on his pad and tore off the top page, handing it to Caitlyn with a business card for the radiology lab. She saw him out and shut the front door, assuming Antonio had stayed holed up in his room to work off his mood.

But when she turned, he was leaning against the wall at the other end of the foyer, watching her with crossed arms and a hooded, hard look. His expression wasn't as black as it had been, but somehow it was far more dangerous.

Startled, she backed up against the door, accidentally trapping her hands behind her. Feeling oddly exposed, she yanked them free and laced her fingers together over her abdomen, right where a strange sort of hum had started.

"I'm not getting a CT scan," he said succinctly. "I didn't ask you to call the doctor so you could railroad me into a bunch of useless tests. I had enough of doctors in Indonesia who couldn't fix me."

She shook her head, not about to back down. This was too important. "But what if the tests help? Don't you want to get your memory back?"

"Of course." A hint of vulnerability flitted through his gaze and the hum inside her abdomen sped up. "There's only one thing that's helped with that so far and it wasn't a doctor."

The atmosphere in the foyer pressed down on her, almost agonizing in its power. She couldn't think when he was like this, so focused and intense, funneling all of his energy toward her. It woke up her nerve endings and they ruffled under the surface of her skin, begging her to move with a restless insistence. But move where?

"What helps?" she asked softly, afraid of spooking him. She couldn't predict if he'd leave or advance on her and, at this point, she couldn't say which she'd prefer.

"Fighting." The word reverberated against the marble, ringing in her ears.

She gasped, hand flying to her mouth. Surely he didn't mean actual fighting. As if he intended to return to his former sport.

"I need to get in the ring again," he confirmed, his dark gaze on hers, searching for something she couldn't give him. Pleading with her to understand. "I have—"

"No," she interrupted as her stomach dropped. "You can't. You have no idea what's going on inside your skull and you want to introduce more trauma? Not a good idea."

He'd only returned to civilization a few days ago, broken on the inside. He needed…something, yes, but it wasn't picking up his former MMA persona as if no time had passed. As if he was still whole and healthy. As if he had nothing important to lose.

"This is not your call, Caitlyn," he said gently. Too gently. He'd already made up his mind. "This is my life, my head. I'm a fighter. It's what I do."

She stared up at him, and the raw emotion swimming through his eyes took her breath. "You haven't been a fighter for a long time, Antonio. You're a businessman now."

That was the man she knew well, the safe, contained version of Antonio. When he'd quit his MMA career to manage what went on in the ring for other fighters, it was the best of both worlds. Antonio still had all the outer trappings of his lean fighting physique, which—*let's be honest*—was wickedly delicious enough to get a nun going, but he'd shed the harsh brutality of Falco.

She liked him as a businessman. Businessmen were constant, committed. The way she'd always thought of Antonio. If he wasn't that man, who was he?

"I might have been before the crash, but I don't remember that part of me." Bleakly, he stared off into the distance and her heart plummeted. "That Antonio might as well be dead. The only Antonio *I* know is the one who lives inside my heart, beating against the walls of my chest, alive but not *whole*. That Antonio screams inside my head, begging to be free of this web of uncertainty."

God, how poetically awful and terrible. Her soul ached to imagine the confusion and pain he must experience every minute of every day, but at the same time, she thrilled in the knowledge that he'd shared even that small piece of himself.

His gaze snapped back to hers and she'd swear on a stack of Bibles he hadn't moved, but his heat wrapped around her, engulfing her, and she was powerless to stop it from affecting her. She wanted to step back, quickly. As fast as her legs could carry her. But he'd backed her against the wall…or she'd backed herself against the wall by starting this madness. By assuming she could convince a man who'd survived a plane crash to see a doctor.

Madness.

Because her body ached for Antonio to step into that scant space between them, which felt uncomfortably slight and yet as massive as the ocean that had separated him from his old life.

She wanted to support him. To care for him. To help him reenter his life in whatever way made sense to him. Who was she to say he shouldn't be in the ring again? Vanessa hadn't liked him fighting, either, but her sister had held many weapons in her arsenal that might have prevented the man she'd married from doing something dangerous.

Caitlyn had nothing.

"Please understand." He held her captive without words, without touching her at all, as his simple plea burned her throat. "I have to unleash my frustration on an opponent who can take it. Who's trained for it. Before I take it out on someone else."

Her teeth caught her lip and bit down as his meaning sank in. He sought a healthy outlet for his confusion, one that was familiar to him. Why was that so bad?

She'd been trying to keep him away from the media, away from his former employees and business partners, who might ask uncomfortable questions he couldn't answer. Perhaps she'd worried unnecessarily. Most likely, he'd be firmly in the public eye for the rest of his life, whether she liked it or not, and she couldn't keep him to herself forever. It was ridiculous to even pretend they could hide away in this house, even for a few days.

And then he reached out, encompassing her forearm with his palm. "I need you—" He swallowed and faltered.

"I need you in my corner, Caitlyn. I don't have anyone else."

Wide-eyed, she covered his strong fingers with hers. Reassuringly, she squeezed, reveling in the contact as warmth flooded the places where their skin touched. *She* was comforting *him* in what was clearly a difficult conversation for them both.

He needed her. More important, he needed her to validate his choices, no matter how crazy they seemed.

A little awed by the realization, she nodded because speaking wasn't an option as he rested his forehead on hers, whispering his gratitude. She closed her eyes against the intimacy of the thank-you, feeling as if she'd just fought an exhausting battle, only to look up and see the opposing general's second flank swarming the battlefield.

"I'll take you to Falco," she promised, her voice croaking, and wished she only meant she would take him to the building housing the empire he'd founded called Falco Fight Club. But she suspected she would really be taking him back to his former self, when he *was* Falco, a champion fighter who regularly took blows to the head.

God help her for enabling this lunacy.

Caitlyn insisted on driving to Falco, and Antonio humored her only because his pounding head had blurred his vision. Slightly. Not enough to give the doctor's ridiculous CT-scan idea any credence. He'd had plenty of brain scans in the past and the final one had ended his career.

He'd given up trying to understand why he could recall the last CT scan he'd endured, but couldn't remember the woman he'd been married to for—what? Four or five years? He didn't even know. He couldn't even fully picture her face, just bits of it in an insane collage.

They picked up Antonio's prescription on the way, but he waited to take a pill since the warning said the medication might make him drowsy. He definitely wanted to be alert for this first trip to his place of business.

The building came into view and Caitlyn pointed at it, saying Antonio had bought the lot and built Falco from the ground up, approving the architect's plans, surveying the drywall as it went up and hand selecting the equipment inside.

He waited for some sense of recognition. Pushed for it with widened eyes and a mostly empty mind. But the simple glass and brick looked like hundreds of other buildings in Los Angeles.

Falco Fight Club. The red-and-black letters marched across the brick, signifying this as the headquarters for the global MMA promotional company Antonio had founded. Under the name, a replica of the falcon tattoo on Antonio's pectoral had apparently been worked in as Falco's logo.

He briefly touched the ink under his shirt. This was part of his past, and likely his future as well, though he knew nothing about the business side of Falco. Nor did he have a driving desire to reclaim the helm...not yet.

He was here for what happened inside the ring.

Grimly, he climbed from the Range Rover Caitlyn drove more carefully than a ninety-year-old priest, and hesitated, suddenly fearful at crossing the threshold. What if he climbed into the ring and none of his memories came back? What if Caitlyn was right and additional trauma to his head actually caused more problems? He was a father now; he had other people to think about besides himself.

Caitlyn's presence wrapped around him before she slipped her smooth hand into his. It felt oddly...right to have her by his side as he faced down his past. She didn't say a word but stood with him as he surveyed the entrance, silently offering her unconditional support, even though she'd been adamantly against him fighting.

Somehow, that made his unsettling confusion acceptable. No matter what happened inside Falco Fight Club, he'd found his old life, and after a year of praying for it, he'd count his blessings.

The falcon emblem on his chest mirrored the one on the bricks in more ways than one— both decorated a shell housing the soul of Antonio Cavallari, and somewhere inside lay the answers he sought. He wouldn't give up until he had reclaimed *all* of his pieces.

"Is the company still in operation?" he asked, wishing he'd unbent from his bad mood enough to ask the question in the car. But his headache had grown worse as the day wore on, and he was weary of dealing with pain and questions and the blankness inside his head.

She nodded. "I get monthly reports from the interim CEO, Thomas Warren. He's been running it in your stead, but I have no idea if he's doing a good job or not. I was hoping you'd want to take over at some point, but I think everyone would understand if you didn't do so right away."

"Do they know?" He inclined his head toward the building, and even that renewed the pounding at his temples. Maybe he should take a painkiller anyway. It might dull the embarrassment and frustration of not knowing who "they" were.

She squeezed his hand and let it go, then shoved hers into her pocket. He missed the feel of her skin on his instantly and almost reached for her but recognized the wisdom in not appearing too intimate in public.

"Thomas called me yesterday after your lawyer gave him the heads-up that you were back," she said. "But I didn't tell him anything other than to confirm it was true, which was all he asked. I didn't know how much you'd planned to divulge."

"Thanks." He didn't know, either, but the truth would likely come out soon enough when Antonio stepped inside and had to be led around his own building like a blind person.

"Antonio." She hesitated for a moment. "I've been trying to shield you from the media, but you should know that coming to Falco is probably going to trip their radar. You should be prepared for a full onslaught at any time."

A crush of people, cameras, microphones, babbling. The chants of "Falco, Falco, Falco." The montage was the clearest yet of elements from his past. The memory washed over him, or rather it was a blend of several memories bleeding together, of him leaving the ring to follow his manager as Rick pushed through the crowd.

With the images came the expected renewed headache. The increased pounding and pressure wasn't so difficult to deal with if it came with new memories. But it was a brutal trade-off.

"I…" He'd been about to say he was used to reporters and cameras. But then he realized. The media wouldn't be interviewing him about his latest bout with Ramirez or Fuentes. He wasn't a fighter anymore.

Instead, the media would ask him painful questions, like, "Why don't you remember your wife?" and "What did you do for a whole year while you were gone?"

They might even ask him something even more difficult to answer, like, "How does it feel to find out you're a father after all this time?" Would the media want to crack open his life and take pictures of his children? He didn't want the babies exposed to anyone who didn't necessarily have their best interests at heart.

Caitlyn had been *shielding* him from the media. As if she wanted to protect him. It snagged a tender place inside, and he had no idea what to do with that.

"I shouldn't have come here," he muttered and turned to climb back into the Range Rover.

Fight or flight. The more he delved into his past, the

more appropriate the name Falco became. Seemed as if Antonio was constantly poised to use his talons or his wings, and he didn't like it. But he had no idea how to change it, how to achieve a happy medium where he dealt with life in a healthy way.

"Wait."

Caitlyn stopped him with a warm hand on his shoulder and the area under her palm tingled. Did all women affect him so greatly, or just this one?

Aggravated because he couldn't remember, Antonio moved out of her reach but paused before sliding into the passenger seat.

"I wasn't trying to talk you out of going inside," she said, concern lacing her tone. Enough so that he turned to face her. "This is important to you, and I think you need to do it. Five minutes. We'll walk around, say hello and then leave. The press won't have time to congregate in that length of time if you'd prefer not to be accosted."

"And then what?" he asked far more sharply than he'd intended, but she didn't flinch. "The hurdles will still be there tomorrow and the next day."

And he didn't just mean the press. All at once, the uphill battle he faced to reclaim his memories, coupled with the constant physical pain, overwhelmed him.

"That will be true whether you take this step or not." She held out her hand for him to clasp, as if she'd known exactly what he needed.

Without hesitation, he slid his hand into hers and held it, wordlessly absorbing her energy and spirit, and it calmed him instantly. Miraculously.

"Walk with me." She pulled him away from the car and shut the door. "I'll do all the talking. If you want to spar with someone, the training facility is adjacent to the administrative offices. I'm sure one of the guys would indulge you in a round. There's always a ton of people either in the rings or strength training on the gym equipment."

"How do you know so much about my company?" hc asked as he let her lead him toward the door, his pulse hammering in his temples. From nerves, trauma, the silky-sweet scent of Caitlyn? He couldn't tell. Maybe it was all three.

"I spent time here occasionally over the past year." A shadow passed through her expression. "I've brought the babies a couple of times, hoping to infuse your heritage into them. Silly, I know. They're too young to understand it."

She laughed and he felt an answering tug at his mouth. How did she do that? He'd been all set to command her to drive away as fast as she could, and when he got home, he'd probably have barred himself in his room to indulge in a fit of bad temper. Instead, Caitlyn had gotten him across the parking lot and pulled a smile from him, as well.

All in the name of physically, mentally and spiritually guiding him through a place she hadn't wanted him to go.

What an amazing, beautiful, selfless woman. The mother of his children. There was nothing temporary about her role; he saw that now. Her love for them shone through in every action, every small gesture.

Caitlyn Hopewell was his children's mother, and it was an odd addition to her attractiveness. But there it was.

That ever-present sense of disloyalty squelched the warmth in his chest that had bloomed at the sound of Caitlyn's laugh. Caitlyn was sensual and beautiful and likely that meant her sister'd had those qualities, as well. But why couldn't he remember being so outrageously attracted to Vanessa? Why couldn't he remember her touch the way he could recall with perfect clarity what Caitlyn's hand felt like on his shoulder? Surely he'd fallen for Vanessa for a myriad of reasons, especially if he'd married the redheaded sister instead of the dark-haired one. His late wife's attributes and personality must have eclipsed Caitlyn's.

But he couldn't fathom how, not when innocently thinking about Caitlyn caused a burn in his gut he couldn't explain away. It was pure, sensual attraction that he wished to explore.

How was he supposed to move past his relationship with Vanessa and potentially have a new one—especially if the woman was Caitlyn—when thinking about moving on caused a wretched sense of unfaithfulness?

Five

Antonio stepped through the glass doors to Falco with a silent sense of awe. The reception area held a hushed purpose, as if to say important matters happened between these walls, and it hit him oddly to imagine he owned all of this, had made it happen, had created this company himself through his own ingenuity and resolve.

White marble stretched under his feet, edged with red and black. Framed promotional pictures lined the walls on both sides, similar to the ones in his home gym, featuring fierce-faced fighters with raised gloves or crossed arms sporting bulging biceps. Many wore enormous title belts with distinctive, rounded shields in the center, proclaiming the fighter a world champion.

His own face stared back at him from three of the frames, one each for his three welterweight titles. The memory of posing for the shots crowded into his head, crystal clear.

But he couldn't remember picking out the marble under

his feet or the lot under the foundation or ever having walked into this building before today. It was becoming evident that his most severe memory loss encompassed the events that had happened after that final knockout Caitlyn had spoken of, the one that had ended his fighting career.

Perhaps the CT scan wasn't such a far-fetched next step. If there was something in his brain locking up his memories of that period, shouldn't he explore options to remove the block? Of course, he barely remembered Vanessa and he didn't remember Caitlyn at all, though he'd clearly known them both prior to his career-ending coma. So nothing was guaranteed.

After all, none of the Indonesian doctors had helped. Nothing had helped. And he hated hoping for a cure that would eventually amount to nothing.

In deference to the holidays, the reception area held a small decorated tree, and holly boughs covered nearly every surface. A classic Bing Crosby tune filtered through the sound system and he recognized it, of course, because his brain retaining Christmas songs made perfect sense. The receptionist looked up from her desk, blonde and perky, smiling with genuine happiness when she saw Antonio.

"Mr. Cavallari!" She shook her head, her wide-eyed gaze searching his face. "It's as if the past year never happened. I can't believe it. You look exactly the same."

Antonio nodded, because what else would he do when he couldn't remember this woman's name, though he'd probably hired her.

"Hi, Mandy," Caitlyn said smoothly, as if she'd read his mind. "Antonio would like to see what you've done with the place in his absence. I assured him that Thomas and his stellar team kept things in order, but there's nothing like an in-person tour, right?"

Rescued again. Antonio squelched the gratefulness

flooding his chest, because how long could Caitlyn's savior superpowers actually last? It was a fluke anyway. There was no way she'd picked up on his distress. They barely knew each other and besides, her ability to read his mind had to be flawed; *he* didn't even know what was in his head most of the time.

"Of course." The receptionist—Mandy—smiled at Caitlyn and picked up the phone on the desk to murmur into it, then glanced up again. "Thomas will be here momentarily to show you around. Glad you're…um…*here*, Mr. Cavallari."

Here, meaning not dead. That was definitely a plus and cheered him slightly. "Thanks, Mandy. I plan to be around for a long time."

A man with a graying crew cut wearing an expensive, tailored suit bustled into the reception area. *Thomas*.

A memory of the two of them standing in nearly this same spot popped into Antonio's head, from Thomas's first day on the job. Relief stung the back of Antonio's throat. His memories were in there somewhere. It just took the right combination of criteria for them to battle to the forefront.

Thomas Warren was flanked by a couple of younger men in sweatpants and hoodies. Fighters. They wore almost identical expressions with a slight menacing edge, and they both leaned into the room, fists lightly curled as if preparing to start swinging.

Antonio recognized the stance instantly—he'd entered thousands of rooms that way. Still did, even now. Or perhaps he'd only picked it up again recently. Had he lost that ready-to-fly edge in the past few years, only to regain it after awakening to a blank world where simply entering a room brought on a barrage of questions and few answers?

These were the pieces of Antonio Cavallari he hoped to recover inside this building.

"Thomas." Antonio held out his hand to the older man, who shook Antonio's hand with a critical once-over.

"It's true." The interim CEO of Falco Fight Club narrowed his gaze, mouth slightly open as he fixated on Antonio's face. "I guess you can call me a doubting Thomas because I really didn't believe it until I saw you for myself. Come, let me show you the improvements we've made in your…ah, absence."

Seemed as if everyone was going to stumble over the proper verbiage to explain they'd assumed Antonio had died in the plane crash. He didn't blame them; he didn't have any clue what you were supposed to say, either.

"Let's put pretense aside," Antonio said before he'd fully determined what he planned to say. "You thought I was dead and spent the past year accordingly. I may disagree with some, or even all, of your decisions, but I fail to see how I could find fault with them. You did what you thought was right and I have no intention of walking in here to undo everything you've done."

Thomas's eyebrows rose. "Fair enough. It is an unprecedented situation and I appreciate that we might both need to maintain flexibility."

Thomas inclined his head and indicated Antonio should follow him into the interior of the building.

The two fighters fell in behind as well, and Antonio had the distinct sense the men were either intended as intimidation or accessory. It didn't matter which; either one was as laughable as it was baffling.

The short tour generated little in the way of jogging his memories, but the visit to Falco itself had already yielded a valuable harvest. Antonio had the unique opportunity to appreciate what he'd built using his own fortitude and business savvy as he surveyed it for what was, for all intents and purposes, the first time.

The vast influence of Falco unrolled before him as he

learned of his vision for bringing glory back to the sport of mixed martial arts with a promotional powerhouse that had no ties to a media conglomerate. Untainted by corporate politics or the need for a healthy bottom line, Antonio had pushed boundaries, opening MMA to unconventional fighting disciplines, training some of the most elite fighters in the world and gaining entry to off-the-beaten-path venues. Most important, he'd insisted all his fighters be allowed to compete for titles based on their records, not handshake promotional deals.

And he'd been wildly successful, beyond anything he'd envisioned when Caitlyn mentioned Falco was where he'd made all his money. When he'd asked Thomas to show him the books, his eye had shot straight to the profit line, as if he'd last glanced at a balance sheet yesterday. The number of decimal places couldn't be right, and Antonio had nearly chalked it up to a clerical error until he glanced at the rest of the line items.

Not a mistake. Billions of dollars flowed through his company. It was dizzying. He should have paid more attention to the balances of his accounts when Caitlyn had transferred control of his estate back to him at his lawyer's office the other day.

No wonder Caitlyn hadn't taken the first opportunity to get out of Dodge when he'd offered to relieve her of baby duty. He could easily give her eight or nine figures for her trouble and never think twice about it, which was probably what she was hoping for. She seemed to genuinely care about the children, but everyone wanted something, and that something tended to be money.

"I want to see the training facility," Antonio announced abruptly.

"Absolutely." Thomas led the way to the adjacent building.

Energy bolted through his body as he anticipated climbing between the ropes. That had been his sole purpose in coming here and it had thus far been eclipsed by a slow slide back into Businessman Antonio.

Which didn't seem as bad as it once might have.

Maybe part of his journey lay in coupling both halves of his soul—the fighter and the suit—under one banner. But it wouldn't be today. He needed to get his wits about him, what few remained, and the ring was the only place where he'd experienced any peace in the past year.

As he entered the training facility, Antonio's lungs hitched as his eye was drawn to the equipment closet, to the three rings, one with a regulation metal cage surrounding it, to the workout area. Exactly where he'd known they would all be placed. Because he truly remembered, or because he'd modeled the layout on another facility from before the career-ending knockout?

Eager to find out, he strode through the cavernous room, drawing the attention of the muscled men—and surprisingly, a few women—engaged in various activities. One by one, weights drifted to the ground and sparring partners halted, gloves down, as they stared at him.

"That's right," he called to the room at large. "I've arisen from my watery grave. Who's brave enough to go a round with a ghost?"

"Cavallari, you sly dog." A grinning Hispanic male, early twenties, jogged over from his spot at a weight bench and punched Antonio on the arm as if he'd done it often. "They told us you were dead. What have you been doing, hiding out to get back in professional shape without any pressure? Smart."

What a ridiculous notion. Ridiculously brilliant. Maybe he'd adopt it as his easy out if the media did start harassing him about his whereabouts over the past year.

"Hey, Rodrigo," Caitlyn called, and when Antonio

glanced at her, she winked, and then murmured under her breath, "Rodrigo was a good friend. Before."

When they got home, he'd treat her to the most expensive bottle of wine in his cellar. And then when she was good and looped, he'd carefully extract her real agenda.

No matter how much she seemed to love his kids, no one did nice things without a motive. He wanted to know what hers was.

"Are you my volunteer?" Antonio jerked his head at the nearest ring, eyes on his potential sparring partner.

"Sure, boss." Rodrigo shadowboxed a couple of jabs at Antonio's gut. "Like old times. Just go easy on me if your secret training put you out of my league."

Rodrigo's grin belied the seriousness of the statement—did he not believe Antonio had actually trained over the past year or did he assume that regardless, they'd still be matched in skill? Apparently, they'd sparred before and had been on pretty equal ground.

"Likewise," Antonio commented, mirroring Rodrigo's grin because it felt expected. Honestly, he had no idea how they'd match up. He couldn't wait to find out.

Something inside rotated into place, as if two gears had been grinding together haphazardly, and all at once, the teeth aligned, humming like a well-oiled machine.

His headache had almost receded and if God had been listening to his pleas at all, the next few minutes would knock loose a precious memory or two.

Before long, Antonio had slipped into the shorts Caitlyn had insisted he bring from home. She watched him face off against Rodrigo in the large ring, both men barechested and barefoot. It hadn't taken the office grapevine but about five minutes to circulate the news that Antonio Cavallari was both back and in the ring. Nearly everyone from FFC's administrative building had crowded into the training facility and around the cage with expectant faces, murmuring about Antonio's return.

You couldn't have pried most of the women's gazes from Antonio with a crowbar, Caitlyn's included, though she at least tried to hide it. But he was magnificent, sinewy and hard, with that fierce tattoo so prominent against his golden body. His still-longish hair was slicked back from his forehead, highlighting his striking eyes as they glittered like black diamonds.

Apparently she liked him as a fighter just as much as she liked the savvy businessman. Maybe more. Her raw reaction at the sight of Antonio in the ring was powerful and uncomfortably warm. Hot, even. And far lower than seemed appropriate in public.

It was shameful. Shameful to be so affected by her sister's husband, shameful that she'd carried a yet-to-be-extinguished torch for Antonio all of these years. Most shameful of all was that at least half of his appeal lay in his primal stance as he waited for an opening to do bodily harm to another human. She'd always thought of him as the perfect man—committed, beautiful, steady. And it frightened her to be so attracted to him for purely carnal reasons.

But she couldn't stop the flood of elemental longing any more than she could explain how over-the-top sexy the man had become once he slipped into his glory in the ring.

She'd never seen him fight live. Once he and Vanessa had hooked up, she'd spent a lot of time feeling sorry for herself and as little time as possible around the two of them. It was too hard to be reminded that he'd picked the glamorous Hopewell sister instead of the quiet, unassuming one. Not that she blamed him; most men had overlooked Caitlyn in favor of Vanessa, and Caitlyn had never been bitter about it. Until Antonio.

She'd spent the entirety of their marriage hiding her hurt and disappointment and jealousy, the entirety of their relationship wishing she could have her sister's marriage... and then the past year feeling guilty and sick about the uncharitable thoughts she'd had.

Now she just wanted to feel as if she didn't have to apologize for being alive when her sister wasn't. For being a woman affected by a prime specimen of man as he engaged in physical combat. Was that so wrong?

The men circled each other, trash-talking. Suddenly, Antonio lashed out in a blur of intricately executed moves, both beautiful and lethally graceful. Her breath caught as she drank in the visual panorama. Antonio's body moved fluidly, as if it had been made specifically for this purpose, and it was stunning to behold.

In enabling him to return to the ring, she'd unwittingly exposed herself to a piece of his soul that was the opposite of harsh, the opposite of brutal. It was breathtaking.

Caitlyn blinked as Rodrigo hit the mat without having lodged one defense.

Violence was unfolding before her very eyes and the only thing she'd noticed was how exquisitely Antonio had executed it. Something was very wrong with her.

The crowd murmured as Rodrigo shook his head and climbed to his feet, rubbing his jaw.

"Lucky shot, boss," he grumbled.

Not that she had any basis for judgment, but Caitlyn didn't think so. As the men went at it again, Antonio's superior skill and style couldn't be mistaken, even by an untrained eye such as hers. Rodrigo landed a couple of shots, but the younger man called a halt to the match after only a few more minutes, breathing heavily. Caitlyn grimaced at his split lip.

Rodrigo and Antonio shook hands and the crowd slowly dispersed, many of them stopping to welcome Antonio back or clap him on the shoulder with a few congratulatory words about his performance.

Caitlyn hung back, remaining as unobtrusive as possible while Antonio excused himself to shower and change. No one was paying attention to her anyway, which she considered a blessing as long as her insides were still so unsettled. This whole Falco Fight Club experience had shown her something about herself that she didn't understand and didn't know what to do with.

Antonio returned. His gaze cut through the crowd and locked on to hers, his eyes dark with something untamed and unnameable and she shivered. It was as if he knew exactly where she was in the crowd. And exactly what she'd been thinking about while watching him fight.

Her cheeks heated and she blessed his distance because, hopefully, that meant he couldn't tell. But the distance disappeared as he strode directly to her.

Though clothed, his potency hadn't diminished in the slightest. Because she knew what his hard body looked like under his crisp white shirt and slacks. Heat rolled between them and his gaze fell to her mouth for a moment as if he was thinking about dropping a kiss there.

Her lips tingled under his scrutiny. Madness. She'd fallen under some kind of spell that caused her imagination to run away with her, obviously.

"I'm ready to go home," he murmured and the moment broke apart. "I've had enough for one day."

"Sure," she managed to get out around the tight, hot lump in her throat.

Goody. Now they could cram themselves into a tiny Range Rover for the drive home, where his masculine scent would overpower her, and she'd spend the drive reminding herself that no matter how sexy he was, the complications between them were legion.

Which was exactly what happened. She gripped the wheel, white-knuckling it onto the main street and, thankfully, Antonio fell silent.

Too silent. He'd just reentered his old world in the most immersive way possible. She desperately wanted to ask him about it.

Had he remembered any of Falco? All of it? What had it felt like for him to get in the ring again? Antonio hadn't fought professionally in years and, as far as Caitlyn knew, Vanessa had forbid him from even messing around with the guys in the ring because she feared he'd get hurt again.

Part of Caitlyn wondered if she'd helped facilitate his return to Falco because it was something her sister never would have done. As if it was some kind of sick contest to see if Antonio would realize Caitlyn was the better woman for him.

But she had no idea how to navigate the heavy vibe in the Range Rover, so she kept her mouth shut and let the silence ride.

When they got home, she followed him into the house from the garage, unable to stand the silence any longer. "How's your head?"

That was a safe enough topic, wasn't it?

He paused in the kitchen to get a glass of water and gulped the entire thing down before answering. "It hurts."

She leaned a hip on the granite countertop as close to him as she dared and crossed her arms over her still-unsettled insides. "Why don't you take a painkiller and rest."

"Because I'm not ninety and waiting around to die," he said shortly, then frowned. "Sorry, I don't mean to snap."

The line between his eyebrows concerned her and she regretted not encouraging him to talk to her while they'd been in the car. Her own uncertainties weren't an excuse to be selfish. "It's okay. You've had a difficult day."

His gaze latched on to hers and he surveyed her with a focused, hooded expression that pulled at something deep in her core. In or out of the ring—didn't matter. He exuded a primal energy that she couldn't stop herself from reacting to, and it was as frightening as it was thrilling.

The way Antonio made her feel had nothing to do with the safe, nebulous fantasy she'd carried around in her heart for years. *That*, she understood. The raw, ferocious draw between them, she didn't.

"Difficult?" he repeated. "Really? What gives you that impression?"

"Uh…because you're snapping at me?" When the corners of his mouth lifted, she smiled involuntarily in return. "It couldn't have been easy to get into the ring today in front of all your colleagues. How long has it been since you last went a round?"

"A couple of weeks. I trained six hours a day in Indonesia over the past few months. It was part of my rehabilitation."

"Oh, you never mentioned that." And why would he? She wasn't his confidante. But she'd kind of hoped he saw her in that role, as someone he could turn to, who would be there for him in a confusing world.

"It wasn't worth mentioning." A smile still played with his lips and she couldn't tear her gaze from his mouth as he talked. "Indonesia was about survival. Only. I fight—then and now—because I have to."

The confessions of his deepest self were as affecting as watching him fight had been. She wanted more but was afraid of what it might mean to get it. "I remember you said you needed to get in the ring to blow off frustration. Did it work?"

"Partially," he allowed. "I need a more skilled partner."

"Yes, even I could see that Rodrigo was outmatched."

A blanket of intimacy settled around them as a full, genuine smile bloomed on his face, and she reveled in it.

Brigitte bustled into the kitchen at that moment, shattering the mood. "Oh, you're back. Grand. Do you want to spend time with the babies before dinner?"

Taking a guilty step backward, Caitlyn tore her gaze from Antonio to focus on the au pair. "Um, yes. Of course."

She always played with the babies before dinner while Brigitte helped the chef, Francesco, put the children's meal together. What was wrong with Caitlyn that she hadn't noticed the time? Well, duh—Antonio was what was wrong with her.

"They're in their cribs waiting for you," Brigitte said sunnily and went to the fridge to pull out covered bowls of premashed fruit and veggies.

"Come with me." Caitlyn put a hand on Antonio's arm before she thought better of it. Heat prickled her palm and she snatched it back. "It'll be fun. Low pressure."

Fun, plus an excuse to stay in his presence under the pretense of guiding his steps toward fatherhood—but with the added distance the babies would automatically create.

Then she remembered his headache. "You don't have to if you'd rather be alone. I don't want to push you into a role you're not ready for."

"I'd like to," he said, surprising her.

He followed her upstairs and into the nursery. Leon stood in the center of his crib, both chubby hands gripping the edge to support his wobbly legs as he yowled like a wet cat. Annabelle sat with her back to the room banging one of the crib slats with a rattle while sweet Antonio Junior lay on his back staring at the mobile above his crib.

"There you go," Caitlyn murmured to their father. "This is a perfect encapsulation of your children's personalities. Leon does not like being forced to do something and he isn't a bit hesitant to tell you how unhappy he is. He'll be the first to learn how to climb out of his crib, mark my words. God help us then."

"Why?" Antonio eyed first his son and then Caitlyn as

she boosted Leon from his crib and into her arms, which predictably, quieted down his protests.

"Because then he'll be a holy terror, climbing out in the middle of the night while we're asleep." She nodded to the baby. "Would you like to hold him?"

"Yes," he said decisively and then his brows drew together as Caitlyn handed over the baby. "Do I have to do anything?"

"Nothing special, just make sure he feels secure."

She laughed as Leon peered up at his father suspiciously, as if trying to figure out whether he was okay with this new person. They'd learn the verdict in about two seconds.

Thankfully, Leon waved his fist around, which was his way of saying things were cool. Antonio's gaze never left his son's face, and his clear adoration shot straight through Caitlyn's heart with a painful, wonderful arrow.

Caitlyn spun to busy herself with Antonio Junior before the tears pricking at her eyelids actually fell in a mortifying display of sentiment. It was just a dad with his kid. Why should it be so tender and meaningful?

There were so many reasons locked up in that question, she could hardly start answering it—but first and foremost, because it was her kid, too, one she'd created with this man in a most unconventional way, sure, but that didn't make it any less powerful to watch the two interact.

Then there was the compelling contrast between this tender version of Antonio and the fierce warrior he'd been in the ring. The dichotomy created an even more compelling man, and he was already so mesmerizing, she could hardly think.

Antonio Junior hadn't made a sound since they'd entered the room, so Caitlyn checked on him as she often did, just to be sure he was still breathing. He'd always been quiet, carrying the weight of the world on his shoulders, and it bothered her that he'd adopted such a grave demeanor.

He definitely took after his father in that respect, where Leon was a demanding prima donna like Vanessa.

"That's my serious little man," she crooned to Antonio Junior and slid her fingertips across his fine dark hair as he refocused his gaze from the mobile to Caitlyn.

The sheer beauty of her child nearly took her breath. She'd always thought he looked like Antonio, but it had been an academic observation based on memory and expectation—they both had dark hair and dark eyes; of course the comparisons would come.

"Is he serious?" Antonio asked with genuine curiosity.

"Very. He's also quiet. Annabelle would probably be content to sit in her crib until the cows came home as long as she could make noise," Caitlyn called over her shoulder and, dang it, her voice caught on the emotion still clogging her throat. She cleared it, hoping Antonio had been too caught up in Leon to notice. "That's her favorite thing. Noise. She likes it best when she can bang on something and then imitate the noise with her voice and, trust me, she practices a lot."

"I don't mind," Antonio said softly, and she sensed him come up behind her long before she heard his quiet intake of breath. He peered over her shoulder into Annabelle's crib. "Hi, there, sweetheart."

Annabelle tipped her head up to focus on her father, her upside-down face beaming. "Gah."

"Is that her imitation of banging the rattle?" Antonio asked with a laugh. "Because she should practice some more."

"No, that's how she says hello."

Caitlyn's throat tightened again, which was silly when she was only explaining her children's quirks. But their father didn't know any of these things—because he'd been lost and alone half a world away while she'd lived in his house, cared for his children and spent his money. She wanted to make that up to him as best she could.

"Come on, you big flirt." Caitlyn hoisted Annabelle out of the crib and set her on the soft pink blanket already spread out on the nursery floor. "I realize pink is clichéd for a girl, but I thought Annabelle needed girlie things with two brothers."

"You don't have to justify your choices." Antonio crouched down on the blanket and settled Leon next to his sister. "I'd be the last person to tell you you're doing it wrong, and even if I have a conflicting opinion, I'd prefer to talk through it, not issue countercommands. You've done the best you can, and it couldn't have been easy to do it alone."

"It wasn't." One tear spilled over before she could catch it. "I worried every day that I wasn't enough for them."

Antonio glanced up from his perch on the fluffy pink blanket, which should have looked ridiculous but didn't in the slightest. "You've been amazing. More than enough. Look at how perfect these babies are. Healthy, happy. What more could you have provided?"

"A father," she whispered. And somehow the fates had granted that wish in the most unexpected, flawless way possible. "They deserve two parents."

A shadow passed over his face. "And for now, that's what they have."

For now? Was that a cryptic comment about the future of her place in this family?

"No matter what happens, I will always be their mother," she stated firmly, and if only her voice hadn't cracked, it might have sounded as authoritative out loud as it had in her head.

They needed to talk about the future, but she was afraid to bring it up, afraid to overload him with one more thing he didn't want to deal with, afraid he was only letting her stay because it was Christmas and she'd begged him not to kick her out.

But she had to get over it and go to the mat for her children. If anyone could understand the bone-deep need to fight for what you wanted, it would surely be Antonio.

"Yes," he said quietly. "You *are* their mother."

And that took the wind out of her sails so fast, she couldn't breathe. "Okay, then."

She'd have to bring up the future another time, after she'd recovered from all of this.

Six

Antonio's headache persisted through dinner, but he couldn't stomach the idea of taking the pills now that he actually had them. He'd lost so much of his past; losing his present to drowsiness held little appeal. Instead, he bided his time until Caitlyn and Brigitte put the babies to bed and then he cornered Caitlyn in the sunroom.

He hoped she wouldn't mind the interruption. It was time to dig into what Caitlyn wanted from him in exchange for the role she'd played thus far in his life and the lives of his children. And did she see a continued role? If so, what role did she envision for herself?

The sun had set long ago and Caitlyn read by low lamplight. He started to say her name but the words dried up on his tongue. Something inside lurched sweetly, as confusing as it was intriguing. Silently, he watched her, loath to alert her to his presence until he was good and finished sating himself on her ethereal beauty.

But she glanced up almost instantly, as if she'd sensed

him. He knew the feeling. There was an undeniable draw between them, and he'd bet every last dollar that she felt it, too. Maybe it was time to dig into that as well, and find out what role *he* wanted her to play.

"Have a glass with me?" He held up the uncorked bottle of wine he'd judiciously selected from his extensive wine cellar.

"Um, sure." Her fair skin bloomed with that blush he liked far more than he should. But what had brought it out? He had a perverse need to find out.

Which seemed to be the theme of this nighttime rendezvous. He'd barely scratched the surface of what made Caitlyn Hopewell tick, and exposing her layers appealed to him immensely.

Antonio poured two glasses of the deep red cabernet and handed one to Caitlyn, then settled into the other chair, separated from hers by a small wooden end table. For a moment, he watched the moonlight dance on the silvery surf so beautifully framed by the wall of glass opposite the chairs.

"I bought this house specifically for the view from this room," he commented instead of diving right in. "It's my favorite spot."

"Mine, too," Caitlyn agreed quietly.

"I figured. This is where I find you most often." He sipped his wine, rolling it around on his tongue as the easy silence stretched. For once, Caitlyn didn't seem determined to fill the gap with nervous chatter.

It was nice to sit with no expectations and not worry about his missing memories. His headache eased the longer he watched the waves crash on the shore below.

"Did you have something on your mind?" she blurted out and then sighed. "I mean, other than the regular stuff, like becoming a father and having amnesia and learning to live in civilization again and—"

"Caitlyn." He touched the rim of his glass to hers in silent apology for the interruption, but he wasn't really sorry. He liked that she gave him so many opportunities to say her name. "I wanted to have a bottle of wine with you. As you pointed out, if nothing else, we're a family by default. Nothing wrong with acting like one."

She didn't relax. "Except we're not a family, not really. You were all set to send me on my way until I convinced you to let me stay through the holidays. Then what, Antonio? I need to know what you plan to do."

Nothing like laying it on the line. Apparently, the easy silence hadn't been so easy for her. If she wasn't keen on a social drink, they didn't have to play nice. Shame. He'd have preferred to have the wine flowing before getting to the reason he'd tracked her down.

But clearly, her ability to read him wasn't a fluke, as he'd assumed earlier today.

"I'm not sure," he said carefully. "It's not January yet and I have a lot to consider. Tell me what you'd like to see happen."

Her fingers gripped the stem of the wineglass until her nail beds turned white. "That's difficult to answer."

Because she didn't want to come right out and say that on the first of January, she'd take a wire transfer with nine zeros tacked onto the end? "Then, maybe you can answer this for me. Why did you rescue me at Falco so many times today? It was as if you could read the room and tell exactly when I was floundering."

"Oh, um…" Her eyebrows drew together as her gaze flew to his face, searching it, and unexpected rawness sprang into the depths of her eyes. "I don't know. It was painfully obvious when you didn't remember someone. I hated that you were uncertain."

That rawness—it nearly eviscerated him with its strength. What did it mean? He had no context for it, not with her, not with any woman. And he wanted to know if it signified the same intense desire to explore each other, the way it did in him.

The draw between them grew tighter as he contemplated her. "Obvious?"

"Well, probably not to everyone," she corrected quickly. "To me anyway. I was, uh…paying attention."

Her gaze traveled down his body, and she didn't try to hide it, probably because she had no idea how to play coy. Heat flared in his loins as he became extremely aware of how the lamp highlighted the curves under her clothes. "I never thanked you for paying such close *attention*. I'm curious, though. What do you hope to gain from helping me?"

"Gain?" She cocked her head, confusion evident. "I'm helping you navigate your life because you need me. You told me so. I want to help."

"Why?"

"Because I like the fact that you need me!" Her eyelids flew shut and she shook her head. Leaping to her feet, she backed away. "I didn't mean to say that."

"Caitlyn." He'd upset her, and he didn't like the way it snagged at his gut to be responsible for the distress around her mouth and eyes.

He'd much rather be responsible for the raw intensity he'd glimpsed a moment ago.

When he slid from his chair and approached her, she stood her ground despite the fact that her body was poised to flee.

"Wait," he murmured. "What did you mean to say?"

She wouldn't meet his gaze. "I meant to say that the children are my first priority."

No, there was more here, more she didn't want to say, more she didn't want him to discover—and that unidentified something called to him.

Instinct alone guided his hand to her chin and he tipped

her head up to evaluate her stricken expression. "Mine, too. That's why I ask these questions. I want to know whether you're helping me in hopes of a nice payout. Or some other, yet-to-be-determined motive."

"Really, Antonio?" Fire flared in her blue eyes, surprising him in its intensity. "Do you have any context for what being a mother means? What it means to me personally?"

Her lips curled into a harsh smile and he couldn't stop watching her, fascinated by the physical changes in her as she schooled him. Even more surprising, she didn't pull away but pushed her chin deeper into his grip.

"Leon, Annabelle and Antonio Junior are my *children*," she continued, her voice dipping lower with each impassioned word. "Just as much as they're yours. More so. I carried them in my womb and I've raised them. I could do it on an accountant's salary and would have if the judge hadn't granted me conservatorship of their inheritance. Keep your money. This is about love."

Love. A nebulous notion that he should understand but didn't.

With that one word, the atmosphere in the sunroom shifted, growing heavier with awareness. Her body leaned toward his, bristling with vibrancy. No longer poised to flee but to fight.

It reached out and punched him with a dark thrill. She wasn't backing down. She was prepared to meet him halfway, taking whatever he dished out. But what would she do with it?

"Hmm." The sound purred from his throat as he slanted her chin a touch higher. "Let's examine that. What do you know about love?"

More important, did she know the things he wanted to learn?

"I know enough," she retorted. "I know when I look at those babies, my heart feels as if it's about to explode with so many wonderful, terrible emotions. I know what it feels like to lose my sister to an early death and sob for days and days because I can't ever tell her I love her again."

Yes, that tightness in his chest when he'd gazed at his own flesh and blood encapsulated in a tiny person for the first time. It *was* wonderful and terrible. And inexplicably, that decided it. She was telling the truth about her motives, and all interest in grilling her over them evaporated.

Now his agenda included one thing and one thing only—Caitlyn and getting more of her soft skin under his fingers.

Love for a child he understood, but it wasn't the full extent of the kind of love possible. The kind of love he must have had for Vanessa. *That* was the concept that stayed maddeningly out of reach. "What about love for a man? Romantically."

"What, as if you're going to prove my motives are ugly because I've never been in love?" Fiercely, she eyed him. "I know how it feels to want a man to tell you he loves you. You want it so badly that you can't breathe. You want him to touch you and kiss you. It hurts deep down every second that you don't get it. And when you do get it, you want it to last forever."

Electricity arced between them and he ached to close the distance between them, to give her everything on her checklist, right here, right now.

"Is that what you wanted to hear?" she said, her chest rising and falling with quickened breath. "Love is equal parts need and commitment. What do *you* know about love?"

"Nothing," he growled, and instantly, the reality of it crushed through his chest.

The love that she'd painted with her impassioned speech—he wanted that. Wanted to know that he *could* feel like that. But love grew over time, over shared experiences, over shared memories.

He'd been robbed of that when he crashed in the ocean. But he had a chance to start over with someone else, to move on from the past he couldn't reclaim.

This nighttime interlude had started out as a way to get her to explain her motives, but instead, she'd uncovered his. Everything he wanted was right here, gripped in his hand. So he took it.

Hauling Caitlyn forward, he fused his mouth to hers. Hungrily, desperately, he kissed her, and his body ignited in a firestorm of sensation. Her mouth came alive under his, taking and giving with each stroke, matching him in the power of her appetite. He soared into the heavens in the most intense flight he'd ever experienced.

His eyes slammed shut as he savored the tight, heated pulls in his groin that could only be eased by burying himself in this woman, body and soul. *More*. He worked her mouth open and her tongue met his in the middle in a perfect, hot clash of flesh. Her eagerness coursed through him, spurring him on, begging him to take her deeper.

His mind drained of everything except her. He felt alive in the most elemental way, as if he'd been snatched from the jaws of hell for this moment, this woman.

Scrabbling for purchase, he slid his arms around her, aligning her with his body and dragging her into the most intimate of embraces. She clung to his shoulders and the contact sparked through his shirt. The contrast of her soft curves sliding against his brutally hardened torso and thighs drove him wild with sharp-edged need.

So frustrating. Too many clothes in the way. His fingertips explored her automatically, mindlessly, craving her. He wanted every millimeter of her beautiful skin exposed, wanted to taste it, feel it, rake it with his gaze and incite that gorgeous blush she could never seem to stop.

The kiss abruptly ended. Caitlyn tore out of his arms, hair in wild disarray from his questing fingers. Chest heaving, she stared at him, eyes limpid and heated.

And then she fled without a word.

Still mortified over her brazen behavior, Caitlyn curled in a ball on her bed, praying none of the babies would wake up tonight. Praying that Antonio didn't take her display of wantonness as an invitation to knock on her door. Because she didn't know if she'd open it. Or never come out.

She'd kissed her sister's husband. And the guilt was killing her—almost as much as the fact that she wouldn't stop herself from doing it again.

That kiss had rocked her to the core.

And shattered all her harmless fantasies about what it might be like to kiss Antonio.

The gap between imagination and reality was so wide, she couldn't see across it. Never would she have imagined her body capable of feeling such raw *need*. Or such a desire to let Antonio take her further into the descent of sensual pleasure, a place she'd never gone with any man.

The way he made her feel scared her, no doubt. But she scared herself even more. She was afraid of her own impaired judgment. If she gave in to that swirl of dark desire—which had seemed like a very real possibility when Antonio had taken her into his arms—what happened then? Was Antonio gearing up for a marriage proposal? She had no idea how any of this worked. Where his thoughts were on the matter. How you even brought up such important subjects as commitment and love when a man had done nothing more than kiss you.

She needed these questions answered before she let these confusing new feelings brainwash her. The confusion was made even worse by the fact that it was *Antonio* on the other end of the equation. A different, harder, sexier, more over-the-top Antonio, who wasn't necessarily the man he'd been. She had no idea how to handle any of this.

And while she'd long ago accepted that she was already half in love with him, he hadn't professed any such thing to her. Sex was a big deal and until she knew he got that, no more kissing. Otherwise, she might find herself on the wrong side of a broken heart—as she'd always feared.

Along with a guilty conscience she couldn't shake, it was too much.

So they'd just have to pretend that scorching, mind-altering kiss had never happened.

By morning, she'd figured out that was impossible. The long, need-soaked night had not been kind.

Today's goal: get Antonio into a public place so he couldn't entice her again.

When he entered the breakfast nook, fresh from the shower, her heart did a crazy, erratic dance. It was sinful how perfect he was, how well his shoulders filled out a simple T-shirt, how his sinewy arms made her want to run her fingertips across them. Those arms... They'd held her expertly last night as he'd treated her to the most passionate kiss of her life.

How did the sight of him muddle her insides so much?

"Good morning," he murmured, his gaze full of knowledge.

"Hi," she squeaked in return. What did that dark, enigmatic look mean? That he remembered the taste of their kiss and wanted more?

Or was that a classic case of projection since that was what *she* was thinking? Would he even bring up the kiss, or was he of the same mind that it was better to forget about it?

Quickly, she tore her gaze from his and concentrated on her...oatmeal. At least that was what she vaguely recalled she'd been eating before he'd waltzed in and stolen her ability to use her brain.

"Would you like to go Christmas shopping with me today?" she asked and winced at the desperation in the question. As if she was dying to spend the day in his company instead of the truth—public places were her new best friend.

He pursed his perfect lips, which made it really hard not to stare at them. *Oatmeal.* She put her head down and shoveled some in her mouth.

"I'd like that," he said easily. "Will we shop for the children? Or are they too young for gifts?"

"Oh, no. It's their first Christmas. I planned to shower them with presents and lots of brightly wrapped boxes. You know how kids only like to play with the boxes? I thought it would be fun to have empty boxes as well as toys. Of course, I came up with all of that before you returned, so if it's too extravagant—"

"Caitlyn."

She didn't look up. Didn't have to in order to know she was rambling again. Her name was like a code word. Anytime she heard it, it meant *shut up.*

With a soft rush of cloth, he crossed the breakfast nook, pausing by her chair. He tilted her chin to force her to meet his gaze. The way he'd done last night, but this morning, she didn't have the fuel of righteous indignation to keep her semisane. Caught in the grip of his powerful presence, she watched him, unable to look away or breathe. His fingers were like live electrical conduits, zapping her skin with energy, and she was pretty sure the heat had climbed into her cheeks.

"Let's just go shopping, okay?" he asked. "Money is not subject to discussion today."

"Oh. Um, really?" That certainly wasn't the tune he'd

been singing last night. "I told you, I don't want your money, nor am I okay with treating you like a blank check."

She *had* said that, hadn't she? The atmosphere last night had been so vibrant and intense, there was no telling what she'd actually communicated now that she thought back.

"I believe you. So let's be clear. I'm paying. You are shopping." His smile broadened as she opened her mouth. "And not arguing," he added quickly before she could interrupt.

"So you don't have my name in your head next to a little check box labeled 'gold digger' anymore?" she asked suspiciously.

He shook his head and dropped his hand, which she instantly wished he'd put back simply because she liked his touch.

"I'm sorry. I was less than tactful last night. We still have the future to sort out, but I'm less concerned about that today than I was yesterday. I'm willing to see what happens."

"You know I'm breast-feeding the babies, right?" she blurted out, and yeah, that heat was definitely in her cheeks.

His gaze narrowed, but to his credit, he didn't outwardly react to such an intimate topic. "All three of them?"

She scowled. "Yes, all three of them. Why in the world would I be selective?"

For some reason, that amused him. "I wasn't suggesting you should be. Forgive my surprise. It just seems like a huge undertaking. Though, admittedly, my understanding of the mechanics is limited."

Yeah, she'd bet he understood breasts better than most men. "It's a sacrifice, for sure, but one I'm more than willing to make. But the point is, I can't just stop. So there's not a lot of room for seeing how it goes. I'm their mother, not an employee."

He nodded. "I'm beginning to see that point more clearly."

At last. There was no telling if he'd actually softened his stance or whether she could explain her feelings any better now than she'd thus far been able to. But the time seemed right to try.

She shut her eyes for a beat and laid it on the line. "Well, thank you for that. You asked me last night what I envision and honestly, I see us co-parenting."

"You mean long-term?" Even that didn't ruffle his composure, which, hopefully, meant it wasn't too far out of a suggestion in his mind.

"Forever. They're my children," she said simply. "I want to shop for Annabelle's prom dress, see them graduate from college, be there when they get married. The works. There's not one single thing I'd agree to miss."

His silence wasn't very reassuring. Finally, he nodded once. "I don't know how to do that. But I'm willing to talk about it after the holidays, like we agreed. It will give us time to think about what that looks like."

Breath she hadn't realized she was holding whooshed out. It was something. Not the full-bore yes she'd have preferred but more than she'd had five minutes ago.

"That's great. Thank you. It means a lot to me."

"It means a lot to me that you're willing to be their mother." His dark, hooded expression sought hers and held again and she shivered under the intensity. "They need a mother. Who better than the one who carried them for nine months?"

"That's exactly what I've been trying to tell you," she said and wished she could have pulled that off with a smirk, but it probably just sounded grateful.

"Let me eat some breakfast and we'll go shopping." He smiled as Francesco hustled into the breakfast nook, carrying a bowl of oatmeal and some coffee with two teaspoons of sugar, milk and a shot of espresso, the way Antonio liked it.

Not that she'd memorized his likes and dislikes over the years, but she found it interesting that his coffee preference hadn't changed even through the nightmare of amnesia.

"I'll drive," she told him. "Unless your headache is better?"

"It's not as bad today." He glanced at her. "I took a painkiller last night. Figured it was the only way I'd get to sleep after you ran out on me."

Amusement danced through his gaze along with a hint of heat that she had no trouble understanding. And on cue, there came the stupid blush. "I'm sorry. That was juvenile."

"Why did you take off, then?" Casually, he spooned up some oatmeal as if the answer didn't matter, but she caught the tightness around his mouth.

"It was too much," she said carefully. And honestly. "We have a lot of challenges in front of us. I'd like to focus on them without…complications."

That part wasn't the whole truth, but it was certainly true enough.

"That's a good point." Antonio polished off his breakfast without fanfare and without arguing.

Caitlyn frowned. Was she that easy to resist?

It didn't matter. No more kissing. That was the rule and she was sticking to it.

She stood and moved toward the door of the breakfast nook, hoping it didn't appear too much as if she was running away again, but Antonio confused her and she wanted to find a place where she could breathe for a few minutes. "I'll be ready to go shopping in about thirty minutes, if that's okay."

"Caitlyn."

She paused but didn't turn around.

"You focus on your challenges your way, and I'll focus on my challenges my way."

"What's that supposed to mean?" she whispered, afraid she wasn't going to like the answer.

"It means I'm going to kiss you again. The complications aren't great enough to stop me. You'd best think of another argument if you don't want me to."

Seven

The Malibu Country Mart at Christmastime might not have been the smartest choice for keeping her distance from Antonio. For the fourth time, the crush of holiday shoppers forced them together, and for the fourth time, his thigh brushed Caitlyn's hand.

She snatched it back before considering how telling a gesture it was.

Of course, his parting comment at breakfast had obviously been designed to throw her off balance, so alerting him to the fact that he'd succeeded shouldn't be that big of a deal.

"There's Toy Crazy," she squawked and cleared her throat, pointing with her still-tingling finger. "Let's hit that first."

Antonio nodded without comment about her affected voice, bless him, and they walked in tandem to the store.

A Salvation Army bell ringer called out season's greetings as they passed, and the holiday decor added a cheerful mien to the shopping center that Caitlyn wished she could enjoy. She loved Christmas, loved the holiday spirit and had been looking forward to the babies' first experience with the festivities.

Now everything with Antonio was weird and uncertain and she hated that. For so long she'd dreamed of having a relationship with him, and nothing had happened like she would have thought. *He* was nothing like she would have thought, so different than the man he'd been before the crash. Darker, fiercer Antonio wasn't the tame businessman her sister had married, and Vanessa was far more suited to handle this version of the man than Caitlyn was.

Antonio had flat-out told her he was going to kiss her again. What did she do with that? How did she come up with a better argument than "It's complicated"? Especially when there wasn't a better argument.

"After you," Antonio murmured and allowed Caitlyn to enter the toy store ahead of him, then followed her closely as they wandered into the fray.

Dolls and rocking horses and toy trains dominated the floor space, jockeying for attention amidst the shoppers. Caitlyn grabbed a cart and jostled through the aisles in search of the perfect toys for their children. True to his words at breakfast, Antonio didn't allow her to look at prices, and insisted she put everything in the cart she wanted.

Somewhere along the way, the sensual tension faded and the task became fun. They were just two parents picking out presents for their kids: swapping suggestions, agreeing with each other's ideas, nixing the toys that one of them felt wasn't age appropriate—mostly Caitlyn took on that role, especially after Antonio joyfully picked out remote-control cars for Leon and Antonio Junior. Honestly. The boys couldn't even walk yet.

Before long, the cart overflowed and Caitlyn had shared

more smiles with Antonio than she'd expected, given yesterday's kiss.

"I don't think anything else will fit," she announced.

"Then, I suppose we're finished." Antonio nodded toward the front of the store. "Unless you want to get another cart and keep going."

She laughed. "No, I think this is enough to spoil three children rotten."

Antonio smiled and pushed the cart toward the register. He'd manhandled it away from Caitlyn about halfway through without asking, insisting it had grown too heavy for her to maneuver. How could she argue with chivalry?

After they paid and Caitlyn got over her sticker shock, she let Antonio carry the umpteen bags.

But she didn't make it two feet toward the door. Antonio nearly plowed into her when she stopped. 'Twas the season to spend money as if it was going out of style, but it was also the season to spread good cheer to those who wouldn't be waking up to their parents' overindulgence.

"I just remembered that I wanted to donate something to Toys for Tots." Caitlyn picked up a Barbie doll and a GI Joe action figure located near the register. "I'll pay for this out of my own money."

Antonio's brows drew together. "What's Toys for Tots?"

He didn't remember Toys for Tots? Amnesia was such a strange beast, constantly surprising her with the holes it had created in Antonio's mind. Her heart twisted anew as she imagined how difficult his daily life must still be.

"It's a charity sponsored by the US Marines that gives toys to underprivileged kids. Not everyone has a billionaire for a father," she joked. "I like to donate every year, but I selfishly got caught up in my own children this year and nearly forgot."

His expression flickered with a dozen inexplicable emotions.

"Wait here," he instructed. "I'll be right back."

Mystified, she watched him thread back through the crowd and say something to the girl behind the register. Wide-eyed, she nodded and called to another worker. They spoke furiously to each other and then the second worker came alongside the first to speak to Antonio. He handed her something and then returned to Caitlyn's side with a small smile.

"Sorry, but you can't use your own money to buy toys for the kids without fathers."

Kids without fathers. That wasn't what she'd said, but he'd interpreted the term *underprivileged* in a way that had affected him, obviously. And many of the Toys for Tots recipients probably *didn't* have fathers.

"Don't argue with me," she told him sternly. "I didn't say anything about you paying for the babies' gifts, but this is something for me to do on my own."

"I don't mean I don't want you to. I mean, you can't. I bought out the whole store," he explained, and didn't even have the grace to look chagrined.

"You...what?"

"I told the clerk that she should check out the people already in the store and I'd buy whatever was left." He looked downright gleeful. "So we're going to hang out until they clear the store and then she's going to run my credit card."

Her heart thumped strangely. "That's...extravagant. And generous. What brought that on?"

He shrugged. "I don't think I've ever done anything for others before. That charity event you mentioned, the one where I wore the pink shirt. On the day we met," he prompted, as if she'd ever forget. "I did that because it was part of my contract. Not because I believed in the cause. I'm a father now. It means something to me and I want to be a better person than I was."

Tears pricked her eyes and she fought to keep them from falling. "You already are, Antonio."

Somehow her hand ended up in his and he squeezed it tight. "You're the one who brought it up."

What, as if she had something to do with Antonio's beautiful gesture? "Not so you could unload an entire toy store on the marines!"

He laughed and it rumbled through her warmly. *This* was what she'd dreamed of all those lonely nights when she imagined what it would be like to have a relationship with Antonio. Here they were, holding hands, standing near each other, and it was comfortable. Nice.

Not desperate and sensual and dark the way that kiss had been. Which one was the real Antonio?

His thumb stroked her knuckle and heat curled through her midsection. Okay, so he had the capacity to be both, which wasn't an easy thing to reconcile.

"I'll call someone to pick up the toys after the customers are gone and arrange for everything to be taken to the drop-off location," he said.

Yeah, there was nothing wrong with that part of his memory—he had no trouble recalling how to be large and in charge. And she hated that she found that shockingly attractive, too. As much as his generosity and his warrior-like persona and the way he was with the babies.

Who was she kidding? *All* of him was attractive.

When they got home, she spent an hour with the babies feeding them, which was time with her children that she treasured. They wouldn't breast-feed forever and while it had its challenges, such as having to use a breast pump after she'd had wine with Antonio the other night, she would be sad when this special bonding period was over.

Brigitte took over when Caitlyn was finished and they chatted for a few minutes. Leon was teething and making his displeasure known. Brigitte made a few suggestions and they agreed to try a different approach.

Should they include Antonio in discussions about the children's care? Caitlyn hadn't even thought to ask him but she really should. That was what being co-parents was all about.

She went in search of him and found him in his gym. Shirtless. And putting his hard body through a punishing round of inverted push-ups. Muscles bunched as he lowered himself to the ground and back up. His torso rippled and his skin glistened with his effort.

Dear Lord. A more exquisitely built man did not exist anywhere in the world.

Her mouth dried up. She couldn't peel her eyes from his body. Watching him put a burn in her core that ached with unfulfilled need. Somehow, the fact that he didn't know she was there heightened the experience, heating her further.

What was she *doing*?

She backed away, horrified to be gawking like a teenager. Horrified that she'd allowed herself to have a carnal reaction to Antonio.

"Caitlyn."

She glanced up. He'd climbed to his feet and stood watching her with a slightly amused expression. His torso heaved with exertion, and the falcon on his pectoral seemed poised to fly off his chest with each breath.

"Did you want something?" he asked, eyebrows raised.

So many things… "Uh—"

Wide-eyed, she watched him approach and speaking wasn't much of an option. His masculinity wrapped around her in a sensual cloak that settled heavily along her skin, warming it.

"Maybe you wanted to work out with me?" he asked, his head cocked in contemplation.

He was too close. Her body woke up in thrumming anticipation.

"I…um…do Pilates." *What did that have to do with anything, dummy?* She could still lift weights or something in Antonio's company, couldn't she? She shook her head. What was she thinking? That wasn't even why she'd tracked him down.

He reached out and toyed with a lock of her hair, smoothing it from her cheek, letting his fingers trail across her throat as he tucked the strand behind her back.

"Maybe you're here to deliver that argument we talked about earlier?" he murmured.

"Argument?"

Her mind went blank as Antonio's hand slipped from her shoulder to her waist. His naked chest was right there, within her reach. Her fingertips strained to trace the ink that bled into his skin, branding him as Falco. A fierce bird of prey.

"Against me kissing you. If you've got one, now would be the time to say your piece."

She glanced up into his eyes and the typhoon of desire swirling in their dark depths slammed through her. That sensual flare—it was desire *for her.*

She was his prey. She should be frightened. She was… and yet perversely curious what *would* happen next if she let things roll.

"We're, uh… That is…" She yelped as his arm slid around her waist, tugging her closer.

Her breasts brushed his bare torso, and even through her clothes, the contact ignited her already tingling core, flooding her with damp warmth.

"Caitlyn," he murmured. "Don't deny this. Hush now, and let me kiss you."

And before she could blink, he cupped her chin and lifted her head, bringing her mouth to his in one expert shot. The touch of his lips sang through her and she fell into Antonio, into the dark need, into her own pleasure.

Hot and hungry, he kissed her, hefting her deeper in his arms so their bodies snugged tight. She couldn't stop herself from spreading a palm on his heated flesh, right across his heart. Where the falcon lived.

His tongue coupled with hers, sliding against hers with rough insistence, and the sparks it generated ripped a moan from her throat.

Her core liquefied. No man had ever made her feel like this, so desperate and incomplete, as if she'd never be whole without him. She wanted...more. Wanted things she had little concept of. Wanted him to teach her about the pleasure she sought but hadn't yet realized.

Antonio gripped her shirt at the waist and pulled it from her pants before she could protest. Suddenly, his fingertips slid up her spine, magic against her bare flesh. She reveled in it, losing herself in his touch. He palmed her rib cage and thumbed one breast through her bra. Her core throbbed in time with her thundering pulse. Her head lolled backward as he mouthed down her throat to suck at the hollow of her shoulder blade, his unshaven jaw scrubbing her sensitive skin, heightening the pleasure tenfold.

That questing thumb worked its way under her bra and the shock of his rough, insistent touch against her nipple rocketed through her with a spike of dangerous lust.

"Antonio," she croaked and somehow got a grip on his wrist to pull it free from her clothing. "That's too far. It's too much. I can't—"

She bit off the rest—she sounded exactly like the inexperienced virgin she was. She peeled her hands from his chest and tore out of his grip.

"Don't run away," he commanded quietly. "Not this time. I enjoy kissing you. I want to make love to you. But you keep stopping me. Why?"

Afflicted, she stared at him, totally at a loss. "You want to…"

She couldn't even say that out loud. *He wanted to sleep with her*. Of course he did; she'd led him on like a wicked temptress who was perfectly prepared to strip naked right there in his gym and go at it on the floor.

This was her fault. She had no clue how to handle a man like Antonio, who was built like a woman's fantasy come to life. Who probably thought of sex as the next logical step in this type of attraction. No wonder she was screwing this up.

"I'm not like that," she said firmly. "I don't run around sleeping with people indiscriminately."

Something dangerous whipped through his expression. "I'm not 'people' and I object to being classified as such. You're cheapening what's happening between us. Also, I don't think that's the reason. You're afraid to be intimate with me."

He was offended. And disappointed in her. It scratched at her insides painfully. He'd cut through her surface protests to find the truth of her uncertainty. The realization that he understood her so well, even better than she'd understood her reticence, coated her throat, turning it raw.

"Yes," she whispered. "I need space."

She left the gym and he didn't try to stop her. Good. She needed to sort out her confusion. Antonio wasn't some random guy who'd love her and leave her, and of course he'd seen right through that excuse. Good grief, he had *commitment* written all over him—it was a huge part of his appeal.

Still was, but the physicality of her attraction far eclipsed it. Somehow. He'd brought out a part of her she'd never known existed. Around Antonio, she became a sensual, carnal woman that she didn't recognize, who liked his fierce side, his raw masculinity. Who wanted to delve into the pleasures of his touch with no regard to the emotional connection she thought she'd valued above anything else. And it scared her.

Because she didn't want to be like Vanessa. And yet, Caitlyn craved the type of relationship her sister had had with Antonio. It was a paradox, one she didn't know how to resolve.

Antonio had offered himself up on a silver platter. And she never dreamed she'd be fighting herself over whether to accept.

Antonio gave Caitlyn her space.

It was the last thing he wanted to do, but he had enough wits about him to recognize that Caitlyn required delicacy. Not his forte. But he'd learn it to get what he wanted.

The long night stretched, lonely and uncomfortable. The enormous four-poster bed would fit five people, but there was only one person he wanted in it. He had the vague sense that he must have slept in this bed with Vanessa, but he didn't think of his late wife at all. Instead, his vivid fantasies involved a dark-haired beauty who'd tied him up in knots.

Twice.

The first kiss had floored him. The second kiss had thrown him into a whole other level of senselessness. What had started as a way to help him move on from his marriage had exploded into something far more intriguing than he'd dreamed. When he kissed Caitlyn, her essence crawled inside him, haunting him. Pleasing and thrilling at the same time.

He wanted more. So much more. He shifted, unable to find a comfortable position, and the too-soft mattress doubled as a torture device. His half-aroused state didn't help.

The next morning, he bought a town car and hired a full-time driver to shuttle him back and forth to Falco. He still didn't feel comfortable driving, not with the head-aches that sometimes cropped up out of the blue. Naviga-tion sometimes tripped him up as well, especially while trying to get to a place he didn't remember. His house—no problem. Falco wasn't on the approved list of memories his brain had apparently created.

Fighting was his only outlet for the constant frustra-tions. And his opportunities for it were limited.

Once at Falco, he first arranged for a private detective to start searching for the remaining two unaccounted-for passengers from his flight to Thailand. He gave the highly recommended man one instruction—spare no expense. If those two people were out there, Antonio would help them get back their lives.

Then he spent the afternoon with Thomas untangling legalities. They worked through the brunt of it until Anto-nio thought his head would explode with details and pain. This office job was where he belonged, where he'd built a company out of the ashes of his first love.

He didn't want it.

In reality, Antonio longed to climb back in the ring. The business side of this promotional venue he'd created didn't call to him as it once must have. Some aspects felt comfortable and familiar, though he didn't have conscious memories of strategy and balance sheets. Surely sitting be-hind his desk and monitoring his empire had once made him supremely happy.

As Thomas gathered up his paperwork, Antonio swiv-eled the high-backed chair toward the window, which overlooked a landscaped courtyard with a wishing-pool fountain in the center. He must have enjoyed this view often, as Caitlyn mentioned that he'd been a workaholic, often clocking eighty-hour weeks.

"Thomas, what would it take to get me back in rota-tion?" Antonio asked without taking his gaze off the gurgling fountain. Not only was it a shocking request in and of itself, but worse, the man who owned an MMA promotional company should probably know the answer already.

"You want to fight again?" Thomas kept any surprise from his tone, which Antonio appreciated. "As a contender? Or just exhibition?"

His mouth quirked involuntarily. "It's not worth doing if you're not going for the title."

The ins and outs of being a professional fighter he had no problems remembering. The pain and the training and the brutal conditioning...all worth it for a shot at glory.

But Antonio had underlying reasons. Reasons why he was a fighter in the first place. It was a part of him, an indelible piece of his makeup that even a near lobotomy of his memory couldn't extricate.

Thomas cleared his throat. "Well, you certainly proved the other day that you're in good enough shape for it. But you stopped fighting for a reason. What's changed?"

"*I* have. Make it happen."

After Thomas left, restlessness drove Antonio to the training facility, where several people called out greetings, none of whom he recognized, and without his mind-reading guide to assist, there was no chance he'd come up with names. If only Caitlyn hadn't requested her space, he'd have gladly brought her with him.

Trainers worked with fighters of all shapes and sizes, some in the rings, some at the bags. Along with the grunts and slaps of flesh, a sense of purpose permeated the atmosphere. Falco had been born out of Antonio's love of mixed martial arts, but he felt far more comfortable in this half of it than in the CEO's office.

He watched a couple of heavyweights duke it out in the circular-cage ring. Round, so one fighter couldn't force the other into an inescapable corner as so often happened in traditional boxing. MMA strove to even the playing field, to create fairness. The two heavyweights sparred under the watchful eye of a middle-aged man who moved with the fighters gracefully and knowledgeably. A former fighter, clearly, and Antonio liked his coaching style instantly.

Both men in the ring were good and they likely practiced together often. But one was better, with a stellar command of his body and a force of will the second man couldn't match.

Even without clear memories of planning or creating this place, Antonio recognized that he'd spared no expense when purchasing and maintaining the equipment. He'd also managed to attract world-class athletes and trainers, who'd sustained his company while he'd been in Indonesia.

Everyone here had come to improve their technique, to become better fighters, to win. Including Antonio. What happened in the ring made sense, followed a set of rules, a flow. The discipline and repetition settled him and allowed his damaged mind to take a breather.

"Who wants a piece of me?" he called.

"I'm up for it, if you are, old man."

Slowly, Antonio turned to face one of Thomas's right-hand men. A dark gray hoodie partially obscured the younger man's face, but his slight smirk beamed brightly from the depths.

The fighter vibrated with animosity, and Antonio's radar blipped. The man didn't like him. Dirty fight. Excellent. Darkness rose inside him and he didn't squelch it.

He'd been itching for this since his last round with Ravi in Punggur Besar. Rodrigo hadn't matched even a tenth of Antonio's skill and the fight had left him unsatisfied. Plus, Antonio and Rodrigo must have been friendly at some point in the past and that alone had caused Antonio to hold back.

There would be no holding back required with this matchup.

Antonio let his gaze travel down the length of his opponent and snorted his derision. "Hope your moves back up your mouth."

"Only one way to find out."

"What do they call you?" His real name was irrelevant, but the nicknames fighters adopted often gave clues about their style, their mind-set.

"Cutter." The insolent lift of his chin revealed eyes so light blue, they were almost colorless. "Because you're gonna walk away with my cuts all over your face."

Or in some cases, when you were good at reading your competition, nicknames revealed their weaknesses. Cutter was arrogant. Overconfident. Eager to prove himself against the legendary Falco.

Of course, Antonio had known all of that the moment Cutter had labeled him "old man." And this punk was about to be schooled on what age meant for a man's technique and skill.

In minutes, Antonio and Cutter had suited up and squared off. Antonio sized him up quickly now that his opponent wasn't hiding under shapeless clothing. Muscular but not too bulky. Blond hair shaved close to his scalp. Viking-style tattoos across his torso and wrapped around his biceps. Feral sneer firmly in place. Nothing to differentiate him from the dozens of other fighters in his age and weight class—which was probably what pissed Cutter off the most.

The metal cage gleamed around them, providing a safe backdrop for the two men to tear each other up, no holds barred. No chance of being thrown from the ring…and no chance of escape.

There was nowhere to hide and nowhere to run. And blood would be spilled before long.

The younger man feinted and went low. Amateur. Antonio circled away and spun to catch him off guard with a sideways kick to his hip.

Cutter's retribution came in a series of attacks that kept Antonio busy deflecting. Duck. Spin. Feint. The rhythm became comfortable. Mindless.

In a split second, Antonio found a hole. *Attack.* His opponent was a lightweight, so Antonio had a few pounds on him, which he used ruthlessly to force Cutter against the fence. Going for the man's mouth was a no-brainer.

Antonio's fist connected and Cutter's flesh separated. The scent of blood rolled over him.

Cutter sprang forward with an amazing show of strength, fury lacing his expression and weighting his punches. A lucky cuff caught Antonio across the temple before he could block.

Pain exploded in his head, blurring his vision. Images of Vanessa's red hair ricocheted through his consciousness. Images of her in various scenarios. The two of them shouting at each other. Of her talking. Laughing. Of Antonio with her, skin bared, his hand on her flesh, mouth on hers.

Something about the memories pricked at him, sitting strangely. Something wasn't right. He couldn't—

He had no time to think.

Show no weakness. Blindly, he circled away, trying to give himself a moment to let his mind clear. The moment he regained his faculties, he went on the offensive. Uppercut, double kick. *No mercy.*

Often two fighters left the ring shaking hands. MMA was more gentlemanly than outsiders would assume. That wasn't the case in this ring.

In moments, it was finished. Antonio wiped the trickle of blood leaking into his right eye. Cutter lay crumpled on the mat, groaning.

Endorphins soared through his body like bullets. Memories of his wife crowded his mind. The metallic scent of blood stung his nose and he craved more.

"Anyone else want a go at me?" Antonio challenged.

No one volunteered.

Eight

Antonio sneaked into the house and closed himself off in his bedroom to clean up before anyone saw him. Anyone, meaning Caitlyn. The split skin near his eyebrow wasn't life threatening but it wasn't pretty, either. Nor was he good company, not with adrenaline still swirling through his body like a tornado.

A long, hot shower gave him decompression time, allowing him to force back the base urge to smack something again and again. Once he got going, it was hard to shut it off.

But he couldn't live in the ring. He had to find a balance between the need to fight and the rest of his life. Until he could, what kind of father would he be? How could he willingly expose his children to that?

Someone knocked on his bedroom door as he exited the bathroom, toweling off his damp hair. For modesty's sake, he draped the towel over his lower half and pulled open the door.

"Hi." Caitlyn's eyes strayed to his torso, lingered and cut back up again quickly. Pink bloomed in her cheeks.

He loved that blush, and with his body already caught in an adrenaline storm, it set off fireworks. His groin filled, primed for a whole different sort of one-on-one. Not a good combination when in the company of a woman who'd asked for space.

But then, she was also a woman who'd sought him out—in his bedroom. Maybe she'd gotten her space and was done with it.

Her eyebrows drew together as she focused on his face. "What happened? You're bleeding."

"I ran into something." He shrugged as her gaze narrowed. "Another guy's fist. I went to Falco this afternoon."

Her expression didn't change. "Do you need antiseptic? A Band-Aid?"

He bit back a smile. "No self-respecting fighter walks around with a Band-Aid on his face. Thanks for the concern, but it doesn't hurt."

It didn't hurt because his body was still flying on a postmatch trip that ignored the pain of a cut. Instead, he was solely focused on the ache caused by Caitlyn's nearness. She was exactly what his queued-up body craved.

"Come in," he murmured thickly and held the door open wider.

She shook her head, eyes wide. "I don't think that's a good idea."

Oh, it was a very good idea. Obviously she thought so, too, or she wouldn't have knocked on his door. "Then, why *are* you here, Caitlyn?"

The question seemed to confuse her. She bit her lip and it drew his gaze to her mouth, causing him to imagine replacing her teeth with his.

She glanced away and cleared her throat. "I, uh, meant

to talk to you about something, but I didn't realize you'd be…undressed."

"Didn't you?" He cocked his head. "That's what generally happens behind closed doors. Here, let me demonstrate."

But when he reached for the towel, intending to drop it and see where it led, she squeezed her eyelids shut. "No, no! That's okay. I get the point. I shouldn't have come to your bedroom, not after you'd just come back from Falco. I didn't realize you'd gone there, but you didn't come down for dinner, and I was worried and you're hurt and…this was a mistake."

Caitlyn whirled as if about to flee. Again.

Antonio shot out his hand to grip her arm before she took a step. "Caitlyn. Stop running away."

He needed her in a raw, elemental way. In other, more emotional ways he couldn't fully grasp. He didn't think it was one-sided, and the longer this back-and-forth went on, the clearer it became that they needed to deal with it head-on.

Smoothly, he turned her around to face him, searching her gaze for clues to her constant caginess. Confusion and something else skated through her expression.

"Come inside," he pleaded again.

If only he could get her on this side of the threshold, he'd feel less as if he was losing a grip on his sanity. If only he could get her to understand he was desperate to explore things he didn't fully grasp, things only she could teach him because she was the only woman he wanted.

"I can't." Her eyes were huge and troubled and her gaze flicked to the wound near his eyebrow. "I'm…scared."

The admission pinged through him, drawing blood with its claws of condemnation. He dropped his hand from her arm, flexing his raw fist, which smarted from connecting with bone in Cutter's face. Antonio lived and breathed to inflict bodily harm on other human beings, and she saw that about him.

She'd needed space because the falcon inside him frightened her. It *should* scare her.

He'd forced her to watch him fight the other day, forced her to remain in his presence now with evidence of his brutal nature plain as day on his face. Practically forced her into his room so he could have his carnal way with her because of his own selfish desires.

But she didn't leave when he let go. She had every right to. She deserved someone gentle and kind.

"I won't hurt you," he said brusquely, and cleared his throat. He'd done nothing to assure her otherwise. "I hate that you think I might."

Her rounded gaze flew to his and the glint of moisture nearly undid him.

"I'm not scared of *you*," she corrected, but her voice cracked halfway through. "Never of you. I…"

She swallowed and he watched the delicate muscles of her beautiful throat work. If she wasn't scared of him, what was it? And why was it so difficult for her to articulate?

"Then, tell me," he commanded softly, and reached out to grasp her hand in his so he could draw her forward. Almost over the threshold. She didn't resist, but neither did she rush. "What's going on in your mind when I do this?"

Slowly, he took her hand and placed it flat on his chest, over his thundering heart. Her touch nearly drove him to the carpet, but he locked his knees, sensing that if he could keep his wits about him, paradise might be within their reach.

Mute, she stared at her splayed hand under his. Her fingertips curled slightly as if she wanted to grip harder but couldn't.

"It's like granite," she whispered. "That's what I think

about. So hard. But underneath lies something so amazing."

"What?"

"You. Antonio." His name fluttered from her throat on a half groan and the sound almost broke him open.

"You say that as if my name is poetry." It was just a simple name. But one he'd sought in the reaches of his messed-up mind for so long. Hearing it on her lips… It was an elemental thrill.

He was Antonio. And yet not. Because he couldn't fully remember all of the parts that created the whole.

"*All* of you is poetic," she murmured, and drew in a ragged breath. "The way you walk, the way you hold your children. How you move in the ring. I couldn't stop watching you and it was, um…nice."

"You liked watching me fight?" The idea was ludicrous. But her dreamy smile spoke volumes.

"I didn't think I would, but it was amazing." She sighed, a breathy sound that hardened him instantly. "Watching you execute those perfect moves, your body so fluid and in such harmony. It's like a perfect song lyric that when you hear it for the first time, it climbs inside your heart and lives there."

His own breath came more quickly as he stared at her with dawning comprehension. "You have feelings for me."

That was what he'd seen in her expression, what he couldn't quite grasp. It was a wondrous, blessed revelation. As obvious all at once as the sun bursting over the horizon to announce daytime. But he had no context for how he felt. And he wanted to.

Blinking slowly, she bit her lip again and nodded. "I've tried not to. But I can't help it."

A hundred questions rocketed through his mind, but he stuck with the most important.

"Then, why?" he asked hoarsely. "Why do you run away? Why are you so scared of what's happening?"

"I..." She glanced off and the moment of honesty, of her raw confession, started slipping away.

Desperate not to lose it, he cupped her face in both hands and brought it to his, a breath away. "What, Caitlyn? Tell me. Please. I'm losing my mind here. And I don't have much left to lose."

His wry joke earned him a watery smile.

"I'm scared of *me*," she whispered. "I want...things. Things I barely understand. It's like in all the fairy tales where they tell the girl not to touch the spindle or not to eat the apple. I never understood why they couldn't help themselves. Because I never understood what it meant to truly *desire* something. Or someone. Until you. I don't know what to do."

She wanted him. And that made all the difference.

"There's only one right answer to that."

He leaned into the space between them and laid his lips on hers for a scant second, kissing her with only a thousandth of the passion he wished he could unleash. But didn't because she wasn't fully inside the room.

Once she stepped over the threshold, all bets were off.

Pulling back with an iron will that could only be developed by years of ruthless training, he evaluated her. "Do you like kissing me?"

"Yes," she murmured. "More than I should."

"Then, come inside. Let me kiss you. Let me give you that experience you described. Let me be the man who touches you and loves you."

He wanted that—badly. Wanted to feel her skin next to his, to feel alive alongside her. To feel as if the things she spoke of were more than just words but concepts his soul recognized.

Her eyes closed and her lips pursed as if in invitation,

as if she yearned for him to kiss her again. But then her eyes blinked open and she swallowed. Hard.

"I need to tell you something else." Her gaze sought his and held. "I've never had a lover before."

Antonio's expression didn't waver, bless him. "You're a virgin?"

Caitlyn nodded. Her tongue was stuck to the roof of her mouth, glued there by nerves and who knew what else— three or four of the seven deadly sins, most likely.

"That explains a lot. I'm sorry you didn't trust me with that fact sooner. That's why you asked for space." His chiseled lips turned down. "I didn't give it to you."

Her heart fluttered. Antonio had the patience of Job.

"You did," she corrected hurriedly. "You've been perfect. I'm the problem. That's what I've been trying to tell you. I don't have any experience at…you know. And I'm nervous. You're this beautiful, wonderful man with all these expectations about being with me, probably because I've led you on, and I'm… Well, I'm not Vanessa, that's for sure—"

"Caitlyn." The quirk of his eyebrow rendered her speechless, as he'd probably intended. "Are you trying to tell me that you think I'll compare you unfavorably to Vanessa?"

"Uh…" Clearly, yes wasn't the right answer. But it was the only one she had. "She was so gorgeous, with a body men salivated over. She knew how to please a man in bed, too, which she liked to brag about. It's hard to imagine following that."

His quick smile knocked her off-kilter. Was it *that* funny?

"Isn't it ironic, then," he mused, "that I can't remember Vanessa?"

"At all?" He couldn't remember his wife, the one he'd

ended his career for, whose babies he'd wanted to have so badly, he'd agreed to surrogacy?

Her gaze flicked to the year-old scar disappearing into his hairline. What kind of whack to the head had he endured that his memories were that insubstantial? It must have been vicious.

"Some." His tone grew somber. "I see flashes of her red hair and remember bits and pieces, like her laugh. It's all jumbled in my head. Sometimes it's her face and sometimes her body. But I don't remember being in love with her. I feel so disconnected from her, as if she wasn't real. I don't remember feeling like you said I should, as if I want to be with her so badly I can't breathe."

The despondency in his voice caught in her chest and made it hurt. "I'm sorry, Antonio. I didn't realize you hadn't regained your memories of her. That must be very difficult."

"What's difficult is that I want to move on." His lashes lowered and he speared her with that dark, enigmatic glance that set her blood on low simmer. "I want to be in the here and now, not stuck dwelling on the past I can't remember. I've found someone new, someone I *do* want so badly I can't breathe. I want to love her and fulfill her and let her do the same to me. But I can't seem to get her into my arms."

"Me?" she whispered.

Heat climbed into her cheeks, on cue. *Duh.* Of course he meant her. But her brain wasn't working quite right. Too busy filtering through the divine idea that Antonio wanted to love her.

"Yes, you." His thumb feathered across her hot cheek. "I not only can't compare you to Vanessa, I don't want to. I want what's possible now, for as long as we have together. I want to learn about the kind of love that you talked about. Teach me."

"How can I teach you anything? I'm not the one with experience."

His gorgeous lips turned upward into a killer smile. "I'm not the one with any experience I can remember. In a way, this will be the first time for both of us."

For some reason, that appealed to her. Immensely.

He didn't remember Vanessa and wanted to learn everything about love, sex, relationships over again. It was like the slate being wiped clean—Caitlyn could make this experience anything and everything she could imagine, be as wicked in his arms as she wished and wrap it up in a beautiful emotional connection that could last an eternity.

He'd come back from the dead a different person, and she'd often dwelt on the darker changes. It had never occurred to her that amnesia would be a positive in this one case.

Except he'd been born with a body designed for pleasure, and just as he'd not forgotten how to breathe, he likely hadn't lost any knowledge of how to make a woman quiver with desire. She couldn't do the same to him, no way.

"Are you sure this is what you want? With me? I mean, you might not precisely remember Vanessa, but you have to recall other women." *Shut up.* Nobody brought up former lovers on the brink of becoming the next one. She sighed. "See. I'm a big mess. That's so not attractive, I realize."

He glanced down at the two feet of space between them. "We've been standing in this doorway for ten minutes now, and for nine minutes and fifty-five seconds of it, I've been in danger of losing this towel due to the serious arousal you've caused me. Stop worrying so much about things that don't matter. Don't deny us any longer, Caitlyn."

He stepped aside, opening the doorway for her to enter if she chose.

This was it. Her opportunity to grab what she'd longed for. To put her guilt to rest and finally become a full-fledged, sexually realized woman at the hands of a master. A man who was probably the great love of her life, the only one she might ever love.

And his pretty speech about learning how to love at *her* hands surely meant he was open and willing to returning her feelings. He'd loved Vanessa, had married her and obviously yearned to have that sort of connection again. The sort of connection Caitlyn had dreamed of.

It was all within her reach.

Yet she hesitated, long enough for his eyebrows to rise.

What would happen if she stepped over the threshold, signaling to Antonio that she was ready to embark on a romantic relationship, and if it didn't work out? How would she co-parent their children with a broken heart? The past few years had been difficult enough when she'd revered him from afar. How much harder would it be to actually love and be loved by a man like Antonio, only to lose him because she wasn't the kind of woman who could handle him?

And what if he cut her out of her children's lives in retribution?

This was why she never got very far in a relationship with any man, including Antonio when she'd first met him. She was terrified of what came *after* she opened herself body and soul to someone.

As she let her gaze rest on his bare torso, on that glorious inked falcon, she wanted to let him melt her resistance.

Because it would be impossible to walk away.

She took a breath to calm her racing heart, which didn't work, and walked into Antonio's bedroom.

Nine

The door clicked shut behind her and Caitlyn froze.

She was inside a man's bedroom. She wouldn't leave it a virgin. She'd been saving herself for the right man, a man she was ready, willing and eager to love forever, and here he was…but this wasn't the safe fantasy she'd harbored for years. Was she *really* ready for this?

Oh, my. Antonio was going to see her naked, with her C-section scars and ridiculously shaped breasts that had served as a milk source for three hungry mouths for months.

Nearing full-blown panic, she tried to suck in a deep, calming breath. And choked on it as she thought back to getting dressed this morning. What underwear had she put on?

"Caitlyn."

She whirled. Antonio leaned against the door, arms crossed over his cut torso, towel dipping dangerously low. Her mouth went sticky and she averted her gaze. Then shifted her gaze back because, dang it, *surely* it was okay to look at him if they were about to make love. Maybe it was even expected. Part of foreplay.

"Do you want a glass of wine?" he asked casually.

"To drink?" When he laughed, she thought about punching him but would probably only hurt her hand. Mortified, she scowled. "I didn't know what you meant! Maybe it's some kind of sex thing, like you want me to pour it on you and lick it off."

His eyebrows rose and he treated her to a thoroughly wicked once-over. "Would you? Lick it off?"

The image of her tongue swirling over the ink on his chest popped into her mind and she couldn't shake it. As she imagined the taste of his golden skin melded with fruity red wine, her insides contracted. "Maybe. *Was* it a sex thing?"

He shrugged, a smile still playing about his expressive mouth. "As much as I want you right now, it could be. Seems a little messy, though. Let's save that for another time."

"How many times do you envision there being?"

"A thousand." His expression darkened carnally as if he was imagining each time individually and it was hot. "The things I want to do to you, to experience with you, might very well take a lifetime."

She couldn't blink, couldn't look away. Couldn't quite believe the sincerity ringing from his voice. She rubbed at the ache in her chest as she internalized that she'd heard precisely what he'd meant for her to hear. "A lifetime?"

Of course, it was what she'd yearned for. But it was another thing entirely to hear it from Antonio's mouth.

He tilted his head quizzically. "You aren't the kind of person who sleeps around indiscriminately. Neither am I. I want to be with you from now on. Awake, asleep. In bed, out of bed. Which part is confusing you?"

"All of it. Starting with 'hi' when I first knocked on the door," she muttered.

"So that wasn't a good subject, obviously. Here's what we're going to do instead," he said decisively, because of course he could read her like a book. "We're going to have a glass of wine. Then we're going to take this as slowly as you want to."

"Why?" Could she have sounded more suspicious? He was saying all the right things and she was botching this.

"The wine is to relax you," he explained, not seeming at all bothered by her lack of decorum. "Actually, both parts are to relax you. And both parts get me where I want to be. Inside you. Anticipation will make it sweeter, so I'm quite happy with the idea of taking my time. I've got a whole night and I'm not afraid to use it."

Dumbfounded, she let him lead her to his sitting area overlooking the coastline and sank onto the love seat he pointed to. Apparently, Antonio was botchproof. Good thing. She'd probably do ten more things to increase her mortification level before the night was through.

He selected a bottle of red wine from the rack on the wet bar and pulled the cork. Since his back was to her, she watched his bare torso unashamedly. Too quickly, he returned with two glasses full of deep red wine, handed her one and settled in next to her on the love seat. Clad in a towel.

It should be weird. He was completely naked underneath the terry cloth, which gaped at his thigh, revealing the muscular stretch of leg that led to his...good parts.

He glanced at her and then followed her line of vision. "Curious?"

Yes, wine was a fantastic idea. The alcohol needed to be swimming through her bloodstream, not sitting in a glass untouched. She gulped as much as she could get down, for fortification.

Because, oh, yes, she was curious. Burning with it.

"I've never seen a naked man before," she croaked.

Not enough wine, obviously, if she was still going to utter gems like that.

"Not even in pictures?"

She shook her head. "I'm a novice. I tried to tell you."

Antonio set down his glass on the side table with a hard click and then took her free hand in his. "Listen to me, because I don't want there to be any confusion about this."

Heart hammering in her throat, she stared at him as something tender sprang into his gaze.

"It means everything to me that no other man has ever touched you. That I get to be the first. It's an honor and I intend to treat it as such. You should never feel as if you have to apologize for this gift you're giving me."

"I…um." What did you say that *that*? "Okay."

That must have been the magic word. His thumb brushed over her knuckles and he let go of her hand to run his fingertips over the back of her wrist.

And kept going up her bare arm, watching her with that dark intensity as he touched her. Without a word, he took the glass from her suddenly nerveless fingers and set it next to his. A breath later, his mouth descended and took hers in a slow, deliberate kiss that melted her bones.

His sweet lips… They molded hers, explored. Slowly, as promised.

"Wait," he murmured, and his heat left her as he rose to click off the lights. Moonlight poured in from outside the glass, illuminating the love seat and throwing the rest of the room into shadow.

Antonio returned with the comforter from his bed and a couple of small squares that she eyed curiously until she realized what they were. Condoms. This had just turned real and her throat closed.

He spread the comforter in front of the floor-to-ceiling

window and stretched out on it, beckoning her to join him. "Just to set the mood."

But the sight of Antonio bathed in the glow from the moon froze her completely. He was beautiful, mystical. Too perfect to be real. She just wanted to soak him in, to gorge herself on his splendor.

He seemed to sense her thoughts and lay still, allowing her to gaze at him as much as she wanted. The scar marking the location of his once-broken leg forked up his calf, as seductively savage as the rest of him.

After an eternity, he reached for his towel and held it in both hands, poised to take it off. "Do you want to see all of me?"

Too numb to speak, she nodded, but before she could properly school her expression or her thoughts or her... anything, the towel fell away and... *Oh, my.* He was utterly divine in all his glory, hard everywhere, with a jutting erection she'd felt when he'd kissed her in the gym, but never in a million years would she have thought it would look like *that*.

She couldn't stop drinking him in. And he didn't seem to be in a hurry to stop her.

"By the way," he murmured, "you know you're going to do this for me in a minute, right?"

"Do what?" Then she clued in. "You mean lie in front of the window naked so you can stare at me?"

A wolfish smile bloomed on his face. "Let me know when you're ready."

"I don't think I'll ever be ready for that," she muttered.

He flipped onto his hands and knees and crawled to her, kneeling between her legs. "Then, I'll have to fix that. Because I want to see you in the moonlight. I want to watch your face as I make love to you. And you will most definitely need to be naked for that."

With exquisite care, he cupped her face with both hands and brought her lips to his.

This kiss was nothing like the one a minute ago, when there'd still been a towel and some modesty between them. There was nothing but Antonio between her legs, and when his mouth claimed hers in a scorching kiss, he palmed the small of her back and shoved her to the edge of the couch, almost flush with his body. Close, so close, and she arched involuntarily, seeking his heat.

His tongue plunged toward hers, possessing her with his taste, with his intoxicating desire. Moaning, she slid her arms around his strong torso, reveling in the feel of his sleek, heated skin under her palms. A small movement forward, just the slightest tilt of her hips, and his erection would brush her center.

And she ached for that contact. Desire emboldened her and she strained for it.

When it came, she gasped. He must have sensed her instant need for more because he pressed harder, rubbing in small circles. Heat exploded at her core and her head tipped back in shock.

He followed the line of her throat with his luscious lips, laving the tender skin expertly until he got a mouthful of her blouse. She nearly wept as his mouth lifted.

"I'm going to take this off," he murmured and fingered the first button for emphasis. "Okay?"

She nodded, appreciative that he respected her nerves enough to ask. Plus, she was very interested in getting his magic mouth back on her skin. "Seems fair. You're not wearing a shirt."

His warm chuckle had a hint of wicked that shuddered through her. Now, *that* was delightful.

"I'm not wearing anything. If you want to talk about fair…"

"You know what, you're right."

This imbalance *wasn't* fair. She stood quickly without thought of his proximity, and it was a testament to his superior balance that she didn't bowl him over.

He sat back on his muscular haunches, completely at ease in his own skin. She wanted to be that confident. To feel as if she belonged here, able to handle a man as virile and gorgeous as Antonio. There was only one way. She had to get over this virgin hump and take this night—her destiny, her *pleasure*—into her own hands. It wasn't Antonio's job to lead her through this.

He desired her. It was in his expression, in his words. In the hard flesh at his center. What purpose did it serve to protect her maidenly modesty? None.

She wanted him to take her in the basest sense. *Now*. And she wanted it to be hot. Sinful. Explosive. He could make that happen, she had no doubt. But he was holding back. She could feel it.

"I'm ready," she announced, and though her hands shook, she slipped the first button on her blouse from its mooring.

His eyelids lowered a touch as he watched her move on to the next button. "Ready?"

Third button. Fourth. "For you to see me. In the moonlight."

Heat flared in his expression and he hummed his approval. The sexy sound empowered her. Last button.

She slipped the blouse from her frame, gaze glued to his, and let it float from her fingers. That wasn't so bad. The clasp on her bra was a little harder to undo even though it was in front, and she couldn't even blame that on being a novice; she'd definitely taken her bra off a million times in her life, but never in front of a man, and this was it—the first time a man would see her bare breasts—and suddenly, the clasp came apart in her hands.

Well, that was the point, wasn't it?

Nothing left to do but shed the hideous nursing bra. In retrospect, stripping out of it probably increased her sexiness quotient. She dropped it on the ground near her blouse and fought the urge to cover herself when Antonio's heavy-lidded gaze swept her with clear appreciation.

"You might want to hurry," he muttered, hands clenched on his thighs as he looked up at her from his prone position. "I'm about to lose my mind."

"Really?" That sounded...lovely. "Am I making you crazy?"

The thought pleased her. Imagine. Caitlyn Hopewell was driving a man insane with a slow striptease. It practically made her giddy.

He groaned. "Completely. You're killing me. If you had any idea how much I want to— " He shook his head, teeth gritted. "Never mind. You take this at your pace. I'll be the one over here practicing my patience."

"No. Tell me. What do you want to do?" She fingered the clasp on her jeans, toying with it the way she imagined a more experienced woman might do. "I might let you."

"Oh, yeah?" he growled. "Lose those pants and let's rumble, my darling."

The endearment rolled through her and left a whole lot of heat and pleasure in its wake. "I like it when you talk to me like that."

"You do, huh?" Amusement curled his lips upward. "Not well enough, since you're still dressed."

"Well, you still haven't told me what you want to do." The curiosity was killing her. So she shoved off her pants, careful to take her nonsexy underwear along for the ride, and kicked them both away.

She couldn't get more naked. With the moon as the only source of light, her flaws weren't as noticeable and the lines of her postpregnancy body smoothed out. And that was when it dawned on her—that had been the whole purpose of lights-out. Was there nothing that the man missed?

Antonio worshipped her with his gaze and she let him, keeping her arms by her sides. The way he looked at her made her feel beautiful. As though she had nothing to hide.

"Now then. Tell me," she commanded, proud that her voice didn't waver. "What sorts of wicked activities do you have in store? Because I've waited a lifetime to be thoroughly ravished and I'm a little anxious to get started."

Groaning, Antonio tried to keep his faculties about him as he surveyed the very tempting woman on display before him wearing nothing but moonlight and a smile.

Blood and adrenaline pounded through his veins. He'd kept a very tight hold on his body since he'd opened the bedroom door. Caitlyn had just pushed him to the brink with a unique mix of innocence and friskiness that belied her lack of experience.

He hadn't expected it to be such a turn-on.

Or for her to systematically break down his resistance until he held on to his self-control by the barest edge. He wanted her more fiercely than he'd ever wanted anything—including his memories. His muscles strained to pounce. To possess. To claim. To relentlessly drive her to the threshold of madness the way she'd driven him.

But he couldn't because Caitlyn deserved something special for her first time. She deserved someone gentle. Restrained. Refined.

She had to make do with Antonio Cavallari instead.

"I…" He nearly swallowed his tongue as Caitlyn sauntered toward him, invitation in her eyes that he couldn't misread even in the pale light. "My intentions are to make love to you. There's nothing wicked about that."

The hard floor beneath the comforter ground into his knees, but he couldn't have moved if his life depended on it. He should have prepared better for this, changed out the furniture. Caitlyn's first experience with sex should happen in a bed, but he refused to make love to her in the same place he'd been with another woman. Whether he could remember it or not. It was a matter of principle.

"Why not? What if I want wicked?" she murmured and halted directly in front of him, then folded her legs under her to mirror his pose. Knee to knee. She pierced him with a gaze far too knowing for a woman of her innocence. "Listen to me so there's no confusion about this, Antonio. I watched you in the ring and it was brutal. But it was beautiful at the same time. Like you. It was an unsettling, thrilling experience. There's probably something wrong with me that I like the primal part of you. But I don't care."

Without hesitation, she traced the falcon tearing across his flesh, watching him as she touched him, and he sucked in a breath as his skin pulsed under her fingers.

"I want Falco," she said simply. "And Antonio. I'll only have one first time. Make it memorable. Give me all of it and don't hold back."

His iron will dissolved under the onslaught of her sensuous plea. With equal parts desperation and need, he hauled her into his arms and fell into her, into the innocence that called to him. Not to destroy, but to absorb. She was perfectly whole and exquisite and the shattered pieces of his soul cried out for her.

Hungrily, he kissed her, twining her body with his so he could feel her. His skin screamed for more of the sweet friction against hers. He palmed her heavy breasts, which filled his hands and then some. They were gorgeous, full, with huge nipples that his mouth strained to taste.

Unable to wait, he sucked one between his lips. She gasped and her back arched instantly. *Yes*. Amazingly responsive, as he'd fantasized. He moved to the other breast, and the sensation of his tongue curling around her hard nipple had him pulsing with need.

The groan ripped from his throat and he murmured her name as he eased her back against the comforter. Moonlight played with her features as she lay there, exactly as he'd envisioned, and it was almost too much to take in. The mother of his children. His savior. Soon to be lover.

He needed her. Needed to be inside her, with her, loving her. But first things first. He bent one of her legs back and knelt to swirl his tongue at her center.

She froze and made mewling sounds in her throat.

"Shh, my darling," he murmured and kissed her inner thigh. "You asked for wicked." He kissed the other and opened her legs farther. "Close your eyes and imagine me in the ring. What about it excited you?"

"You were so graceful," she murmured. "Like an apparition. But so very real and raw. It made me hot. All over."

"Like this?"

Slowly, he touched her again with the tip of his tongue. She shuddered but didn't tense up this time. He went a little farther, lapping a little harder. Her hips rolled and she sighed in pleasure.

"That's right, sweetheart. Lie still, think about me and let me taste you." He cupped her hips and tilted her up to his lips to feast.

She thrashed under his onslaught, but since her shudders brought her center closer and closer each time, he took full advantage of it instead of scolding her for doing the opposite of lying still. Honey gathered under his tongue a moment before she cried out.

Her climax went on and on and his own body throbbed in response, aching for a release in kind inside this woman.

Shaking with the effort, he managed to roll on a condom without breaking it—a minor miracle, given that he couldn't precisely remember the technique—and stretched out next to her to take her into his arms.

"Ready?" he asked hoarsely, shocked he could speak at all.

"There's more?" Since the question was laced with wry humor, he hoped that meant she was kidding.

"Oh, yes, there's more," he said fiercely. "I'm dying to show you."

She feathered a thumb across his lips, sparking sensation to the point of pain. "Show me, Antonio."

More roughly than he'd intended, he nudged a knee between her thighs and rolled, poised to thrust with all his pent-up energy. But he held back at the last second, somehow, and kissed her with every ounce of that longing instead. When she responded with a throaty moan that he felt in his groin, he couldn't wait. He pushed as slowly as he could into her center.

She wasn't on board with slow.

Her hips rose up to meet him, accepting him, encouraging him, and with a groan, he sheathed himself completely. Then forced his muscles to pause, though every fiber of his being screamed to let loose, to drive them both to completion with frenzied coupling.

He sought her gaze. "Tell me it's okay."

She nodded and let out a breath, her eyes shining as she peered up at him, hair a dark mass around her ethereal face. *She* was the apparition, a heavenly body trapped on this plane, and he'd been lucky enough to find her.

"It doesn't feel like I would have thought," she commented.

That made two of them.

Emotion he couldn't name wrenched at his heart, threatening to pull it from his chest. *Love.* He wanted it to be love, to know that he could feel such things and wasn't irreparably damaged.

But the sense he had of his previous experiences didn't match this. Not even close. This was so much bigger, so overwhelming. What if he *was* damaged? What if his memories never returned? How would he know if he was loving Caitlyn the way she deserved?

"You feel amazing," she murmured. Experimentally, she wiggled her hips. "What does it feel like to you?"

Her innocent movements set off a riptide of heat. "Let's compare notes later."

Settling her firmly under him, he began to move, rendering them both speechless. She arched against him, nails biting into his shoulders, those perfect, full breasts peaked against his torso.

Thrust for thrust, she met him, never retreating, never yielding. *More. Faster.* His body took from hers and she gave endlessly. Palming her rear, he changed the angle. Reversed the dynamic so he was doing the giving. Spiraling her higher into the heavens where she'd already taken him.

He needed to discharge, to explode. But he couldn't… not yet. He tasted blood on his lip where he'd bitten down with the effort to hold back. Animalistic sounds growled from his throat as he bent one of her legs back to go deeper still.

Exquisite pleasure rolled over him, and he needed more. Relentlessly, he rolled his hips to meet hers, and when she tightened around him with a small moan, he lost control.

Groaning as he spilled his release, he collapsed to the side, rolling her with him as he lost all feeling in his extremities.

In the aftermath, they lay together, and he gently spooned her into his body to hold her tightly. She snuggled in willingly with a small sigh of contentment.

He let her essence bleed through him as he lay with his eyes shut, absorbing her. If he never had to move from this spot, it would be too soon.

An instant later, he cursed his own selfishness. "Can I get you anything?"

What did you give a woman who had just offered up her virginity? Diamond earrings? A washcloth? She was likely bruised and raw. It wasn't as if he'd been gentle, not the way he'd pretended he was going to be.

"I'm fine, thanks. Don't you dare move." She wiggled closer to him. "Your body heat feels good against my sore muscles."

"I should have gone slower." Remorse crashed through his breastbone. He'd taken her innocence like the brute that he was. "I'm sorry I hurt you."

"Don't you dare apologize. Some of it hurt, but in a good way. It was amazing. Perfect. Beautiful. Everything I've ever dreamed of." Threading her fingers through his, she raised his hand to her lips. "Thank you for that."

Emotion clogged his throat and he swallowed against it, fighting to keep himself level.

The things she made him feel… He wished he could understand them. Could draw on his past to make sense of the swirl in his belly when he looked at her. But he couldn't.

All he knew was that Caitlyn was a miracle. Everything he'd prayed to find when he'd set off from Indonesia in search of his life.

He stroked her side and with moonlight spilling over them both, he murmured the million-dollar question. "Why me? Of all the men in the world you could have chosen for your first experience."

"I always wanted it to be you," she said slowly. "Well, not *always*. Vanessa was…rather free with her affections, even back in high school. I didn't like how broken up she always was after, and I vowed to save myself for the right man. The first moment I met you, I had this strange shock of recognition, like *there you are*."

His hand stilled. "The first moment? You mean the pink-shirt meeting?"

She nodded and her hair brushed his chin. "After that, no other man could compare. I've had a crush on you for a long time."

"Even while I was married?" It should have seemed wrong, but it thrilled him for some reason. Caitlyn had been saving herself for *him*, even through his marriage to someone else. It spoke to her constancy and devotion, and it humbled him.

"I didn't say I was a saint. I had a lot of mixed feelings about it. You know, I cried for almost two days straight when they came to tell me the plane had crashed. I thought I'd lost you forever," she whispered brokenly.

In the long pause, he gathered her in his arms and held her as close as physically possible as his heart thumped in tandem with hers.

While he'd been lost and alone, Caitlyn had been here in his house, mourning him. He'd thought no one cared. But she had. She still did.

It was a far better gift than her virginity.

Ten

The next morning, Caitlyn awoke at dawn, stiff and sore from a night sleeping on the floor entwined with Antonio. And every inch of her body felt glorious.

Antonio had kissed her soundly before sending her off to her own room, presumably to keep the rest of the household in the dark about the new relationship that had bloomed between them. She showered under the hottest stream of water she could stand, letting the water ease her aches. Her thoughts never strayed far from the sexy man down the hall.

He might even be in his own shower, naked, with water sluicing down his gorgeous body. Feeling a little scandalous, she allowed the image to play through her mind… because she could. She knew what every inch of that man's flesh looked like, thank you very much.

She'd slept with Antonio. Her sister's husband, whom she had always coveted. There was probably a special place in hell for a woman who did that. And she hated to admit that she'd loved every second of it.

When she emerged, steam had obscured the mirror. She wiped it with a towel and stared at herself in the glass. Odd. She didn't look any different than she had yesterday morning, and it was a bit of a shock to see her same face reflected back at her.

By all rights, there should be *some* external mark to account for the rite of passage she'd undertaken. What, she couldn't say. But a man had loved her thoroughly last night. He'd filled her body with his, tasted her intimately, brought her to a shuddering climax. Twice. It was an earth-shaking event worthy of distinction. Maybe she should get a tattoo to commemorate the experience.

A dove on her breast, maybe.

Silly. She was already picking out matching tattoos after sleeping with a man one night.

But it had been so incredible. Now she totally got why he'd said he planned to do it a thousand more times. Once could never be enough.

She'd just pretend he'd never been married to Vanessa. Block it out and never think about it. Vanessa was gone, and Caitlyn and Antonio deserved to move on. Together. It wasn't a crime.

At breakfast, the babies played with their bananas and Cheerios as always, Brigitte chattered up a storm as she did every morning and Caitlyn sat in her usual spot at the table. But the secret looks Antonio shot her gave every-thing a rosy, sensual glow, and she was very much afraid she was grinning at him like a besotted fool.

Perhaps she should be more covert if the goal was to keep their relationship on the down low.

"Caitlyn and I are going shopping today," Antonio an-nounced out of the blue when everyone finished eating.

"We are?" Did they have some Christmas presents to

buy that she'd forgotten about? "It's two days until Christmas. The stores will be insane."

"I believe I have adequately demonstrated my ability to dispense with holiday crowds," he countered with a smirk.

"So that's your solution to everything now? Just buy out the whole store?"

"When I find something that works, I stick with it. You might consider thanking me for that." His dark gaze flickered with promise, and yesterday, such innuendo might have made her blush, but she was a worldly woman now. So she stuck her tongue out at him instead.

Brigitte watched all of this with unabashed fascination, probably interpreting the exchange in the wrong way. "Well. You two have *fun*."

Or the right way, depending on how you looked at it.

Antonio herded her into the Range Rover, and she dutifully drove, navigating through the paparazzi outside the gate. She wasn't used to all of this. The cameras had camped out there ever since the first time Antonio had gone to Falco.

As always, Antonio ignored them. Oh, his lawyer and Thomas Warren had fielded a ton of questions on Antonio's behalf, but he wasn't in a hurry to take that part of his life back. He liked his privacy, which suited Caitlyn fine.

Once they were clear of the knot of people and vans, she asked, "What are we shopping for?"

"Bedroom furniture."

She glanced at him askance and flicked her gaze back to the road immediately. "Because there's something wrong with the furniture you already have?"

"Yes. It's Vanessa's," he explained quietly, oblivious of the sword he'd just stuck through her abdomen. "Every stick of furniture in that room will be gone by the time we return. I already arranged it. Help me pick out something new."

Oh. So that was why they'd slept on the floor. He didn't

want to sleep with Caitlyn in the bed he'd shared with his wife. He'd probably considered it the height of betrayal.

Her throat burned with sudden unshed tears. "That's…"

There were no words to explain the hard twist of her heart. Vanessa had been his wife first, and there was nothing she could do to change that. After all, Antonio hadn't chosen her when he'd had the opportunity. Caitlyn was the backup sister.

And Antonio had done something unbelievably considerate in removing the remnants of his first marriage. He'd told her last night that he wanted to move on. She couldn't blame him for choices he'd made either before the crash or after.

He deserved a fresh start after the horrors he'd endured. If he wanted new bedroom furniture because the old pieces had belonged to his first wife, she'd help him redecorate once a week until he was happy. And keep her mouth shut about how hard it was on her to constantly recall that she was living her sister's life by default.

A clerk approached them the moment they stepped into the hushed store. Expensive plank flooring and discreet lighting lent to the moneyed atmosphere, and the high-end pieces on display even smelled expensive. It would be a Christmas miracle if Antonio walked out of here with a full bedroom set for less than fifty thousand dollars.

"What are you looking for today?" the salesclerk asked politely. "A new sofa to accommodate extra party guests, perhaps?"

"We're in need of new bedroom furniture," Antonio said as Caitlyn did a double take.

What was this "we" stuff?

"Absolutely, sir." The clerk eyed them both. "Can you give me an idea what style you might be looking for? Art deco, maybe? American heritage or contemporary?"

"Caitlyn, did you have a particular style in mind?" Antonio asked, and put a palm to the small of her back as if she had every right to be included in the decision. As if they were a couple shopping for furniture together.

"I, um…don't know what you'd like," she admitted, which seemed ridiculous to say when she'd not only studied him surreptitiously for years, she'd also just had sex with him. Shouldn't she know what he liked?

"I'd like something that puts a smile on your face." The look he gave her curled her toes and rendered her speechless. To the clerk, he nodded and said, "Show her everything and make sure she's given the opportunity to pick colors and such. I assume you do custom orders."

Dollar signs sprang into the clerk's eyes. "Of course. Down to the throw pillows. Please call me Judy. And you are?"

"This is Ms. Hopewell," Antonio said smoothly. "And she's the star of this show. She doesn't walk out of here without an entire bedroom set. When she's finished picking what she wants, you let me know and I'll pay for it."

"Excuse us a moment." Caitlyn pulled Antonio to the side. "What are you doing?" she whispered hotly. "I can't pick out your bedroom furniture. It's too…"

Intimate. Fast. Expensive.

"I want you to," he insisted. "After all, you're going to be using it."

She shut her eyes for a moment as she envisioned exactly what he meant by that. "But it's not going to be *mine*. I have a bedroom."

"Not anymore." Antonio's eyebrows drew together as her eyes widened. "I'm messing this up, aren't I? I should have talked to you about this at home. I want you to move into my bedroom. Permanently."

Warmth spread through her abdomen. The staff would know instantly that they were together, so maybe he *didn't* intend for their relationship to be a secret.

But what *was* their relationship? She knew he was the committed sort—it wasn't a surprise that he wanted something permanent. But it would be nice to have specifics. She'd never done this before. Was this his subtle way of asking her to be his girlfriend? Or was this the precursor to a marriage proposal?

Yes. Yes. Yes. No matter what he was asking, the answer was yes.

This definitely wasn't the time nor the place to hash this out, but she couldn't be upset. He wanted her to be a part of his life. Permanently. There was no possible way to misinterpret *that*. Who cared what label they slapped on it? Her heart flipped over and back again, unable to find the right spot in her chest now that everything she'd ever dreamed for herself had fallen in her lap.

He took her hand and squeezed it. "Help me make it a place we can be together without shadows of the past."

Her unsettled heart climbed into her throat as the sentiment crashed through her happiness. If only new furniture could actually achieve that.

She could never be rid of Vanessa's shadow. She was living her sister's life, the one Vanessa couldn't live because she'd died. A life Caitlyn never should have had, despite desperately wanting it. The enormous burden of guilt settled over her anew.

And the worst part was, she couldn't even tell Antonio how she felt, because he definitely didn't need an extra layer of guilt. He couldn't even *remember* Vanessa and it weighed on him.

This was going to go down far worse than the toy store. Picking out a forty-dollar toy for their children didn't carry a million heavy implications the way picking out furniture did.

"Please." Antonio's plea slid through her. "I need to feel as if I'm not still adrift and alone. I need you."

She shut her eyes and let Antonio bleed through her. This wasn't just about furniture. *Nothing* in their interaction was surface level. Or simple. Regardless, there was no point in acting as if there was a choice here. She lacked the strength—or the desire—to deny him anything.

"Okay." She blew out a breath and turned back to the expectant clerk. "I'm ready."

Panic ruffled her nerves. This was so far out of her realm of experience. She was shopping for furniture with a man. With Antonio.

But he was holding her hand and smiling at her as though she'd just given him the world's best Christmas present. She couldn't let her guilt or the circumstances ruin this. She couldn't let him down.

"Right this way." Judy escorted her to the left, already chattering about fabric and colors and who knew what.

At the end of the day, she'd be sleeping in Antonio's bed. Honestly, who cared what the furniture looked like when her full attention would be firmly fixed on the amazing, sensitive man lying on the next pillow?

As dawn broke through the glass wall overlooking the pounding Malibu surf, Caitlyn curled around Antonio's slumbering form and watched him breathe. The way she'd done yesterday morning. Because it could never be enough. He didn't get any less beautiful, and it was her God-given right to gawk at the man she was sleeping with, wasn't it?

His sooty lashes rested above his cheekbones and his lips pursed as if he was dreaming about kissing her. Funny, that was exactly what she'd dreamed about, too.

So she indulged them both and kissed him awake. "Merry Christmas."

His dark eyes blinked open and he smiled sleepily. "Is it already the twenty-fifth? I lost track."

"We've been busy."

Once she'd gotten over herself, the redecoration effort had consumed them both as they'd laughed and argued good-naturedly over the style and placement of the purchases. Then Antonio had gotten started on artwork, perusing gallery upon gallery until he'd found precisely what he wanted.

Late last night, they'd tossed the final teal pillow onto the couch in the sitting area and declared it done. The finished product looked nothing like the former space. Vanessa's taste had run to heavy and ornate baroque. Caitlyn had selected more simple lines and colors: a four-poster bed with simple square posts. A compact dresser in espresso-colored wood with silver pulls. Teal and dark brown accents.

It had been a magical, breathless few days. But as she'd suspected, Antonio was the best thing in the room. Every day was Christmas, as far as she was concerned.

Antonio rolled onto his side and pulled her into his arms. "Then, Merry Christmas to you, too."

She snuggled into his warm body. "We don't have to get up right away, do we?"

"Not for years and years. The kids won't know about Santa until they're, like, three or four, right?"

She loved it when he talked like that, as if they were a family who would be together forever, come what may. He hadn't mentioned the word *marriage*. But she hoped that was where they were headed.

"Ha. We'll be lucky if they aren't up at 5:00 a.m. next year, pounding down the stairs on their little toddler feet to see what Santa brought."

With a gleam in his eye that was impossible to misread, he winked. "Then, we better make good use of our one bye year."

So slowly she thought she might weep, he took her lips

in a long kiss that set off a freight train of heat through her blood.

It was so much more powerful to know what this kind of kiss led to as she fell into the sensual pleasure of his lips thoroughly claiming hers. His tongue was hot and rough and she reveled in the shock of it invading her mouth. Thrilled in it. Because while it mated with hers, it was so unbelievably arousing to recall that he'd also tasted her intimately with that same tongue.

His thigh slid between her legs, insistent and tight against her core. She moaned and arched into the pleasure as sparks exploded under his ministrations. Silently, she urged him on, riding his muscular thigh with small rolls of her hips. She needed…more. But she didn't have to tell him because he seemed to know instinctively what she wanted, as if he could read her mind.

He replaced his thigh with one strong hand and instantly, he found her sensitive bud, rolling it between his fingers as if he'd been born to touch her exactly in this way.

She gasped and her eyelids fluttered shut as waves of heat broke over her skin like the surf on the shore below their window. The man must have a deal with the devil. How else could he be so beautifully built, so incredibly successful at both of his chosen professions *and* be so *good* at making her feel like this?

Murmuring flowery Italian phrases like a prayer against her lips, he touched her intimately and pleasured her until she feared her skin would incinerate and leave her in ashes. Then he trailed his lips down her throat and set that magic mouth on one of her incredibly sensitive breasts. As soon as he curled his hard tongue around a nipple, she detonated like the Fourth of July.

The climax overwhelmed her, tensing her muscles and sending shooting stars across her vision.

"Antonio," she whispered. Or screamed. Hard to tell

when her entire body sang his name so loudly, it deafened her.

"Yes, my darling. I'm here." He rolled her to her back and covered her with his unbelievable body, resting his weight on his forearms so he wouldn't crush her.

But it was far too late to prevent that. As he positioned himself to slide into her, joy burst open inside her chest and streamed through her entire body. Oh, she'd been crushed, all right.

Crushed by the overwhelming sensations of being completely, fully in love. That desperation of wanting him from afar—that wasn't love. That was infatuation, and there was no comparison.

Antonio filled her to the hilt, and she rocked her hips to draw him deeper still, a technique she'd discovered by accident last night. And judging by his answering groan, he approved of it just as much this morning as he had last night.

She shut her eyes and savored the fullness of him as he shifted to hit her sweet spot. A sigh escaped her lips. Perfection. Was it always like this, like being touched physically and spiritually at the same time? Or did she and Antonio have a bond other people never experienced?

It was an academic question because she'd never know. This was the only man she'd ever love. The only man she'd ever be intimate with. She trusted him fully, knew he'd be there for her, steadfast and strong. Waiting for him had been worth it. She couldn't imagine being with anyone else like this, opening her body and her heart to another person in this beautiful expression of their love.

His thrusts grew more insistent, more urgent, and she bowed to meet him, taking pleasure, giving it until they came together one final time in a shuddery dual climax that left her boneless and replete.

They lay in each other's arms, silent but in perfect harmony until her muscles regained enough strength for her to move. But she didn't go very far. She pillowed her head on his shoulder and thanked whatever fates had seen fit to grant her this second chance to be with Antonio.

As he'd done yesterday morning, Antonio flipped on the wall-mounted flat-screen TV to watch the news. Habitual, he'd told her when she asked, since returning from Indonesia—to break the silence.

"You don't need that noise anymore," she said and grabbed the remote with every intention of powering it off again.

But in the split second before she hit the button, the news anchor mentioned Antonio's name.

"What are they saying?" He sat up against the headboard and focused his attention on the newscast.

"...the identity of the anonymous donor who had the entire inventory of a toy store delivered to Toys for Tots." The blonde on the screen smiled as a photo of Antonio appeared next to her head. "It will be a merry Christmas indeed for thousands of local children who have this secret Santa to thank. Antonio Cavallari made headlines recently by returning to LA after being presumed dead in a plane crash over a year ago—"

"They shouldn't have tracked down who donated those toys." Antonio frowned. "It was anonymous for a reason."

The newshounds had finally scented Antonio's story due to his generous gesture, which, as he pointed out, should have remained anonymous. He could have paraded around naked in front of Falco and generated less interest apparently, but the one thing he hadn't wanted advertised was what had garnered coverage. The nerve.

A photo of Vanessa flashed on the screen and she flipped the channel. The guilt was bad enough. She didn't need her sister staring at her from beyond the grave. "Enough of that."

But Antonio wasn't even looking at the TV. His gaze was squarely on Caitlyn. "You're very good for me, you know that?"

He tucked a lock of her hair behind her ear and then lifted the long strands from her neck to press a kiss to her throat. She shuddered as he gathered her closer, fanning the ashes of their lovemaking, which apparently hadn't fully cooled.

"I have something for you," he said, his lips sparking against her skin.

"And it's exactly what I wanted," she murmured, arching into his mouth, silently encouraging him to trail those lips down her throat.

It could never be enough. He could touch her every minute of every day, crawl inside her ten more times before they left this bed, and she'd never reach the saturation point.

He laughed and reached behind him to pull a long, flat box from the bedside dresser drawer.

Entranced by the possibilities, Caitlyn ripped off the green foil wrapping paper and lifted the lid. A silver chain lay on the velvet interior.

Antonio withdrew it from the box and held it up so she could see the silver-filigreed initial charms hanging from it. "There's an *A*, an *L* and another *A*."

"Oh," she breathed as her heart surged. "One for each of the babies."

He fingered an *A* and tilted it so the light glinted off the polished white stone set in the center. "When I was in Indonesia, I trained in a makeshift dirt ring. Oftentimes, when we sparred, we'd uncover rocks buried in the soil. I carried one in my pocket when I left in search of where I belonged. It was symbolic of what I hoped I'd find when I got to America. Myself, buried beneath the layers of damaged memories."

Speechless, she stared at him as her pulse pounded.

"I had the jeweler cut and polish my stone. Each letter holds a fragment of it." His gaze far away and troubled, he set the *A* swinging with a small tip of his finger. "If Vanessa had been carrying the babies, they would have died along with her."

True. And horrifying. She'd never thought about her decision to be their surrogate in quite that way. When Vanessa had asked her, Caitlyn had agreed because she loved her sister, but honestly, the thought of getting to carry Antonio's baby had tipped the scales. It had been a win-win in her book, but the reality had so much more positives wound up in that she couldn't feel guilty about it any longer.

He bunched the chain in his fist and drew the covers back from her naked form. She was too emotional to do anything but watch. He knelt to lay his lips on her C-section scars for an eternity, and then his dark gaze swept upward to fixate on her. "My children are a piece of me that I never would have had without you. I cannot ever repay you for what you've given me. This is but a small token."

Tears splashed down her face unchecked as Antonio leaned up to hook the chain around her neck. Everything inside swelled up and over, pouring out of her mouth.

"I love you," she choked out.

She didn't care if he didn't say it back. Didn't care if the timing was wrong. Didn't care if it was only the emotion of the moment that had dragged it out of her. It was the pure honest truth, and she couldn't have held back the tide of her feelings even with a dam the size of Asia.

His gaze flicked to hers and a wealth of emotions swam through his dark eyes. "I wish I could say the same. I'd like to. But it would be unfair."

She nodded and a few more tears splashed down on the teal comforter she'd painstakingly selected. His heart still belonged to Vanessa. It was a poetic kind of justice for her sister. And for Caitlyn, truth be told.

"It's okay. I'm not trying to pressure you. But I thought you should know how I feel."

He gathered her close and held her as if he never planned to let go. "Yet another gift you've given me without expectation of anything in return. You're an amazing woman, Caitlyn."

She laid her cheek over the falcon and listened to his heartbeat. He just needed time to get over Vanessa. She'd *help* him get over her so that strong, beautiful heart could belong to Caitlyn forever. And then she'd be complete.

"Let's go spend Christmas with our family," Caitlyn suggested, and Antonio's rumbled agreement vibrated against her cheek.

The day after Christmas, Antonio couldn't stand his own company any longer and the only solution for his foul mood was to go to Falco. Without Caitlyn.

She sent him off with a kiss and nary a backward glance, as if she really had no clue he was about to lose his mind. Seemed as if he'd done a spectacular job keeping his doubts and trepidation to himself.

He had to do something different to regain his memories. It wasn't fair to Caitlyn that she was stuck in a relationship with a man who had no concrete memories of his marriage and therefore no guideposts to help him move on.

He wanted to. Desperately. He'd hoped finally getting Caitlyn into his arms would do the trick. Instead, all he'd accomplished was to make things worse.

She was in love with him. And the way he felt about her—*wonderful and terrifying emotions* was a stellar way to describe it. When he looked at her, it was as if every star in the sky shined all at once, lighting up the darkness. *She* was his star. The only constellation in his life that would ever make sense. Because he'd done exactly what he'd set out to do. He'd created new memories, new experiences with her.

Surely this was love.

But he'd been in love with Vanessa, or so Caitlyn had told him. Why couldn't he remember her clearly? It seemed wrong to tell Caitlyn about his feelings, his fledging certainty that he was in love with her, too, to promise her any sort of future, when he'd done the same with Vanessa... only to lose all consciousness of that relationship.

What if he did that to Caitlyn one day? What if he got in the ring with Cutter again and the next blow to his head erased his memories of her?

He couldn't stand the thought.

At Falco, he sat in the chair behind his desk. It was a sleek behemoth with a front piece that went all the way to the ground, hiding his lower half from view to visitors. Why had such obscurity appealed to him? He had no idea, but Caitlyn had told him he'd selected it along with all of the other furniture in the office.

Perhaps he'd shopped for furniture with Vanessa, too, as he'd done with Caitlyn. He yearned for his relationship with Caitlyn to feel special and unique. But how would he know either way?

This frustration was useless, and nothing he'd done thus far today came close to handling his memory problems differently. So he picked up the phone and scheduled the CT scan for the following week after the holidays.

It might not help, but he couldn't live in this fog of uncertainty any longer. He'd promised Caitlyn they would talk about the future after the first of the year and he'd been entertaining the notion of taking her to someplace she'd enjoy for New Year's Eve, like Paris or Madrid. Just the two of them.

Antonio pulled the ring box from his pocket and flipped

the lid. The fifteen-karat diamond dazzled like a perfect, round star against the midnight velvet. The moment he'd seen it in the case as he'd waited for the jeweler to retrieve Caitlyn's custom-made necklace, he'd known. That was the ring he wanted on Caitlyn's finger forever, as a physical symbol that she belonged to him and he needed her. He imagined her eyes filling with all that sweet, endless emotion as she realized he was asking her to marry him.

But he couldn't ask her until he exorcised the ghost of his first wife.

He pushed away from the desk and strode outside to get some fresh air. Street sounds and the ever-present sting of smog and pollution invaded what little serenity he might have found outdoors.

A flash of red hair in his peripheral vision put a hitch in his gut. An otherworldly sense of dread overwhelmed him.

Slowly, he turned to see a woman approaching him, a quizzical, hopeful slant to her expression. Long legged, slim build, beautiful porcelain face, fall of bright red hair to her waist.

Vanessa.

Oh, God. *It was his wife.* In the flesh. A million irreconcilable images flew through his head as he stared at her. Pain knifed through his temples.

"Antonio," she whispered, her voice scratchy and trembling. She searched his gaze hungrily. "I saw the news report and couldn't believe it. I had to find you, to see you for myself."

"Vanessa," he croaked, and his throat seized up.

She recoiled as if he'd backhanded her across the face. "What is that, a joke?"

"You're supposed to be dead. Caitlyn told me they found your body."

Caitlyn. Horrified, he stared at the redhead filling his vision. Caitlyn was the mother of his children, his lover.

She lived in his house, in his heart…and there was no room for Vanessa. How could this be *possible*?

"I'm not Vanessa, Antonio. What's going on? It's me." Confusion threw her expression into shadow when he shook his head. "Shayla."

The name exploded in his head. Across his soul. *Shayla.*

Laughing, moaning, murmuring his name—dozens of memories of her scrolled through his mind. Her body twining with his. Her full breasts on unashamed display, head thrown back as she rode him, taking her pleasure as if she had done it often, as if she had a right to use his body.

And of course she *had* done it often.

Shayla. His mistress. Vanessa—his wife.

The images in his head of the redheaded woman were so jumbled and nonsensical because he'd had incomplete, fragmented memories of *two different women*.

Eleven

A swirl of nausea squeezed Antonio's stomach as his eyes shut against the shocking revelation. He couldn't look at her, couldn't take the idea that he'd been intimate with her.

He'd been carrying on an affair with this woman. Cheating on his wife with her.

It was repulsive. Wrong. Not something he'd ever have imagined himself doing.

But clearly, that hadn't always been his opinion of adultery.

Gagging against the bile rising in his throat, he turned away from Shayla's prying, too-familiar gaze.

"What's the matter?" she asked. "Aren't you happy to see me? Vanessa is gone and we can finally be together."

"I don't…" *Remember you.* But it was a lie. He remembered her all too well.

Oblivious of his consternation, she put a manicured hand on his arm. He fought the urge to shake it off because it wasn't her fault he'd forsaken his marriage vows.

His skin crawled under her fingers.

He yanked his arm away and her hand fell to her side as hurt clouded her expression.

"I'm sorry," he said roughly, as pain ice-picked through his skull. "Things are not like you assume."

She cocked her head. "I don't understand what's wrong. You're alive and it's a miracle. Why didn't you call me? I've thought you were dead for over a year. Do you have any idea what I've gone through?"

His short bark of laughter startled them both. "Shayla, I—" God, he couldn't even say her name without wanting to cut out his tongue. Swallowing, he tried again. "I have amnesia."

It was the first time he'd uttered that word out loud. And oddly, naming it, *owning* it, diminished its power. Not completely, but his spine straightened and he nodded at her stunned flinch.

"Yes, you heard correctly," he told her a bit more firmly. "The plane crash dumped me on the shore of an island in Indonesia with few memories. I only found my way home a few weeks ago."

"You don't remember me." Her expression caved in and tears shimmered in her eyes. "Of all the things... I thought we'd pick up where we left—I mean, Vanessa is dead. When I heard you'd survived the crash, I figured you—"

"I remember you," he broke in. "But I didn't until I saw you."

As he'd remembered his lawyer and Thomas. But he hadn't remembered Caitlyn. Or Rodrigo. Which led to the most important question—

Would he remember Vanessa if he saw *her*?

A perverse need to know overtook him.

"I'm sorry," he told the tearful redhead before him, determined to get home and discover what else he could extract from the sieve in his brain. "There's nothing here for you any longer. I'm not in love with you and I never will be."

She laughed bitterly. "Funny, that's almost exactly what you said before you left to go to Thailand. Except you were talking about Vanessa at the time. Didn't stop you from running off on your lovers' retreat."

The words blasted through his head, but in his voice as he said them to Shayla one night.

I'm not in love with her and I never will be. There's nothing left for me in that cold, empty house. The Malibu house. He'd meant the one he'd shared with Vanessa. The one he now shared with Caitlyn and his children.

He'd told Shayla he wasn't in love with Vanessa. Truth? It might explain why he couldn't recall what that had felt like. Or had it been something he'd told his mistress to string her along?

After all, he'd gone to Thailand with Vanessa. Had fathered children with her. All while conducting a hot-and-heavy affair with this woman.

What kind of man did such things? When he'd come to LA to find out who he was, he'd never imagined he'd discover such dishonesty and selfishness in his past. Who had he *been* before the crash?

Some aspects, like being a fighter, he didn't have to question. That was a part of him. Was being an adulterer part of him, too? A part he couldn't remove any easier than he could stop fighting? He owed it to himself, his children and Caitlyn to learn everything he could about what kind of person Antonio Cavallari had been. So he could chart a course for the kind of man he wanted to be in the future.

"I'm sorry," he repeated. "I have to go. Please don't contact me again. Our relationship, whatever it was, is over."

"Yeah." She sighed. "It has been for more than a year. I mistakenly assumed we had a second chance this time.

A real one. You were never going to divorce Vanessa, not with the baby on the way."

That resonated. Divorce wasn't something the man he *knew* he was deep inside would tolerate. "No, I wouldn't have. And turns out there were three babies. Triplets."

Her smile was small but genuine. "Congratulations. Didn't see that coming. Vanessa was smarter than I would have given her credit for. That's triple the amount of child support if you ever did divorce her. I wish I knew how she'd pulled that off."

Child support. A fight with Vanessa where that term had been launched at him like a grenade... The details slammed through his head. Shayla's name had come up. Vanessa was furious because he'd sworn he'd end things with "that woman," but he apparently hadn't. Then Vanessa had taunted him with the pregnancy, saying it was insurance. Against what?

He couldn't remember that much of the conversation.

"The triplets were an accident," he assured her. "A happy one."

She nodded and he watched her walk away, then strode to the town car so the driver could take him home, where he would get some answers to the mysteries locked in his mind, once and for all.

Once he got into the house, he disappeared into the media room to queue up episodes of the TV show Vanessa had starred in. He should have done this weeks ago. Why hadn't he?

He'd told himself it wouldn't do any good. That his memories of Vanessa were so scattered and fragmented that seeing her wouldn't help. It was a lie, one he'd convinced himself of for his own self-preservation.

Vanessa walked onto the sixty-inch screen as his pulse thundered in his throat. Slim, redheaded, with delicate features. The way she held herself, something about her demeanor, was horribly familiar…because she looked like a redheaded version of Caitlyn.

Pain knifed through his temples, throbbing in tandem with his pulse.

His memories of Shayla and Vanessa split instantly. Distinct and whole, the snippets of scenes and his interactions with each woman flooded his consciousness. He let them flow despite the enormous shock to his system, absorbing, reliving. And he didn't like the realizations that followed.

Maybe he hadn't wanted to remember either his wife or his mistress. Maybe he'd known subconsciously that he didn't deserve someone as innocent as Caitlyn and he'd suppressed his memories on purpose to avoid facing the dark choices he'd made before the crash.

Grief clawed at his throat.

He had to tell Caitlyn. She should know what kind of man he'd been. What kind of man he still was. Amnesia hadn't made him into someone different. Just someone who didn't remember his sins.

He powered off the TV and sat on the plush couch in full darkness for an eternity, hating himself. Hating his choices, hating that he couldn't remember why he'd made them. Because that was part of the key in moving toward the future—understanding the past.

The door to the media room opened and Caitlyn's dark head poked through. "Hey, I didn't know you were back, but I saw the car and—"

"Come in," he commanded unevenly. "Please."

She was here. Might as well lay it all on the line. The hordes of paparazzi hanging out at Falco had likely snapped a picture of his conversation with Shayla, and he'd rather Caitlyn hear about it from him.

She came into the room, reaching for the lamp switch. He caught her arm before she could turn it on. Dark was appropriate.

"What's wrong?" she asked, concern coating her voice.

It was a painful, unintentional echo of Shayla's question. Apparently, they could both read him well. Better than he could read himself. "I need to talk to you."

How did you approach such a subject? He hadn't dishonored *her*. But she'd likely be outraged on her sister's behalf. Regardless, she had to know the truth.

"Sure." She perched on the couch, her features barely discernible in the faint light from the still-open door. He could sense her, smell her light coconut shampoo, and his heart ached to bury himself in her, no talking, no specters of the past between them.

But he'd probably never touch her again. She deserved better than he was capable of giving her.

"I…ran into someone today. A woman. From before the crash. I…remembered her."

"That's great!" Caitlyn's sweet voice knifed through him.

"No, it's not. I was having an affair with her," he said bluntly. Harshly. But there were no punches to be pulled here, no matter how difficult it was to keep swinging.

"An affair?"

Her confusion mirrored his but must have been ten times worse because she'd only just learned of it. He'd had hours to reconcile how truly sinful he was.

"Yes. A long-standing one, apparently." Remorse nearly overwhelmed him.

She grew quiet and he wished he hadn't insisted on no lights. Was she upset? She should be. But the darkness left him only his own guilt for company.

"I don't understand," she finally said. "You and Vanessa were happy. You were in love."

"I wasn't. Happy," he clarified. "Or in love."

That was perhaps the most painful realization of all. His confusion about love stemmed wholly from not ever having been in love before. When his memories of Vanessa resurfaced, he'd recognized the truth Shayla had revealed. He hadn't loved Vanessa.

He couldn't compare how he felt now to the past because there was nothing to compare it to. His feelings for Caitlyn were unprecedented.

And he was most definitely in love with her.

Otherwise it wouldn't be breaking his heart to tell her who he was, deep down inside where he couldn't change it.

"Why didn't you get a divorce, then?" Her voice had grown faint, as if she'd drawn in on herself.

"I don't know," he admitted quietly. "Too Catholic, maybe. And there was a baby on the way. I'm still missing huge pieces of my memories of the past, pieces I might never recover."

They lapsed into silence and he ached to bridge it, but this was an unprecedented situation, too. She should be allowed to react however she wanted.

"Did Vanessa know?" Her voice cracked and he realized she was crying as she sniffled quietly.

His gut twisted, and her pain was far worse than the pain he'd caused himself. She was hurting. More than he would have anticipated. Of course he hadn't thought this would go over well, but he'd expected her to be angry, not injured. His nails dug into his palms as he struggled to keep from touching her, comforting her. He was the source of her hurt, not the solution.

"She knew." And he wished he understood the dynamics of his marriage, why Vanessa would have stayed in a marriage where her husband didn't love her and was having an affair with another woman. He didn't even remember if she'd professed to love him. "I'm sorry to drop this on you with no warning. It's not how I envisioned this going between us."

They should have been talking about the trip he'd hoped to surprise her with, the imminent marriage proposal.

"It's a lot to take in, Antonio." Her voice fractured again on the last syllable of his name. "I don't know what to say."

Frustration and grief and anguish rose up inside, riling his temper as he tried to reconcile how to get through this, how to move forward when all he wanted was to hear her say it was okay, that she still loved him. That it didn't matter who he'd been. "Say how you feel. Are you mad at me? Hurt? You want to punch me?"

"I feel as if I don't know you. Commitment isn't important to you like it is to me. I wish I'd never slept with you," she admitted on a whisper that turned his whole body cold. "I can't deal with all of this. Not right now."

She slid to her feet and left the media room with a rush of quiet sobbing.

His guiding star had left him in the dark, and he felt further away from finding himself than ever. Ironic that he'd spent so long fighting to remember and now all he wished for was the ability to forget.

Dry-eyed, Caitlyn fed the babies. It was the only accomplishment she could list for the afternoon.

She rocked Annabelle, staring blindly at the wall as she tried to quiet the storm of misery zinging through her heart. If only she could crawl into bed and shut out the world, she might figure out how to get through this.

But she couldn't. Children still needed to be fed no matter what pain had just ripped a hole in your chest. Christmas decorations still had to be put away, leaving an empty hole where the holiday cheer had been. Life went on, oblivious of how one simple phrase had destroyed her world.

I was having an affair with her.

For years, Caitlyn had envied her sister's marriage. For

years, Caitlyn had lived with her unrequited feelings for Antonio. *For years*, she'd suffered crippling guilt over both.

And it was all a lie.

Her sister's marriage had been a sham. The strong, beautiful commitment she'd imagined was an illusion. The man she'd thought so steadfast and constant? An adulterer. Antonio wasn't perfect in the way she'd thought he was, and her guilt had been all for nothing.

Nothing. That guilt certainly hadn't served to keep her out of Antonio's bed. Oh, no, she'd hopped right into his arms with practically no resistance. She'd given her virginity to a man who thought so little of marriage vows that he couldn't honor them. Who thought so little of love that he hadn't considered it a necessity when choosing a wife.

It was reprehensible.

And none of it made *sense*. The awful words pouring out of Antonio's mouth: the admission that he hadn't been in love with Vanessa, the affair, the reasons for not divorcing—they didn't mesh with the man she'd fallen in love with.

She'd known Antonio for seven years. Was she really such a bad judge of character that she could love a man who'd treated her sister like that? How could she forgive any of this?

She wished she could cry. But everything was too numb.

After the babies had been fed, she slumped in the rocking chair as Leon, Annabelle and Antonio Junior crawled around on a blanket in the center of the nursery. It had been only a couple of hours since Antonio had told her. But it felt like a year.

"May I come in?"

Her gaze cut to the door. As if her thoughts had conjured him, Antonio stood just inside it, his expression blank.

For an instant, her heart lurched as she drank him in. Apparently, nothing could kill the reaction she still had to him. A sobering realization. As was the fact that he hadn't tracked her down with some magical solution to the giant cloud over them now, as much as she might wish that such a thing existed. No, he was here because they always played with the babies before dinner. It had become a ritual all five of them enjoyed, and he would still want to spend time with his children no matter what else happened.

Life went on. And they were co-parents of small children. Forever.

"Of course you can come in," she said. "This is your house."

He winced and she almost apologized for the bitter tone. But she didn't have the energy and she wasn't all that sorry. The old Caitlyn would have apologized. The old Caitlyn always had a kind word for everyone and lived in a rosy world of rainbows and unicorns, obviously.

All that had gotten her was devastated and broken-hearted. Why hadn't someone warned her that a commitment had absolutely nothing hidden inside it to guard against being hurt? Actually, it was worse because then you had to figure out how to live with your hurt.

Antonio crouched on the blanket and handed Leon a rattle, murmuring encouraging words as his son crawled toward it. Annabelle hummed as she explored the perimeter of the blanket and Antonio Junior lay on his back in the center of the room, examining the ceiling with his unique brand of concentration.

Not so unique, actually. His father had that same ability to hone in on something and it was nearly hypnotic.

She tamped down the tide of sheer grief. Antonio wasn't who she thought he was. He hadn't been probably since the beginning. She had to get past it, forgive him and get over her disappointment so they could move on. Didn't she?

The clock on the wall ticked loudly, marking off second after interminable second. They bled into a minute, then another. The silence stretched, heavy and thick. But this was how it had to go. They'd play with the babies and eat dinner. Then what? They shared a bedroom. Would they get ready for bed and lay next to each other with the silence and the big letter *A* for *affair* creating an invisible boundary between them?

"I can't do this." She was on her feet, hands clenched in tight fists, before she fully registered moving. "It's like waiting for the executioner's ax to fall."

Antonio glanced up at her, his mouth set in a hard line. It ruined the beauty of his face. He was obviously as miserable as she was. She hated that she noticed and hated even more that she apparently still cared.

"What is? Hanging out with our kids?"

"No. This." She swirled a taut hand in the air to encompass the room at large, but she meant the two of them and the big question marks surrounding their relationship, how they moved forward, all of it. "I can't do this with you. I'm not Vanessa. I won't put up with affairs and I'm not okay with it."

She'd yearned for her sister's life and now she had it. The whole kit and caboodle. Clearly she needed to be more careful what she wished for. Yet it was such a suitable penance. She bit back hysterical laughter.

"I'm not asking you to be okay with it," he countered quietly with a glance at Annabelle who had pulled up on her crib with a loud squeal of achievement. "*I'm* not okay with it. And you should know, it wasn't affairs. Just one. I told her not to contact me anymore. I don't want anything to do with her."

Did he honestly expect any of that to make a *difference*?

"I need to move back into my own bedroom." Her throat hitched as she said the words and she wished she could take them back, but it was the smartest move for her sanity. "I can't be with you anymore, not like we were."

And there it was. She'd held this man in her arms, cradled him with her body, loved him, slept with him, tasted him. Never in a million years would she have imagined she'd be the one to call off their relationship. In the end, she'd been painfully spot on—she wasn't the right kind of woman for Antonio Cavallari.

Grimly, he crossed his arms. "What will we be like, then?"

She shook her head blindly. "Parents. Roommates. I don't know. I just know I can't sleep in that bedroom. I can't—"

A sob broke through, ending whatever she'd been about to say. Head bowed, she buried her head in her hands, squeezing her eyes shut. She sensed Antonio's presence as he approached, but he didn't touch her.

She wished he would. Wished they were still in a place where he could comfort her. But was glad he didn't. It would only confuse things.

"Caitlyn."

She blinked up at him through watery eyes.

His dark gaze zeroed in on her, overwhelming her with unvoiced conflict and soul-deep wounds. Even now, with these irreparable ruptures between them, she could read him.

"Will you fight me for custody of the children?" he asked softly.

She gasped. "What? Why in the world would I do that?"

"What kind of father could I possibly be?" Resolute and stoic, he stared her down. "I have an uncontrollable urge to decimate other men in the ring. I have amnesia. I defiled my marriage with a tasteless affair. Any judge would grant your petition to take my children and likely award you as much money as you ask for to raise them. If I were you, I would have already taken steps to remove them from my influence."

"Antonio." Her chest constricted as she searched his ravaged expression. "None of that makes you a bad father. Your children need you."

I need you.

But she bit it back. She needed the man she'd *thought* he was, the one who made her feel treasured because he'd chosen her. Because of all the people in his life he could have reached out to, he'd taken her hand and asked her to stand with him when he had gone to Falco the first time. He'd asked her to see the doctor with him. He'd been alone and frightened and he hadn't wanted anyone else but her.

Then he'd destroyed her trust by morphing into someone else. Someone who didn't respect and honor marriage the way she did. Who hadn't loved his wife.

If he couldn't love Vanessa, what hope did Caitlyn have that he could ever feel that way about her? And she wouldn't settle for anything less than a man's love. Yet, how could she trust him if he *did* say that he loved her?

It was a vicious cycle, one she couldn't find a way to break, no matter how many times she went over it in her head. All this time, she'd thought he couldn't tell her he loved her because his heart still belonged to Vanessa. The reality was…indescribable.

Antonio glanced at the babies, and all the love she knew he felt for them radiated from every pore of his being. He was capable of love. Just not loving her.

"No, I need *them*," he said. "As long as you're not going to take them from me, I can handle anything else."

It was a strange reversal of some of their earlier conversations, when she'd been terrified he'd find a way to dismiss her from her children's lives. She knew what that clawing, desperate panic felt like and it softened her. More than she'd have liked.

A harder, more cynical person might have taken the information he'd laid out and run with it, ensuring that she got exactly what he said—custody and Antonio's money. It would be a fit punishment for his crimes.

But she wasn't that person, and as she stood close enough to touch him, close enough to smell his heady masculine scent, her heart twisted.

She still loved him. Nothing he'd said to her today could erase that.

"I will never take your children from you," she promised and her voice cracked. "But I can't have a romantic relationship with you. We have to figure out a way to live together as parents and nothing else. Can we?"

He stepped back, hands at his sides and his beautiful face a mask. "I'll respect whatever decision you make."

Her heart wept over his matter-of-fact tone, as if he had no interest in fighting for her. But what would she have said if he told her no, that it was totally unacceptable to end their relationship? That he loved her and wanted her in his bed, come hell or high water?

She'd have refused.

So here they were. Parents. And nothing else.

That made her want to weep more than anything else that had happened today.

Twelve

Antonio stood outside Caitlyn's old bedroom at 1:00 a.m., hands on the wood, listening to her breathe. God, this separation was an eternal hell.

After two days of staying out of her way, he was done with it.

She was awake and lying there in despair. He could sense it. Her essence had floated down the hall to him on a whisper of misery, and he'd caught it easily because he'd been lying awake in his own bed in similar turmoil.

His headaches had grown worse since they'd been apart, and his pillow still smelled like Caitlyn even after ten washings. She haunted him, asleep or awake. Didn't matter. She was so close, yet so far, and his body never quite got used to the fact that she wasn't easily accessible any longer. He still rolled over in the night, seeking her heat and the bone-deep contentment that came with touching her.

Only to come up empty-handed and empty hearted. The

only thing in life that made sense was gone, and it hurt worse than any physical pain he'd ever endured.

The pounding in his temples wouldn't ease no matter how many rounds he went in the ring at Falco. He'd even resorted to a pain pill earlier that evening, to no avail.

The only thing that ever worked to take away his headache was Caitlyn.

He pushed the door open and stepped inside her room. She didn't move, but the quick intake of her breath told him she knew he was there.

"I can't sleep," he said inanely.

Her scent filled his head, pulsing through it with sweet memories, and it was worse than being in his lonely bed without her. This was too close. And not close enough.

It was maddening.

"I'm sorry." Her voice whispered across his skin, raising the hair. "But you can't come in here in the middle of the night."

"This is my house," he growled as his temper got the best of him. It was the wrong tactic; he knew that. But she was killing him. "I need to talk to you."

"Can't it wait?"

It was a reasonable request for one o'clock in the morning. "No, it can't. Please, Caitlyn. What can I say, what can I do? I'm sorry. I hate that I did something so inexcusable. Can't you get past it?"

"I don't think so." The quiet words cut through him. "We don't have the same views on commitment, and that's not something that I can get past. You told me you believed in forever and I believed you. Now I can't trust you, and without that, what kind of relationship would we have? I'm not like Vanessa."

Why couldn't she see that he didn't want her to be like Vanessa? At one point in time, he'd liked a certain kind of woman, clearly. But he didn't remember why and didn't want to.

He wanted Caitlyn.

And she didn't want him. Because of something he'd done a long time ago. Something he couldn't undo. Something that haunted him, something he hated about himself. He'd surgically extract whatever she objected to if he could. If it would make a difference.

But it wouldn't, and this was one fight he lacked the skill to win.

Without another word, he left her there in the dark because he couldn't stand the space between them any longer. Couldn't stand that he didn't know what to do.

He had to change her mind. She was everything to him and he needed her. Loved her.

For the first time in his life, he was pinned against the fence, strength draining away, and his opponent was too big to overcome.

But he refused to go down for the count. He needed to do something big and drastic to win her back. But what?

After a long night of tossing and turning, Caitlyn gave up at 5:00 a.m. She'd slept in this bed pre-Antonio for over a year and had never thought twice about it. A few days in paradise, also known as the bedroom down the hall, and suddenly there was no sleep to be had in this old room.

And she wasn't fooled into thinking it was the mattress. Her inability to sleep had everything to do with the black swirl of her thoughts and the cutting pain in her chest after shutting down Antonio's middle-of-the-night plea. Closing her eyes only made it worse.

Caitlyn padded to the sunroom and tried to get in the mood for Pilates before Leon woke up. But all she could think about was the first time Antonio had kissed her. He'd backed her up against a wall, literally and figuratively, in this very room, demanding she tell him about love. So she'd spilled her heart and turned the question back to him, expecting a profound tribute straight from the poetry books. An ode to his late wife about his devotion and the wonders of their marriage.

What do you know about love? she'd asked.

Nothing, he'd returned.

She'd assumed he didn't remember love and stupidly thought he was asking her to help him. But really, he'd meant he'd never loved Vanessa. How awful it must have been for her sister, to be stuck in a loveless marriage with a man who wouldn't divorce her solely because of the baby on the way. Instead, he'd forced her to put up with his infidelity.

How had Vanessa done it? How had she woken up each morning, her mind ripe with the knowledge that her husband had been intimate with another woman? Unrequited love was something Caitlyn had a special empathy for. Had her sister cried herself to sleep at night, the way Caitlyn had over the past few days? Why hadn't Vanessa told her what was going on?

Inexplicably, she wished her sister was here so she could bury her head in Vanessa's shoulder and weep out all her troubles. Which was the worst kind of juxtaposition. If Vanessa was alive, Caitlyn's troubles would be nonexistent. She'd still be laboring under the false premise that marriage, commitment, love and sex were all tied up with a big, magnificent bow.

Leon woke up early. While Caitlyn fed him, her mind wandered back to Vanessa and it suddenly hit her that her sister's possessions sat tucked away in the attic. Her sister might be gone, but Caitlyn could still surround herself with Vanessa. Maybe it would help ease Caitlyn's bruised and battered soul.

She turned the babies over to Brigitte, who bundled

them up for a ride in the triple-seated stroller, and then escaped to the attic. *Attic* might be a little grandiose of a term—it was really a small, unfinished room above the second floor, accessible by a narrow staircase next to the linen closet.

Caitlyn hadn't been in here for over a year, not since she'd moved the bulk of Vanessa's things after the plane crash. A coating of dust covered the items farthest from the entrance. The boxes near the front had been placed there recently and weren't as grimy. Shortly after Antonio had returned, Caitlyn had asked the housekeeper to pack up the rest of her sister's things.

Sitting down cross-legged, she opened the nearest untaped box. Clothes. She pulled out one of her sister's silk blouses and held it to her cheek. The heavy, exotic perfume Vanessa had favored wafted from the fabric. All at once, Caitlyn recalled the last time she'd smelled it, when she'd been four months pregnant and had come to say goodbye before Vanessa and Antonio left for Thailand.

Tears slid down her face and she suspected the majority of them were because she missed Antonio. Not Vanessa. Apparently, her shame knew no bounds, but he'd been so lost last night. She'd wanted to tell him she wished there was a way to get past it, too. But she couldn't see it.

The clothes weren't helping. Pushing that box to the side, she dived into the next one, which was full of Vanessa's toiletries, including two small, jeweled bottles of her perfume. Caitlyn pulled them out to give to Annabelle. The perfume would likely not last that long, but the bottles were encrusted with real semiprecious stones and the pair would be a lovely keepsake for their daughter.

Perhaps the children she shared with Vanessa were actually the answer Caitlyn had been seeking about how she was supposed to find the strength to live in the same house with Antonio. Had Vanessa considered the babies a good enough reason to stay with her husband despite the emotional pain he'd caused her? Leon, Annabelle and Antonio Junior were certainly the reason why Caitlyn was still here after all. She couldn't imagine not waking up each day and seeing the faces of her kids. It was worth the sword through her heart every time she saw their father to get daily access to her children.

Maybe it had also been worth it to Vanessa to keep her family intact. Maybe that was why she hadn't pressed for a divorce and stayed with Antonio even after she found out about his affair.

Drained, Caitlyn rested her head on the box. Her weight threw it off balance and it tumbled to spill its contents into her lap.

A leather-bound book landed on top. It looked like an old-fashioned journal. Curious, Caitlyn leafed through it and recognized her sister's handwriting.

"Sept 4: Ronald doesn't think the Paramount people will consider me for the lead in *Bright Things*. The role is too opposite from Janelle. I should fire him, but he's my third agent in two years. Ugh. I really want that movie!"

Interesting. Caitlyn wouldn't have considered Vanessa the type to record her innermost thoughts, especially not in written form when her sister had been so attached to her smartphone, but here it was, in blue pen. With all of the email hacking and cloud-storage security breaches that plagued celebrities, Vanessa might have felt paper had a measure of privacy she couldn't get any other way. Feeling a little voyeuristic, Caitlyn read a few more entries at the beginning and then skipped ahead.

Wow, she hadn't realized how much Vanessa had wanted to move on from Janelle, the character she'd played on the prime-time drama *Beacon Street*. Her sister had never said anything about how trapped she'd felt.

It kind of stung to find out Vanessa hadn't confided in

Caitlyn about her career woes. Or much of anything, apparently. The journal was full of surprises. Caitlyn would have said they were pretty close before the crash, but obviously Vanessa had kept a lot of things hidden.

Antonio's name caught her eye and she paused mid–page flip.

"I told Antonio about Mark. He totally freaked out, worse than I expected. Simple solution to the problem, I told him. If he'd just stop this ridiculous nonsense about reviving his glory days in the ring, I'd agree to stop seeing Mark. Which won't be hard. He's nowhere near as good as Antonio in bed, but I had to do something to get my stupid husband's attention!"

Caitlyn went cold, then hot.

Her sister had been having an affair, too?

Dread twisted her stomach inside out as she flipped to the beginning of the entry. It was dated over two years ago. Well before Vanessa had approached Caitlyn about being a surrogate. Her sister's marriage problems had extended that far back?

She kept reading entry after entry with slick apprehension souring her mouth.

"Antonio is still really upset about Mark. He demanded I quit *Beacon Street*. I laughed. As if I'd ruin my career for him just so my darling husband didn't have to watch me on-screen with the man I'm sleeping with? Whatever."

And then a few pages later: "Antonio is so horrible. Not only is he still talking about fighting again—which I will not put up with!—he's found what he thinks is the best way to get back at me for Mark. He's having an affair with a woman who looks like me. On purpose. It's so juvenile. He's so not the type to be this vindictive. But I left him no choice, he said in that imperious voice that never fails to piss me off."

Antonio had started his affair in retaliation for Vanessa's. It didn't change how she felt about infidelity, but it changed how she felt about her sister. And her sister's views on marriage, which clearly didn't mirror Caitlyn's.

Information overload. Wave after wave of it crashed over her. So Antonio had wanted to get back in the ring even before the crash—did he remember that?

Her throat and eyes both burning uncontrollably, Caitlyn forced herself to read to the end. Without checking her strength, she threw the leather-bound confessional at the wall, unable to hold the evidence of how little she'd actually known her sister.

She'd walked into this attic hoping to find some comfort for the task ahead of her—living with a man she loved but couldn't fathom how to trust—and instead found out her sister hadn't been sitting around pining for her husband. In fact, Vanessa had had skeletons of her own in her closet.

Hot, angry tears coursed down Caitlyn's face, and she couldn't stop the flood of grief. Didn't want to. Nothing was as she'd thought. Vanessa had pushed Antonio into the arms of another woman first by forbidding him from doing something he loved and then punishing him via a romance with her costar. It didn't make Antonio's choices right, but against everything Caitlyn would have expected, she had sympathy for him nonetheless.

It was too much. She sank into a heap and wept.

She registered Antonio's presence only a moment before he gathered her into his arms, rocking her against his strong chest. Ashamed that her soul had latched on to his touch like a greedy miser being showered with gold, she clung to him as he murmured her name. She cried on his expensive shirt and he didn't even seem to notice the huge wet spot under her cheek.

His fingers tangled in her hair as he cupped her head gently, massaging with his strong fingers. Tiny needles of awareness spiked through her skin, energizing her with the power of his sweet touch, but she ignored it. He didn't speak and somehow that made it okay to just be, no words, no excuses, no reasons to shove him away yet again.

When the storm passed, she peeked up at his blank expression. "Where did you come from? I didn't think you were home."

"I just got back," he said gruffly. "I…heard you and I couldn't stay away. I know you can take care of yourself, but I needed to check on you. Don't say I should have left you alone and let you cry because that was not going to happen."

"It's okay. I'm glad you found me."

"I doubt that's true when I'm the reason you're crying."

His arms dropped away and she missed them, almost calling out for him to encompass her again with that blanket of serenity. But she didn't. There was still so much unsaid between them. So much swirling through her heart that she could hardly think.

She shook her head. "Not this time. Vanessa—" her deep breath fractured on another half sob "—was sleeping with her costar. Mark—"

"Van Allsberg." Antonio's expression wavered between outrage and bleak resignation. "I remember now. I didn't until you said his name. I almost got in the car to drive to his house and take him apart for touching my wife. How did you find out?" he asked quietly as he sat back on his heels.

"She wrote in a journal." Bitterness laced her tone involuntarily. Vanessa had been very free with information when the page was her only audience. "I read it. It was illuminating."

Caitlyn's chest hurt as she watched the pain filter through his entire body anew, as if he was experiencing it for the first time. And perhaps amnesia was like that, continually forcing Antonio to relive events he should have been able to put behind him. Distance didn't exist for him the way it did for other people, who could grow numb to the pain—or deal with it—over time.

Unwittingly, she'd forced him to do the same by jumping on the self-righteous bandwagon, lambasting him for an affair that had happened a long time ago when in reality, she'd known nothing of the difficulties in his marriage. She'd been judge, jury and executioner without all of the facts.

She stared at the exposed beams of the ceiling until she thought she could talk without crying. "Her affair was your punishment for daring to express your interest in fighting again."

"I... It was?" Frustration knitted his features into an unrecognizable state. "I thought…"

His anguish ripped through her, and before she could list the hundreds of reasons why it was a bad idea, she grabbed his hand, holding it tightly in hers as if she could communicate all her angst through that small bit of contact.

"You made mistakes, Antonio. But there were extenuating circumstances."

It didn't negate the sacredness of marriage vows, but it did throw a lot of light on how Antonio's choices had come about.

"That's no excuse," he bit out savagely. "There *is* no excuse. That's why I can't forgive myself."

That speared through her gut and left a gaping wound in its wake.

His distress wasn't faked. Cautiously, she searched his face, his body language, and the truth was there in every fiber of his being. He clearly didn't think the affair was okay now, despite having thought differently back then.

Not only had the affair happened a long time ago, she'd refused to take into account that Antonio wasn't the same person he'd been while married to her sister. As many times as she'd noted he was different, in this, she'd convicted him of being the same.

Amnesia had taken pieces of his memory, and perhaps what was left had reshaped him. Could she find a way to trust the Antonio who had returned to her from the grave and allow the old one to stay buried?

"Antonio." He didn't look at her, but she went on anyway. "You should know something. She said you talked her into going to Thailand as a way to reconnect. You wanted to try again, just the two of you."

He nodded. "I don't remember. But I'm glad that Vanessa died knowing that I was committed to her."

That gelled with the Antonio she'd always known. A man who valued commitment, who despite the rockiness of his marriage had wanted to try again. "I'm sorry I dredged up all of this pain again."

He huffed out an unamused half laugh, scrubbing his face with his free hand. "You don't have to apologize. I remember so little about Vanessa in the first place. Hell, practically everything I know is from things you've told me. So the fairy tale you painted wasn't true. That's actually easier to deal with than the reverse."

"The reverse?"

With a small smile, he stared at the dusty attic floor between them. "That Vanessa was the love of my life but I would never remember what that felt like. That I'd never be able to move on until I properly mourned our relationship. Now I know all I had with her was a dysfunctional marriage that I can put behind me. The future seems a lot brighter knowing that the best relationship of my life is yet to come."

The cloud of pain seemed to lift from his features as he spoke, and she couldn't look away from his expression. It was fresh, beautiful, hopeful.

His strength was amazing and it bolstered hers. "I like the sound of that."

He tipped up her chin and feathered a thumb across her cheek. Lovingly. She fell into his gaze, mesmerized, forgetting for a moment that things were still unsettled between them. Then it all crashed down again: the disappointment, the heartache. The sense that they'd both cleansed a lot from the past but the future still had so many question marks.

Did she have what it took to put the affair behind her, as he seemed to want her to? As he seemed to do so easily himself?

"Caitlyn," he murmured and hesitated for an eternity, his gaze playing over her face as if he couldn't make up his mind what to say. Finally, he sighed. "I'm miserable without you. Can't sleep, can't eat. I deserve this purgatory you've cast me into, but you have to know that our relationship isn't going down without a fight."

"I'm miserable, too." She bowed her head. "But part of that misery is because I don't know how I'm supposed to feel about all of this. The revelations in Vanessa's journal don't change anything. Marriage is a sacred thing. Sex is, too. I have a hard time trusting that you truly believe that. I have a hard time trusting that if you and I fall into a rough spot in the future, you won't console yourself with another woman."

It was the old adage: once a cheater, always a cheater. Except she'd never thought she'd be wondering how true it was. People could and did change all the time, especially when presented with the best kind of motivation. Just look at her—she'd never envisioned being a mother, and it had taken a huge mind-set change to prepare for it.

He winced and nodded. "I deserve that, too. So that's why I went to Falco this morning and spent hours locked in a room with Thomas Warren and the other executives to hash out the details required to sell Falco Fight Club."

"You...what?" She couldn't catch her breath.

"I want it gone." Grimly, he sliced the air with a flat palm. "It's a brutal, bloody sport. I've got kids now, and limiting their exposure to MMA is always in the back of my mind. But that's not the reason I want to sell."

Sell. The word reverberated in her heart and nearly made her sick.

"Antonio! You can't sell Falco." It would be akin to her announcing she wanted to sell one of the babies. It was lunacy. "That place is a part of you. I watched you fight. You love it. It's as if you were born to be in the ring."

"Exactly. I sign everyone's paychecks. Who's going to tell me no if I say I want to get back into rotation? As long as I own Falco, I have a guaranteed path into the ring."

"You're not making any sense. All of that sounds like a *good* thing. If you want to get in the ring again, I won't stop you. I'll support it," she countered fiercely. "I'm not Vanessa."

Caitlyn would never be so daft as to forbid Antonio to return to the ring if that was what he wanted. Love didn't bind a man's wings and then selfishly expect him to fall in line.

"No, you're not." He knelt on one knee and cupped her face in his hands, holding her steady as he treated her to a beautiful, tender smile. "That's why I'm selling. I want to show you that I can stop fighting. Don't you see? If I can shut off such a deep-seated piece of my soul, I can also remove the part that believed infidelity was okay."

Her eyelids flew shut as she processed that. "Why would you do that just for me?"

"It wasn't just for you. I need to prove it to myself, too." His smile faltered. "As hard as it's been to live without you, it's been even harder to live with myself, knowing that I have the capacity to do something so wrong. This is the only way I can come to you again and ask you to reconsider being with me. How else could you believe me when I say I'd never have an affair again? I needed to prove in a concrete way that I love you."

Stricken, she stared at him as tears spilled over and splashed down her face.

He'd done this for her, as a gesture to show that he loved her. That she could give him another chance and she could trust him because he'd truly changed.

And he *had* changed. She'd recognized that from the very beginning.

He wasn't the same Antonio. It was blatantly, wonderfully obvious that he'd become someone else. Someone better, stronger, who knew the meaning of love to a far greater degree than she did.

He'd fought the demon of amnesia to find his family and fought to regain a foothold in his life. Antonio had been nothing but brutally honest with Caitlyn from day one, and just as he'd been honest about his affair, she could trust that he was telling the truth that he'd never do that to her. Perhaps she should look within for the root of her issues.

She'd feared for a long time that she wasn't woman enough, strong enough or just plain *enough* for a powerful, complex man like Antonio. Because she wasn't Vanessa and couldn't be like her sister.

But the dynamic between Caitlyn and Antonio would never follow the same path as his first marriage because her relationship with Antonio had no parallel to the one he'd had with her sister. He loved *Caitlyn*, enough to do something crazy like sell his company, which he'd never have considered for Vanessa.

No, she wasn't Vanessa, who had no clue how to love a man like Antonio. Caitlyn did.

Antonio was a fighter. And so was she.

"No," she said firmly. "I refuse to stand by and let you do this. It's not necessary."

"Then, what can I do, Caitlyn?" Frustrated, he started to drop his hands, but she snatched them back and threw her arms around him.

"You can love me." His embrace tightened and she melted into it as all her reservations vanished. "Forever. That's what I want."

She loved Antonio, and forgiveness was a part of that. She wouldn't withhold it a moment longer.

He murmured her name, his lips in her hair as he shifted her more deeply in his lap. "You've already got that. You should ask for the moon because I would give it to you."

"You're more than enough. You're all I've ever wanted."

Antonio stood with her in his arms and navigated the narrow stairway from the attic with all the grace and finesse she'd come to expect from such a magnificent man.

Caitlyn silently said goodbye to her sister and left the past in the dusty attic where it belonged. She had the family of her dreams and she'd never let it go again.

Epilogue

The announcer took the mic and announced, "And by unanimous decision, the winner is Antonio Cavallari!"

With his name buzzing in his ears, Antonio raised his aching hands to the roaring crowd in a classic fighter's victory pose, but his gaze only sought one face—Caitlyn's. The lights of the packed arena blinded him, as did the trickle of blood from his eyebrow, but he ignored it all until he located her in her usual ringside spot.

His wife of six months shot him that sexy, sleepy smile that had replaced her maidenly blush. Sometimes he missed that blush, but not very often, because she backed up the smile with abandon behind closed doors. He grinned back. He couldn't wait to get her alone later. But it would have to wait because a hundred people wanted a piece of the new welterweight champion.

After an hour of interviews, in which he was asked over and over again the secret to revitalizing his career, and then showering through the pain of his cuts and bruises and Thomas Warren's incessant chatter about another champion coming out of Falco, Antonio finally threaded through the animated crowd to press up against Caitlyn's back.

Exactly where he wanted to be.

She leaned into him, and he slipped his arms around her. The silk of her blue dress felt like heaven under his battered hands, but her skin would feel even better, and he let all his desire for her surge through his veins because she could take it. Later, she would beg for him to love her, meet him in his urgency. Because she was his missing piece, and without her, he'd still be wandering through the confusion inside his head, trying to figure out where he belonged.

"Congratulations," she murmured and turned her head to press a kiss to his throat. "How does it feel to be the king of the comeback?"

"Feels as if it's been too long since you were naked," he grumbled in her ear, careful not to say it too loudly when Brigitte was only a few feet away with the babies.

The au pair had one hand on the three-seated stroller, expertly splitting her attention between her charges and the young featherweight fighter engaging her in conversation. Matteo Long was a rising star in Antonio's empire, and his children's caregiver could do worse.

Caitlyn had continually insisted the kids should be immersed in their father's world so they could learn for themselves the artistry and discipline of Antonio's passion. The fact that she truly understood what made him tick was yet another reason he loved his wife completely.

And his love for her and his children had finally gotten him into a doctor's office to get that CT scan. That had led to more tests and procedures that had eventually uncovered the medical reason for Antonio's headaches—and a solution. He rarely had them these days, which was a blessing for an athlete going after a title.

His private detective hadn't turned up evidence of other survivors from the plane crash. So Antonio had let that quest go—his own amazing story was enough.

Turning in his arms, Caitlyn fingered the chain around her neck where she wore his wedding band while he was in the ring and undid the clasp. Encircling the band, she slid it on his finger and said, "Till death do us part."

It was a ritual they performed often, reminiscent of their wedding ceremony. A tactile reminder of their love, commitment and marriage vows. He'd insisted on it.

Not that he needed any reminders. He still hadn't fully regained his memories from before the crash and had accepted that he likely never would. Odd flashes came to him at strange times, but it didn't matter what his brain resurfaced.

Caitlyn was the only woman he could never forget.

* * * * *

*If you liked this tale of family drama and romance,
pick up these other stories from*
So You Think You Can Write *winner*
Kat Cantrell

*MARRIAGE WITH BENEFITS
THE THINGS SHE SAYS
THE BABY DEAL
PREGNANT BY MORNING*

Available now from Harlequin Desire!

And don't miss the next
BILLIONAIRES AND BABIES *story,*
TWIN HEIRS TO HIS THRONE,
from USA TODAY *bestselling author Olivia Gates*
Available January 2016!

COMING NEXT MONTH FROM

HARLEQUIN®

Desire

Available January 5, 2016

#2419 TWIN HEIRS TO HIS THRONE
Billionaires and Babies • by Olivia Gates
Prince Voronov disappeared after he broke Kassandra's heart, leaving her pregnant and alone. Now the future king has returned to claim his twin heirs. Will he reclaim Kassandra's heart as part of the bargain?

#2420 NANNY MAKES THREE
Texas Cattleman's Club: Lies and Lullabies
by Cat Schield
Hadley Stratton is more than the nanny Liam Ward hired for his unexpected newborn niece. She's also the girl who got away...and the rich rancher is not going to let that happen twice!

#2421 A BABY FOR THE BOSS
Pregnant by the Boss • by Maureen Child
Is his one-time fling and current employee guilty of corporate espionage? Billionaire boss Mike Ryan believes so, but he'll need to reevaluate everything when he learns she's carrying his child...

#2422 PREGNANT BY THE RIVAL CEO
by Karen Booth
Anna Langford wants the deal—even though it means working with the guy she's never forgotten. But what starts as business turns into romance—until Anna learns of Jacob's ruthless motives and her unplanned pregnancy!

#2423 THAT NIGHT WITH THE RICH RANCHER
Lone Star Legends • by Sara Orwig
Tony can't believe the vision in red who won him at the bachelor auction. One night with Lindsay—his stubborn next-door neighbor—is all he'd signed up for. But her makeover has him forgetting all about their family feud!

#2424 TRAPPED WITH THE TYCOON
Mafia Moguls • by Jules Bennett
All that stands between mafia boss Braden O'Shea and what he wants is employee Zara Perkins. But when they're snowed in together, seduction becomes his only goal. Will he choose his family...or the woman he can't resist?

REQUEST YOUR FREE BOOKS!
2 FREE NOVELS PLUS 2 FREE GIFTS!

HARLEQUIN®

Desire

ALWAYS POWERFUL, PASSIONATE AND PROVOCATIVE

YES! Please send me 2 FREE Harlequin® Desire novels and my 2 FREE gifts (gifts are worth about $10). After receiving them, if I don't wish to receive any more books, I can return the shipping statement marked "cancel." If I don't cancel, I will receive 6 brand-new novels every month and be billed just $4.55 per book in the U.S. or $5.24 per book in Canada. That's a savings of at least 13% off the cover price! It's quite a bargain! Shipping and handling is just 50¢ per book in the U.S. and 75¢ per book in Canada.* I understand that accepting the 2 free books and gifts places me under no obligation to buy anything. I can always return a shipment and cancel at any time. Even if I never buy another book, the two free books and gifts are mine to keep forever.

225/326 HDN GH2P

Name _____ (PLEASE PRINT) _____

Address _____ Apt. #

City _____ State/Prov. _____ Zip/Postal Code

Signature (if under 18, a parent or guardian must sign)

Mail to the Reader Service:
IN U.S.A.: P.O. Box 1867, Buffalo, NY 14240-1867
IN CANADA: P.O. Box 609, Fort Erie, Ontario L2A 5X3

Want to try two free books from another line?
Call 1-800-873-8635 or visit www.ReaderService.com.

* Terms and prices subject to change without notice. Prices do not include applicable taxes. Sales tax applicable in N.Y. Canadian residents will be charged applicable taxes. Offer not valid in Quebec. This offer is limited to one order per household. Not valid for current subscribers to Harlequin Desire books. All orders subject to credit approval. Credit or debit balances in a customer's account(s) may be offset by any other outstanding balance owed by or to the customer. Please allow 4 to 6 weeks for delivery. Offer available while quantities last.

Your Privacy—The Reader Service is committed to protecting your privacy. Our Privacy Policy is available online at www.ReaderService.com or upon request from the Reader Service.

We make a portion of our mailing list available to reputable third parties that offer products we believe may interest you. If you prefer that we not exchange your name with third parties, or if you wish to clarify or modify your communication preferences, please visit us at www.ReaderService.com/consumerschoice or write to us at Reader Service Preference Service, P.O. Box 9062, Buffalo, NY 14240-9062. Include your complete name and address.

HD15

Kassandra fumbled for the remote, pushing every button before she managed to turn off the TV.

But it was too late. She'd seen him. For the first time since she'd walked out of his hospital room twenty-six months ago. That had been the last time the world had seen him, too. He'd dropped off the radar completely ever since. Now her retinas burned with the image of Leonid striding out of his imposing Fifth Avenue headquarters.

The man she'd known had been crackling with vitality, a smile of whimsy and assurance always hovering on his lips and sparkling in the depths of his eyes. This man was totally detached, as if he was no longer part of the world. Or as if it was beneath his notice. And there'd been another change. The stalking swagger was gone. In its place was a deliberate, almost menacing prowl.

This wasn't the man she'd known.

Or rather, the man she'd thought she'd known.

She'd long ago faced the fact that she'd known nothing of him. Not before she'd been with him, or while they'd been together, or after he'd shoved her away and vanished.

HDEXP1215

Kassandra had withdrawn from the world, too. She'd been pathetic enough to be literally sick with worry about him, to pine for him until she'd wasted away. Until she'd almost miscarried. That scare had finally jolted her to the one reality she'd been certain of. That she'd wanted that baby with everything in her and would never risk losing it. That day at the doctor's, she'd found out she wasn't carrying one baby, but two.

She'd reclaimed herself and her stability, had become even more successful career-wise, but most important, she'd become a mother to two perfect daughters. Eva and Zoya. She'd given them both names meaning life, as they'd given *her* new life.

Then Zorya had suddenly filled the news with a declaration of its intention to reinstate the monarchy. With every rapid development, foreboding had filled her. Even when she'd had no reason to think it would make Leonid resurface.

The doorbell rang.

It had become a ritual for her neighbor to come by and have a cup of tea so they could unwind together after their hectic days.

Rushing to the door, she opened it with a ready smile. "We should…"

Air clogged her lungs. All her nerves fired, short-circuiting her every muscle, especially her heart.

Leonid.

Right there. On her doorstep.

Don't miss TWIN HEIRS TO HS THRONE
by USA TODAY bestselling author Olivia Gates,
available January 2016 wherever
Harlequin® Desire books and ebooks are sold.
www.Harlequin.com

THE WORLD IS BETTER WITH

Romance

Harlequin has everything from contemporary, passionate and heartwarming to suspenseful and inspirational stories.

Whatever your mood, we have a romance just for you!

Connect with us to find your next great read, special offers and more.

f /HarlequinBooks

🐦 @HarlequinBooks

www.HarlequinBlog.com

www.Harlequin.com/Newsletters

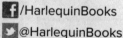

⬦HARLEQUIN®

A *Romance* FOR EVERY MOOD™

www.Harlequin.com

SERIESHALOAD2015

Turn your love of reading into rewards you'll love with
Harlequin My Rewards

**Join for FREE today at
www.HarlequinMyRewards.com**

Earn **FREE BOOKS** of your choice.

Experience **EXCLUSIVE OFFERS** and contests.

Enjoy **BOOK RECOMMENDATIONS**
selected just for you.

PLUS! Sign up now
and get **500** points
right away!

Earn **FREE REWARDS** Join Today! HarlequinMyRewards.com

MYR16R

P9-CLK-753

Nobody Knows My Name

"To be James Baldwin is to touch on so many hidden places in Europe, America, the Negro, the white man—to be forced to understand so much."

—Alfred Kazin

"This author retains a place in an extremely select group: that composed of the few genuinely indispensable American writers."

—*Saturday Review*

"He has not himself lost access to the sources of his being—which is what makes him read and awaited by perhaps a wider range of people than any other major American writer."

—*The Nation*

"He is thought-provoking, tantalizing, irritating, abusing and amusing. And he uses words as the sea uses waves, to flow and beat, advance and retreat, rise and take a bow in disappearing . . . the thought becomes poetry and the poetry illuminates the thought."

—Langston Hughes

"He has become one of the few writers of our time."

—Norman Mailer

OTHER DELL TITLES BY JAMES BALDWIN:

James Baldwin

NOBODY KNOWS MY NAME

MORE NOTES OF A NATIVE SON

LAUREL

Acknowledgments

Acknowledgment is made to the following publications in whose pages these essays first appeared. *The New York Times Book Review* for "The Discovery of What It Means to Be an American" (January 25, 1959); *Encounter* for "Princes and Powers"; *Esquire* for "Fifth Avenue Uptown: a Letter from Harlem" (July, 1960), reprinted by permission; *The New York Times Magazine* for "East River Downtown: Postscript to a Letter from Harlem" (which appeared as "A Negro Assays the Negro Mood," March 12, 1961); *Harper's Magazine* for "A Fly in Buttermilk" (which appeared as "The Hard Kind of Courage," October, 1958); *The Partisan Review* for "Nobody Knows My Name: a Letter from the South" (Winter, 1959) and "Faulkner and Desegregation" (Winter, 1956); Kalamazoo College for "In Search of a Majority" delivered there as an address; *Esquire* for "Notes for a Hypothetical Novel" (delivered as an address at the third annual *Esquire* Magazine symposium on "The Role of the Writer in America" at San Francisco State College, October 22, 1960); *The New Leader* for "The Male Prison" (which appeared as "Gide As Husband and Homosexual," December 13, 1954); *Esquire* for "The Northern Protestant" (which appeared as "The Precarious Vogue of Ingmar Bergman," April, 1960), reprinted by permission; *The Reporter* for "Eight Men" (which appeared as "The Survival of Richard Wright," March 16, 1961); *La Preuve* for "The Exile" (February, 1961); and *Esquire* for "The Black Boy Looks at the White Boy" (May, 1961), reprinted by permission.

CONTENTS

INTRODUCTION

These essays were written over the last six years, in various places and in many states of mind. These years seemed, on the whole, rather sad and aimless to me. My life in Europe was ending, not because I had decided that it should, but because it became clearer and clearer —as I dealt with the streets, the climate, and the temperament of Paris, fled to Spain and Corsica and Scandinavia—that something had ended for me. I rather think now, to tell the sober truth, that it was merely my youth, first youth, anyway, that was ending and I hated to see it go. In the context of my life, the end of my youth was signaled by the reluctant realization that I had, indeed, become a writer; so far, so good: now I would have to go the distance.

In America, the color of my skin had stood between myself and me; in Europe, that barrier was down. Nothing is more desirable than to be released from an affliction, but nothing is more frightening than to be divested of a crutch. It turned out that the question of who I was was not solved because I had removed myself from the social forces which menaced me—anyway, these forces had become interior, and I had dragged them across the ocean with me. The question of who I was had at last become a personal question, and the answer was to be found in me.

I think that there is always something frightening about this realization. I know it frightened me—that was one of the reasons that I dawdled in the European haven for so long. And yet, I could not escape the knowledge, though God knows I tried, that if I was still in need of havens, my journey had been for nothing. Havens are high-priced. The price exacted of the haven-dweller is that he contrive to delude himself into believing that he has found a haven. It would seem, unless one looks more deeply at the phenomenon, that most people are able to delude themselves and get through their lives quite happily. But I still believe that the unexamined life is not worth living: and I know that self-delusion, in the service of no matter what small or lofty cause, is a price no writer can afford. His subject is himself and the world and it requires every ounce of stamina he can summon to attempt to look on himself and the world as they are.

What it came to for me was that I no longer needed to fear leaving Europe, no longer needed to hide myself from the high and dangerous winds of the world. The world was enormous and I could go anywhere in it I chose—including America: and I decided to return here because I was afraid to. But the question which confronted me, nibbled at me, in my stony Corsican exile was: Am I afraid of returning to America? Or am I afraid of journeying any further with myself? Once this question had presented itself it would not be appeased, it had to be answered.

"Be careful what you set your heart upon," someone once said to me, "for it will surely be yours." Well, I had said that I was going to be a writer, God, Satan, and Mississippi notwithstanding, and that color did not matter, and that I was going to be free. And, here I was, left with only myself to deal with. It was entirely up to me.

These essays are a very small part of a private logbook. The question of color takes up much space in these pages, but the question of color, especially in this country, operates to hide the graver questions of the self. That is precisely why what we like to call "the Negro problem" is so tenacious in American life, and so dangerous. But my own experience proves to me that the connection between American whites and blacks is far deeper and more passionate than any of us like to think. And, even in icy Sweden, I found myself talking with a man whose endless questioning has given him himself, and who reminded me of black Baptist preachers. The questions which one asks oneself begin, at last, to illuminate the world, and become one's key to the experience of others. One can only face in others what one can face in oneself. On this confrontation depends the measure of our wisdom and compassion. This energy is all that one finds in the rubble of vanished civilizations, and the only hope for ours.

JAMES BALDWIN

PART ONE

SITTING IN THE HOUSE

1. THE DISCOVERY OF WHAT
IT MEANS TO BE AN AMERICAN

"It is a complex fate to be an American," Henry James observed, and the principal discovery an American writer makes in Europe is just how complex this fate is. America's history, her aspirations, her peculiar triumphs, her even more peculiar defeats, and her position in the world —yesterday and today—are all so profoundly and stubbornly unique that the very word "America" remains a new, almost completely undefined and extremely controversial proper noun. No one in the world seems to know exactly what it describes, not even we motley millions who call ourselves Americans.

I left America because I doubted my ability to survive the fury of the color problem here. (Sometimes I still do.) I wanted to prevent myself from becoming *merely* a Negro; or, even, merely a Negro writer. I wanted to find out in what way the *specialness* of my experience could be made to connect me with other people instead of dividing me from them. (I was as isolated from Negroes as I was from whites, which is what happens when a Negro begins, at bottom, to believe what white people say about him.)

In my necessity to find the terms on which my experience could be related to that of others, Negroes and whites, writers and non-writers, I proved, to my astonishment, to be as American as any Texas G.I. And I found my experience was shared by every American writer I knew in Paris. Like me, they had been divorced from their origins, and it turned out to make very little difference that the origins of white Americans were European and mine were African—they were no more at home in Europe than I was.

The fact that I was the son of a slave and they were the sons of free men meant less, by the time we confronted each other on European soil, than the fact that we were both searching for our separate identities. When we had found these, we seemed to be saying, why, then, we would no longer need to cling to the shame and bitterness which had divided us so long.

It became terribly clear in Europe, as it never had been here, that we knew more about each other than any European ever could. And it also became clear that, no matter where our fathers had been born, or what they had endured, the fact of Europe had formed us both, was part of our identity and part of our inheritance.

I had been in Paris a couple of years before any of this became clear to me. When it did, I, like many a writer before me upon the discovery that his props have all been knocked out from under him, suffered a species of breakdown and was carried off to the mountains of Switzerland. There, in that absolutely alabaster landscape, armed with two Bessie Smith records and a typewriter, I began to try to re-create the life that I had first known as a child and from which I had spent so many years in flight.

It was Bessie Smith, through her tone and her cadence, who helped me to dig back to the way I myself must have spoken when I was a pickaninny, and to remember the things I had heard and seen and felt. I had buried them very deep. I had never listened to Bessie Smith in America (in the same way that, for years, I would not touch watermelon), but in Europe she helped to reconcile me to being a "nigger."

I do not think that I could have made this reconciliation here. Once I was able to accept my role—as distinguished, I must say, from my "place"—in the extraordinary drama which is America, I was released from the illusion that I hated America.

The story of what can happen to an American Negro writer in Europe simply illustrates, in some relief, what can happen to any American writer there. It is not meant, of course, to imply that it happens to them all, for Europe can be very crippling, too; and, anyway, a writer, when he has made his first breakthrough, has simply won a crucial skirmish in a dangerous, unending and unpredictable battle. Still, the breakthrough is important, and the point is that an American writer, in order to achieve it, very often has to leave this country.

The American writer, in Europe, is released, first of all, from the necessity of apologizing for himself. It is not until he *is* released from the habit of flexing his muscles and proving that he is just a "regular guy" that he realizes how crippling this habit has been. It is not necessary for him, there, to pretend to be something he is not, for the artist does not encounter in Europe the same suspicion he encounters here. Whatever the Europeans may actually think of artists, they have killed enough of them off by now to know that they are as real—and as persistent—as rain, snow, taxes or businessmen.

Of course, the reason for Europe's comparative clarity concerning the different functions of men in society is that European society has always been divided into classes in a way that American society never has been. A European writer considers himself to be part of an old and honorable tradition—of intellectual activity, of letters—and his choice of a vocation does not cause him any uneasy wonder as to whether or not it will cost him all his friends. But this tradition does not exist in America.

On the contrary, we have a very deep-seated distrust of real intellectual effort (probably because we suspect that it will destroy, as I hope it does, that myth of America to which we cling so desperately). An American writer fights his way to one of the lowest rungs on the American social ladder by means of pure bull-headedness and an indescribable series of odd jobs. He probably *has* been a "regular fellow" for much of his adult life, and it is not easy for him to step out of that lukewarm bath.

We must, however, consider a rather serious paradox: though American society is more mobile than Europe's, it is easier to cut across social and occupational lines there than it is here. This has something to do, I think, with the problem of status in American life. Where everyone has status, it is also perfectly possible, after all, that no one has. It seems inevitable, in any case, that a man may become uneasy as to just what his status is.

But Europeans have lived with the idea of status for a long time. A man can be as proud of being a good waiter as of being a good actor, and in neither case feel threatened. And this means that the actor and the waiter can have a freer and more genuinely friendly relationship in Europe than they are likely to have here. The waiter does not feel, with obscure resentment, that the actor has "made it," and the actor is not tormented by the fear that he may find himself, tomorrow, once again a waiter.

This lack of what may roughly be called social paranoia causes the American writer in Europe to feel—almost certainly for the first time in his life—that he can reach out to everyone, that he is accessible to everyone and open to everything. This is an extraordinary feeling. He feels, so to speak, his own weight, his own value.

It is as though he suddenly came out of a dark tunnel and found himself beneath the open sky. And, in fact, in Paris, I began to see the sky for what seemed to be the first time. It was borne in on me—and it did not make me feel melancholy—that this sky had been there before I was born and would be there when I was dead. And it was up to me, therefore, to make of my brief opportunity the most that could be made.

I was born in New York, but have lived only in pockets

of it. In Paris, I lived in all parts of the city—on the Right Bank and the Left, among the bourgeoisie and among *les misérables,* and knew all kinds of people, from pimps and prostitutes in Pigalle to Egyptian bankers in Neuilly. This may sound extremely unprincipled or even obscurely immoral: I found it healthy. I love to talk to people, all kinds of people, and almost everyone, as I hope we still know, loves a man who loves to listen.

This perpetual dealing with people very different from myself caused a shattering in me of preconceptions I scarcely knew I held. The writer is meeting in Europe people who are not American, whose sense of reality is entirely different from his own. They may love or hate or admire or fear or envy this country—they see it, in any case, from another point of view, and this forces the writer to reconsider many things he had always taken for granted. This reassessment, which can be very painful, is also very valuable.

This freedom, like all freedom, has its dangers and its responsibilities. One day it begins to be borne in on the writer, and with great force, that he is living in Europe as an American. If he were living there as a European, he would be living on a different and far less attractive continent.

This crucial day may be the day on which an Algerian taxi-driver tells him how it feels to be an Algerian in Paris. It may be the day on which he passes a café terrace and catches a glimpse of the tense, intelligent and troubled face of Albert Camus. Or it may be the day on which someone asks him to explain Little Rock and he begins to feel that it would be simpler—and, corny as the words may sound, more honorable—to *go* to Little Rock than sit in Europe, on an American passport, trying to explain it.

This is a personal day, a terrible day, the day to which his entire sojourn has been tending. It is the day he realizes that there are no untroubled countries in this fearfully troubled world; that if he has been preparing himself for anything in Europe, he has been preparing himself—for America. In short, the freedom that the American writer finds in Europe brings him, full circle, back to himself, with the responsibility for his development where it always was: in his own hands.

Even the most incorrigible maverick has to be born somewhere. He may leave the group that produced him— he may be forced to—but nothing will efface his origins, the marks of which he carries with him everywhere. I think it is important to know this and even find it a matter for rejoicing, as the strongest people do, regardless of their station. On this acceptance, literally, the life of a writer depends.

The charge has often been made against American writers that they do not describe society, and have no interest in it. They only describe individuals in opposition to it, or isolated from it. Of course, what the American writer is describing is his own situation. But what is *Anna Karenina* describing if not the tragic fate of the isolated individual, at odds with her time and place?

The real difference is that Tolstoy was describing an old and dense society in which everything seemed—to the people in it, though not to Tolstoy—to be fixed forever. And the book is a masterpiece because Tolstoy was able to fathom, and make us see, the hidden laws which really governed this society and made Anna's doom inevitable.

American writers do not have a fixed society to describe. The only society they know is one in which nothing is fixed and in which the individual must fight for his identity. This is a rich confusion, indeed, and it creates for the American writer unprecedented opportunities.

That the tensions of American life, as well as the possibilities, are tremendous is certainly not even a question. But these are dealt with in contemporary literature mainly compulsively; that is, the book is more likely to be a symptom of our tension than an examination of it. The time has come, God knows, for us to examine ourselves, but we can only do this if we are willing to free ourselves of the myth of America and try to find out what is really happening here.

Every society is really governed by hidden laws, by unspoken but profound assumptions on the part of the people, and ours is no exception. It is up to the American writer to find out what these laws and assumptions are. In a society much given to smashing taboos without thereby managing to be liberated from them, it will be no easy matter.

It is no wonder, in the meantime, that the American writer keeps running off to Europe. He needs sustenance for his journey and the best models he can find. Europe has what we do not have yet, a sense of the mysterious and inexorable limits of life, a sense, in a word, of tragedy. And we have what they sorely need: a new sense of life's possibilities.

In this endeavor to wed the vision of the Old World with that of the New, it is the writer, not the statesman, who is our strongest arm. Though we do not wholly believe it yet, the interior life is a real life, and the intangible dreams of people have a tangible effect on the world.

2. PRINCES AND POWERS

The Conference of Negro-African Writers and Artists *(Le Congrès des Ecrivains et Artistes Noirs)* opened on Wednesday, September 19, 1956, in the Sorbonne's Amphitheatre Descartes, in Paris. It was one of those bright, warm days which one likes to think of as typical of the atmosphere of the intellectual capital of the Western world. There were people on the café terraces, boys and girls on the boulevards, bicycles racing by on their fantastically urgent errands. Everyone and everything wore a cheerful aspect, even the houses of Paris, which did not show their age. Those who were unable to pay the steep rents of these houses were enabled, by the weather, to enjoy the streets, to sit, unnoticed, in the parks. The boys and girls and old men and women who had nowhere at all to go and nothing whatever to do, for whom no provision had been made, or could be, added to the beauty of the Paris scene by walking along the river. The newspaper vendors seemed cheerful; so did the people who bought the newspapers. Even the men and women queueing up before bakeries—for there was a bread strike in Paris—did so as though they had long been used to it.

The conference was to open at nine o'clock. By ten o'clock the lecture hall was already unbearably hot, people choked the entrances and covered the wooden steps. It was hectic with the activity attendant upon the setting up of tape recorders, with the testing of earphones, with the lighting of flash-bulbs. Electricity, in fact, filled the hall. Of the people there that first day, I should judge that not quite two-thirds were colored.

Behind the table at the front of the hall sat eight colored men. These included the American novelist Richard Wright; Alioune Diop, the editor of *Présence Africaine* and one of the principal organizers of the conference; poets Leopold Senghor, from Senegal, and Aimé Cesaire, from Martinique, and the poet and novelist Jacques Alexis, from Haiti. From Haiti, also, came the President of the conference, Dr. Price-Mars, a very old and very handsome man.

It was well past ten o'clock when the conference actually opened. Alioune Diop, who is tall, very dark and self-contained, and who rather resembles, in his extreme sobriety, an old-time Baptist minister, made the opening address. He referred to the present gathering as a kind of second Bandung. As at Bandung, the people gathered together here held in common the fact of their subjugation to Europe, or, at the very least, to the European vision of the world. Out of the fact that European well-being had been, for centuries, so crucially dependent on this subjugation had come that *racisme* from which all black men suffered. Then he spoke of the changes which had taken place during the last decade regarding the fate and the aspirations of non-European peoples, especially the blacks. "The blacks," he said, "whom history has treated in a rather cavalier fashion. I would even say that history has treated black men in a resolutely spiteful fashion were it not for the fact that this history with a large *H* is nothing more, after all, than the Western interpretation of the life of the world." He spoke of the variety of cultures the conference represented, saying that they were genuine cultures and that the ignorance of the West regarding them was largely a matter of convenience.

Yet, in speaking of the relation between politics and culture, he pointed out that the loss of vitality from which all Negro cultures were suffering was due to the fact that their political destinies were not in their hands. A people deprived of political sovereignty finds it very nearly impossible to re-create, for itself, the image of its past, this perpetual re-creation being an absolute necessity for, if not indeed the definition of, a living culture. And one of the questions, then, said Diop, which would often be raised during this conference was the question of assimilation. Assimilation was frequently but another name for the very special brand of relations between human beings which had been imposed by colonialism. These relations demanded that the individual, torn from the context to which he owed his identity, should replace his habits of feeling, thinking, and acting by another set of habits which belonged to the strangers who dominated him. He cited the example of certain natives of the Belgian Congo, who, *accablé des complexes,* wished for an assimilation so complete that they would no longer be distinguishable from white men. This, said Diop, indicated the blind horror which the spiritual heritage of Africa inspired in their breasts.

The question of assimilation could not, however, be posed this way. It was not a question, on the one hand, of simply being swallowed up, of disappearing in the maw of Western culture, nor was it, on the other hand, a question of rejecting assimilation in order to be isolated within African culture. Neither was it a question of deciding which African values were to be retained and which European values were to be adopted. Life was not that simple.

It was due to the crisis which their cultures were now undergoing that black intellectuals had come together. They were here to define and accept their responsibilities, to assess the riches and the promise of their cultures, and to open, in effect, a dialogue with Europe. He ended with a brief and rather moving reference to the fifteen-year struggle of himself and his confreres to bring about this day.

His speech won a great deal of applause. Yet, I felt that among the dark people in the hall there was, perhaps, some disappointment that he had not been more specific, more bitter, in a word, more demagogical; whereas, among the whites in the hall, there was certainly expressed in their applause a somewhat shamefaced and uneasy relief. And, indeed, the atmosphere was strange. No one, black or white, seemed quite to believe what was happening and everyone was tense with the question of which direction the conference would take. Hanging in the air, as real as the heat from which we suffered, were the great specters of America and Russia, of the battle going on between them for the domination of the world. The resolution of this battle might very well depend on the earth's non-European population, a population vastly outnumbering Europe's, and which had suffered such injustices at European hands. With the best will in the world, no one now living could undo what past generations had accomplished. The great question was what, exactly, *had* they accomplished: whether the evil, of which there had been so much, alone lived after them, whether the good, and there had been some, had been interred with their bones.

Of the messages from well-wishers which were read immediately after Diop's speech, the one which caused the greatest stir came from America's W. E. B. Du Bois. "I am not present at your meeting," he began, "because the U.S. government will not give me a passport." The reading was interrupted at this point by great waves of laughter, by no means good-natured, and by a roar of applause, which, as it clearly could not have been intended for the State Department, was intended to express admiration for Du Bois' plain speaking. "Any American Negro traveling abroad today must either not care about Negroes or say what the State Department wishes him to say." This, of course, drew more applause. It also very neatly compromised whatever effectiveness the five-man American delegation then sitting in the hall might have hoped to have. It was less Du Bois' extremely ill-considered communication which did this than the incontestable fact that he had not been allowed to leave his country. It was a fact which could scarcely be explained or defended, particularly as one would have also had to explain just how the reasons for Du Bois' absence differed from those which had prevented the arrival of the delegation from South Africa. The very attempt at such an explanation, especially for people whose distrust of the West, however richly justified, also tends to make them dangerously blind and hasty, was to be suspected of "caring nothing about Negroes," of saying what the State Department "wished" you to say. It was a fact which increased and seemed to justify the distrust with which all Americans are regarded abroad, and it made yet deeper, for the five American Negroes present, that gulf which yawns between the American Negro and all other men of color. This is a very sad and dangerous state of affairs, for the American Negro is possibly the only man of color who can speak of the West with real authority, whose experience, painful as it is, also proves the vitality of the so transgressed Western ideals. The fact that Du Bois was not there and could not, therefore, be engaged in debate, naturally made the more seductive his closing argument: which was that, the future of Africa being socialist, African writers should take the road taken by Russia, Poland, China, etc., and not be "betrayed backward by the U.S. into colonialism."

When the morning session ended and I was spewed forth with the mob into the bright courtyard, Richard Wright introduced me to the American delegation. And it seemed quite unbelievable for a moment that the five men standing with Wright (and Wright and myself) were defined, and had been brought together in this courtyard by our relation to the African continent. The chief of the delegation, John Davis, was to be asked just *why* he considered himself a Negro—he was to be told that he certainly did not look like one. He *is* a Negro, of course, from the remarkable legal point of view which obtains in the United States, but, more importantly, as he tried to make clear to his interlocutor, he was a Negro by choice and by depth of involvement—by experience, in fact. But the question of choice in such a context can scarcely be coherent for an African and the experience referred to, which produces a John Davis, remains a closed book for him. Mr. Davis might have been rather darker, as were the others—Mercer Cook, William Fontaine, Horace Bond, and James Ivy—and it would not have helped matters very much.

For what, at bottom, distinguished the Americans from the Negroes who surrounded us, men from Nigeria, Senegal, Barbados, Martinique—so many names for so many disciplines—was the banal and abruptly quite overwhelming fact that we had been born in a society, which, in a way quite inconceivable for Africans, and no longer real for Europeans, was open, and, in a sense which has nothing to do with justice or injustice, was free. It was a society, in short, in which nothing was fixed and we had therefore been born to a greater number of possibilities, wretched as these possibilities seemed at the instant of our birth. Moreover, the land of our forefathers' exile had been made, by that travail, our home. It may have been the popular impulse to keep us at the bottom of the perpetually shifting and bewildered populace; but we were, on the other hand, almost personally indispensable to each of them, simply because, without us, they could never have been certain, in such a confusion, where the bottom was; and nothing, in any case, could take away our title to the land which we, too, had purchased with our blood. This results in a psychology very different—at its best and at its worst—from the psychology which is produced by a sense of having been invaded and overrun, the sense of having no recourse whatever against oppression other than overthrowing the machinery of the oppressor. We had been dealing with, had been made and mangled by, another machinery altogether. It had never

been in our interest to overthrow it. It had been necessary to make the machinery work for our benefit and the
possibility of its doing so had been, so to speak, built in.

We could, therefore, in a way, be considered the connecting link between Africa and the West, the most real
and certainly the most shocking of all African contributions to Western cultural life. The articulation of this
reality, however, was another matter. But it was clear
that our relation to the mysterious continent of Africa
would not be clarified until we had found some means
of saying, to ourselves and to the world, more about the
mysterious American continent than had ever been said
before.

M. Lasebikan, from Nigeria, spoke that afternoon on
the tonal structure of Youriba poetry, a language spoken
by five million people in his country. Lasebikan was a very
winning and unassuming personality, dressed in a most
arresting costume. What looked like a white lace poncho
covered him from head to foot; beneath this he was
wearing a very subdued but very ornately figured silk
robe, which looked Chinese, and he wore a red velvet
toque, a sign, someone told me, that he was a Moham-
medan.

The Youriba language, he told us, had only become a
written language in the middle of the last century and
this had been done by missionaries. His face expressed
some sorrow at this point, due, it developed, to the fact
that this had not already been accomplished by the Youriba people. However—and his face brightened again—
he lived in the hope that one day an excavation would
bring to light a great literature written by the Youriba
people. In the meantime, with great good nature, he re-
signed himself to sharing with us that literature which already existed. I doubt that I learned much about the
tonal structure of Youriba poetry, but I found myself fascinated by the sensibility which had produced it. M. Lasebikan spoke first in Youriba and then in English. It

was perhaps because he so clearly loved his subject that he not only succeeded in conveying the poetry of this extremely strange language, he also conveyed something of the style of life out of which it came. The poems quoted ranged from the devotional to a poem which described the pounding of yams. And one somehow felt the loneliness and the yearning of the first and the peaceful, rhythmic domesticity of the second. There was a poem about the memory of a battle, a poem about a faithless friend, and a poem celebrating the variety to be found in life, which conceived of this variety in rather startling terms: "Some would have been great eaters, but they haven't got the food; some, great drinkers, but they haven't got the wine." Some of the poetry demanded the use of a marvelously ornate drum, on which were many little bells. It was not the drum it once had been, he told us, but despite whatever mishap had befallen it, I could have listened to him play it for the rest of the afternoon.

He was followed by Leopold Senghor. Senghor is a very dark and impressive figure in a smooth, bespectacled kind of way, and he is very highly regarded as a poet. He was to speak on West African writers and artists.

He began by invoking what he called the "spirit of Bandung." In referring to Bandung, he was referring less, he said, to the liberation of black peoples than he was saluting the reality and the toughness of their culture, which, despite the vicissitudes of their history, had refused to perish. We were now witnessing, in fact, the beginning of its renaissance. This renaissance would owe less to politics than it would to black writers and artists. The "spirit of Bandung" had had the effect of "sending them to school to Africa."

One of the things, said Senghor—perhaps *the* thing—which distinguishes Africans from Europeans is the comparative urgency of their ability to feel. *"Sentir c'est apercevoir"*: it is perhaps a tribute to his personal force that this phrase then meant something which makes the literal English translation quite inadequate, seeming to

leave too great a distance between the feeling and the
perception. The feeling and the perception, for Africans,
is one and the same thing. This is the difference between
European and African reasoning: the reasoning of the
African is not compartmentalized, and, to illustrate this,
Senghor here used the image of the bloodstream in which
all things mingle and flow to and through the heart. He
told us that the difference between the function of the
arts in Europe and their function in Africa lay in the
fact that, in Africa, the function of the arts is more present and pervasive, is infinitely less special, "is done by
all, for all." Thus, art for art's sake is not a concept
which makes any sense in Africa. The division between
art and life out of which such a concept comes does not
exist there. Art itself is taken to be perishable, to be made
again each time it disappears or is destroyed. What is
clung to is the spirit which makes art possible. And the
African idea of this spirit is very different from the European idea. European art attempts to imitate nature.
African art is concerned with reaching beyond and beneath nature, to contact, and itself become a part of *la
force vitale*. The artistic image is not intended to represent the thing itself, but, rather, the reality of the force
the thing contains. Thus, the moon is fecundity, the ele-
phant is force.

Much of this made great sense to me, even though
Senghor was speaking of, and out of, a way of life which
I could only very dimly and perhaps somewhat wistfully
imagine. It was the esthetic which attracted me, the idea
that the work of art expresses, contains, and is itself a
part of that energy which is life. Yet, I was aware that
Senghor's thought had come into my mind translated.
What he had been speaking of was something more di-
rect and less isolated than the line in which my imagination immediately began to move. The distortions used
by African artists to create a work of art are not at all
the same distortions which have become one of the principal aims of almost every artist in the West today. (They

are not the same distortions even when they have been copied from Africa.) And this was due entirely to the different situations in which each had his being. Poems and stories, in the only situation I know anything about, were never told, except, rarely, to children, and, at the risk of mayhem, in bars. They were written to be read, alone, and by a handful of people at that—there was really beginning to be something suspect in being read by more than a handful. These creations no more insisted on the actual presence of other human beings than they demanded the collaboration of a dancer and a drum. They could not be said to celebrate the society any more than the homage which Western artists sometimes receive can be said to have anything to do with society's celebration of a work of art. The only thing in Western life which seemed even faintly to approximate Senghor's intense sketch of the creative interdependence, the active, actual, joyful intercourse obtaining among African artists and what only a Westerner would call their public, was the atmosphere sometimes created among jazz musicians and their fans during, say, a jam session. But the ghastly isolation of the jazz musician, the neurotic intensity of his listeners, was proof enough that what Senghor meant when he spoke of social art had no reality whatever in Western life. He was speaking out of his past, which had been lived where art was naturally and spontaneously social, where artistic creation did not presuppose divorce. (Yet he was not there. Here he was, in Paris, speaking the adopted language in which he also wrote his poetry.)

Just what the specific relation of an artist to his culture says about that culture is a very pretty question. The culture which had produced Senghor seemed, on the face of it, to have a greater coherence as regarded assumptions, traditions, customs, and beliefs than did the Western culture to which it stood in so problematical a relation. And this might very well mean that the culture represented by Senghor was healthier than the culture represented by the hall in which he spoke. But the leap to this conclusion, than which nothing would have seemed easier, was frustrated by the question of just what health is in relation to a culture. Senghor's culture, for example, did not seem to need the lonely activity of the singular intelligence on which the cultural life—the moral life —of the West depends. And a really cohesive society, one of the attributes, perhaps, of what is taken to be a "healthy" culture, has, generally, and, I suspect, necessarily, a much lower level of tolerance for the maverick, the dissenter, the man who steals the fire, than have societies in which, the common ground of belief having all but vanished, each man, in awful and brutal isolation, is for himself, to flower or to perish. Or, not impossibly, to make real and fruitful again that vanished common ground, which, as I take it, is nothing more or less than the culture itself, endangered and rendered nearly inaccessible by the complexities it has, itself, inevitably created.

Nothing is more undeniable than the fact that cultures vanish, undergo crises; are, in any case, in a perpetual state of change and fermentation, being perpetually driven, God knows where, by forces within and without. And one of the results, surely, of the present tension between the society represented by Senghor and the society represented by the Salle Descartes was just this perceptible drop, during the last decade, of the Western level of tolerance. I wondered what this would mean—for Africa, for us. I wondered just what effect the concept of art expressed by Senghor would have on that renaissance he had predicted and just what transformations this concept itself would undergo as it encountered the complexities of the century into which it was moving with such speed.

The evening debate rang perpetual changes on two questions. These questions—each of which splintered, each time it was asked, into a thousand more—were, first: What *is* a culture? This is a difficult question under the most serene circumstances—under which circumstances, incidentally, it mostly fails to present itself. (This implies, perhaps, one of the possible definitions of a culture, at least at a certain stage of its development.) In the context of the conference, it was a question which was helplessly at the mercy of another one. And the second question was this: Is it possible to describe as a culture what may simply be, after all, a history of oppression? That is, is this history and these present facts, which involve so many millions of people who are divided from each other by so many miles of the globe, which operates, and has operated, under such very different conditions, to such different effects, and which has produced so many different subhistories, problems, traditions, possibilities, aspirations, assumptions, languages, hybrids—is this history enough to have made of the earth's black populations anything that can legitimately be described as a culture? For what, beyond the fact that all black men at one time or another left Africa, or have remained there, do they really have in common?

And yet, it became clear as the debate wore on, that there *was* something which all black men held in common, something which cut across opposing points of view, and placed in the same context their widely dissimilar experience. What they held in common was their precarious, their unutterably painful relation to the white world. What they held in common was the necessity to remake the world in their own image, to impose this image on the world, and no longer be controlled by the vision of the world, and of themselves, held by other people. What, in sum, black men held in common was their ache to come into the world as men. And this ache united people who might otherwise have been divided as to what a man should be.

Yet, whether or not this could properly be described as a *cultural* reality remained another question. Haiti's Jacques Alexis made the rather desperate observation that a cultural survey must have *something* to survey; but then seemed confounded, as, indeed, we all were, by the dimensions of the particular cultural survey in progress. It was necessary, for example, before one could relate the culture of Haiti to that of Africa, to know what the Haitian culture was. Within Haiti there were a great many cultures. Frenchmen, Negroes, and Indians had bequeathed it quite dissimilar ways of life; Catholics, voodooists, and animists cut across class and color lines. Alexis described as "pockets" of culture those related and yet quite specific and dissimilar ways of life to be found within the borders of any country in the world and wished to know by what alchemy these opposing ways of life became a national culture. And he wished to know, too, what relation national culture bore to national independence—was it possible, really, to speak of a national culture when speaking of nations which were not free?

Senghor remarked, apropos of this question, that one of the great difficulties posed by this problem of cultures within cultures, particularly within the borders of Africa herself, was the difficulty of establishing and maintaining contact with the people if one's language had been formed in Europe. And he went on, somewhat later, to make the point that the heritage of the American Negro was an African heritage. He used, as proof of this, a poem of Richard Wright's which was, he said, involved with African tensions and symbols, even though Wright himself had not been aware of this. He suggested that the study of African sources might prove extremely illuminating for American Negroes. For, he suggested, in the same way that white classics exist—classic here taken to mean an enduring revelation and statement of a specific, peculiar, cultural sensibility—black classics must also exist. This raised in my mind the question of whether or not white classics *did* exist, and, with this question, I began to see the implications of Senghor's claim.

For, if white classics existed, in distinction, that is, to merely French or English classics, these could only be the classics produced by Greece and Rome. If *Black Boy*, said

Senghor, were to be analyzed, it would undoubtedly reveal the African heritage to which it owed its existence; in the same way, I supposed, that Dickens' *A Tale Of Two Cities,* would, upon analysis, reveal its debt to Aeschylus. It did not seem very important.

And yet, I realized, the question had simply never come up in relation to European literature. It was not, now, the European necessity to go rummaging in the past, and through all the countries of the world, bitterly staking out claims to its cultural possessions.

Yet *Black Boy* owed its existence to a great many other factors, by no means so tenuous or so problematical; in so handsomely presenting Wright with his African heritage, Senghor rather seemed to be taking away his identity. *Black Boy* is the study of the growing up of a Negro boy in the Deep South, and is one of the major American autobiographies. I had never thought of it, as Senghor clearly did, as one of the major *African* autobiographies, only one more document, in fact, like one more book in the Bible, speaking of the African's long persecution and exile.

Senghor chose to overlook several gaps in his argument, not the least of which was the fact that Wright had not been in a position, as Europeans had been, to remain in contact with his hypothetical African heritage. The Greco-Roman tradition had, after all, been *written down;* it was by this means that it had kept itself alive. Granted that there was something African in *Black Boy,* as there was undoubtedly something African in all American Negroes, the great question of what this was, and how it had survived, remained wide open. Moreover, *Black Boy* had been written in the English language which Americans had inherited from England, that is, if you like, from Greece and Rome; its form, psychology, moral attitude, preoccupations, in short, its cultural validity, were all due to forces which had nothing to do with Africa. Or was it simply that we had been rendered unable to recognize Africa in it?—for it seemed that in

Senghor's vast re-creation of the world, the footfall of
the African would prove to have covered more territory
than the footfall of the Roman.

Thursday's great event was Aimé Cesaire's speech in
the afternoon, dealing with the relation between colonization and culture. Cesaire is a caramel-colored man
from Martinique, probably around forty, with a great
tendency to roundness and smoothness, physically speaking, and with the rather vaguely benign air of a school-
teacher. All this changes the moment he begins to speak.
It becomes at once apparent that his curious, slow-mov-
ing blandness is related to the grace and patience of a
jungle cat and that the intelligence behind those spectacles is of a very penetrating and demagogic order.

The cultural crisis through which we are passing today
can be summed up thus, said Cesaire: that culture which
is strongest from the material and technological point of
view threatens to crush all weaker cultures, particularly
in a world in which, distance counting for nothing, the
technologically weaker cultures have no means of protecting themselves. All cultures have, furthermore, an
economic, social, and political base, and no culture can
continue to live if its political destiny is not in its own
hands. "Any political and social regime which destroys
the self-determination of a people also destroys the creative power of that people." When this has happened the
culture of that people has been destroyed. And it is simply not true that the colonizers bring to the colonized a
new culture to replace the old one, a culture not being
something given to a people, but, on the contrary and by
definition, something that they make themselves. Nor is
it, in any case, in the nature of colonialism to wish or to
permit such a degree of well-being among the colonized.
The well-being of the colonized is desirable only insofar
as this well-being enriches the dominant country, the
necessity of which is simply to remain dominant. Now the
civilizations of Europe, said Cesaire, speaking very clear-

ly and intensely to a packed and attentive hall, evolved
an economy based on capital and the capital was based
on black labor; and thus, regardless of whatever arguments Europeans use to defend themselves, and in spite
of the absurd palliatives with which they have sometimes
tried to soften the blow, the fact, of their domination, in
order to accomplish and maintain this domination—in
order, in fact, to make money—they destroyed, with utter
ruthlessness, everything that stood in their way, languages, customs, tribes, lives; and not only put nothing
in its place, but erected, on the contrary, the most tremendous barriers between themselves and the people
they ruled. Europeans never had the remotest intention
of raising Africans to the Western level, of sharing with
them the instruments of physical, political or economic
power. It was precisely their intention, their necessity, to
keep the people they ruled in a state of cultural anarchy,
that is, simply in a barbaric state. "The famous inferiority complex one is pleased to observe as a characteristic
of the colonized is no accident but something very definitely desired and deliberately inculcated by the coloniz-
er." He was interrupted at this point—not for the first
time—by prolonged applause.

"The situation, therefore, in the colonial countries, is
tragic," Cesaire continued. "Wherever colonization is a
fact the indigenous culture begins to rot. And, among
these ruins, something begins to be born which is not a
culture but a kind of subculture, a subculture which is
condemned to exist on the margin allowed it by European culture. This then becomes the province of a few
men, the elite, who find themselves placed in the most
artificial conditions, deprived of any revivifying contact
with the masses of the people. Under such conditions,
this subculture has no chance whatever of growing into
an active, living culture." And what, he asked, before
this situation, can be done?

The answer would not be simple. "In every society
there is always a delicate balance between the old and

the new, a balance which is perpetually being reestablished, which is reestablished by each generation. Black
societies, cultures, civilizations, will not escape this law."
Cesaire spoke of the energy already proved by black cultures in the past, and, declining to believe that this energy no longer existed, declined also to believe that the
total obliteration of the existing culture was a condition
for the renaissance of black people. "In the culture to be
born there will no doubt be old and new elements. How
these elements will be mixed is not a question to which
any individual can respond. The response must be given
by the community. But we can say this: that the response
will be given, and not verbally, but in tangible facts, and
by action."

He was interrupted by applause again. He paused,
faintly smiling, and reached his peroration: "We find
ourselves today in a cultural chaos. And this is our role:
to liberate the forces which, alone, can organize from this
chaos a new synthesis, a synthesis which will deserve the
name of a culture, a synthesis which will be the reconciliation—*et dépassement*—of the old and the new. We
are here to proclaim the right of our people to speak, to
let our people, black people, make their entrance on the
great stage of history."

This speech, which was very brilliantly delivered, and
which had the further advantage of being, in the main,
unanswerable (and the advantage, also, of being very
little concerned, at bottom, with culture) wrung from
the audience which heard it the most violent reaction of
joy. Cesaire had spoken for those who could not speak
and those who could not speak thronged around the table to shake his hand, and kiss him. I myself felt stirred
in a very strange and disagreeable way. For Cesaire's case
against Europe, which was watertight, was also a very
easy case to make. The anatomizing of the great injustice
which is the irreducible fact of colonialism was yet not
enough to give the victims of that injustice a new sense
of themselves. One may say, of course, that the very fact

that Cesaire had spoken so thrillingly, and in one of the great institutions of Western learning, invested them with this new sense, but I do not think this is so. He had certainly played very skillfully on their emotions and their hopes, but he had not raised the central, tremendous question, which was, simply: What *had* this colonial experience made of them and what were they now to do with it? For they were all, now, whether they liked it or not, related to Europe, stained by European visions and standards, and their relation to themselves, and to each other, and to their past had changed. Their relation to their poets had also changed, as had the relation of their poets to them. Cesaire's speech left out of account one of the great effects of the colonial experience: its creation, precisely, of men like himself. His real relation to the people who thronged about him now had been changed, by this experience, into something very different from what it once had been. What made him so attractive now was the fact that he, without having ceased to be one of them, yet seemed to move with the European authority. He had penetrated into the heart of the great wilderness which was Europe and stolen the sacred fire. And this, which was the promise of their freedom, was also the assurance of his power.

Friday's session began in a rather tense atmosphere and this tension continued throughout the day. Diop opened the session by pointing out that each speaker spoke only for himself and could not be considered as speaking for the conference. I imagined that this had something to do with Cesaire's speech of the day before and with some of its effects, among which, apparently, had been a rather sharp exchange between Cesaire and the American delegation.

This was the session during which it became apparent that there was a religious war going on at the conference, a war which suggested, in miniature, some of the tensions dividing Africa. A Protestant minister from the

Cameroons, Pastor T. Ekollo, had been forced by the hostility of the audience the day before to abandon a dissertation in defense of Christianity in Africa. He was visibly upset still. "There will be Christians in Africa, even when there is not a white man there," he said, with a tense defiance, and added, with an unconsciously despairing irony to which, however, no one reacted, "supposing that to be possible." He had been asked how he could defend Christianity in view of what Christians had done in his country. To which his answer was that the doctrine of Christianity was of more moment than the crimes committed by Christians. The necessity which confronted Africans was to make Christianity real in their own lives, without reference to the crimes committed by others. The audience was extremely cold and hostile, forcing him again, in effect, from the floor. But I felt that this also had something to do with Pastor Ekollo's rather petulant and not notably Christian attitude toward them.

Dr. Marcus James, a priest of the Anglican church from Jamaica, picked up where Ekollo left off. Dr. James is a round, very pleasant-looking, chocolate-colored man, with spectacles. He began with a quotation to the effect that, when the Christian arrived in Africa, he had the Bible and the African had the land; but that, before long, the African had the Bible and the Christian had the land. There was a great deal of laughter at this, in which Dr. James joined. But the postscript to be added today, he said, is that the African not only has the Bible but has found in it a potential weapon for the recovery of his land. The Christians in the hall, who seemed to be in the minority, applauded and stomped their feet at this, but many others now rose and left.

Dr. James did not seem to be distressed and went on to discuss the relationship between Christianity and democracy. In Africa, he said, there was none whatever. Africans do not, in fact, believe that Christianity is any longer real for Europeans, due to the immense scaffold-

ing with which they have covered it, and the fact that
this religion has no effect whatever on their conduct.
There are, nevertheless, more than twenty million Christians in Africa, and Dr. James believed that the future
of their country was very largely up to them. The task of
making Christianity real in Africa was made the more
difficult in that they could expect no help whatever from
Europe: "Christianity, as practiced by Europeans in
Africa, is a cruel travesty."

This bitter observation, which was uttered in sorrow,
gained a great deal of force from the fact that so genial
a man had felt compelled to make it. It made vivid, unanswerable, in a way which rage could not have done,
how little the West has respected its own ideals in dealing with subject peoples, and suggested that there was
a price we would pay for this. He speculated a little on
what African Christianity might become, and how it
might contribute to the rebirth of Christianity everywhere; and left his audience to chew on this momentous
speculation: Considering, he said, that what Africa
wishes to wrest from Europe is power, will it be necessary
for Africa to take the same bloody road which Europe
has followed? Or will it be possible for her to work out
some means of avoiding this?

M. Wahal, from the Sudan, spoke in the afternoon on
the role of the law in culture, using as an illustration
the role the law had played in the history of the American Negro. He spoke at length on the role of French law
in Africa, pointing out that French law is simply not
equipped to deal with the complexity of the African situation. And what is even worse, of course, is that it
makes virtually no attempt to do so. The result is that
French law, in Africa, is simply a legal means of adminis-
tering injustice. It is not a solution, either, simply to re-
vert to African tribal custom, which is also helpless before the complexities of present-day African life. Wahal
spoke with a quiet matter-of-fact-ness, which lent great
force to the ugly story he was telling, and he concluded

by saying that the question was ultimately a political one and that there was no hope of solving it within the framework of the present colonial system.

He was followed by George Lamming. Lamming is tall, raw-boned, untidy, and intense, and one of his real distinctions is his refusal to be intimidated by the fact that he is a genuine writer. He proposed to raise certain questions pertaining to the quality of life to be lived by black people in that hypothetical tomorrow when they would no longer be ruled by whites. "The profession of letters is an untidy one," he began, looking as though he had dressed to prove it. He directed his speech to Aimé Cesaire and Jacques Alexis in particular, and quoted Djuna Barnes: "Too great a sense of identity makes a man feel he can do no wrong. And too little does the same." He suggested that it was important to bear in mind that the word Negro meant black—and meant nothing more than that; and commented on the great variety of heritages, experiences, and points of view which the conference had brought together under the heading of this single noun. He wished to suggest that the nature of power was unrelated to pigmentation, that bad faith was a phenomenon which was independent of race. He found—from the point of view of an untidy man of letters—something crippling in the obsession from which Negroes suffered as regards the existence and the attitudes of the Other—this Other being everyone who was not Negro. That black people faced great problems was surely not to be denied and yet the greatest problem facing us was what *we,* Negroes, would do among ourselves "when there was no longer any colonial horse to ride." He pointed out that this was the horse on which a great many Negroes, who were in what he called "the skin trade," hoped to ride to power, power which would be in no way distinguishable from the power they sought to overthrow.

Lamming was insisting on the respect which is due the

private life. I respected him very much, not only because he raised this question, but because he knew what he was doing. He was concerned with the immensity and the variety of the experience called Negro; he was concerned that one should recognize this variety as wealth. He cited the case of Amos Tutuola's *The Palm-Wine Drunkard,* which he described as a fantasy, made up of legends, anecdotes, episodes, the product, in fact, of an oral story-telling tradition which disappeared from Western life generations ago. Yet "Tutuola really *does* speak English. It is *not* his second language." The English did not find the book strange. On the contrary, they were astonished by how truthfully it seemed to speak to them of their own experience. They felt that Tutuola was closer to the English than he could possibly be to his equivalent in Nigeria; and yet Tutuola's work could elicit this reaction only because, in a way which could never really be understood, but which Tutuola had accepted, he was closer to his equivalent in Nigeria than he would ever be to the English. It seemed to me that Lamming was suggesting to the conference a subtle and difficult idea, the idea that part of the great wealth of the Negro experience lay precisely in its double-edgedness. He was suggesting that all Negroes were held in a state of supreme tension between the difficult, dangerous relationship in which they stood to the white world and the relationship, not a whit less painful or dangerous, in which they stood to each other. He was suggesting that in the acceptance of this duality lay their strength, that in this, precisely, lay their means of defining and controlling the world in which they lived.

Lamming was interrupted at about this point, however, for it had lately been decided, in view of the great number of reports still to be read, to limit everyone to twenty minutes. This quite unrealistic rule was not to be observed very closely, especially as regarded the French-speaking delegates. But Lamming put his notes in his pocket and ended by saying that if, as someone had remarked, silence was the only common language, politics, for Negroes, was the only common ground.

The evening session began with a film, which I missed, and was followed by a speech from Cheik Anta Diop, which, in sum, claimed the ancient Egyptian empire as part of the Negro past. I can only say that this question has never greatly exercised my mind, nor did M. Diop succeed in doing so—at least not in the direction he intended. He quite refused to remain within the twenty-minute limit and, while his claims of the deliberate dishonesty of all Egyptian scholars may be quite well founded for all I know, I cannot say that he convinced me. He was, however, a great success in the hall, second only, in fact, to Aimé Césaire.

He was followed by Richard Wright. Wright had been acting as liaison man between the American delegation and the Africans and this had placed him in rather a difficult position, since both factions tended to claim him as their spokesman. It had not, of course, occurred to the Americans that he could be anything less, whereas the Africans automatically claimed him because of his great prestige as a novelist and his reputation for calling a spade a spade—particularly if the spade were white. The consciousness of his peculiar and certainly rather grueling position weighed on him, I think, rather heavily.

He began by confessing that the paper he had written, while on his farm in Normandy, impressed him as being, after the events of the last few days, inadequate. Some of the things he had observed during the course of the conference had raised questions in him which his paper could not have foreseen. He had not, however, rewritten his paper, but would read it now, exactly as it had been written, interrupting himself whenever what he had written and what he had since been made to feel seemed to be at variance. He was exposing, in short, his conscience to the conference and asking help of them in his confusion.

There was, first of all, he said, a painful contradiction in being at once a Westerner and a black man. "I see both worlds from another, and third, point of view." This fact had nothing to do with his will, his desire, or his choice. It was simply that he had been born in the West and the West had formed him.

As a black Westerner, it was difficult to know what one's attitude should be toward three realities which were inextricably woven together in the Western fabric. These were religion, tradition, and imperialism, and in none of these realities had the lives of black men been taken into account: their advent dated back to 1455, when the church had determined to rule all infidels. And it just so happened, said Wright, ironically, that a vast proportion of these infidels were black. Nevertheless, this decision on the part of the church had not been, despite the church's intentions, entirely oppressive, for one of the results of 1455 had, at length, been Calvin and Luther, who shook the authority of the church in insisting on the authority of the individual conscience. This might not, he said accurately, have been precisely their intention, but it had certainly been one of their effects. For, with the authority of the church shaken, men were left prey to many strange and new ideas, ideas which led, finally, to the discrediting of the racial dogma. Neither had this been foreseen, but what men imagine they are doing and what they are doing in fact are rarely the same thing. This was a perfectly valid observation which would, I felt, have been just as valid without the remarkable capsule history with which Wright imagined he supported it.

Wright then went on to speak of the effects of European colonialism in the African colonies. He confessed—bearing in mind always the great gap between human intentions and human effects—that he thought of it as having been, in many ways, liberating, since it smashed old traditions and destroyed old gods. One of the things that surprised him in the last few days had been the realization that most of the delegates to the conference

did not feel as he did. He felt, nevertheless, that, though
Europeans had not realized what they were doing freeing Africans from the "rot" of their past, they had been
accomplishing a good. And yet—he was not certain that
he had the right to say that, having forgotten that Africans are not American Negroes and were not, therefore,
as he somewhat mysteriously considered American Negroes to be, free from their "irrational" past.

In sum, Wright said, he felt that Europe had brought
the Enlightenment to Africa and that "what was good
for Europe was good for all mankind." I felt that this
was, perhaps, a tactless way of phrasing a debatable
idea, but Wright went on to express a notion which I
found even stranger. And this was that the West, having
created an African and Asian elite, should now "give
them their heads" and "refuse to be shocked" at the
"methods they will feel compelled to use" in unifying
their countries. We had not, ourselves, used very pretty
methods. Presumably, this left us in no position to throw
stones at Nehru, Nasser, Sukarno, etc., should they decide,
as they almost surely would, to use dictatorial methods
in order to hasten the "social evolution." In any case,
Wright said, these men, the leaders of their countries,
once the new social order was established, would voluntarily surrender the "personal power." He did not say
what would happen then, but I supposed it would be the
second coming.

Saturday was the last day of the conference, which
was scheduled to end with the invitation to the audience
to engage with the delegates in the Euro-African dialogue. It was a day marked by much confusion and ex-
citement and discontent—this last on the part of people
who felt that the conference had been badly run, or who
had not been allowed to read their reports. (They were
often the same people.) It was marked, too, by rather a
great deal of plain speaking, both on and off, but mostly
off, the record. The hall was even more hot and crowded

than it had been the first day and the photographers were back.

The entire morning was taken up in an attempt to agree on a "cultural inventory." This had to be done before the conference could draft those resolutions which they were, today, to present to the world. This task would have been extremely difficult even had there obtained in the black world a greater unity—geographical, spiritual, and historical—than is actually the case. Under the circumstances, it was an endeavor complicated by the nearly indefinable complexities of the word *culture,* by the fact that no coherent statement had yet been made concerning the relationship of black cultures to each other, and, finally, by the necessity, which had obtained throughout the conference, of avoiding the political issues.

The inability to discuss politics had certainly handicapped the conference, but it could scarcely have been run otherwise. The political question would have caused the conference to lose itself in a war of political ideologies. Moreover, the conference *was* being held in Paris, many of the delegates represented areas which belonged to France, most of them represented areas which were not free. There was also to be considered the delicate position of the American delegation, which had sat throughout the conference uncomfortably aware that they might at any moment be forced to rise and leave the hall.

The declaration of political points of view being thus prohibited, the "cultural" debate which raged in the hall that morning was in perpetual danger of drowning in the sea of the unstated. For, according to his political position, each delegate had a different interpretation of his culture, and a different idea of its future, as well as the means to be used to make that future a reality. A solution of a kind was offered by Senghor's suggestion that two committees be formed, one to take an inventory of the past, and one to deal with present prospects. There

was some feeling that two committees were scarcely necessary. Diop suggested that one committee be formed,
which, if necessary, could divide itself into two. Then
the question arose as to just how the committee should
be appointed, whether by countries or by cultural areas.
It was decided, at length, that the committee should be
set up on the latter basis, and should have resolutions
drafted by noon. "It is by these resolutions," protested
Mercer Cook, "that we shall make ourselves known. It
cannot be done in an hour."

He was entirely right. At eleven-twenty a committee of
eighteen members had been formed. At four o'clock in
the afternoon they were still invisible. By this time, too,
the most tremendous impatience reigned in the crowded
hall, in which, today, Negroes by far outnumbered whites.
At four-twenty-five the impatience of the audience
erupted in whistles, catcalls, and stamping of feet. At
four-thirty, Alioune Diop arrived and officially opened
the meeting. He tried to explain some of the difficulties
such a conference inevitably encountered and assured
the audience that the committee on resolutions would
not be absent much longer. In the meantime, in their absence, and in the absence of Dr. Price-Mars, he proposed
to read a few messages from well-wishers. But the audience was not really interested in these messages and was
manifesting a very definite tendency to get out of hand
again when, at four-fifty-five, Dr. Price-Mars entered. His
arrival had the effect of calming the audience somewhat
and, luckily, the committee on resolutions came in very
shortly afterwards. At five-seven, Diop rose to read the
document which had come one vote short of being unan-
imously approved.

As is the way with documents of this kind, it was carefully worded and slightly repetitious. This did not make
its meaning less clear or diminish its importance.

It spoke first of the great importance of the cultural inventory here begun in relation to the various black cultures which had been "systematically misunderstood, un-

derestimated, sometimes destroyed." This inventory had confirmed the pressing need for a reexamination of the history of these cultures *("la verité historique")* with a view to their reevaluation. The ignorance concerning them, the errors, and the willful distortions, were among the great contributing factors to the crisis through which they now were passing, in relation to themselves and to human culture in general. The active aid of writers, artists, theologians, thinkers, scientists, and technicians was necessary for the revival, the rehabilitation, and the development of these cultures as the first step toward their integration in the active cultural life of the world. Black men, whatever their political and religious beliefs, were united in believing that the health and growth of these cultures could not possibly come about until colonialism, the exploitation of undeveloped peoples, and racial discrimination had come to an end. (At this point the conference expressed its regret at the involuntary absence of the South African delegation and the reading was interrupted by prolonged and violent applause.) All people, the document continued, had the right to be able to place themselves in fruitful contact with their national cultural values and to benefit from the instruction and education which could be afforded them within this framework. It spoke of the progress which had taken place in the world in the last few years and stated that this progress permitted one to hope for the general abolition of the colonial system and the total and universal end of racial discrimination, and ended: "Our conference, which respects the cultures of all countries and appreciates their contributions to the progress of civilization, engages all black men in the defense, the illustration, and the dissemination throughout the world of the national values of their people. We, black writers and artists, proclaim our brotherhood toward all men and expect of them *('nous attendons d'eux')* the manifestation of this same brotherhood toward our people."

When the applause in which the last words of this

document were very nearly drowned had ended, Diop
pointed out that this was not a declaration of war; it
was, rather, he said, a declaration of love—for the culture, European, which had been of such importance in
the history of mankind. But it had been very keenly felt
that it was now necessary for black men to make the effort to define themselves *au lieu d'être toujours defini
par les autres.* Black men had resolved "to take their destinies into their own hands." He spoke of plans for the
setting up of an international association for the dissemination of black culture and, at five-twenty-two, Dr.
Price-Mars officially closed the conference and opened
the floor to the audience for the Euro-African dialogue.

Someone, a European, addressed this question to Aimé
Cesaire: How, he asked, do you explain the fact that
many Europeans—as well as many Africans, *bien en-
tendu*—reject what is referred to as European culture?
A European himself, he was far from certain that such a
thing as a European culture existed. It was possible to
be a European without accepting the Greco-Roman tradition. Neither did he believe in race. He wanted to
know in what, exactly, this Negro-African culture consisted and, more, why it was judged necessary to save it.
He ended, somewhat vaguely, by saying that, in his opinion, it was human values which had to be preserved,
human needs which had to be respected and expressed.

This admirable but quite inadequate psychologist pre-
cipitated something of a storm. Diop tried to answer the
first part of his question by pointing out that, in their
attitudes toward their cultures, a great diversity of view-
points also obtained among black men. Then an enormous, handsome, extremely impressive black man whom
I had not remarked before, who was also named Cesaire,
stated that the contemporary crisis of black cultures had
been brought about by Europe's nineteenth- and twentieth-century attempts to impose their culture on other
peoples. They did this without any recognition of the
cultural validity of these peoples and thus aroused their

resistance. In the case of Africa, where culture was fluid and largely unwritten, resistance had been most difficult. "Which is why," he said, "we are here. We are the most characteristic products of this crisis." And then a rage seemed to shake him, and he continued in a voice thick with fury, "Nothing will ever make us believe that our beliefs . . . are merely frivolous superstitions. No power will ever cause us to admit that we are lower than any other people." He then made a reference to the present Arab struggle against the French which I did not understand, and ended, "What we are doing is holding on to what is ours. Little," he added, sardonically, "but it belongs to us."

Aimé Cesaire, to whom the question had been addressed, was finally able to answer it. He pointed out, with a deliberate, mocking logic, that the rejection by a European of European culture was of the utmost unimportance. "Reject it or not, he is still a European, even his rejection is a European rejection. We do not choose our cultures, we belong to them." As to the speaker's implied idea of cultural relativity, and the progressive role this idea can sometimes play, he cited the French objection to this idea. It is an idea which, by making all cultures, as such, equal, undermines French justification for its presence in Africa. He also suggested that the speaker had implied that this conference was primarily interested in an idealistic reconstruction of the past. "But our attitude," said Cesaire, "toward colonialism and racial discrimination is very concrete. Our aims cannot be realized without this concreteness." And as for the question of race: "No one is suggesting that there is such a thing as a pure race, or that culture is a racial product. We are not Negroes by our own desire, but, in effect, because of Europe. What unites all Negroes is the injustices they have suffered at European hands."

The moment Cesaire finished, Cheik Anta Diop passionately demanded if it were a heresy from a Marxist point of view to try to hang on to a national culture.

"Where," he asked, "is the European nation which, in order to progress, surrendered its past?"

There was no answer to this question, nor were there any further questions from the audience. Richard Wright spoke briefly, saying that this conference marked a turning point in the history of Euro-African relations: it marked, in fact, the beginning of the end of the European domination. He spoke of the great diversity of techniques and approaches now at the command of black people, with particular emphasis on the role the American Negro could be expected to play. Among black people, the American Negro was in the technological vanguard and this could prove of inestimable value to the developing African sovereignties. And the dialogue ended immediately afterward, at six-fifty-five, with Senghor's statement that this was the first of many such conferences, the first of many dialogues. As night was falling we poured into the Paris streets. Boys and girls, old men and women, bicycles, terraces, all were there, and the people were queueing up before the bakeries for bread.

3. FIFTH AVENUE, UPTOWN:

A Letter From Harlem

There is a housing project standing now where the house in which we grew up once stood, and one of those stunted city trees is snarling where our doorway used to be. This is on the rehabilitated side of the avenue. The other side of the avenue—for progress takes time—has not been rehabilitated yet and it looks exactly as it looked in the days when we sat with our noses pressed against the windowpane, longing to be allowed to go "across the street." The grocery store which gave us credit is still there, and there can be no doubt that it is still giving credit. The people in the project certainly need it—far more, indeed, than they ever needed the project. The last time I passed by, the Jewish proprietor was still standing among his shelves, looking sadder and heavier but scarcely any older. Farther down the block stands the shoe-repair store in which our shoes were repaired until reparation became impossible and in which, then, we bought all our "new" ones. The Negro proprietor is still in the window, head down, working at the leather.

These two, I imagine, could tell a long tale if they would (perhaps they would be glad to if they could), having watched so many, for so long, struggling in the fishhooks, the barbed wire, of this avenue.

The avenue is elsewhere the renowned and elegant Fifth. The area I am describing, which, in today's gang parlance, would be called "the turf," is bounded by Lenox

Avenue on the west, the Harlem River on the east, 135th Street on the north, and 130th Street on the south. We never lived beyond these boundaries; this is where we grew up. Walking along 145th Street—for example—familiar as it is, and similar, does not have the same impact because I do not know any of the people on the block. But when I turn east on 131st Street and Lenox Avenue, there is first a soda-pop joint, then a shoeshine "parlor," then a grocery store, then a dry cleaners', then the houses. All along the street there are people who watched me grow up, people who grew up with me, people I watched grow up along with my brothers and sisters; and, sometimes in my arms, sometimes underfoot, sometimes at my shoulder—or on it—their children, a riot, a forest of children, who include my nieces and nephews.

When we reach the end of this long block, we find ourselves on wide, filthy, hostile Fifth Avenue, facing that project which hangs over the avenue like a monument to the folly, and the cowardice, of good intentions. All along the block, for anyone who knows it, are immense human gaps, like craters. These gaps are not created merely by those who have moved away, inevitably into some other ghetto; or by those who have risen, almost always into a greater capacity for self-loathing and self-delusion; or yet by those who, by whatever means—World War II, the Korean war, a policeman's gun or billy, a gang war, a brawl, madness, an overdose of heroin, or, simply, unnatural exhaustion—are dead. I am talking about those who are left, and I am talking principally about the young. What are they doing? Well, some, a minority, are fanatical churchgoers, members of the more extreme of the Holy Roller sects. Many, many more are "moslems," by affiliation or sympathy, that is to say that they are united by nothing more—and nothing less—than a hatred of the white world and all its works. They are present, for example, at every Buy Black street-corner meeting—meetings in which the speaker urges his hearers to cease trading with white men and establish a separate economy. Neither the speaker nor his hearers can possibly do this, of course, since Negroes do not own General Motors or RCA or the A & P, nor, indeed, do they own more than a wholly insufficient fraction of anything else in Harlem (those who *do* own anything are more interested in their profits than in their fellows). But these meetings nevertheless keep alive in the participators a certain pride of bitterness without which, however futile this bitterness may be, they could scarcely remain alive at all. Many have given up. They stay home and watch the TV screen, living on the earnings of their parents, cousins, brothers, or uncles, and only leave the house to go to the movies or to the nearest bar. "How're you making it?" one may ask, running into them along the block, or in the bar. "Oh, I'm TV-ing it"; with the saddest, sweetest, most shamefaced of smiles, and from a great distance. This distance one is compelled to respect; anyone who has traveled so far will not easily be dragged again into the world. There are further retreats, of course, than the TV screen or the bar. There are those who are simply sitting on their stoops, "stoned," animated for a moment only, and hideously, by the approach of someone who may lend them the money for a "fix." Or by the approach of someone from whom they can purchase it, one of the shrewd ones, on the way to prison or just coming out.

And the others, who have avoided all of these deaths, get up in the morning and go downtown to meet "the man." They work in the white man's world all day and come home in the evening to this fetid block. They struggle to instill in their children some private sense of honor or dignity which will help the child to survive. This means, of course, that they must struggle, stolidly, incessantly, to keep this sense alive in themselves, in spite of the insults, the indifference, and the cruelty they are certain to encounter in their working day. They patiently browbeat the landlord into fixing the heat, the plaster, the plumbing; this demands prodigious patience; nor is patience usually enough. In trying to make their hovels habitable, they are perpetually throwing good money after bad. Such frustration, so long endured, is driving many strong, admirable men and women whose only crime is color to the very gates of paranoia.

One remembers them from another time—playing handball in the playground, going to church, wondering if they were going to be promoted at school. One remembers them going off to war—gladly, to escape this block. One remembers their return. Perhaps one remembers their wedding day. And one sees where the girl is now —vainly looking for salvation from some other embittered, trussed, and struggling boy—and sees the all-but-abandoned children in the streets.

Now I am perfectly aware that there are other slums in which white men are fighting for their lives, and mainly losing. I know that blood is also flowing through those streets and that the human damage there is incalculable. People are continually pointing out to me the wretchedness of white people in order to console me for the wretchedness of blacks. But an itemized account of the American failure does not console me and it should not console anyone else. That hundreds of thousands of white people are living, in effect, no better than the "niggers" is not a fact to be regarded with complacency. The social and moral bankruptcy suggested by this fact is of the bitterest, most terrifying kind.

The people, however, who believe that this democratic anguish has some consoling value are always pointing out that So-and-So, white, and So-and-So, black, rose from the slums into the big time. The existence—the public existence—of, say, Frank Sinatra and Sammy Davis, Jr. proves to them that America is still the land of opportunity and that inequalities vanish before the determined will. It proves nothing of the sort. The determined will is rare—at the moment, in this country, it is unspeakably rare—and the inequalities suffered by the many are in no way justified by the rise of a few. A few have always risen—in every country, every era, and in the teeth of regimes which can by no stretch of the imagination be thought of as free. Not all of these people, it is worth remembering, left the world better than they found it. The determined will is rare, but it is not invariably benevolent. Furthermore, the American equation of success with the big time reveals an awful disrespect for human life and human achievement. This equation has placed our cities among the most dangerous in the world and has placed our youth among the most empty and most bewildered. The situation of our youth is not mysterious. Children have never been very good at listening to their elders, but they have never failed to imitate them. They must, they have no other models. That is exactly what our children are doing. They are imitating our immorality, our disrespect for the pain of others.

All other slum dwellers, when the bank account permits it, can move out of the slum and vanish altogether from the eye of persecution. No Negro in this country has ever made that much money and it will be a long time before any Negro does. The Negroes in Harlem, who have no money, spend what they have on such gimcracks as they are sold. These include "wider" TV screens, more "faithful" hi-fi sets, more "powerful" cars, all of which, of course, are obsolete long before they are paid for. Anyone who has ever struggled with poverty knows how extremely expensive it is to be poor; and if one is a member of a captive population, economically speaking, one's feet have simply been placed on the treadmill forever. One is victimized, economically, in a thousand ways—rent, for example, or car insurance. Go shopping one day in Harlem—for anything—and compare Harlem prices and quality with those downtown.

The people who have managed to get off this block have only got as far as a more respectable ghetto. This respectable ghetto does not even have the advantages of the disreputable one—friends, neighbors, a familiar church, and friendly tradesmen; and it is not, moreover, in the nature of any ghetto to remain respectable long. Every Sunday, people who have left the block take the lonely ride back, dragging their increasingly discontented children with them. They spend the day talking, not always with words, about the trouble they've seen and the trouble—one must watch their eyes as they watch their children—they are only too likely to see. For children do not like ghettos. It takes them nearly no time to discover exactly why they are there.

The projects in Harlem are hated. They are hated almost as much as policemen, and this is saying a great deal. And they are hated for the same reason: both reveal, unbearably, the real attitude of the white world, no matter how many liberal speeches are made, no matter how many lofty editorials are written, no matter how many civil-rights commissions are set up.

The projects are hideous, of course, there being a law, apparently respected throughout the world, that popular housing shall be as cheerless as a prison. They are lumped all over Harlem, colorless, bleak, high, and revolting. The wide windows look out on Harlem's invincible and indescribable squalor: the Park Avenue railroad tracks, around which, about forty years ago, the present dark community began; the unrehabilitated houses, bowed down, it would seem, under the great weight of frustration and bitterness they contain; the dark, the ominous schoolhouses from which the child may emerge maimed, blinded, hooked, or enraged for life; and the churches, churches, block upon block of churches, niched in the walls like cannon in the walls of a fortress. Even if the administration of the projects were not so insanely humiliating (for example: one must report raises in salary to the management, which will then eat up the profit by raising one's rent; the management has the right to know who is staying in your apartment; the management can ask you to leave, at their discre-

tion), the projects would still be hated because they are
an insult to the meanest intelligence.

Harlem got its first private project, Riverton*—which
is now, naturally, a slum—about twelve years ago because at that time Negroes were not allowed to live in
Stuyvesant Town. Harlem watched Riverton go up,
therefore, in the most violent bitterness of spirit, and
hated it long before the builders arrived. They began
hating it at about the time people began moving out of
their condemned houses to make room for this additional
proof of how thoroughly the white world despised them.
And they had scarcely moved in, naturally, before they
began smashing windows, defacing walls, urinating in
the elevators, and fornicating in the playgrounds. Liberals, both white and black, were appalled at the spectacle.
I was appalled by the liberal innocence—or cynicism,
which comes out in practice as much the same thing.
Other people were delighted to be able to point to proof
positive that nothing could be done to better the lot
of the colored people. They were, and are, right in one
respect: that nothing can be done as long as they are
treated like colored people. The people in Harlem know
they are living there because white people do not think
they are good enough to live anywhere else. No amount
of "improvement" can sweeten this fact. Whatever
money is now being earmarked to improve this, or any
other ghetto, might as well be burnt. A ghetto can be improved in one way only: out of existence.

Similarly, the only way to police a ghetto is to be oppressive. None of the Police Commissioner's men, even

*The inhabitants of Riverton were much embittered by this description; they
have, apparently, forgotten how their project came into being; and have re-
peatedly informed me that I cannot possibly be referring to Riverton, but to
another housing project which is directly across the street. It is quite clear,
I think, that I have no interest in accusing any individuals or families of the
depredations herein described: but neither can I deny the evidence of my own
eyes. Nor do I blame anyone in Harlem for making the best of a dreadful bargain. But anyone who lives in Harlem and imagines that he has not struck
this bargain, or that what he takes to be his status (in whose eyes?) protects
him against the common pain, demoralization, and danger, is simply self
deluded

with the best will in the world, have any way of understanding the lives led by the people they swagger about in twos and threes controlling. Their very presence is an insult, and it would be, even if they spent their entire day feeding gumdrops to children. They represent the force of the white world, and that world's real intentions are, simply, for that world's criminal profit and ease, to keep the black man corraled up here, in his place. The badge, the gun in the holster, and the swinging club make vivid what will happen should his rebellion become overt. Rare, indeed, is the Harlem citizen, from the most circumspect church member to the most shiftless adolescent, who does not have a long tale to tell of police incompetence, injustice, or brutality. I myself have witnessed and endured it more than once. The businessmen and racketeers also have a story. And so do the prostitutes. (And this is not, perhaps, the place to discuss Harlem's very complex attitude toward black policemen, nor the reasons, according to Harlem, that they are nearly all downtown.)

It is hard, on the other hand, to blame the policeman, blank, good-natured, thoughtless, and insuperably innocent, for being such a perfect representative of the people he serves. He, too, believes in good intentions and is astounded and offended when they are not taken for the deed. He has never, himself, done anything for which to be hated—which of us has?—and yet he is facing, daily and nightly, people who would gladly see him dead, and he knows it. There is no way for him not to know it: there are few things under heaven more unnerving than the silent, accumulating contempt and hatred of a people. He moves through Harlem, therefore, like an occupying soldier in a bitterly hostile country; which is precisely what, and where, he is, and is the reason he walks in twos and threes. And he is not the only one who knows why he is always in company: the people who are watching him know why, too. Any street meeting, sacred or secular, which he and his colleagues uneasily cover has as its explicit or implicit burden the cruelty and injustice of the white domination. And these days, of course, in terms increasingly vivid and jubilant, it speaks of the end of that domination. The white policeman standing on a Harlem street corner finds himself at the very center of the revolution now occurring in the world. He is not prepared for it—naturally, nobody is—and, what is possibly much more to the point, he is exposed, as few white people are, to the anguish of the black people around him. Even if he is gifted with the merest mustard grain of imagination, something must seep in. He cannot avoid observing that some of the children, in spite of their color, remind him of children he has known and loved, perhaps even of his own children. He knows that he certainly does not want *his* children living this way. He can retreat from his uneasiness in only one direction: into a callousness which very shortly becomes second nature. He becomes more callous, the population becomes more hostile, the situation grows more tense, and the police force is increased. One day, to everyone's astonishment, someone drops a match in the powder keg and everything blows up. Before the dust has settled or the blood congealed, editorials, speeches, and civil-rights commissions are loud in the land, demanding to know what happened. What happened is that Negroes want to be treated like men.

Negroes want to be treated like men: a perfectly straightforward statement, containing only seven words. People who have mastered Kant, Hegel, Shakespeare, Marx, Freud, and the Bible find this statement utterly impenetrable. The idea seems to threaten profound, barely conscious assumptions. A kind of panic paralyzes their features, as though they found themselves trapped on the edge of a steep place. I once tried to describe to a very well-known American intellectual the conditions among Negroes in the South. My recital disturbed him and made him indignant; and he asked me in perfect innocence, "Why don't all the Negroes in the South

move North?" I tried to explain what *has* happened, unfailingly, whenever a significant body of Negroes move
North. They do not escape Jim Crow: they merely encounter another, not-less-deadly variety. They do not
move to Chicago, they move to the South Side; they do
not move to New York, they move to Harlem. The pressure within the ghetto causes the ghetto walls to expand,
and this expansion is always violent. White people hold
the line as long as they can, and in as many ways as they
can, from verbal intimidation to physical violence. But
inevitably the border which has divided the ghetto from
the rest of the world falls into the hands of the ghetto.
The white people fall back bitterly before the black
horde; the landlords make a tidy profit by raising the
rent, chopping up the rooms, and all but dispensing with
the upkeep; and what has once been a neighborhood
turns into a "turf." This is precisely what happened
when the Puerto Ricans arrived in their thousands—and
the bitterness thus caused is, as I write, being fought out
all up and down those streets.

Northerners indulge in an extremely dangerous lux-
ury. They seem to feel that because they fought on the
right side during the Civil War, and won, they have
earned the right merely to deplore what is going on in
the South, without taking any responsibility for it; and
that they can ignore what is happening in Northern cities because what is happening in Little Rock or Birmingham is worse. Well, in the first place, it is not possible for
anyone who has not endured both to know which is
"worse." I know Negroes who prefer the South and
white Southerners, because "At least there, you haven't
got to play any guessing games!" The guessing games referred to have driven more than one Negro into the nar-
cotics ward, the madhouse, or the river. I know another
Negro, a man very dear to me, who says, with conviction
and with truth, "The spirit of the South is the spirit of
America." He was born in the North and did his military training in the South. He did not, as far as I can

gather, find the South "worse"; he found it, if anything, all too familiar. In the second place, though, even if Birmingham *is* worse, no doubt Johannesburg, South Africa, beats it by several miles, and Buchenwald was one of the worst things that ever happened in the entire history of the world. The world has never lacked for horrifying examples; but I do not believe that these examples are meant to be used as justification for our own crimes. This perpetual justification empties the heart of all human feeling. The emptier our hearts become, the greater will be our crimes. Thirdly, the South is not merely an embarrassingly backward region, but a part of this country, and what happens there concerns every one of us.

As far as the color problem is concerned, there is but one great difference between the Southern white and the Northerner: the Southerner remembers, historically and in his own psyche, a kind of Eden in which he loved black people and they loved him. Historically, the flaming sword laid across this Eden is the Civil War. Personally, it is the Southerner's sexual coming of age, when, without any warning, unbreakable taboos are set up between himself and his past. Everything, thereafter, is permitted him except the love he remembers and has never ceased to need. The resulting, indescribable torment affects every Southern mind and is the basis of the Southern hysteria.

None of this is true for the Northerner. Negroes represent nothing to him personally, except, perhaps, the dangers of carnality. He never sees Negroes. Southerners see them all the time. Northerners never think about them whereas Southerners are never really thinking of anything else. Negroes are, therefore, ignored in the North and are under surveillance in the South, and suffer hideously in both places. Neither the Southerner nor the Northerner is able to look on the Negro simply as a man. It seems to be indispensable to the national self-esteem that the Negro be considered either as a kind of ward (in which case we are told how many Negroes, comparatively, bought Cadillacs last year and how few, comparatively, were lynched), or as a victim (in which case we are promised that he will never vote in our assemblies or go to school with our kids). They are two sides of the same coin and the South will not change—*cannot* change—until the North changes. The country will not change until it reexamines itself and discovers what it really means by freedom. In the meantime, generations keep being born, bitterness is increased by incompetence, pride, and folly, and the world shrinks around us.

It is a terrible, an inexorable, law that one cannot deny the humanity of another without diminishing one's own: in the face of one's victim, one sees oneself. Walk through the streets of Harlem and see what we, this nation, have become.

4. EAST RIVER, DOWNTOWN:

Postscript to a Letter From Harlem

The fact that American Negroes rioted in the U.N. while Adlai Stevenson was addressing the Assembly shocked and baffled most white Americans. Stevenson's speech, and the spectacular disturbance in the gallery, were both touched off by the death, in Katanga, the day before, of Patrice Lumumba. Stevenson stated, in the course of his address, that the United States was "against" colonialism. God knows what the African nations, who hold 25 per cent of the voting stock in the U.N. were thinking— they may, for example, have been thinking of the U.S. abstention when the vote on Algerian freedom was before the Assembly—but I think I have a fairly accurate notion of what the Negroes in the gallery were thinking. I had intended to be there myself. It was my first reaction upon hearing of Lumumba's death. I was curious about the impact of this political assassination on Negroes in Harlem, for Lumumba had—has—captured the popular imagination there. I was curious to know if Lumumba's death, which is surely among the most sinister of recent events, would elicit from "our" side anything more than the usual, well-meaning rhetoric. And I was curious about the African reaction.

However, the chaos on my desk prevented my being in the U.N. gallery. Had I been there, I, too, in the eyes of most Americans, would have been merely a pawn in the hands of the Communists. The climate and the events of the last decade, and the steady pressure of the "cold" war, have given Americans yet another means of avoiding self-examination, and so it has been decided that the riots were "Communist" inspired. Nor was it long, naturally, before prominent Negroes rushed forward to assure the republic that the U.N. rioters do not represent the real feeling of the Negro community.

According, then, to what I take to be the prevailing view, these rioters were merely a handful of irresponsible, Stalinist-corrupted *provocateurs*.

I find this view amazing. It is a view which even a minimal effort at observation would immediately contradict. One has only, for example, to walk through Harlem and ask oneself two questions. The first question is: Would *I* like to live here? And the second question is: Why don't those who now live here move out? The answer to both questions is immediately obvious. Unless one takes refuge in the theory—however disguised—that Negroes are, somehow, different from white people, I do not see how one can escape the conclusion that the Negro's status in this country is not only a cruel injustice but a grave national liability.

Now, I do not doubt that, among the people at the U.N. that day, there were Stalinist and professional revolutionists acting out of the most cynical motives. Wherever there is great social discontent, these people are, sooner or later, to be found. Their presence is not as frightening as the discontent which creates their opportunity. What I find appalling—and really dangerous— is the American assumption that the Negro is so contented with his lot here that only the cynical agents of a foreign power can rouse him to protest. It is a notion which contains a gratuitous insult, implying, as it does, that Negroes can make no move unless they are manipulated. It forcibly suggests that the Southern attitude toward the Negro is also, essentially, the national attitude. When the South has trouble with its Negroes—when the Negroes refuse to remain in their "place"—it blames "outside" agitators and "Northern interference." When the nation has trouble with the Northern Negro, it blames the Kremlin. And this, by no means incidentally, is a very dangerous thing to do. We thus give credit to the Communists for attitudes and victories which are not theirs. We make of them the champions of the oppressed, and they could not, of course, be more delighted.

If, as is only too likely, one prefers not to visit Harlem and expose oneself to the anguish there, one has only to consider the two most powerful movements among Negroes in this country today. At one pole, there is the Negro student movement. This movement, I believe, will prove to be the very last attempt made by American Negroes to achieve acceptance in the republic, to force the country to honor its own ideals. The movement does not have as its goal the consumption of over-cooked hamburgers and tasteless coffee at various sleazy lunch counters. Neither do Negroes, who have, largely, been produced by miscegenation, share the white man's helplessly hypocritical attitudes toward the time-honored and universal mingling. The goal of the student movement is nothing less than the liberation of the entire country from its most crippling attitudes and habits. The reason that it is important—of the utmost importance—for white people, here, to see the Negroes as people like themselves is that white people will not, otherwise, be able to see themselves as they are.

At the other pole is the Muslim movement, which daily becomes more powerful. The Muslims do not expect anything at all from the white people of this country. They do not believe that the American professions of democracy or equality have ever been even remotely sincere. They insist on the total separation of the races. This is to be achieved by the acquisition of land from the United States—land which is owed the Negroes as "back wages" for the labor wrested from them when they were slaves, and for their unrecognized and unhonored contributions to the wealth and power of this country. The

student movement depends, at bottom, on an act of
faith, an ability to see, beneath the cruelty and hysteria
and apathy of white people, their bafflement and pain
and essential decency. This is superbly difficult. It demands a perpetually cultivated spiritual resilience, for
the bulk of the evidence contradicts the vision. But the
Muslim movement has all the evidence on its side. Unless one supposes that the idea of black supremacy has
virtues denied to the idea of white supremacy, one cannot possibly accept the deadly conclusions a Muslim
draws from this evidence. On the other hand, it is quite
impossible to argue with a Muslim concerning the actual
state of Negroes in this country—the truth, after all, is
the truth.

This is the great power a Muslim speaker has over his
audience. His audience has not heard this truth—the
truth about their daily lives—honored by anyone else.
Almost anyone else, black or white, prefers to soften this
truth, and point to a new day which is coming in America. But this day has been coming for nearly one hundred
years. Viewed solely in the light of this country's moral
professions, this lapse is inexcusable. Even more important, however, is the fact that there is desperately little
in the record to indicate that white America ever seriously desired—or desires—to see this day arrive.

Usually, for example, those white people who are in
favor of integration prove to be in favor of it later, in
some other city, some other town, some other building,
some other school. The arguments, or rationalizations,
with which they attempt to disguise their panic cannot
be respected. Northerners proffer their indignation about
the South as a kind of badge, as proof of good intentions;
never suspecting that they thus increase, in the heart of
the Negro they are speaking to, a kind of helpless pain
and rage—and pity. Negroes know how little most white
people are prepared to implement their words with
deeds, how little, when the chips are down, they are prepared to risk. And this long history of moral evasion has

had an unhealthy effect on the total life of the country, and has eroded whatever respect Negroes may once have felt for white people.

We are beginning, therefore, to witness in this country a new thing. "I am not at all sure," states one prominent Negro, who is *not* a Muslim, "that I *want* to be integrated into a burning house." "I might," says another, "consider being integrated into something else, an American society more real and more honest—but *this?* No, thank you, man, who *needs* it?" And this searching disaffection has everything to do with the emergence of Africa: "At the rate things are going here, all of Africa will be free before we can get a lousy cup of coffee."

Now, of course, it is easy to say—and it is true enough, as far as it goes—that the American Negro deludes himself if he imagines himself capable of any loyalty other than his loyalty to the United States. He is an American, too, and he will survive or perish with the country. This seems an unanswerable argument. But, while I have no wish whatever to question the loyalty of American Negroes, I think this argument may be examined with some profit. The argument is used, I think, too often and too glibly. It obscures the effects of the passage of time, and the great changes that have taken place in the world.

In the first place, as the homeless wanderers of the twentieth century prove, the question of nationality no longer necessarily involves the question of allegiance. Allegiance, after all, has to work two ways; and one can grow weary of an allegiance which is not reciprocal. I have the right and the duty, for example, in my country, to vote; but it is my country's responsibility to protect my right to vote. People now approaching, or past, middle age, who have spent their lives in such struggles, have thereby acquired an understanding of America, and a belief in her potential which cannot now be shaken. (There are exceptions to this, however, W. E. B. Du Bois, for example. It is easy to dismiss him as a Stalinist; but it is more interesting to consider just why so intelligent a man became so disillusioned.) But I very strongly doubt that any Negro youth, now approaching maturity, and with the whole, vast world before him, is willing, say, to settle for Jim Crow in Miami, when he can—or, before the travel ban, *could*—feast at the welcome table in Havana. And he need not, to prefer Havana, have any pro-Communist, or, for that matter, pro-Cuban, or pro-Castro sympathies: he need merely prefer not to be treated as a second-class citizen.

These are extremely unattractive facts, but they *are* facts, and no purpose is served by denying them. Neither, as I have already tried to indicate, is any purpose served by pretending that Negroes who refuse to be bound by this country's peculiar attitudes are subversive. They have every right to refuse to be bound by a set of attitudes as useless now and as obsolete as the pillory. Finally, the time is forever behind us when Negroes could be expected to "wait." What is demanded now, and at once, is not that Negroes continue to adjust themselves to the cruel racial pressures of life in the United States but that the United States readjust itself to the facts of life in the present world.

One of these facts is that the American Negro can no longer, nor will he ever again, be controlled by white America's image of him. This fact has everything to do with the rise of Africa in world affairs. At the time that I was growing up, Negroes in this country were taught to be ashamed of Africa. They were taught it bluntly, as I was, for example, by being told that Africa had never contributed "anything" to civilization. Or once was taught the same lesson more obliquely, and even more effectively, by watching nearly naked, dancing, comic-opera, cannibalistic savages in the movies. They were nearly always all bad, sometimes funny, sometimes both. If one of them was good, his goodness was proved by his loyalty to the white man. A baffling sort of goodness, particularly as one's father, who certainly wanted one to be "good," was more than likely to come home cursing—

cursing the white man. One's hair was always being attacked with hard brushes and combs and Vaseline: it was shameful to have "nappy" hair. One's legs and arms and face were always being greased, so that one would not look "ashy" in the wintertime. One was always being mercilessly scrubbed and polished, as though in the hope that a stain could thus be washed away—I hazard that the Negro children of my generation, anyway, had an earlier and more painful acquaintance with soap than any other children anywhere. The women were forever straightening and curling their hair, and using bleaching creams. And yet it was clear that none of this effort would release one from the stigma and danger of being a Negro; this effort merely increased the shame and rage. There was not, no matter where one turned, any acceptable image of oneself, no proof of one's existence. One had the choice, either of "acting just like a nigger" or of *not* acting just like a nigger—and only those who have tried it know how impossible it is to tell the difference.

My first hero was Joe Louis. I was ashamed of Father Divine. Haile Selassie was the first black emperor I ever saw—in a newsreel; he was pleading vainly with the West to prevent the rape of his country. And the extraordinary complex of tensions thus set up in the breast, between hatred of whites and contempt for blacks, is very hard to describe. Some of the most energetic people of my generation were destroyed by this interior warfare.

But none of this is so for those who are young now. The power of the white world to control their identities was crumbling as they were born; and by the time they were able to react to the world, Africa was on the stage of history. This could not but have an extraordinary effect on their own morale, for it meant that they were not merely the descendants of slaves in a white, Protestant, and puritan country: they were also related to kings and princes in an ancestral homeland, far away. And this has proved to be a great antidote to the poison of self-hatred.

It also signals, at last, the end of the Negro situation in this country, as we have so far known it. Any effort, from here on out, to keep the Negro in his "place" can only have the most extreme and unlucky repercussions. This being so, it would seem to me that the most intelligent effort we can now make is to give up this doomed endeavor and study how we can most quickly end this division in our house. The Negroes who rioted in the U.N. are but a very small echo of the black discontent now abroad in the world. If we are not able, and quickly, to face and begin to eliminate the sources of this discontent in our own country, we will never be able to do it on the great stage of the world.

5. A FLY IN BUTTERMILK

"You can take the child out of the country," my elders were fond of saying, "but you can't take the country out of the child." They were speaking of their own antecedents, I supposed; it didn't, anyway, seem possible that they could be warning me; I took myself out of the country and went to Paris. It was there I discovered that the old folks knew what they had been talking about: I found myself, willy-nilly, alchemized into an American the moment I touched French soil.

Now, back again after nearly nine years, it was ironical to reflect that if I had not lived in France for so long I would never have found it necessary—or possible—to visit the American South. The South had always frightened me. How deeply it had frightened me—though I had never seen it—and how soon, was one of the things my dreams revealed to me while I was there. And this made me think of the privacy and mystery of childhood all over again, in a new way. I wondered where children got their strength—the strength, in this case, to walk through mobs to get to school.

"You've got to remember," said an older Negro friend to me, in Washington, "that no matter what you see or how it makes you feel, it can't be compared to twenty-five, thirty years ago—you remember those photographs of Negroes hanging from trees?" I looked at him differently. *I* had seen the photographs—but *he* might have been one of them. "I remember," he said, "when conduc-

tors on streetcars wore pistols and had police powers."
And he remembered a great deal more. He remembered,
for example, hearing Booker T. Washington speak, and
the day-to-day progress of the Scottsboro case, and the
rise and bloody fall of Bessie Smith. These had been
books and headlines and music for me but it now developed that they were also a part of my identity.

"You're just one generation away from the South, you
know. You'll find," he added, kindly, "that people will
be willing to talk to you . . . if they don't feel that you
look down on them just because you're from the North."

The first Negro I encountered, an educator, didn't
give me any opportunity to look down. He forced me to
admit, at once, that I had never been to college; that
Northern Negroes lived herded together, like pigs in a
pen; that the campus on which we met was a tribute
to the industry and determination of Southern Negroes.
"Negroes in the South form a *community*." My humilia-
tion was complete with his discovery that I couldn't even
drive a car. I couldn't ask him anything. He made me
feel so hopeless an example of the general Northern
spinelessness that it would have seemed a spiteful coun-
terattack to have asked him to discuss the integration
problem which had placed his city in the headlines.

At the same time, I felt that there was nothing which
bothered him more; but perhaps he did not really know
what he thought about it; or thought too many things at
once. His campus risked being very different twenty years
from now. Its special function would be gone—and so
would his position, arrived at with such pain. The new
day a-coming was not for him. I don't think this fact
made him bitter but I think it frightened him and made
him sad; for the future is like heaven—everyone exalts
it but no one wants to go there now. And I imagine that
he shared the attitude, which I was to encounter so often
later, toward the children who were helping to bring this
future about; admiration before the general spectacle
and skepticism before the individual case.

That evening I went to visit G., one of the "integrated" children, a boy of about fifteen. I had already heard something of his first day in school, the peculiar problems his presence caused, and his own extraordinary bearing.

He seemed extraordinary at first mainly by his silence. He was tall for his age and, typically, seemed to be constructed mainly of sharp angles, such as elbows and knees. Dark gingerbread sort of coloring, with ordinary hair, and a face disquietingly impassive, save for his very dark, very large eyes. I got the impression, each time that he raised them, not so much that they spoke but that they registered volumes; each time he dropped them it was as though he had retired into the library.

We sat in the living room, his mother, younger brother and sister, and I, while G. sat on the sofa, doing his homework. The father was at work and the older sister had not yet come home. The boy had looked up once, as I came in, to say, "Good evening, sir," and then left all the rest to his mother.

Mrs. R. was a very strong-willed woman, handsome, quiet-looking, dressed in black. Nothing, she told me, beyond name-calling, had marked G.'s first day at school; but on the second day she received the last of several threatening phone calls. She was told that if she didn't want her son "cut to ribbons" she had better keep him at home. She heeded this warning to the extent of calling the chief of police.

"He told me to go on and send him. He said he'd be there when the cutting started. So I sent him." Even more remarkably perhaps, G. went.

No one cut him, in fact no one touched him. The students formed a wall between G. and the entrances, saying only enough, apparently, to make their intention clearly understood, watching him, and keeping him outside. (I asked him, "What did you feel when they blocked your way?" G. looked up at me, very briefly, with no expression on his face, and told me, "Nothing, sir.")

At last the principal appeared and took him by the hand and they entered the school, while the children shouted behind them, "Nigger-lover!"

G. was alone all day at school.

"But I thought you already knew some of the kids there," I said. I had been told that he had friends among the white students because of their previous competition in a Soapbox Derby.

"Well, none of them are in his classes," his mother told me—a shade too quickly, as though she did not want to dwell on the idea of G.'s daily isolation.

"We don't have the same schedule," G. said. It was as though he were coming to his mother's rescue. Then, unwillingly, with a kind of interior shrug, "Some of the guys had lunch with me but then the other kids called them names." He went back to his homework.

I began to realize that there were not only a great many things G. would not tell me, there was much that he would never tell his mother.

"But nobody bothers you, anyway?"

"No," he said. "They just—call names. I don't let it bother me."

Nevertheless, the principal frequently escorts him through the halls. One day, when G. was alone, a boy tripped him and knocked him down and G. reported this to the principal. The white boy denied it but a few days later, while G. and the principal were together, he came over and said, "I'm sorry I tripped you; I won't do it again," and they shook hands. But it doesn't seem that this boy has as yet developed into a friend. And it is clear that G. will not allow himself to expect this.

I asked Mrs. R. what had prompted her to have her son reassigned to a previously all-white high school. She sighed, paused; then, sharply, "Well, it's not because I'm so anxious to have him around white people." Then she laughed. "I really don't know how I'd feel if I was to carry a white baby around who was calling me Grandma." G. laughed, too, for the first time. "White people say," the mother went on, "that that's all a Negro wants. I don't think they believe that themselves."

Then we switched from the mysterious question of what white folks believe to the relatively solid ground of what she, herself, knows and fears.

"You see that boy? Well, he's always been a straight-A student. He didn't hardly have to work at it. You see the way he's so quiet now on the sofa, with his books? Well, when he was going to —— High School, he didn't have no homework or if he did, he could get it done in five minutes. Then, there he was, out in the streets, getting into mischief, and all he did all day in school was just keep clowning to make the other boys laugh. He wasn't learning nothing and didn't nobody care if he *never* learned nothing and I could just see what was going to happen to him if he kept on like that."

The boy was very quiet.

"What were you learning in —— High?" I asked him.

"Nothing!" he exploded, with a very un-boyish laugh. I asked him to tell me about it.

"Well, the teacher comes in," he said, "and she gives you something to read and she goes out. She leaves some other student in charge . . ." ("You can just imagine how much reading gets done," Mrs. R. interposed.) "At the end of the period," G. continued, "she comes back and tells you something to read for the next day."

So, having nothing else to do, G. began amusing his classmates and his mother began to be afraid. G. is just about at the age when boys begin dropping out of school. Perhaps they get a girl into trouble; she also drops out; the boy gets work for a time or gets into trouble for a long time. I was told that forty-five girls had left school for the maternity ward the year before. A week or ten days before I arrived in the city eighteen boys from G.'s former high school had been sentenced to the chain gang.

"My boy's a good boy," said Mrs. R., "and I wanted to see him have a chance."

"Don't the teachers care about the students?" I asked. This brought forth more laughter. How could they care? How much could they do if they *did* care? There were too many children, from shaky homes and worn-out parents, in aging, inadequate plants. They could be considered, most of them, as already doomed. Besides, the teachers' jobs were safe. They were responsible only to the principal, an appointed official, whose judgment, apparently, was never questioned by his (white) superiors or confreres.

The principal of G.'s former high school was about seventy-five when he was finally retired and his idea of discipline was to have two boys beat each other—"under his supervision"—with leather belts. This once happened with G., with no other results than that his parents gave the principal a tongue-lashing. It happened with two boys of G.'s acquaintance with the result that, after school, one boy beat the other so badly that he had to be sent to the hospital. The teachers have themselves arrived at a dead end, for in a segregated school system they cannot rise any higher, and the students are aware of this. Both students and teachers soon cease to struggle.

"If a boy can wash a blackboard," a teacher was heard to say, "I'll promote him."

I asked Mrs. R. how other Negroes felt about her having had G. reassigned.

"Well, a lot of them don't like it," she said—though I gathered that they did not say so to her. As school time approached, more and more people asked her, "Are you going to send him?" "Well," she told them, "the man says the door is open and I feel like, yes, I'm going to go on and send him."

Out of a population of some fifty thousand Negroes, there had been only forty-five applications. People had said that they would send their children, had talked about it, had made plans; but, as the time drew near, when the application blanks were actually in their hands, they said, "I don't believe I'll sign this right now. I'll sign it later." Or, "I been thinking about this. I don't believe I'll send him right now."

"Why?" I asked. But to this she couldn't, or wouldn't, give me any answer.

I asked if there had been any reprisals taken against herself or her husband, if she was worried while G. was at school all day. She said that, no, there had been no reprisals, though some white people, under the pretext of giving her good advice, had expressed disapproval of her action. But she herself doesn't have a job and so doesn't risk losing one. Nor, she told me, had anyone said anything to her husband, who, however, by her own proud suggestion, is extremely closemouthed. And it developed later that he was not working at his regular trade but at something else.

As to whether she was worried, "No," she told me; in much the same way that G., when asked about the blockade, had said, "Nothing, sir." In her case it was easier to see what she meant: she hoped for the best and would not allow herself, in the meantime, to lose her head. "I don't feel like nothing's going to happen," she said, soberly. "I *hope* not. But I know if anybody tries to harm me or any one of my children, I'm going to strike back with all my strength. I'm going to strike them in God's name."

G., in the meantime, on the sofa with his books, was preparing himself for the next school day. His face was as impassive as ever and I found myself wondering—again —how he managed to face what must surely have been the worst moment of his day—the morning, when he opened his eyes and realized that it was all to be gone through again. Insults, and incipient violence, teachers, and—exams.

"One among so many," his mother said, "that's kind of rough."

"Do you think you'll make it?" I asked him. "Would you rather go back to —— High?"

"No," he said, "I'll make it. I ain't going back."

"He ain't thinking about going back," said his mother —proudly and sadly. I began to suspect that the boy managed to support the extreme tension of his situation by means of a nearly fanatical concentration on his schoolwork; by holding in the center of his mind the issue on which, when the deal went down, others would be *forced* to judge him. Pride and silence were his weapons. Pride comes naturally, and soon, to a Negro, but even his mother, I felt, was worried about G.'s silence, though she was too wise to break it. For what was all this doing to him really?

"It's hard enough," the boy said later, still in control but with flashing eyes, "to keep quiet and keep walking when they call you nigger. But if anybody ever spits on me, I *know* I'll have to fight."

His mother laughs, laughs to ease them both, then looks at me and says, "I wonder sometimes what makes white folks so mean."

This is a recurring question among Negroes, even among the most "liberated"—which epithet is meant, of course, to describe the writer. The next day, with this question (more elegantly phrased) still beating in my mind, I visited the principal of G.'s new high school. But he didn't look "mean" and he wasn't "mean": he was a thin, young man of about my age, bewildered and in trouble. I asked him how things were working out, what he thought about it, what he thought would happen— in the long run, or the short.

"Well, I've got a job to do," he told me, "and I'm going to do it." He said that there hadn't been any trouble and that he didn't expect any. "Many students, after all, never see G. at all." None of the children have harmed him and the teachers are, apparently, carrying out their rather tall orders, which are to be kind to G. and, at the same time, to treat him like any other student.

I asked him to describe to me the incident, on the second day of school, when G.'s entrance had been blocked

by the students. He told me that it was nothing at all—
"It was a gesture more than anything else." He had simply walked out and spoken to the students and brought
G. inside. "I've seen them do the same thing to other
kids when they were kidding," he said. I imagine that
he would like to be able to place this incident in the same
cheerful if rowdy category, despite the shouts (which he
does not mention) of "nigger-lover!"

Which epithet does not, in any case, describe him at
all.

"Why," I asked, "is G. the only Negro student here?"
According to this city's pupil-assignment plan, a plan designed to allow the least possible integration over the
longest possible period of time, G. was the only Negro
student who qualified.

"And, anyway," he said, "I don't think it's right for
colored children to come to white schools just *because*
they're white."

"Well," I began, "even if you don't like it . . ."

"Oh," he said quickly, raising his head and looking at
me sideways, "I never said I didn't like it."

And then he explained to me, with difficulty, that it
was simply contrary to everything he'd ever seen or believed. He'd never dreamed of a mingling of the races;
had never lived that way himself and didn't suppose that
he ever would; in the same way, he added, perhaps a
trifle defensively, that he only associated with a certain
stratum of white people. But, "I've never seen a colored
person toward whom I had any hatred or ill-will."

His eyes searched mine as he said this and I knew that
he was wondering if I believed him.

I certainly did believe him; he impressed me as being
a very gentle and honorable man. But I could not avoid
wondering if he had ever really *looked* at a Negro and
wondered about the life, the aspirations, the universal
humanity hidden behind the dark skin. As I wondered,
when he told me that race relations in his city were "excellent" and had not been strained by recent develop-

ments, how on earth he managed to hold on to this delusion.

I later got back to my interrupted question, which I phrased more tactfully.

"Even though it's very difficult for all concerned—this situation—doesn't it occur to you that the reason colored children wish to come to white schools isn't because they want to be with white people but simply because they want a better education?"

"Oh, I don't know," he replied, "it seems to me that colored schools are just as good as white schools." I wanted to ask him on what evidence he had arrived at this conclusion and also how they could possibly be "as good" in view of the kind of life they came out of, and perpetuated, and the dim prospects faced by all but the most exceptional or ruthless Negro students. But I only suggested that G. and his family, who certainly should have known, so thoroughly disagreed with him that they had been willing to risk G.'s present well-being and his future psychological and mental health in order to bring about a change in his environment. Nor did I mention the lack of enthusiasm evinced by G.'s mother when musing on the prospect of a fair grandchild. There seemed no point in making this man any more a victim of his heritage than he so gallantly was already.

"Still," I said at last, after a rather painful pause, "I should think that the trouble in this situation is that it's very hard for *you* to face a child and treat him unjustly because of something for which he is no more responsible than—than *you* are."

The eyes came to life then, or a veil fell, and I found myself staring at a man in anguish. The eyes were full of pain and bewilderment and he nodded his head. This was the impossibility which he faced every day. And I imagined that his tribe would increase, in sudden leaps and bounds was already increasing.

For segregation has worked brilliantly in the South,

and, in fact, in the nation, to this extent: it has allowed white people, with scarcely any pangs of conscience whatever, to *create*, in every generation, only the Negro they wished to see. As the walls come down they will be forced to take another, harder look at the shiftless and the menial and will be forced into a wonder concerning them which cannot fail to be agonizing. It is not an easy thing to be forced to reexamine a way of life and to speculate, in a personal way, on the general injustice.

"What do you think," I asked him, "will happen? What do you think the future holds?"

He gave a strained laugh and said he didn't know. "I don't want to think about it." Then, "I'm a religious man," he said, "and I believe the Creator will always help us find a way to solve our problems. If a man loses that, he's lost everything he had." I agreed, struck by the look in his eyes.

"You're from the North?" he asked me, abruptly.

"Yes," I said.

"Well," he said, "you've got your troubles too."

"Ah, yes, we certainly do," I admitted, and shook hands and left him. I did not say what I was thinking, that our troubles were the same trouble and that, unless we were very swift and honest, what is happening in the South today will be happening in the North tomorrow.

6. NOBODY KNOWS MY NAME:

A Letter from the South

I walked down the street, didn't have on no hat,
Asking everybody I meet,
Where's my man at?

—Ma Rainey

Negroes in the North are right when they refer to the South as the Old Country. A Negro born in the North who finds himself in the South is in a position similar to that of the son of the Italian emigrant who finds himself in Italy, near the village where his father first saw the light of day. Both are in countries they have never seen, but which they cannot fail to recognize. The landscape has always been familiar; the speech is archaic, but it rings a bell; and so do the ways of the people, though their ways are not his ways. Everywhere he turns, the revenant finds himself reflected. He sees himself as he was before he was born, perhaps; or as the man he would have become, had he actually been born in this place. He sees the world, from an angle odd indeed, in which his fathers awaited his arrival, perhaps in the very house in which he narrowly avoided being born. He sees, in effect, his ancestors, who, in everything they do and are, proclaim his inescapable identity. And the Northern Negro in the South sees, whatever he or anyone else may wish to believe, that his ancestors are both white and black. The white men, flesh of his flesh, hate him for that very reason. On the other hand, there is scarcely any way for him to join the black community in the South: for both he and this community are in the grip of the immense illusion that their state is more miserable than his own.

This illusion owes everything to the great American illusion that our state is a state to be envied by other people: we are powerful, and we are rich. But our power makes us uncomfortable and we handle it very ineptly. The principal effect of our material well-being has been to set the children's teeth on edge. If we ourselves were not so fond of this illusion, we might understand ourselves and other peoples better than we do, and be enabled to help them understand us. I am very often tempted to believe that this illusion is all that is left of the great dream that was to have become America; whether this is so or not, this illusion certainly prevents us from making America what we say we want it to be.

But let us put aside, for the moment, these subversive speculations. In the fall of last year, my plane hovered over the rust-red earth of Georgia. I was past thirty, and I had never seen this land before. I pressed my face against the window, watching the earth come closer; soon we were just above the tops of trees. I could not suppress the thought that this earth had acquired its color from the blood that had dripped down from these trees. My mind was filled with the image of a black man, younger than I, perhaps, or my own age, hanging from a tree, while white men watched him and cut his sex from him with a knife.

My father must have seen such sights—he was very old when he died—or heard of them, or had this danger touch him. The Negro poet I talked to in Washington, much younger than my father, perhaps twenty years older than myself, remembered such things very vividly, had a long tale to tell, and counseled me to think back on those days as a means of steadying the soul. I was to remember that time, whatever else it had failed to do, nevertheless had passed, that the situation, whether or not it was better, was certainly no longer the same. I was to remember that Southern Negroes had endured things I could not imagine; but this did not really place me at such a great disadvantage, since they clearly had been unable to imagine what awaited them in Harlem. I remembered the Scottsboro case, which I had followed as a child. I remembered Angelo Herndon and wondered, again, whatever had become of him. I remembered the soldier in uniform blinded by an enraged white man, just after the Second World War. There had been many such incidents after the First War, which was one of the reasons I had been born in Harlem. I remembered Willie McGhee, Emmett Till, and the others. My younger brothers had visited Atlanta some years before. I remembered what they had told me about it. One of my brothers, in uniform, had had his front teeth kicked out by a white officer. I remembered my mother telling us how she had wept and prayed and tried to kiss the venom out of her suicidally embittered son. (She managed to do it, too; heaven only knows what she herself was feeling, whose father and brothers had lived and died down here.) I remembered myself as a very small boy, already so bitter about the pledge of allegiance that I could scarcely bring myself to say it, and never, never believed it.

I was, in short, but one generation removed from the South, which was now undergoing a new convulsion over whether black children had the same rights, or capacities, for education as did the children of white people. This is a criminally frivolous dispute, absolutely unworthy of this nation; and it is being carried on, in complete bad faith, by completely uneducated people. (We do not trust educated people and rarely, alas, produce them, for we do not trust the independence of mind which alone makes a genuine education possible.) Educated people, of any color, are so extremely rare that it is unquestionably one of the first tasks of a nation to open all of its schools to all of its citizens. But the dispute has actually nothing to do with education, as some among the eminently uneducated know. It has to do with

political power and it has to do with sex. And this is a
nation which, most unluckily, knows very little about
either.

The city of Atlanta, according to my notes, is "big,
wholly segregated, sprawling; population variously given
as six hundred thousand or one million, depending on
whether one goes beyond or remains within the city limits. Negroes 25 to 30 per cent of the population. Racial
relations, on the record, can be described as fair, considering that this is the state of Georgia. Growing industrial
town. Racial relations manipulated by the mayor and a
fairly strong Negro middle class. This works mainly in
the areas of compromise and concession and has very
little effect on the bulk of the Negro population and none
whatever on the rest of the state. No integration, pending or actual." Also, it seemed to me that the Negroes in
Atlanta were "very vividly *city* Negroes"—they seemed
less patient than their rural brethren, more dangerous,
or at least more unpredictable. And: "Have seen one
wealthy Negro section, very pretty, but with an unpaved
road. . . . The section in which I am living is composed
of frame houses in various stages of disrepair and neglect,
in which two and three families live, often sharing a
single toilet. This is the other side of the tracks; literally,
I mean. It is located, as I am told is the case in many
Southern cities, just beyond the underpass." Atlanta
contains a high proportion of Negroes who own their
own homes and exist, visibly anyway, independently of
the white world. Southern towns distrust this class and
do everything in their power to prevent its appearance.
But it is a class which has a certain usefulness in Southern cities. There is an incipient war, in fact, between
Southern cities and Southern towns—between the city,
that is, and the state—which we will discuss later. Little
Rock is an ominous example of this and it is likely—indeed, it is certain—that we will see many more such examples before the present crisis is over.

Before arriving in Atlanta I had spent several days in

Charlotte, North Carolina. This is a bourgeois town, Pres-
byterian, pretty—if you like towns—and socially so her-
metic that it contains scarcely a single decent restaurant.
I was told that Negroes there are not even licensed to
become electricians or plumbers. I was also told, several
times, by white people, that "race relations" there were
excellent. I failed to find a single Negro who agreed with
this, which is the usual story of "race relations" in this
country. Charlotte, a town of 165,000, was in a ferment
when I was there because, of its 50,000 Negroes, four
had been assigned to previously all-white schools, one to
each school. In fact, by the time I got there, there were
only three. Dorothy Counts, the daughter of a Presbyter-
ian minister, after several days of being stoned and spat
on by the mob—"spit," a woman told me, "was hanging
from the hem of Dorothy's dress"—had withdrawn from
Harding High. Several white students, I was told, had
called—not called *on*—Miss Counts, to beg her to stick
it out. Harry Golden, editor of *The Carolina Israelite*,
suggested that the "hoodlum element" might not so have
shamed the town and the nation if several of the town's
leading businessmen had personally escorted Miss
Counts to school.

I saw the Negro schools in Charlotte, saw, on street
corners, several of their alumnae, and read about others
who had been sentenced to the chain gang. This solved
the mystery of just what made Negro parents send their
children out to face mobs. White people do not understand this because they do not know, and do not want to
know, that the alternative to this ordeal is nothing less
than a lifelong ordeal. Those Negro parents who spend
their days trembling for their children and the rest of
their time praying that their children have not been too
badly damaged inside, are not doing this out of "ideals"
or "convictions" or because they are in the grip of a perverse desire to send their children where "they are not
wanted." They are doing it because they want the child
to receive the education which will allow him to defeat,

possibly escape, and not impossibly help one day abolish the stifling environment in which they see, daily, so many children perish.

This is certainly not the purpose, still less the effect, of most Negro schools. It is hard enough, God knows, under the best of circumstances, to get an education in this country. White children are graduated yearly who can neither read, write, nor think, and who are in a state of the most abysmal ignorance concerning the world around them. But at least they are white. They are under the illusion—which, since they are so badly educated, sometimes has a fatal tenacity—that they can do whatever they want to do. Perhaps that is exactly what they *are* doing, in which case we had best all go down in prayer.

The level of Negro education, obviously, is even lower than the general level. The general level is low because, as I have said, Americans have so little respect for genuine intellectual effort. The Negro level is low because the education of Negroes occurs in, and is designed to perpetuate, a segregated society. This, in the first place, and no matter how much money the South boasts of spending on Negro schools, is utterly demoralizing. It creates a situation in which the Negro teacher is soon as powerless as his students. (There are exceptions among the teachers as there are among the students, but, in this country surely, schools have not been built for the exceptional. And, though white people often seem to expect Negroes to produce nothing but exceptions, the fact is that Negroes are really just like everybody else. Some of them are exceptional and most of them are not.)

The teachers are answerable to the Negro principal, whose power over the teachers is absolute but whose power with the school board is slight. As for this principal, he has arrived at the summit of his career; rarely indeed can he go any higher. He has his pension to look forward to, and he consoles himself, meanwhile, with his status among the "better class of Negroes." This class in-

cludes few, if any, of his students and by no means all of
his teachers. The teachers, as long as they remain in this
school system, and they certainly do not have much
choice, can only aspire to become the principal one day.
Since not all of them will make it, a great deal of the
energy which ought to go into their vocation goes into
the usual bitter, purposeless rivalry. They are underpaid
and ill treated by the white world and rubbed raw by it
every day; and it is altogether understandable that they,
very shortly, cannot bear the sight of their students. The
children know this; it is hard to fool young people. They
also know why they are going to an overcrowded, out-
moded plant, in classes so large that even the most strict-
ly attentive student, the most gifted teacher cannot but
feel himself slowly drowning in the sea of general helplessness.

It is not to be wondered at, therefore, that the violent
distractions of puberty, occurring in such a cage, annu-
ally take their toll, sending female children into the maternity wards and male children into the streets. It is not
to be wondered at that a boy, one day, decides that if all
this studying is going to prepare him only to be a porter
or an elevator boy—or his teacher—well, then, the hell
with it. And there they go, with an overwhelming bitterness which they will dissemble all their lives, an unceasing effort which completes their ruin. They become the
menial or the criminal or the shiftless, the Negroes
whom segregation has produced and whom the South
uses to prove that segregation is right.

In Charlotte, too, I received some notion of what the
South means by "time to adjust." The NAACP there had
been trying for six years before Black Monday to make
the city fathers honor the "separate but equal" statute
and do something about the situation in Negro schools.
Nothing whatever was done. After Black Monday, Charlotte begged for "time": and what she did with this time
was work out legal stratagems designed to get the least
possible integration over the longest possible period. In

August of 1955, Governor Hodges, a moderate, went on
the air with the suggestion that Negroes segregate themselves voluntarily—for the good, as he put it, of both
races. Negroes seemed to be unmoved by this moderate
proposal, the Klan reappeared in the counties and was
still active there when I left. So, no doubt, are the boys
on the chain gang.

But "Charlotte," I was told, "is not the South." I was
told, "You haven't seen the South yet." Charlotte seemed
quite Southern enough for me, but, in fact, the people in
Charlotte were right. One of the reasons for this is that
the South is not the monolithic structure which, from the
North, it appears to be, but a most various and divided
region. It clings to the myth of its past but it is being
inexorably changed, meanwhile, by an entirely unmythi-
cal present: its habits and its self-interest are at war.
Everyone in the South feels this and this is why there is
such panic on the bottom and such impotence on the
top.

It must also be said that the racial setup in the South
is not, for a Negro, very different from the racial setup
in the North. It is the etiquette which is baffling, not the
spirit. Segregation is unofficial in the North and official
in the South, a crucial difference that does nothing, nevertheless, to alleviate the lot of most Northern Negroes.
But we will return to this question when we discuss the
relationship between the Southern cities and states.

Atlanta, however, *is* the South. It is the South in this
respect, that it has a very bitter interracial history. This
is written in the faces of the people and one feels it in
the air. It was on the outskirts of Atlanta that I first felt
how the Southern landscape—the trees, the silence, the
liquid heat, and the fact that one always seems to be
traveling great distances—seems designed for violence,
seems, almost, to demand it. What passions cannot be
unleashed on a dark road in a Southern night! Everything seems so sensual, so languid, and so private. Desire
can be acted out here; over this fence, behind that tree,

in the darkness, there; and no one will see, no one will ever know. Only the night is watching and the night was made for desire. Protestantism is the wrong religion for people in such climates; America is perhaps the last nation in which such a climate belongs. In the Southern night everything seems possible, the most private, unspeakable longings; but then arrives the Southern day, as hard and brazen as the night was soft and dark. It brings what was done in the dark to light. It must have seemed something like this for those people who made the region what it is today. It must have caused them great pain. Perhaps the master who had coupled with his slave saw his guilt in his wife's pale eyes in the morning. And the wife saw his children in the slave quarters, saw the way his concubine, the sensual-looking black girl, looked at her—a woman, after all, and scarcely less sensual, but white. The youth, nursed and raised by the black Mammy whose arms had then held all that there was of warmth and love and desire, and still confounded by the dreadful taboos set up between himself and her progeny, must have wondered, after his first experiment with black flesh, where, under the blazing heavens, he could hide. And the white man must have seen his guilt written somewhere else, seen it all the time, even if his sin was merely lust, even if his sin lay in nothing but his power: in the eyes of the black man. He may not have stolen his woman, but he had certainly stolen his freedom—this black man, who had a body like his, and passions like his, and a ruder, more erotic beauty. How many times has the Southern day come up to find that black man, sexless, hanging from a tree!

It was an old black man in Atlanta who looked into my eyes and directed me into my first segregated bus. I have spent a long time thinking about that man. I never saw him again. I cannot describe the look which passed between us, as I asked him for directions, but it made me think, at once, of Shakespeare's "the oldest have borne most." It made me think of the blues: *Now, when a woman gets the blues, Lord, she hangs her head and cries. But when a man gets the blues, Lord, he grabs a train and rides.* It was borne in on me, suddenly, just why these men had so often been grabbing freight trains as the evening sun went down. And it was, perhaps, because I was getting on a segregated bus, and wondering how Negroes had borne this and other indignities for so long, that this man so struck me. He seemed to know what I was feeling. His eyes seemed to say that what I was feeling he had been feeling, at much higher pressure, all his life. But my eyes would never see the hell his eyes had seen. And this hell was, simply, that he had never in his life owned anything, not his wife, not his house, not his child, which could not, at any instant, be taken from him by the power of white people. This is what paternalism means. And for the rest of the time that I was in the South I watched the eyes of old black men.

Atlanta's well-to-do Negroes never takes buses, for they all have cars. The section in which they live is quite far away from the poor Negro section. They own, or at least are paying for, their own homes. They drive to work and back, and have cocktails and dinner with each other. They see very little of the white world; but they are cut off from the black world, too.

Now, of course, this last statement is not literally true. The teachers teach Negroes, the lawyers defend them. The ministers preach to them and bury them, and others insure their lives, pull their teeth, and cure their ailments. Some of the lawyers work with the NAACP and help push test cases through the courts. (If anything, by the way, disproves the charge of "extremism" which has so often been made against this organization, it is the fantastic care and patience such legal efforts demand.) Many of the teachers work very hard to bolster the morale of their students and prepare them for their new responsibilities; nor did those I met fool themselves about the hideous system under which they work. So when I

say that they are cut off from the black world, I am not
sneering, which, indeed, I scarcely have any right to do.
I am talking about their position as a class—*if* they are a
class—and their role in a very complex and shaky social
structure.

The wealthier Negroes are, at the moment, very useful
for the administration of the city of Atlanta, for they
represent there the potential, at least, of interracial communication. That this phrase is a euphemism, in Atlanta
as elsewhere, becomes clear when one considers how as-
tonishingly little has been communicated in all these generations. What the phrase almost always has reference to
is the fact that, in a given time and place, the Negro
vote is of sufficient value to force politicians to bargain
for it. What interracial communication also refers to is
that Atlanta is really growing and thriving, and because
it wants to make even more money, it would like to prevent incidents that disturb the peace, discourage invest-
ments, and permit test cases, which the city of Atlanta
would certainly lose, to come to the courts. Once this
happens, as it certainly will one day, the state of Georgia
will be up in arms and the present administration of the
city will be out of power. I did not meet a soul in Atlanta
(I naturally did not meet any members of the White
Citizen's Council, not, anyway, to talk to) who did not
pray that the present mayor would be re-elected. Not
that they loved him particularly, but it is his administration which holds off the holocaust.

Now this places Atlanta's wealthy Negroes in a really
quite sinister position. Though both they and the mayor
are devoted to keeping the peace, their aims and his are
not, and cannot be, the same. Many of those lawyers are
working day and night on test cases which the mayor is
doing his best to keep out of court. The teachers spend
their working day attempting to destroy in their students
—and it is not too much to say, in themselves—those
habits of inferiority which form one of the principal
cornerstones of segregation as it is practiced in the South.

Many of the parents listen to speeches by people like Senator Russell and find themselves unable to sleep at night. They are in the extraordinary position of being compelled to work for the destruction of all they have bought so dearly—their homes, their comfort, the safety of their children. But the safety of their children is merely comparative; it is all that their comparative strength as a class has bought them so far; and they are not safe, really, as long as the bulk of Atlanta's Negroes live in such darkness. On any night, in that other part of town, a policeman may beat up one Negro too many, or some Negro or some white man may simply go berserk. This is all it takes to drive so delicately balanced a city mad. And the island on which these Negroes have built their handsome houses will simply disappear.

This is not at all in the interests of Atlanta, and almost everyone there knows it. Left to itself, the city might grudgingly work out compromises designed to reduce the tension and raise the level of Negro life. But it is not left to itself; it belongs to the state of Georgia. The Negro vote has no power in the state, and the governor of Georgia—that "third-rate man," Atlantans call him—makes great political capital out of keeping the Negroes in their place. When six Negro ministers attempted to create a test case by ignoring the segregation ordinance on the buses, the governor was ready to declare martial law and hold the ministers incommunicado. It was the mayor who prevented this, who somehow squashed all publicity, treated the ministers with every outward sign of respect, and it is his office which is preventing the case from coming into court. And remember that it was the governor of Arkansas, in an insane bid for political power, who created the present crisis in Little Rock—against the will of most of its citizens and against the will of the mayor.

This war between the Southern cities and states is of the utmost importance, not only for the South, but for the nation. The Southern states are still very largely gov-

erned by people whose political lives, insofar, at least, as
they are able to conceive of life or politics, are dependent
on the people in the rural regions. It might, indeed, be
more honorable to try to guide these people out of their
pain and ignorance instead of locking them within it,
and battening on it; but it is, admittedly, a difficult task
to try to tell people the truth and it is clear that most
Southern politicians have no intention of attempting it.
The attitude of these people can only have the effect of
stiffening the already implacable Negro resistance, and
this attitude is absolutely certain, sooner or later, to create great trouble in the cities. When a race riot occurs in
Atlanta, it will not spread merely to Birmingham, for example. (Birmingham is a doomed city.) The trouble will
spread to every metropolitan center in the nation which
has a significant Negro population. And this is not only
because the ties between Northern and Southern Negroes
are still very close. It is because the nation, the entire
nation, has spent a hundred years avoiding the question
of the place of the black man in it.

That this has done terrible things to black men is not
even a question. "Integration," said a very light Negro
to me in Alabama, "has always worked very well in the
South, after the sun goes down." "It's not miscegenation," said another Negro to me, "unless a black man's
involved." Now, I talked to many Southern liberals who
were doing their best to bring integration about in the
South, but met scarcely a single Southerner who did not
weep for the passing of the old order. They were perfectly sincere, too, and, within their limits, they were right.
They pointed out how Negroes and whites in the South
had loved each other, they recounted to me tales of devotion and heroism which the old order had produced,
and which, now, would never come again. But the old
black men I looked at down there—those same black
men that the Southern liberal had loved; for whom, until
now, the Southern liberal—and not only the liberal—
has been willing to undergo great inconvenience and

danger—they were not weeping. Men do not like to be protected, it emasculates them. This is what black men know, it is the reality they have lived with; it is what white men do not want to know. It is not a pretty thing to be a father and be ultimately dependent on the power and kindness of some other man for the well-being of your house.

But what this evasion of the Negro's humanity has done to the nation is not so well known. The really striking thing, for me, in the South was this dreadful paradox, that the black men were stronger than the white. I do not know how they did it, but it certainly has something to do with that as yet unwritten history of the Negro woman. What it comes to, finally, is that the nation has spent a large part of its time and energy looking away from one of the principal facts of its life. This failure to look reality in the face diminishes a nation as it diminishes a person, and it can only be described as unmanly. And in exactly the same way that the South imagines that it "knows" the Negro, the North imagines that it has set him free. Both camps are deluded. Human freedom is a complex, difficult—and private—thing. If we can liken life, for a moment, to a furnace, then freedom is the fire which burns away illusion. Any honest examination of the national life proves how far we are from the standard of human freedom with which we began. The recovery of this standard demands of everyone who loves this country a hard look at himself, for the greatest achievements must begin somewhere, and they always begin with the person. If we are not capable of this examination, we may yet become one of the most distinguished and monumental failures in the history of nations.

7. FAULKNER AND
DESEGREGATION

Any real change implies the breakup of the world as one has always known it, the loss of all that gave one an identity, the end of safety. And at such a moment, unable to see and not daring to imagine what the future will now bring forth, one clings to what one knew, or thought one knew; to what one possessed or dreamed that one possessed. Yet, it is only when a man is able, without bitterness or self-pity, to surrender a dream he has long cherished or a privilege he has long possessed that he is set free—he has set himself free—for higher dreams, for greater privileges. All men have gone through this, go through it, each according to his degree, throughout their lives. It is one of the irreducible facts of life. And remembering this, especially since I am a Negro, affords me almost my only means of understanding what is happening in the minds and hearts of white Southerners today.

For the arguments with which the bulk of relatively articulate white Southerners of good will have met the necessity of desegregation have no value whatever as arguments, being almost entirely and helplessly dishonest, when not, indeed, insane. After more than two hundred years in slavery and ninety years of quasi-freedom, it is hard to think very highly of William Faulkner's advice to "go slow." "They don't mean go slow," Thurgood Marshall is reported to have said, "they mean don't go."

Nor is the squire of Oxford very persuasive when he suggests that white Southerners, left to their own devices, will realize that their own social structure looks silly to the rest of the world and correct it of their own accord. It has looked silly, to use Faulkner's rather strange adjective, for a long time; so far from trying to correct it, Southerners, who seem to be characterized by a species of defiance most perverse when it is most despairing, have clung to it, at incalculable cost to themselves, as the only conceivable and as an absolutely sacrosanct way of life. They have never seriously conceded that their social structure was mad. They have insisted, on the contrary, that everyone who criticized it was mad.

Faulkner goes further. He concedes the madness and moral wrongness of the South but at the same time he raises it to the level of a mystique which makes it somehow unjust to discuss Southern society in the same terms in which one would discuss any other society. "Our position is wrong and untenable," says Faulkner, "but it is not wise to keep an emotional people off balance." This, if it means anything, can only mean that this "emotional people" have been swept "off balance" by the pressure of recent events, that is, the Supreme Court decision outlawing segregation. When the pressure is taken off—and not an instant before—this "emotional people" will presumably find themselves once again on balance and will then be able to free themselves of an "obsolescence in [their] own land" in their own way and, of course, in their own time. The question left begging is what, in their history to date, affords any evidence that they have any desire or capacity to do this. And it is, I suppose, impertinent to ask just what Negroes are supposed to do while the South works out what, in Faulkner's rhetoric, becomes something very closely resembling a high and noble tragedy.

The sad truth is that whatever modifications have been effected in the social structure of the South since the Reconstruction, and any alleviations of the Negro's lot within it, are due to great and incessant pressure, very little of it indeed from within the South. That the North has been guilty of Pharisaism in its dealing with the South does not negate the fact that much of this pressure has come from the North. That some—not nearly as many as Faulkner would like to believe— Southern Negroes prefer, or are afraid of changing, the status quo does not negate the fact that it is the Southern Negro himself who, year upon year, and generation upon generation, has kept the Southern waters troubled. As far as the Negro's life in the South is concerned, the NAACP is the only organization which has struggled, with admirable single-mindedness and skill, to raise him to the level of a citizen. For this reason alone, and quite apart from the individual heroism of many of its Southern members, it cannot be equated, as Faulkner equates it, with the pathological Citizen's Council. One organization is working within the law and the other is working against and outside it. Faulkner's threat to leave the "middle of the road" where he has, presumably, all these years, been working for the benefit of Negroes, reduces itself to a more or less up-to-date version of the Southern threat to secede from the Union.

Faulkner—among so many others!—is so plaintive concerning this "middle of the road" from which "extremist" elements of both races are driving him that it does not seem unfair to ask just what he has been doing there until now. Where is the evidence of the struggle he has been carrying on there on behalf of the Negro? Why, if he and his enlightened confreres in the South have been boring from within to destroy segregation, do they react with such panic when the walls show any signs of falling? Why—and how—does one move from the middle of the road where one was aiding Negroes into the streets—to shoot them?

Now it is easy enough to state flatly that Faulkner's middle of the road does not—cannot—exist and that he is guilty of great emotional and intellectual dishonesty

in pretending that it does. I think this is why he clings to
his fantasy. It is easy enough to accuse him of hypocrisy
when he speaks of man being "indestructible because of
his simple will to freedom." But he is not being hypocritical; he means it. It is only that Man is one thing—a
rather unlucky abstraction in this case—and the Negroes
he has always known, so fatally tied up in his mind with
his grandfather's slaves, are quite another. He is at his
best, and is perfectly sincere, when he declares, in *Harp-
ers*, "To live anywhere in the world today and be against
equality because of race or color is like living in Alaska
and being against snow. We have already got snow. And
as with the Alaskan, merely to live in armistice with it is
not enough. Like the Alaskan, we had better use it." And
though this seems to be flatly opposed to his statement
(in an interview printed in *The Reporter*) that, if it
came to a contest between the federal government and
Mississippi, he would fight for Mississippi, "even if it
meant going out into the streets and shooting Negroes,"
he means that, too. Faulkner means everything he says,
means them all at once, and with very nearly the same
intensity. This is why his statements demand our attention. He has perhaps never before more concretely expressed what it means to be a Southerner.

What seems to define the Southerner, in his own mind
at any rate, is his relationship to the North, that is to the
rest of the Republic, a relationship which can at the very
best be described as uneasy. It is apparently very difficult to be at once a Southerner and an American; so
difficult that many of the South's most independent
minds are forced into the American exile; which is not,
of course, without its aggravating, circular effect on the
interior and public life of the South. A Bostonian, say,
who leaves Boston is not regarded by the citizenry he has
abandoned with the same venomous distrust as is the
Southerner who leaves the South. The citizenry of Boston
do not consider that they have been abandoned, much
less betrayed. It is only the American Southerner who

seems to be fighting, in his own entrails, a peculiar, ghastly, and perpetual war with all the rest of the country. ("Didn't you say," demanded a Southern woman of Robert Penn Warren, "that you was born down here, used to live right near here?" And when he agreed that this was so: "Yes . . . but you never said where you living now!")

The difficulty, perhaps, is that the Southerner clings to two entirely antithetical doctrines, two legends, two histories. Like all other Americans, he must subscribe, and is to some extent controlled by the beliefs and the principles expressed in the Constitution; at the same time, these beliefs and principles seem determined to destroy the South. He is, on the one hand, the proud citizen of a free society and, on the other, is committed to a society which has not yet dared to free itself of the necessity of naked and brutal oppression. He is part of a country which boasts that it has never lost a war; but he is also the representative of a conquered nation. I have not seen a single statement of Faulkner's concerning desegregation which does not inform us that his family has lived in the same part of Mississippi for generations, that his great-grandfather owned slaves, and that his ancestors fought and died in the Civil War. And so compelling is the image of ruin, gallantry and death thus evoked that it demands a positive effort of the imagination to remember that slaveholding Southerners were not the only people who perished in that war. Negroes and Northerners were also blown to bits. American history, as opposed to Southern history, proves that Southerners were not the only slaveholders, Negroes were not even the only slaves. And the segregation which Faulkner sanctifies by references to Shiloh, Chickamauga, and Gettysburg does not extend back that far, is in fact scarcely as old as the century. The "racial condition" which Faulkner will not have changed by "mere force of law or economic threat" was imposed by precisely these means. The Southern tradition, which is, after all, all that Faulkner is talking about, is not a tradition at all: when Faulkner evokes it, he is simply evoking a legend which contains an accusation. And that accusation, stated far more simply than it should be, is that the North, in winning the war, left the South only one means of asserting its identity and that means was the Negro.

"My people owned slaves," says Faulkner, "and the very obligation we have to take care of these people is morally bad." "This problem is . . . far beyond the moral one it is and still was a hundred years ago, in 1860, when many Southerners, including Robert Lee, recognized it as a moral one at the very instant they in turn elected to champion the underdog because that underdog was blood and kin and home." But the North escaped scot-free. For one thing, in freeing the slave, it established a moral superiority over the South which the South has not learned to live with until today; and this despite—or possibly because of—the fact that this moral superiority was bought, after all, rather cheaply. The North was no better prepared than the South, as it turned out, to make citizens of former slaves, but it was able, as the South was not, to wash its hands of the matter. Men who knew that slavery was wrong were forced, nevertheless, to fight to perpetuate it because they were unable to turn against "blood and kin and home." And when blood and kin and home were defeated, they found themselves, more than ever, committed: committed, in effect, to a way of life which was as unjust and crippling as it was inescapable. In sum, the North, by freeing the slaves of their masters, robbed the masters of any possibility of freeing themselves of the slaves.

When Faulkner speaks, then, of the "middle of the road," he is simply speaking of the hope—which was always unrealistic and is now all but smashed—that the white Southerner, with no coercion from the rest of the nation, will lift himself above his ancient, crippling bitterness and refuse to add to his already intolerable burden of blood-guiltiness. But this hope would seem to be absolutely dependent on a social and psychological stasis which simply does not exist. "Things have been getting better," Faulkner tells us, "for a long time. Only six Negroes were killed by whites in Mississippi last year, according to police figures." Faulkner surely knows how little consolation this offers a Negro and he also knows something about "police figures" in the Deep South. And he knows, too, that murder is not the worst thing that can happen to a man, black or white. But murder may be the worst thing a man can do. Faulkner is not trying to save Negroes, who are, in his view, already saved; who, having refused to be destroyed by terror, are far stronger than the terrified white populace; and who have, moreover, fatally, from his point of view, the weight of the federal government behind them. He is trying to save "whatever good remains in those white people." The time he pleads for is the time in which the Southerner will come to terms with himself, will cease fleeing from his conscience, and achieve, in the words of Robert Penn Warren, "moral identity." And he surely believes, with Warren, that "Then in a country where moral identity is hard to come by, the South, because it has had to deal concretely with a moral problem, may offer some leadership. And we need any we can get, if we are to break out of the national rhythm, the rhythm between complacency and panic."

But the time Faulkner asks for does not exist—and he is not the only Southerner who knows it. There is never time in the future in which we will work out our salvation. The challenge is in the moment, the time is always now.

8. IN SEARCH OF A MAJORITY

An Address

I am supposed to speak this evening on the goals of American society as they involve minority rights, but what I am really going to do is to invite you to join me in a series of speculations. Some of them are dangerous, some of them painful, all of them are reckless. It seems to me that before we can begin to speak of minority rights in this country, we've got to make some attempt to isolate or to define the majority.

Presumably the society in which we live is an expression—in some way—of the majority will. But it is not so easy to locate this majority. The moment one attempts to define this majority one is faced with several conundrums. Majority is not an expression of numbers, of numerical strength, for example. You may far outnumber your opposition and not be able to impose your will on them or even to modify the rigor with which they impose their will on you, i.e., the Negroes in South Africa or in some counties, some sections, of the American South. You may have beneath your hand all the apparatus of power, political, military, state, and still be unable to use these things to achieve your ends, which is the problem faced by de Gaulle in Algeria and the problem which faced Eisenhower when, largely because of his own inaction, he was forced to send paratroopers into Little Rock. Again, the most trenchant observers of the scene in the South, those who are embattled there, feel that the

Southern mobs are not an expression of the Southern
majority will. Their impression is that these mobs fill, so
to speak, a moral vacuum and that the people who form
these mobs would be very happy to be released from their
pain, and their ignorance, if someone arrived to show
them the way. I would be inclined to agree with this,
simply from what we know of human nature. It is not
my impression that people wish to become worse; they
really wish to become better but very often do not know
how. Most people assume the position, in a way, of the
Jews in Egypt, who really wished to get to the Promised
Land but were afraid of the rigors of the journey; and,
of course, before you embark on a journey the terrors of
whatever may overtake you on that journey live in the
imagination and paralyze you. It was through Moses, according to legend, that they discovered, by undertaking
this journey, how much they could endure.

These speculations have led me a little bit ahead of
myself. I suppose it can be said that there was a time in
this country when an entity existed which could be called
the majority, let's say a class, for the lack of a better
word, which created the standards by which the country
lived or which created the standards to which the country aspired. I am referring to or have in mind, perhaps
somewhat arbitrarily, the aristocracies of Virginia and
New England. These were mainly of Anglo-Saxon stock
and they created what Henry James was to refer to, not
very much later, as our Anglo-American heritage, or
Anglo-American connections. Now at no time did these
men ever form anything resembling a popular majority.
Their importance was that they kept alive and they bore
witness to two elements of a man's life which are not
greatly respected among us now: (1) the social forms,
called manners, which prevent us from rubbing too abra-
sively against one another and (2) the interior life, or
the life of the mind. These things were important; these
things were realities for them and no matter how rough-
hewn or dark the country was then, it is important to re-

member that this was also the time when people sat up in log cabins studying very hard by lamplight or candle-light. That they were better educated than we are now can be proved by comparing the political speeches of that time with those of our own day.

Now, what I have been trying to suggest in all this is that the only useful definition of the word "majority" does not refer to numbers, and it does not refer to power. It refers to influence. Someone said, and said it very ac-curately, that what is honored in a country is cultivated there. If we apply this touchstone to American life we can scarcely fail to arrive at a very grim view of it. But I think we have to look grim facts in the face because if we don't, we can never hope to change them.

These vanished aristocracies, these vanished standard bearers, had several limitations, and not the least of these limitations was the fact that their standards were essen-tially nostalgic. They referred to a past condition; they referred to the achievements, the laborious achievements, of a stratified society; and what was evolving in America had nothing to do with the past. So inevitably what hap-pened, putting it far too simply, was that the old forms gave way before the European tidal wave, gave way be-fore the rush of Italians, Greeks, Spaniards, Irishmen, Poles, Persians, Norwegians, Swedes, Danes, wandering Jews from every nation under heaven, Turks, Armenians, Lithuanians, Japanese, Chinese, and Indians. Everybody was here suddenly in the melting pot, as we like to say, but without any intention of being melted. They were here because they had wanted to leave wherever they had been and they were here to make their lives, and achieve their futures, and to establish a new identity. I doubt if history has ever seen such a spectacle, such a conglomeration of hopes, fears, and desires. I suggest, al-so, that they presented a problem for the Puritan God, who had never heard of them and of whom they had never heard. Almost always as they arrived, they took their places as a minority, a minority because their influence was so slight and because it was their necessity to make themselves over in the image of their new and unformed country. There were no longer any universally accepted forms or standards, and since all the roads to the achievement of an identity had vanished, the problem of status in American life became and it remains today acute. In a way, status became a kind of substitute for identity, and because money and the things money can buy is the universally accepted symbol here of status, we are often condemned as materialists. In fact, we are much closer to being metaphysical because nobody has ever expected from things the miracles that we expect.

Now I think it will be taken for granted that the Irish, the Swedes, the Danes, etc., who came here can no longer be considered in any serious way as minorities; and the question of anti-Semitism presents too many special features to be profitably discussed here tonight. The American minorities can be placed on a kind of color wheel. For example, when we think of the American boy, we don't usually think of a Spanish, Turkish, a Greek, or a Mexican type, still less of an Oriental type. We usually think of someone who is kind of a cross between the Teuton and the Celt, and I think it is interesting to consider what this image suggests. Outrageous as this image is, in most cases, it is the national self-image. It is an image which suggests hard work and good clean fun and chastity and piety and success. It leaves out of account, of course, most of the people in the country, and most of the facts of life, and there is not much point in discussing those virtues it suggests, which are mainly honored in the breach. The point is that it has almost nothing to do with what or who an American really is. It has nothing to do with what life is. Beneath this bland, this conqueror image, a great many unadmitted despairs and confusions, and anguish and unadmitted crimes and failures hide. To speak in my own person, as a member of the nation's most oppressed minority, the oldest oppressed minority, I want to suggest most seriously that before we can do very much in the way of clear thinking or clear doing as relates in the minorities in this country, we must first crack the American image and find out and deal with what it hides. We cannot discuss the state of our minorities until we first have some sense of what we are, who we are, what our goals are, and what we take life to be. The question is not what we can do now for the hypothetical Mexican, the hypothetical Negro. The question is what we really want out of life, for ourselves, what we think is real.

Now I think there is a very good reason why the Negro in this country has been treated for such a long time in such a cruel way, and some of the reasons are economic and some of them are political. We have discussed these reasons without ever coming to any kind of resolution for a very long time. Some of them are social, and these reasons are somewhat more important because they have to do with our social panic, with our fear of losing status. This really amounts sometimes to a kind of social paranoia. One cannot afford to lose status on this peculiar ladder, for the prevailing notion of American life seems to involve a kind of rung-by-rung ascension to some hideously desirable state. If this is one's concept of life, obviously one cannot afford to slip back one rung. When one slips, one slips back not a rung but back into chaos and no longer knows who he is. And this reason, this fear, suggests to me one of the real reasons for the status of the Negro in this country. In a way, the Negro tells us where the bottom is: *because he is there,* and *where* he is, beneath us, we know where the limits are and how far we must not fall. We must not fall beneath him. We must never allow ourselves to fall that low, and I am not trying to be cynical or sardonic. I think if one examines the myths which have proliferated in this country concerning the Negro, one discovers beneath these myths a kind of sleeping terror of some condition which we refuse to imagine. In a way, if the Negro were not here, we might be forced to deal within ourselves and our own personalities, with all those vices, all those conundrums, and all those mysteries with which we have invested the Negro race. Uncle Tom is, for example, if he is called uncle, a kind of saint. He is there, he endures, he will forgive us, and this is a key to that image. But if he is not uncle, if he is merely Tom, he is a danger to everybody. He will wreak havoc on the countryside. When he is Uncle Tom he has no sex—when he is Tom, he does—and this obviously says much more about the people who invented this myth than it does about the people who are the object of it.

If you have been watching television lately, I think this is unendurably clear in the faces of those screaming people in the South, who are quite incapable of telling you what it is they are afraid of. They do not really know what it is they are afraid of, but they know they are afraid of something, and they are so frightened that they are nearly out of their minds. And this same fear obtains on one level or another, to varying degrees, throughout the entire country. We would never, never allow Negroes to starve, to grow bitter, and to die in ghettos all over the country if we were not driven by some nameless fear that has nothing to do with Negroes. We would never victimize, as we do, children whose only crime is color and keep them, as we put it, in their place. We wouldn't drive Negroes mad as we do by accepting them in ball parks, and on concert stages, but not in our homes and not in our neighborhoods, and not in our churches. It is only too clear that even with the most malevolent will in the world Negroes can never manage to achieve one-tenth of the harm which we fear. No, it has everything to do with ourselves and this is one of the reasons that for all these generations we have disguised this problem in the most incredible jargon. One of the reasons we are so fond of sociological reports and research and investigational committees is because they hide something. As long as we can deal with the Negro as a kind of statistic, as something to be manipulated, something to be fled from, or something to be given something to, there is something we can avoid, and what we can avoid is what he really, really means to us. The question that still ends these discussions is an extraordinary question: Would you let your sister marry one? The question, by the way, depends on several extraordinary assumptions. First of all it assumes, if I may say so, that I *want* to marry your sister and it also assumes that if I asked your sister to marry me, she would immediately say yes. There is no reason to make either of these assumptions, which are clearly irrational, and the key to why these assumptions are held is not to be found by asking Negroes. The key to why these assumptions are held has something to do with some insecurity in the people who hold them. It is only, after all, too clear that everyone born is going to have a rather difficult time getting through his life. It is only too clear that people fall in love according to some principle that we have not as yet been able to define, to discover or to isolate, and that marriage depends entirely on the two people involved; so that this objection does not hold water. It certainly is not justification for segregated schools or for ghettos or for mobs. I suggest that the role of the Negro in American life has something to do with our concept of what God is, and from my point of view, this concept is not big enough. It has got to be made much bigger than it is because God is, after all, not anybody's toy. To be with God is really to be involved with some enormous, overwhelming desire, and joy, and power which you cannot control, which controls you. I conceive of my own life as a journey toward something I do not understand, which in the going toward, makes me better. I conceive of God, in fact, as a means of liberation and not a means to control others. Love does not begin and end the way we seem to think it does. Love is a battle, love is a war; love is a growing up. No one in the world—in the entire world—knows more— knows Americans better or, odd as this may sound, loves them more than the American Negro. This is because he

has had to watch you, outwit you, deal with you, and
bear you, and sometimes even bleed and die with you,
ever since we got here, that is, since both of us, black
and white, got here—and this is a wedding. Whether I
like it or not, or whether you like it or not, we are bound
together forever. We are part of each other. What is happening to every Negro in the country at any time is also
happening to you. There is no way around this. I am
suggesting that these walls—these artificial walls—which
have been up so long to protect us from something we
fear, must come down. I think that what we really have
to do is to create a country in which there are no minorities—for the first time in the history of the world. The
one thing that all Americans have in common is that
they have no other identity apart from the identity which
is being achieved on this continent. This is not the English necessity, or the Chinese necessity, or the French
necessity, but they are born into a framework which al-
lows them their identity. The necessity of Americans to
achieve an identity is a historical and a present personal
fact and this is the connection between you and me.

This brings me back, in a way, to where I started. I
said that we couldn't talk about minorities until we had
talked about majorities, and I also said that majorities
had nothing to do with numbers or with power, but with
influence, with moral influence, and I want to suggest
this: that the majority for which everyone is seeking
which must reassess and release us from our past and
deal with the present and create standards worthy of
what a man may be—this majority is you. No one else
can do it. The world is before you and you need not take
it or leave it as it was when you came in.

PART TWO

. . . WITH
EVERYTHING
ON MY MIND

9. NOTES FOR A
HYPOTHETICAL NOVEL

AN ADDRESS

We've been talking about writing for the last two days, which is a very reckless thing to do, so that I shall be absolutely reckless tonight and pretend that I'm writing a novel in your presence. I'm going to ramble on a little tonight about my own past, not as though it were my own past exactly, but as a subject for fiction. I'm doing this in a kind of halting attempt to relate the terms of my experience to yours; and to find out what specific principle, if any, unites us in spite of all the obvious disparities, some of which are superficial and some of which are profound, and most of which are entirely misunderstood. We'll come back to that, in any case, this misunderstanding, I mean, in a minute, but I want to warn you that I'm not pretending to be unbiased. I'm certain that there is something which unites all the Americans in this room, though I can't say what it is. But if I were to meet any one of you in some other country, England, Italy, France, or Spain, it would be at once apparent to everybody else, though it might not be to us, that we had something in common which scarcely any other people, or no other people could really share.

Let's pretend that I want to write a novel concerning the people or some of the people with whom I grew up, and since we are only playing let us pretend it's a very

long novel. I want to follow a group of lives almost
from the time they open their eyes on the world until
some point of resolution, say, marriage, or childbirth, or
death. And I want to impose myself on these people as
little as possible. That means that I do not want to tell
them or the reader what principle their lives illustrate,
or what principle is activating their lives, but by examining their lives I hope to be able to make them convey
to me and to the reader what their lives mean.

Now I know that this is not altogether possible. I
mean that I know that my people are controlled by my
point of view and that by the time I begin the novel I
have some idea of what I want the novel to do, or to say,
or to be. But just the same, whatever my point of view
is and whatever my intentions, because I am an American writer my subject and my material inevitably has to
be a handful of incoherent people in an incoherent
country. And I don't mean incoherent in any light sense,
and later on we'll talk about what I mean when I use
that word.

Well, who are these people who fill my past and seem
to clamor to be expressed? I was born on a very wide
avenue in Harlem, and in those days that part of town
was called The Hollow and now it's called Junkie's Hollow. The time was the 1920's, and as I was coming into
the world there was something going on called The Negro Renaissance; and the most distinguished survivor of
that time is Mr. Langston Hughes. This Negro Renaissance is an elegant term which means that white people
had then discovered that Negroes could act and write as
well as sing and dance and this Renaissance was not destined to last very long. Very shortly there was to be a
depression and the artistic Negro, or the noble savage,
was to give way to the militant or the new Negro; and I
want to point out something in passing which I think is
worth our time to look at, which is this: that the country's image of the Negro, which hasn't very much to do
with the Negro, has never failed to reflect with a kind of

frightening accuracy the state of mind of the country. This was the Jazz Age you will remember. It was the epoch of F. Scott Fitzgerald, Josephine Baker had just gone to France, Mussolini had just come to power in Italy, there was a peculiar man in Germany who was plotting and writing, and the lord knows what Lumumba's mother was thinking. And all of these things and a million more which are now known to the novelist, but not to his people, are to have a terrible effect on their lives.

There's a figure I carry in my mind's eye to this day and I don't know why. He can't really be the first person I remember, but he seems to be, apart from my mother and my father, and this is a man about as old perhaps as I am now who's coming up our street, very drunk, falling-down drunk, and it must have been a Saturday and I was sitting in the window. It must have been winter because I remember he had a black overcoat on—because his overcoat was open—and he's stumbling past one of those high, iron railings with spikes on top, and he falls and he bumps his head against one of these railings, and blood comes down his face, and there are kids behind him and they're tormenting him and laughing at him. And that's all I remember and I don't know why. But I only throw him in to dramatize this fact, that however solemn we writers, or myself, I, may sometimes sound, or how pontifical I may sometimes seem to be, on that level from which any genuine work of the imagination springs, I'm really, and we all are, absolutely helpless and ignorant. But this figure is important because he's going to appear in my novel. He can't be kept out of it. He occupies too large a place in my imagination.

And then, of course, I remember the church people because I was practically born in the church, and I seem to have spent most of the time that I was helpless sitting on someone's lap in the church and being beaten over the head whenever I fell asleep, which was usually. I was frightened of all those brothers and sisters of the

church because they were all powerful, I thought they
were. And I had one ally, my brother, who was a very
undependable ally because sometimes I got beaten for
things he did and sometimes he got beaten for things I
did. But we were united in our hatred for the deacons
and the deaconesses and the shouting sisters and of our
father. And one of the reasons for this is that we were
always hungry and he was always inviting those people
over to the house on Sunday for an enormous banquet
and we sat next to the icebox in the kitchen watching all
those hams, and chickens, and biscuits go down those
righteous bellies, which had no bottom.

Now so far, in this hypothetical sketch of an unwritten
and probably unwritable novel, so good. From what
we've already sketched we can begin to anticipate one of
those long, warm, toasty novels. You know, those novels
in which the novelist is looking back on himself, absolutely infatuated with himself as a child and everything
is in sentimentality. But I think we ought to bring ourselves up short because we don't need another version of
A Tree Grows in Brooklyn and we can do without another version of *The Heart Is a Lonely Hunter*. This hypothetical book is aiming at something more implacable
than that. Because no matter how ridiculous this may
sound, that unseen prisoner in Germany is going to have
an effect on the lives of these people. Two Italians are
going to be executed presently in Boston, there's going to
be something called the Scottsboro case which will give
the Communist party hideous opportunities. In short, the
social realities with which these people, the people I remember, whether they knew it or not, were really con-
tending can't be left out of the novel without falsifying
their experience. And—this is very important—this all
has something to do with the sight of that tormented,
falling down, drunken, bleeding man I mentioned at the
beginning. Who is he and what does he mean?

Well, then I remember, principally I remember, the
boys and girls in the streets. The boys and girls on the

streets, at school, in the church. I remember in the beginning I only knew Negroes except for one Jewish boy, the only white boy in an all-Negro elementary school, a kind of survivor of another day in Harlem, and there was an Italian fruit vendor who lived next door to us who had a son with whom I fought every campaign of the Italian-Ethiopian war. Because, remember that we're projecting a novel, and Harlem is in the course of changing all the time, very soon there won't be any white people there, and this is also going to have some effect on the people in my story.

Well, more people now. There was a boy, a member of our church, and he backslid, which means he achieved a sex life and started smoking cigarettes, and he was therefore rejected from the community in which he had been brought up, because Harlem is also reduced to communities. And I've always believed that one of the reasons he died was because of this rejection. In any case, eighteen months after he was thrown out of the church he was dead of tuberculosis.

And there was a girl, who was a nice girl. She was a niece of one of the deaconesses. In fact, she was my girl. We were very young then, we were going to get married and we were always singing, praying and shouting, and we thought we'd live that way forever. But one day she was picked up in a nightgown on Lenox Avenue screaming and cursing and they carried her away to an institution where she still may be.

And by this time I was a big boy, and there were the friends of my brothers, my younger brothers and sisters. And I had danced to Duke Ellington, but they were dancing to Charlie Parker; and I had learned how to drink gin and whiskey, but they were involved with marijuana and the needle. I will not really insist upon continuing this roster. I have not known many survivors. I know mainly about disaster, but then I want to remind you again of that man I mentioned in the beginning, who haunts the imagination of this novelist. The imagination of a novelist has everything to do with what happens to his material.

Now, we're a little beyond the territory of Betty Smith and Carson McCullers, but we are not quite beyond the territory of James T. Farrell or Richard Wright. Let's go a little bit farther. By and by I left Harlem. I left all those deaconesses, all those sisters, and all those churches, and all those tambourines, and I entered or anyway I encountered the white world. Now this white world which I was just encountering was, just the same, one of the forces that had been controlling me from the time I opened my eyes on the world. For it is important to ask, I think, where did these people I'm talking about come from and where did they get their peculiar school of ethics? What was its origin? What did it mean to them? What did it come out of? What function did it serve and why was it happening here? And why were they living where they were and what was it doing to them? All these things which sociologists think they can find out and haven't managed to do, which no chart can tell us. People are not, though in our age we seem to think so, endlessly manipulable. We think that once one has discovered that thirty thousand, let us say, Negroes, Chinese or Puerto Ricans or whatever have syphilis or don't, or are unemployed or not, that we've discovered something about the Negroes, Chinese or Puerto Ricans. But in fact, this is not so. In fact, we've discovered nothing very useful because people cannot be handled in that way.

Anyway, in the beginning I thought that the white world was very different from the world I was moving out of and I turned out to be entirely wrong. It seemed different. It seemed safer, at least the white people seemed safer. It seemed cleaner, it seemed more polite, and, of course, it seemed much richer from the material point of view. But I didn't meet anyone in that world who didn't suffer from the very same affliction that all the people I had fled from suffered from and that was that they didn't know who they were. They wanted to be something that they were not. And very shortly I didn't know who I was, either. I could not be certain whether I was really rich or really poor, really black or really white, really male or really female, really talented or a fraud, really strong or merely stubborn. In short, I had become an American. I had stepped into, I had walked right into, as I inevitably had to do, the bottomless confusion which is both public and private, of the American republic.

Now we've brought this hypothetical hero to this place, now what are we going to do with him, what does all of this mean, what can we make it mean? What's the thread that unites all these peculiar and disparate lives, whether it's from Idaho to San Francisco, from Idaho to New York, from Boston to Birmingham? Because there is something that unites all of these people and places. What does it mean to be an American? What nerve is pressed in you or me when we hear this word?

Earlier I spoke about the disparities and I said I was going to try and give an example of what I meant. Now the most obvious thing that would seem to divide me from the rest of my countrymen is the fact of color. The fact of color has a relevance objectively and some relevance in some other way, some emotional relevance and not only for the South. I mean that it persists as a problem in American life because it means something, it fulfills something in the American personality. It is here because the Americans in some peculiar way believe or think they need it. Maybe we can find out what it is that this problem fulfills in the American personality, what it corroborates and in what way this peculiar thing, until today, helps Americans to feel safe.

When I spoke about incoherence I said I'd try to tell you what I meant by that word. It's a kind of incoherence that occurs, let us say, when I am frightened, I am absolutely frightened to death, and there's something which is happening or about to happen that I don't want to face, or, let us say, which is an even better example, that I have a friend who has just murdered his mother and put her in the closet and I know it, but we're not going to talk about it. Now this means very shortly since, after all, I know the corpse is in the closet, and he knows I know it, and we're sitting around having a few drinks and trying to be buddy-buddy together, that very shortly, we can't talk about anything because we can't talk about that. No matter what I say I may inadvertently stumble on this corpse. And this incoherence which seems to afflict this country is analogous to that. I mean that in order to have a conversation with someone you have to reveal yourself. In order to have a real relationship with somebody you have got to take the risk of being thought, God forbid, "an oddball." You know, you have to take a chance which in some peculiar way we don't seem willing to take. And this is very serious in that it is not so much a writer's problem, that is to say, I don't want to talk about it from the point of view of a writer's problem, because, after all, you didn't ask me to become a writer, but it seems to me that the situation of the writer in this country is symptomatic and reveals, says something, very terrifying about this country. If I were writing hypothetically about a Frenchman I would have in a way a frame of reference and a point of view and in fact it is easier to write about Frenchmen, comparatively speaking, because they interest me so much less. But to try to deal with the American experience, that is to say to deal with this enormous incoherence, these enormous puddings, this shapeless thing, to try and make an American, well listen to them, and try to put that on a page. The truth about dialogue, for example, or the technical side of it, is that you try and make people say what they would say if they could and then you sort of dress it up to look like speech. That is to say that it's really an absolute height, people don't ever talk the way they talk in novels, but I've got to make you believe they do because I can't possibly do a tape recording.

But to try and find out what Americans mean is almost impossible because there are so many things they do not want to face. And not only the Negro thing which is simply the most obvious and perhaps the simplest example, but on the level of private life which is after all where we have to get to in order to write about anything and also the level we have to get to in order to live, it seems to me that the myth, the illusion, that this is a free country, for example, is disastrous. Let me point out to you that freedom is not something that anybody can be given; freedom is something people take and people are as free as they want to be. One hasn't got to have an enormous military machine in order to be unfree when it's simpler to be asleep, when it's simpler to be apathetic, when it's simpler, in fact, not to want to be free, to think that something else is more important. And I'm not using it in a personal sense. It seems to me that the confusion is revealed, for example, in those dreadful speeches by Eisenhower, those incredible speeches by Nixon, they sound very much, after all, like the jargon of the Beat generation, that is, in terms of clarity. Not a pin to be chosen between them, both levels, that is, the highest level presumably, the administration in Washington, and the lowest level in our national life, the people who are called "beatniks" are both involved in saying that something which is really on their heels does not exist. Jack Kerouac says "Holy, holy" and we say Red China does not exist. But it really does. I'm simply trying to point out that it's the symptom of the same madness.

Now, in some way, somehow, the problem the writer has which is, after all, his problem and perhaps not yours is somehow to unite these things, to find the terms of our connection, without which we will perish. The importance of a writer is continuous; I think it's socially debatable and usually socially not terribly rewarding, but that's not the point; his importance, I think, is that he is here to describe things which other people are too busy to describe. It is a function, let's face it, it's a special function. There is no democracy on this level. It's a very difficult thing to do, it's a very special thing to do and people who do it cannot by that token do many other things. But their importance is, and the importance of writers in this country now is this, that this country is yet to be discovered in any real sense. There is an illusion about America, a myth about America to which we are clinging which has nothing to do with the lives we lead and I don't believe that anybody in this country who has really thought about it or really almost anybody who has been brought up against it—and almost all of us have one way or another—this collision between one's image of oneself and what one actually is is always very painful and there are two things you can do about it, you can meet the collision head-on and try and become what you really are or you can retreat and try to remain what you thought you were, which is a fantasy, in which you will certainly perish. Now, I don't want to keep you any longer. But I'd like to leave you with this, I think we have some idea about reality which is not quite true. Without having anything whatever against Cadillacs, refrigerators or all the paraphernalia of American life, I yet suspect that there is something much more important and much more real which produces the Cadillac, refrigerator, atom bomb, and what produces it, after all, is something which we don't seem to want to look at, and that is the person. A country is only as good—I don't care now about the Constitution and the laws, at the moment let us leave these things aside—a country is only as strong as the people who make it up and the country turns into what the people want it to become. Now, this country is going to be transformed. It will not be transformed by an act of God, but by all of us, by you and me. I don't believe any longer that we can afford to say that it is entirely out of our hands. We made the world we're living in and we have to make it over.

10. THE MALE PRISON

There is something immensely humbling in this last document [*Madeleine* by André Gide] from the hand of a
writer whose elaborately graceful fiction very often impressed me as simply cold, solemn and irritatingly pious,
and whose precise memoirs made me accuse him of the
most exasperating egocentricity. He does not, to be sure,
emerge in *Madeleine* as being less egocentric; but one is
compelled to see this egocentricity as one of the conditions of his life and one of the elements of his pain. Nor
can I claim that reading *Madeleine* has caused me to
reevaluate his fiction (though I care more now for *The
Immoralist* than I did when I read it several years ago);
it has only made me feel that such a reevaluation must
be made. For, whatever Gide's shortcomings may have
been, few writers of our time can equal his devotion to a
very high ideal.

It seems to me now that the two things which contributed most heavily to my dislike of Gide—or, rather, to the
discomfort he caused me to feel—were his Protestantism
and his homosexuality. It was clear to me that he had
not got over his Protestantism and that he had not come
to terms with his nature. (For I believed at one time—
rather oddly, considering the examples by which I was
surrounded, to say nothing of the spectacle I myself presented—that people *did* "get over" their earliest impressions and that "coming to terms" with oneself simply demanded a slightly more protracted stiffening of the will.)
It was his Protestantism, I felt, which made him so pious,

which invested all of his work with the air of an endless
winter, and which made it so difficult for me to care
what happened to any of his people.

And his homosexuality, I felt, was his own affair which
he ought to have kept hidden from us, or, if he needed to
be so explicit, he ought at least to have managed to be a
little more scientific—whatever, in the domain of morals,
that word may mean—less illogical, less romantic. He
ought to have leaned less heavily on the examples of
dead, great men, of vanished cultures, and he ought certainly to have known that the examples provided by
natural history do not go far toward illuminating the
physical, psychological and moral complexities faced by
men. If he were going to talk about homosexuality at all,
he ought, in a word, to have sounded a little less *disturbed*.

This is not the place and I am certainly not the man
to assess the work of André Gide. Moreover, I confess
that a great deal of what I felt concerning his work I
still feel. And that argument, for example, as to whether
or not homosexuality is natural seems to me completely
pointless—pointless because I really do not see what difference the answer makes. It seems clear, in any case, at
least in the world we know, that no matter what ency-
clopedias of physiological and scientific knowledge are
brought to bear the answer never can be Yes. And one
of the reasons for this is that it would rob the normal—
who are simply the many—of their very necessary sense of
security and order, of their sense, perhaps, that the race
is and should be devoted to outwitting oblivion—and will
surely manage to do so.

But there are a great many ways of outwitting oblivion, and to ask whether or not homosexuality is natural
is really like asking whether or not it was natural for
Socrates to swallow hemlock, whether or not it was natural for St. Paul to suffer for the Gospel, whether or not it
was natural for the Germans to send upwards of six million people to an extremely twentieth-century death. It

does not seem to me that nature helps us very much when we need illumination in human affairs. I am certainly convinced that it is one of the greatest impulses of mankind to arrive at something higher than a natural state. How to be natural does not seem to me to be a problem —quite the contrary. The great problem is how to be—in the best sense of that kaleidoscopic word—a man.

This problem was at the heart of all Gide's anguish, and it proved itself, like most real problems, to be insoluble. He died, as it were, with the teeth of this problem still buried in his throat. What one learns from *Madeleine* is what it cost him, in terms of unceasing agony, to live with this problem at all. Of what it cost her, his wife, it is scarcely possible to conjecture. But she was not so much a victim of Gide's sexual nature—homosexuals do not choose women for their victims, nor is the difficulty of becoming a victim so great for a woman that she is compelled to turn to homosexuals for this—as she was a victim of his overwhelming guilt, which connected, it would seem, and most unluckily, with her own guilt and shame.

If this meant, as Gide says, that "the spiritual force of my love [for Madeleine] inhibited all carnal desire," it also meant that some corresponding inhibition in her prevented her from seeking carnal satisfaction elsewhere. And if there is scarcely any suggestion throughout this appalling letter that Gide ever really understood that he had married a woman or that he had any apprehension of what a woman was, neither is there any suggestion that she ever, in any way, insisted on or was able to believe in her womanhood and its right to flower.

Her most definite and also most desperate act is the burning of his letters—and the anguish this cost her, and the fact that in this burning she expressed what surely must have seemed to her life's monumental failure and waste—Gide characteristically (indeed, one may say, necessarily) cannot enter into and cannot understand. "They were my most precious belongings," she tells him, and perhaps he cannot be blamed for protecting himself against the knife of this dreadful conjugal confession. But: "It is the best of me that disappears," he tells us, *"and it will no longer counterbalance the worst."* (Italics mine.) He had entrusted, as it were, to her his purity, that part of him that was not carnal; and it is quite clear that, though he suspected it, he could not face the fact that it was only when her purity ended that her life could begin, that the key to her liberation was in his hands.

But if he had ever turned that key madness and despair would have followed for him, his world would have turned completely dark, the string connecting him to heaven would have been cut. And this is because then he could no longer have loved Madeleine as an ideal, as Emanuele, God-with-us, but would have been compelled to love her as a woman, which he could not have done except physically. And then he would have had to hate her, and at that moment those gates which, as it seemed to him, held him back from utter corruption would have been opened. He loved her as a woman, indeed, only in the sense that no man could have held the place in Gide's dark sky which was held by Madeleine. She was his Heaven who would forgive him for his Hell and help him to endure it. As indeed she was and, in the strangest way possible, did—by allowing him to feel guilty about *her* instead of boys on the *Piazza d'Espagne*—with the result that, in Gide's work, both his Heaven and his Hell suffer from a certain lack of urgency.

Gide's relations with Madeleine place his relations with men in rather a bleak light. Since he clearly could not forgive himself for his anomaly, he must certainly have despised them—which almost certainly explains the fascination felt by Gide and so many of his heroes for countries like North Africa. It is not necessary to despise people who are one's inferiors—whose inferiority, by the way, is amply demonstrated by the fact that they appear to relish, without guilt, their sensuality.

It is possible, as it were, to have one's pleasure without paying for it. But to have one's pleasure without paying for it is precisely the way to find oneself reduced to a search for pleasure which grows steadily more desperate and more grotesque. It does not take long, after all, to discover that sex is only sex, that there are few things on earth more futile or more deadening than a meaningless round of conquests. The really horrible thing about the phenomenon of present-day homosexuality, the horrible thing which lies curled like a worm at the heart of Gide's trouble and his work and the reason that he so clung to Madeleine, is that today's unlucky deviate can only save himself by the most tremendous exertion of all his forces from falling into an underworld in which he never meets either men or women, where it is impossible to have either a lover or a friend, where the possibility of genuine human involvement has altogether ceased. When this possibility has ceased, so has the possibility of growth.

And, again: It is one of the facts of life that there are two sexes, which fact has given the world most of its beauty, cost it not a little of its anguish, and contains the hope and glory of the world. And it is with this fact, which might better perhaps be called a mystery, that every human being born must find some way to live. For, no matter what demons drive them, men cannot live without women and women cannot live without men. And this is what is most clearly conveyed in the agony of Gide's last journal. However little he was able to understand it, or, more important perhaps, take upon himself the responsibility for it, Madeleine kept open for him a kind of door of hope, of possibility, the possibility of entering into communion with another sex. This door, which is the door to life and air and freedom from the tyranny of one's own personality, *must* be kept open, and none feel this more keenly than those on whom the door is perpetually threatening or has already seemed to close.

Gide's dilemma, his wrestling, his peculiar, notable

and extremely valuable failure testify—which should not seem odd—to a powerful masculinity and also to the fact that he found no way to escape the prison of that masculinity. And the fact that he endured this prison with such dignity is precisely what ought to humble us all, living as we do in a time and country where communion between the sexes has become so sorely threatened that we depend more and more on the strident exploitation of externals, as, for example, the breasts of Hollywood glamour girls and the mindless grunting and swaggering of Hollywood he-men.

It is important to remember that the prison in which Gide struggled is not really so unique as it would certainly comfort us to believe, is not very different from the prison inhabited by, say, the heroes of Mickey Spillane. Neither can they get through to women, which is the only reason their muscles, their fists and their tommy guns have acquired such fantastic importance. It is worth observing, too, that when men can no longer love women they also cease to love or respect or trust each other, which makes their isolation complete. Nothing is more dangerous than this isolation, for men will commit any crimes whatever rather than endure it. We ought, for our own sakes, to be humbled by Gide's confession as he was humbled by his pain and make the generous effort to understand that his sorrow was not different from the sorrow of all men born. For, if we do not learn this humility, we may very well be strangled by a most petulant and unmasculine pride.

11. THE NORTHERN PROTESTANT

I already knew that Bergman had just completed one movie, was mixing the sound for it, and was scheduled to begin another almost at once. When I called the Filmstaden, he himself, incredibly enough, came to the phone. He sounded tired but very pleasant, and told me he could see me if I came at once.

The Filmstaden is in a suburb of Stockholm called Rasunda, and is the headquarters of the Svensk Filmindustri, which is one of the oldest movie companies in the world. It was here that Victor Sjöström made those remarkable movies which, eventually (under the name of Victor Seastrom) carried him—briefly—to the arid plains of Hollywood. Here Mauritz Stiller directed *The Legend of Gösta Berling,* after which he and the star thus discovered, Garbo, also took themselves west—a disastrous move for Stiller and not, as it was to turn out, altogether the most fruitful move, artistically anyway, that Garbo could have made. Ingrid Bergman left here in 1939. (She is not related to Ingmar Bergman.) The Svensk Filmindustri is proud of these alumni, but they are prouder of no one, at the moment, than they are of Ingmar Bergman, whose films have placed the Swedish film industry back on the international map. And yet, on the whole, they take a remarkably steady view of the Bergman vogue. They realize that it *is* a vogue, they are bracing themselves for the inevitable reaction, and they hope that Bergman is doing the same. He is neither as great nor as limited as the current hue and cry suggests. But he is one of the very few genuine artists now working in films.

He is also, beyond doubt, the freest. Not for him the necessity of working on a shoestring, with unpaid performers, as has been the case with many of the younger French directors. He is backed by a film company; Swedish film companies usually own their laboratories, studios, rental distribution services, and theaters. If they did not they could scarcely afford to make movies at all, movies being more highly taxed in this tiny country than anywhere else in the world—except Denmark—and 60 per cent of the playing time in these company-owned theaters being taken up by foreign films. Nor can the Swedish film industry possibly support anything resembling the American star system. This is healthy for the performers, who never have to sit idly by for a couple of years, waiting for a fat part, and who are able to develop a range and flexibility rarely permitted even to the most gifted of our stars. And, of course, it's fine for Bergman because he is absolutely free to choose his own performers: if he wishes to work, say, with Geraldine Page, studio pressure will not force him into extracting a performance from Kim Novak. If it were not for this freedom we would almost certainly never have heard of Ingmar Bergman. Most of his twenty-odd movies were not successful when they were made, nor are they today his company's biggest money-makers. (His vogue has changed this somewhat, but, as I say, no one expects this vogue to last.) "He wins the prizes and brings us the prestige," was the comment of one of his co-workers, "but it's So-and-So and So-and-So—" and here he named two very popular Swedish directors—"who can be counted on to bring in the money."

I arrived at the Filmstaden a little early; Bergman was still busy and would be a little late in meeting me, I was told. I was taken into his office to wait for him. I welcomed the opportunity of seeing the office without the man.

It is a very small office, most of it taken up by a desk. The desk is placed smack in front of the window—not that it could have been placed anywhere else; this window looks out on the daylight landscape of Bergman's movies. It was gray and glaring the first day I was there, dry and fiery. Leaves kept falling from the trees, each silent descent bringing a little closer the long, dark, Swedish winter. The forest Bergman's characters are always traversing is outside this window and the ominous carriage from which they have yet to escape is still among the properties. I realized, with a small shock, that the landscape of Bergman's mind was simply the landscape in which he had grown up.

On the desk were papers, folders, a few books, all very neatly arranged. Squeezed between the desk and the wall was a spartan cot; a brown leather jacket and a brown knitted cap were lying on it. The visitor's chair in which I sat was placed at an angle to the door, which proximity, each time that I was there, led to much bumping and scraping and smiling exchanges in Esperanto. On the wall were three photographs of Charlie Chaplin and one of Victor Sjöström.

Eventually, he came in, bareheaded, wearing a sweater, a tall man, economically, intimidatingly lean. He must have been the gawkiest of adolescents, his arms and legs still seeming to be very loosely anchored; something in his good-natured, self-possessed directness suggests that he would also have been among the most belligerently opinionated: by no means an easy man to deal with, in any sense, any relationship whatever, there being about him the evangelical distance of someone possessed by a vision. This extremely dangerous quality—authority—has never failed to incite the hostility of the many. And I got the impression that Bergman was in the habit of saying what he felt because he knew that scarcely anyone was listening.

He suggested tea, partly, I think, to give both of us time to become easier with each other, but also because he really needed a cup of tea before going back to work. We walked out of the office and down the road to the canteen.

I had arrived in Stockholm with what turned out to be the "flu" and I kept coughing and sneezing and wiping my eyes. After a while Bergman began to look at me worriedly and said that I sounded very ill.

I hadn't come there to talk about my health and I tried to change the subject. But I was shortly to learn that any subject changing to be done around Bergman is done by Bergman. He was not to be sidetracked.

"Can I do anything for you?" he persisted; and when I did not answer, being both touched and irritated by his question, he smiled and said, "You haven't to be shy. I know what it is like to be ill and alone in a strange city."

It was a hideously, an inevitably self-conscious gesture and yet it touched and disarmed me. I know that his concern, at bottom, had very little to do with me. It had to do with his memories of himself and it expressed his determination never to be guilty of the world's indifference.

He turned and looked out of the canteen window, at the brilliant October trees and the glaring sky, for a few seconds and then turned back to me.

"Well," he asked me, with a small laugh, "are you for me or against me?"

I did not know how to answer this question right away and he continued, "I don't care if you are or not. Well, that's not true. Naturally, I prefer—I would be happier —if you were *for* me. But I have to know."

I told him I was for him, which might, indeed, turn out to be my principal difficulty in writing about him. I had seen many of his movies—but did not intend to try to see them all—and I felt identified, in some way, with what I felt he was trying to do. What he saw when he looked at the world did not seem very different from what *I* saw. Some of his films seemed rather cold to me, somewhat too deliberate. For example, I had possibly heard too much about *The Seventh Seal* before seeing it, but it had impressed me less than some of the others.

"I cannot discuss that film," he said abruptly, and again turned to look out of the window. "I had to do it. I had to be free of that argument, those questions." He looked at me. "It's the same for you when you write a book? You just do it because you must and then, when you have done it, you are relieved, no?"

He laughed and poured some tea. He had made it sound as though we were two urchins playing a deadly and delightful game which must be kept a secret from our elders.

"Those questions?"

"Oh. God and the Devil. Life and Death. Good and Evil." He smiled. *"Those* questions."

I wanted to suggest that his being a pastor's son contributed not a little to his dark preoccupations. But I did not quite know how to go about digging into his private life. I hoped that we would be able to do it by way of the movies.

I began with: "The question of love seems to occupy you a great deal, too."

I don't doubt that it occupies you, too, was what he seemed to be thinking, but he only said, mildly, "Yes." Then, before I could put it another way, "You may find it a bit hard to talk to me. I really do not see much point in talking about my past work. And I cannot talk about work I haven't done yet."

I mentioned his great preoccupation with egotism, so many of his people being centered on themselves, necessarily, and disastrously: Vogler in *The Magician,* Isak Borg in *Wild Strawberries*, the ballerina in *Summer Interlude*.

"I am very fond of *Summer Interlude*," he said. "It is my favorite movie. "I don't mean," he added, "that it's my best. I don't know which movie is my best."

Summer Interlude was made in 1950. It is probably

not Bergman's best movie—I would give that place to
the movie which has been shown in the States as *The
Naked Night*—but it is certainly among the most moving.
Its strength lies in its portrait of the ballerina, uncannily
precise and truthful, and in its perception of the nature
of first love, which first seems to open the universe to us
and then seems to lock us out of it. It is one of the group
of films—including *The Waiting Women, Smiles of a
Summer Night,* and *Brink of Life*—which have a woman,
or women, at their center and in which the men, generally, are rather shadowy. But all the Bergman themes are
in it: his preoccupation with time and the inevitability
of death, the comedy of human entanglements, the nature of illusion, the nature of egotism, the price of art.
These themes also run through the movies which have at
their center a man: *The Naked Night* (which should
really be called *The Clown's Evening*), *Wild Strawberries,
The Face, The Seventh Seal.* In only one of these movies
—*The Face*—is the male-female relation affirmed from
the male point of view; as being, that is, a source of
strength for the man. In the movies concerned with
women, the male-female relation succeeds only through
the passion, wit, or patience of the woman and depends on
how astutely she is able to manipulate the male conceit.
The Naked Night is the most blackly ambivalent of Bergman's films—and surely one of the most brutally erotic
movies ever made—but it is essentially a study of the
masculine helplessness before the female force. *Wild
Strawberries* is inferior to it, I think, being afflicted with
a verbal and visual rhetoric which is Bergman's most
annoying characteristic. But the terrible assessments that
the old Professor is forced to make in it prove that he is not
merely the victim of his women: he is responsible for what
his women have become.

We soon switched from Bergman's movies to the subject of Stockholm.

"It is not a city at all," he said, with intensity. It is ri-

diculous of it to think of itself as a city. It is simply a
rather larger village, set in the middle of some forests and
some lakes. You wonder what it thinks it is doing there,
looking so important."

I was to encounter in many other people this curious
resistance to the idea that Stockholm could possibly become a city. It certainly seemed to be trying to become a
city as fast as it knew how, which is, indeed, the natural
and inevitable fate of any nation's principal commercial
and cultural clearing house. But for Bergman, who is
forty-one, and for people who are considerably younger,
Stockholm seems always to have had the aspect of a village. They do not look forward to seeing it change. Here,
as in other European towns and cities, people can be
heard bitterly complaining about the "Americanization"
which is taking place.

This "Americanization," so far as I could learn, refers
largely to the fact that more and more people are leaving the countryside and moving into Stockholm. Stockholm is not prepared to receive these people, and the inevitable social tensions result, from housing problems to
juvenile delinquency. Of course, there are juke boxes
grinding out the inevitable rock-and-roll tunes, and
there are, too, a few jazz joints which fail, quite, to remind one of anything in the States. And the ghost—one
is tempted to call it the effigy—of the late James Dean,
complete with uniform, masochistic girl friend, motor-
cycle, or (hideously painted) car, has made its appearance on the streets of Stockholm. These do not frighten
me nearly as much as do the originals in New York, since
they have yet to achieve the authentic American bewilderment or the inimitable American snarl. I ought to
add, perhaps, that the American Negro remains, for
them, a kind of *monstre sacré*, which proves, if anything
does, how little they know of the phenomena which they
feel compelled to imitate. They are unlike their American models in many ways: for example, they are not suf-

fering from a lack of order but from an excess of it. Sexually, they are not drowning in taboos; they are anxious, on the contrary, to establish one or two.

But the people in Stockholm are right to be frightened. It is not Stockholm's becoming a city which frightens them. What frightens them is that the pressures under which everyone in this century lives are destroying the old simplicities. This is almost always what people really mean when they speak of Americanization. It is an epithet which is used to mask the fact that the entire social and moral structure that they have built is proving to be absolutely inadequate to the demands now being placed on it. The old cannot imagine a new one, or create it. The young have no confidence in the old; lacking which, they cannot find any standards in themselves by which to live. The most serious result of such a chaos, though it may not seem to be, is the death of love. I do not mean merely the bankruptcy of the concept of romantic love —it is entirely possible that this concept has had its day —but the breakdown of communication between the sexes.

Bergman talked a little about the early stages of his career. He came to the Filmstaden in 1944, when he wrote the script for *Torment*. This was a very promising beginning. But promising beginnings do not mean much, especially in the movies. Promise, anyway, was never what Bergman lacked. He lacked flexibility. Neither he nor anyone else I talked to suggested that he has since acquired much of this quality; and since he was young and profoundly ambitious and thoroughly untried, he lacked confidence. This lack he disguised by tantrums so violent that they are still talked about at the Filmstaden today. His exasperating allergies extended to such things as refusing to work with a carpenter, say, to whom he had never spoken but whose face he disliked. He has been known, upon finding guests at his home, to hide himself in the bathroom until they left. Many of these people never returned and it is hard, of course, to blame them. Nor was he, at this time in his life, particularly respectful of the feelings of his friends.

"He's improved," said a woman who has been working with him for the last several years, "but he was impossible. He could say the most terrible things, he could make you wish you were dead. Especially if you were a woman."

She reflected. "Then, later, he would come and apologize. One just had to accept it, that's all."

He was referred to in those days, without affection as "the young one" or "the kid" or "the demon director." An American property whose movies, in spite of all this temperament, made no money at the box office, would have suffered, at best, the fate of Orson Welles. But Bergman went on working, as screen writer and director in films and as a director on the stage.

"I was an actor for a while," he says, "a terribly bad actor. But it taught me much."

It probably taught him a great deal about how to handle actors, which is one of his great gifts.

He directed plays for the municipal theaters of Hälsingborg, Göteborg, and Malmö, and is now working—or will be as soon as he completes his present film schedule —for the Royal Dramatic Theatre of Stockholm.

Some of the people I met told me that his work on stage is even more exciting than his work in films. They were the same people, usually, who were most concerned for Bergman's future when his present vogue ends. It was as though they were giving him an ace in the hole.

I did not interrogate Bergman on this point, but his record suggests that he is more attracted to films than to the theater. It would seem, too, that the theater very often operates for him as a kind of prolonged rehearsal or preparation for a film already embryonic in his consciousness. This is almost certainly the case with at least two of his theatrical productions. In 1954, he directed, for the municipal theater of Malmö, Franz Lehár's *The*

Merry Widow. The next year he wrote and directed the elaborate period comedy, *Smiles of a Summer Night,* which beautifully utilizes—for Bergman's rather savage purposes—the atmosphere of romantic light opera. In 1956, he published his play *A Medieval Fresco.* This play was not produced, but it forms the basis for *The Seventh Seal,* which he wrote and directed the same year. It is safe, I think, to assume that the play will now never be produced, at least not by Bergman.

He has had many offers, of course, to work in other countries. I asked him if he had considered taking any of them.

He looked out of the window again. "I am home here," he said. "It took me a long time, but now I have all my instruments—everything—where I want them. I know my crew, my crew knows me, I know my actors."

I watched him. Something in me, inevitably, envied him for being able to love his home so directly and for being able to stay at home and work. And, in another way, rather to my surprise, I envied him not at all. Everything in a life depends on how that life accepts its limits: it would have been like envying him his language.

"If I were a violinist," he said after a while, "and I were invited to play in Paris—well, if the condition was that I could not bring my own violin but would have to play a French one—well, then, I could not go." He made a quick gesture toward the window. "This is my violin."

It was getting late. I had the feeling that I should be leaving, though he had not made any such suggestion. We got around to talking about *The Magician.*

"It doesn't have anything to do with hypnotism, does it?" I asked him.

"No. No, of course not."

"Then it's a joke. A long, elaborate metaphor for the condition of the artist—I mean, any time, anywhere, all the time—"

He laughed in much the same conspiratorial way he had laughed when talking about his reasons for doing

The Seventh Seal. "Well, yes. He is always on the very edge of disaster, he is always on the very edge of great things. Always. Isn't it so? It is his element, like water is the element for the fish."

People had been interrupting us from the moment we sat down, and now someone arrived who clearly intended to take Bergman away with him. We made a date to meet early in the coming week. Bergman stood with me until my cab came and told the driver where I lived. I watched him, tall, bare-headed, and fearfully determined, as he walked away. I thought how there was something in the weird, mad, Northern Protestantism which reminded me of the visions of the black preachers of my childhood.

One of the movies which has made the most profound impression on Bergman is Victor Sjöström's *The Phantom Carriage*. It is based on a novel by Selma Lagerlöf which I have not read—and which, as a novel, I cannot imagine. But it makes great sense as a Northern fable; it has the atmosphere of a tale which has been handed down, for generations, from father to son. The premise of the movie is that whoever dies, in his sins, on New Year's Eve, must drive Death's chariot throughout the coming year. The story that the movie tells is how a sinner—beautifully played by Sjöström himself—outwits Death. He outwits Death by virtue, virtue in the biblical, or, rather, in the New Testament sense: he outwits Death by opposing to this anonymous force his weak and ineradicable humanity.

Now this is, of course, precisely the story that Bergman is telling in *The Seventh Seal*. He has managed to utilize the old framework, the old saga, to speak of our condition in the world today and the way in which this loveless and ominous condition can be transcended. This ancient saga is part of his personal past and one of the keys to the people who produced him.

Since I had been so struck by what seemed to be our similarities, I amused myself, on the ride back into town,

by projecting a movie, which, if I were a moviemaker,
would occupy, among my own productions, the place
The Seventh Seal holds among Bergman's. I did not
have, to hold my films together, the Northern sagas; but I
had the Southern music. From the African tom-toms, to
Congo Square, to New Orleans, to Harlem—and, finally,
all the way to Stockholm, and the European sectors of
African towns. My film would begin with slaves, board-
ing the good ship *Jesus:* a white ship, on a dark sea, with
masters as white as the sails of their ships, and slaves as
black as the ocean. There would be one intransigent
slave, an eternal figure, destined to appear, and to be put
to death in every generation. In the hold of the slave
ship, he would be a witch-doctor or a chief or a prince
or a singer; and he would die, be hurled into the ocean,
for protecting a black woman. Who would bear his child,
however, and this child would lead a slave insurrec-
tion; and be hanged. During the Reconstruction, he
would be murdered upon leaving Congress. He would
be a returning soldier during the first World War, and be
buried alive; and then, during the Depression, he would
become a jazz musician, and go mad. Which would bring
him up to our own day—what would his fate be now?
What would I entitle this grim and vengeful fantasy?
What would be happening, during all this time, to the
descendants of the masters? It did not seem likely, after
all, that I would ever be able to make of my past, on
film, what Bergman had been able to make of his. In
some ways, his past is easier to deal with: it was, at once,
more remote and more present. Perhaps what divided
the black Protestant from the white one was the nature
of my still unwieldy, unaccepted bitterness. My hero,
now, my tragic hero, would probably be a junkie—
which, certainly, in one way, suggested the distance covered by America's dark generations. But it was in only one
way, it was not the whole story; and it then occurred to
me that my bitterness might be turned to good account
if I should dare to envision the tragic hero for whom I

was searching—as myself. All art is a kind of confession, more or less oblique. All artists, if they are to survive, are forced, at last, to tell the whole story, to vomit the anguish up. All of it, the literal and the fanciful. Bergman's authority seemed, then, to come from the fact that he was reconciled to this arduous, delicate, and disciplined self-exposure.

Bergman and his father had not got on well when Bergman was young.

"But how do you get along now?" I had asked him.

"Oh, now," he said, "we get on very well. I go to see him often."

I told him that I envied him. He smiled and said, "Oh, it is always like that—when such a battle is over, fathers and sons can be friends."

I did not say that such a reconciliation had probably a great deal to do with one's attitude toward one's past, and the uses to which one could put it. But I now began to feel, as I saw my hotel glaring up out of the Stockholm gloom, that what was lacking in my movie was the American despair, the search, in our country for authority. The blue-jeaned boys on the Stockholm streets were really imitations, so far; but the streets of my native city were filled with youngsters searching desperately for the limits which would tell them who they were, and create for them a challenge to which they could rise. What would a Bergman make of the American confusion? How would he handle a love story occurring in New York?

12. ALAS, POOR RICHARD

I. EIGHT MEN

Unless a writer is extremely old when he dies, in which case he has probably become a neglected institution, his death must always seem untimely. This is because a real writer is always shifting and changing and searching. The world has many labels for him, of which the most treacherous is the label of Success. But the man behind the label knows defeat far more intimately than he knows triumph. He can never be absolutely certain that he has achieved his intention.

This tension and authority—the authority of the frequently defeated—are in the writer's work, and cause one to feel that, at the moment of his death, he was approaching his greatest achievements. I should think that guilt plays some part in this reaction, as well as a certain unadmitted relief. Guilt, because of our failure in a relationship, because it is extremely difficult to deal with writers as people. Writers are said to be extremely egotistical and demanding, and they are indeed, but that does not distinguish them from anyone else. What distinguishes them is what James once described as a kind of "holy stupidity." The writer's greed is appalling. He wants, or seems to want, everything and practically everybody; in another sense, and at the same time, he needs no one at all; and families, friends, and lovers find this extremely hard to take. While he is alive, his work is fatally entangled with his personal fortunes and misfortunes, his personality, and the social facts and attitudes of his time. The unadmitted relief, then, of which I spoke has to do with a certain drop in the intensity of our bewilderment, for the baffling creator no longer stands between us and his works.

He does not, but many other things do, above all our own preoccupations. In the case of Richard Wright, dead in Paris at fifty-two, the fact that he worked during a bewildering and demoralizing era in Western history makes a proper assessment of his work more difficult. In *Eight Men,* the earliest story, "The Man Who Saw the Flood," takes place in the deep South and was first published in 1937. One of the two previously unpublished stories in the book, "Man, God Ain't Like That," begins in Africa, achieves its hideous resolution in Paris, and brings us, with an ironical and fitting grimness, to the threshold of the 1960's. It is because of this story, which is remarkable, and "Man of All Work," which is a masterpiece, that I cannot avoid feeling that Wright, as he died, was acquiring a new tone, and a less uncertain esthetic distance, and a new depth.

Shortly after we learned of Richard Wright's death, a Negro woman who was rereading *Native Son* told me that it meant more to her now than it had when she had first read it. This, she said, was because the specific social climate which had produced it, or with which it was identified, seemed archaic now, was fading from our memories. Now, there was only the book itself to deal with, for it could no longer be read, as it had been read in 1940, as a militant racial manifesto. Today's racial manifestoes were being written very differently, and in many different languages; what mattered about the book now was how accurately or deeply the life of Chicago's South Side had been conveyed.

I think that my friend may prove to be right. Certainly, the two oldest stories in this book, "The Man Who Was Almost a Man," and "The Man Who Saw the Flood," both Depression stories, both occurring in the South, and both, of course, about Negroes, do not seem dated. Perhaps it is odd, but they did not make me think of the 1930's, or even, particularly, of Negroes. They made me think of human loss and helplessness. There is a dry, savage, folkloric humor in "The Man Who Was Almost a Man." It tells the story of a boy who wants a gun, finally manages to get one, and, by a hideous error, shoots a white man's mule. He then takes to the rails, for he would have needed two years to pay for the mule. There is nothing funny about "The Man Who Saw the Flood," which is as spare and moving an account as that delivered by Bessie Smith in "Backwater Blues."

It is strange to begin to suspect, now, that Richard Wright was never, really, the social and polemical writer he took himself to be. In my own relations with him, I was always exasperated by his notions of society, politics, and history, for they seemed to me utterly fanciful. I never believed that he had any real sense of how a society is put together. It had not occurred to me, and perhaps it had not occurred to him, that his major interests as well as his power lay elsewhere. Or perhaps it *had* occurred to me, for I distrusted his association with the French intellectuals, Sartre, de Beauvoir, and company. I am not being vindictive toward them or condescending toward Richard Wright when I say that it seemed to me that there was very little they could give him which he could use. It has always seemed to me that ideas were somewhat more real to them than people; but anyway, and this is a statement made with the very greatest love and respect, I always sensed in Richard Wright a Mississippi pickaninny, mischievous, cunning, and tough. This always seemed to be at the bottom of everything he said and did, like some fantastic jewel buried in high grass. And it was painful to feel that the people of his adopted country were no more capable of seeing this jewel than were the people of his native land, and were in their own way as intimidated by it.

Even more painful was the suspicion that Wright did

not want to know this. The meaning of Europe for an American Negro was one of the things about which Richard Wright and I disagreed most vehemently. He was fond of referring to Paris as the "city of refuge"—which it certainly was, God knows, for the likes of us. But it was not a city of refuge for the French, still less for anyone belonging to France; and it would not have been a city of refuge for us if we had not been armed with American passports. It did not seem worthwhile to me to have fled the native fantasy only to embrace a foreign one. (Someone, some day, should do a study in depth of the role of the American Negro in the mind and life of Europe, and the extraordinary perils, different from those of America but not less grave, which the American Negro encounters in the Old World.)

But now that the storm of Wright's life is over, and politics is ended forever for him, along with the Negro problem and the fearful conundrum of Africa, it seems to have been the tough and intuitive, the genuine Richard Wright, who was being recorded all along. It now begins to seem, for example, that Wright's unrelentingly bleak landscape was not merely that of the Deep South, or of Chicago, but that of the world, of the human heart. The landscape does not change in any of these stories. Even the most good-natured performance this book contains, good-natured by comparison only, "Big Black Good Man," takes place in Copenhagen in the winter, and in the vastly more chilling confines of a Danish hotel-keeper's fears.

In "Man of All Work," a tight, raging, diamond-hard exercise in irony, a Negro male who cannot find a job dresses himself up in his wife's clothes and hires himself out as a cook. ("Who," he demands of his horrified, bedridden wife, "ever looks at us colored folks anyhow?") He gets the job, and Wright uses this incredible situation to reveal, with beautiful spite and accuracy, the private lives of the master race. The story is told entirely in dialogue, which perfectly accomplishes what it sets out to do, racing along like a locomotive and suggesting far more than it states.

The story, without seeming to, goes very deeply into the demoralization of the Negro male and the resulting fragmentization of the Negro family which occurs when the female is forced to play the male role of breadwinner. It is also a maliciously funny indictment of the sexual terror and hostility of American whites: and the horror of the story is increased by its humor.

"Man, God Ain't Like That," is a fable of an African's discovery of God. It is a far more horrible story than "Man of All Work," but it too manages its effects by a kind of Grand Guignol humor, and it too is an unsparing indictment of the frivolity, egotism, and wrongheadedness of white people—in this case, a French artist and his mistress. It too is told entirely in dialogue and recounts how a French artist traveling through Africa picks up an African servant, uses him as a model, and, in order to shock and titillate his jaded European friends, brings the African back to Paris with him.

Whether or not Wright's vision of the African sensibility will be recognized by Africans, I do not know. But certainly he has managed a frightening and truthful comment on the inexorably mysterious and dangerous relationships between ways of life, which are also ways of thought. This story and "Man of All Work" left me wondering how much richer our extremely poor theater might now be if Wright had chosen to work in it.

But "The Man Who Killed a Shadow" is something else again; it is Wright at the mercy of his subject. His great forte, it now seems to me, was an ability to convey inward states by means of externals: "The Man Who Lived Underground," for example, conveys the spiritual horror of a man and a city by a relentless accumulation of details, and by a series of brief, sharply cut-off tableaus, seen through chinks and cracks and keyholes. The specifically sexual horror faced by a Negro cannot be dealt with in this way. "The Man Who Killed a Shadow" is a story of rape and murder, and neither the murderer nor his victim ever comes alive. The entire story seems to be occurring, somehow, beneath cotton. There are many reasons for this. In most of the novels written by Negroes until today (with the exception of Chester Hime's *If He Hollers Let Him Go*) there is a great space where sex ought to be; and what usually fills this space is violence.

This violence, as in so much of Wright's work, is gratuitous and compulsive. It is one of the severest criticisms than can be leveled against his work. The violence is gratuitous and compulsive because the root of the violence is never examined. The root is rage. It is the rage, almost literally the howl, of a man who is being castrated. I do not think that I am the first person to notice this, but there is probably no greater (or more misleading) body of sexual myths in the world today than those which have proliferated around the figure of the American Negro. This means that he is penalized for the guilty imagination of the white people who invest him with their hates and longings, and is the principal target of their sexual paranoia. Thus, when in Wright's pages a Negro male is found hacking a white woman to death, the very gusto with which this is done, and the great attention paid to the details of physical destruction reveal a terrible attempt to break out of the cage in which the American imagination has imprisoned him for so long.

In the meantime, the man I fought so hard and who meant so much to me, is gone. First America, then Europe, then Africa failed him. He lived long enough to find all of the terms on which he had been born become obsolete; presently, all of his attitudes seemed to be historical. But as his life ended, he seems to me to have been approaching a new beginning. He had survived, as it were, his own obsolescence, and his imagination was beginning to grapple with that darkest of all dark strangers for him, the African. The depth thus touched in him brought him a new power and a new tone. He had survived exile on three continents and lived long enough to begin to tell the tale.

II. THE EXILE

I was far from imagining, when I agreed to write this memoir, that it would prove to be such a painful and difficult task. What, after all, can I really say about Richard . . . ? Everything founders in the sea of what might have been. We might have been friends, for example, but I cannot honestly say that we were. There might have been some way of avoiding our quarrel, our rupture; I can only say that I failed to find it. The quarrel having occurred, perhaps there might have been a way to have become reconciled. I think, in fact, that I counted on this coming about in some mysterious, irrevocable way, the way a child dreams of winning, by means of some dazzling exploit, the love of his parents.

However, he is dead now, and so we never shall be reconciled. The debt I owe him can now never be discharged, at least not in the way I hoped to be able to discharge it. In fact, the saddest thing about our relationship is that my only means of discharging my debt to Richard was to become a writer; and this effort revealed, more and more clearly as the years went on, the deep and irreconcilable differences between our points of view.

This might not have been so serious if I had been older when we met. . . . If I had been, that is, less uncertain of myself, and less monstrously egotistical. But when we met, I was twenty, a carnivorous age; he was then as old as I am now, thirty-six; he had been my idol since high school, and I, as the fledgling Negro writer, was very shortly in the position of his protégé. This position was not really fair to either of us. As writers we were about as unlike as any two writers could possibly be. But no one can read the future, and neither of us knew this then. We were linked together, really, because both of us were black. I had made my pilgrimage to meet him because he was the greatest black writer in the world for me. In *Uncle Tom's Children*, in *Native Son*, and, above all, in *Black Boy*, I found expressed, for the first time in my life, the sorrow, the rage, and the murderous bitterness which was eating up my life and the lives of those around me. His work was an immense liberation and revelation for me. He became my ally and my witness, and alas! my father.

I remember our first meeting very well. It was in Brooklyn; it was winter, I was broke, naturally, shabby, hungry, and scared. He appeared from the depths of what I remember as an extremely long apartment. Now his face, voice, manner, figure are all very sadly familiar to me. But they were a great shock to me then. It is always a shock to meet famous men. There is always an irreducible injustice in the encounter, for the famous man cannot possibly fit the image which one has evolved of him. My own image of Richard was almost certainly based on Canada Lee's terrifying stage portrait of Bigger Thomas. Richard was not like that at all. His voice was light and even rather sweet, with a Southern melody in it; his body was more round than square, more square than tall; and his grin was more boyish than I had expected, and more diffident. He had a trick, when he greeted me, of saying, "Hey, boy!" with a kind of pleased, surprised expression on his face. It was very friendly, and it was also, faintly, mockingly conspiratorial—as though we were two black boys, in league against the world, and had just managed to spirit away several loads of watermelon.

We sat in the living room and Richard brought out a bottle of bourbon and ice and glasses. Ellen Wright was somewhere in the back with the baby, and made only one brief appearance near the end of the evening. I did not drink in those days, did not know how to drink, and I was terrified that the liquor, on my empty stomach, would have the most disastrous consequences. Richard talked to me or, rather, drew me out on the subject of the novel I was working on then. I was so afraid of falling off my chair and so anxious for him to be interested in me, that I told him far more about the novel than I, in fact, knew about it, madly improvising, one jump ahead of the bourbon, on all the themes which cluttered up my mind. I am sure that Richard realized this, for he seemed to be amused by me. But I think he liked me. I know that I liked him, then, and later, and all the time. But I also know that, later on, he did not believe this.

He agreed, that night, to read the sixty or seventy pages I had done on my novel as soon as I could send them to him. I didn't dawdle, naturally, about getting the pages in the mail, and Richard commented very kindly and favorably on them, and his support helped me to win the Eugene F. Saxton Fellowship. He was very proud of me then, and I was puffed up with pleasure that he was proud, and was determined to make him prouder still.

But this was not to be, for, as so often happens, my first real triumph turned out to be the herald of my first real defeat. There is very little point, I think, in regretting anything, and yet I do, nevertheless, rather regret that Richard and I had not become friends by this time, for it might have made a great deal of difference. We might at least have caught a glimpse of the difference between my mind and his; and if we could have argued about it then, our quarrel might not have been so painful later. But we had not become friends mainly, indeed, I suppose, because of this very difference, and also because I really was too young to be his friend and adored him too much and was too afraid of him. And this meant that when my first wintry exposure to the publishing world had resulted in the irreparable ruin—carried out by me—of my first novel, I scarcely knew how to face anyone, let alone Richard. I was too ashamed of myself and I was sure that he was ashamed of me, too. This was utter foolishness on my part, for Richard knew far more about first novels and fledgling novelists than that; but I had been out for his approval. It simply had not occurred to me in those days that anyone *could* approve of me if I had tried for something and failed. The young think that failure is the Siberian end of the line, banishment from all the living, and tend to do what I then did—which was to hide.

I, nevertheless, did see him a few days before he went to Paris in 1946. It was a strange meeting, melancholy in the way a theater is melancholy when the run of the play is ended and the cast and crew are about to be dispersed. All the relationships so laboriously created now no longer exist, seem never to have existed; and the future looks gray and problematical indeed. Richard's apartment—by this time, he lived in the Village, on Charles Street—seemed rather like that, dismantled, everything teetering on the edge of oblivion; people rushing in and out, friends, as I supposed, but alas, most of them were merely admirers; and Richard and I seemed really to be at the end of *our* rope, for he had done what he could for me, and it had not worked out, and now he was going away. It seemed to me that he was sailing into the most splendid of futures, for he was going, of all places! to France, and he had been invited there by the French government. But Richard did not seem, though he was jaunty, to be overjoyed. There was a striking sobriety in his face that day. He talked a great deal about a friend of his, who was in trouble with the U.S. Immigration authorities, and was about to be, or already had been, deported. Richard was not being deported, of course, he was traveling to a foreign country as an honored guest; and he was vain enough and young enough and vivid enough to find this very pleasing and exciting. Yet he knew a great deal about exile, all artists do, especially American artists, especially American Negro art-

ists. He had endured already, liberals and literary critics
to the contrary, a long exile in his own country. He must
have wondered what the real thing would be like. And
he must have wondered, too, what would be the unimag-
inable effect on his daughter, who could now be raised
in a country which would not penalize her on account of
her color.

And that day was very nearly the last time Richard
and I spoke to each other without the later, terrible warfare. Two years later, I, too, quit America, never intending to return. The day I got to Paris, before I even
checked in at a hotel, I was carried to the Deux Magots,
where Richard sat, with the editors of *Zero* magazine.
"Hey, boy!" he cried, looking more surprised and pleased
and conspiratorial than ever, and younger and happier.
I took this meeting as a good omen, and I could not possibly have been more wrong.

I later became rather closely associated with *Zero* magazine, and wrote for them the essay called "Everybody's
Protest Novel." On the day the magazine was published,
and before I had seen it, I walked into the Brasserie Lipp.
Richard was there, and he called me over. I will never
forget that interview, but I doubt that I will ever be able
to re-create it.

Richard accused me of having betrayed him, and not
only him but all American Negroes by attacking the idea
of protest literature. It simply had not occurred to me
that the essay could be interpreted in that way. I was
still in that stage when I imagined that whatever was
clear to me had only to be pointed out to become immediately clear to everyone. I was young enough to be
proud of the essay and, sad and incomprehensible as it
now sounds, I really think that I had rather expected to
be patted on the head for my original point of view. It
had not occurred to me that this point of view, which I
had come to, after all, with some effort and some pain,
could be looked on as treacherous or subversive. Again,

I had mentioned Richard's *Native Son* at the end of the essay because it was the most important and most celebrated novel of Negro life to have appeared in America. Richard thought that I had attacked it, whereas, as far as I was concerned, I had scarcely even criticized it. And Richard thought that I was trying to destroy his novel and his reputation; but it had not entered my mind that either of these *could* be destroyed, and certainly not by me. And yet, what made the interview so ghastly was not merely the foregoing or the fact that I could find no words with which to defend myself. What made it most painful was that Richard was right to be hurt, I was wrong to have hurt him. He saw clearly enough, far more clearly than I had dared to allow myself to see, what I had done: I had used his work as a kind of springboard into my own. His work was a road-block in my road, the sphinx, really, whose riddles I had to answer before I could become myself. I thought confusedly then, and feel very definitely now, that this was the greatest tribute I could have paid him. But it is not an easy tribute to bear and I do not know how I will take it when my time comes. For, finally, Richard was hurt because I had not given him credit for any human feelings or failings. And indeed I had not, he had never really been a human being for me, he had been an idol. And idols are created in order to be destroyed.

This quarrel was never really patched up, though it must be said that, over a period of years, we tried. "What do you mean, *protest!*" Richard cried. "*All* literature is protest. You can't name a single novel that isn't protest." To this I could only weakly counter that all literature might be protest but all protest was not literature. "Oh," he would say then, looking, as he so often did, bewilderingly juvenile, "here you come again with all that art for art's sake crap." This never failed to make me furious, and my anger, for some reason, always seemed to amuse him. Our rare, best times came when we man-

aged to exasperate each other to the point of helpless
hilarity. "Roots," Richard would snort, when I had finally worked my way around to this dreary subject,
"what—roots! Next thing you'll be telling me is that
all colored folks have rhythm." Once, one evening, we
managed to throw the whole terrifying subject to the
winds, and Richard, Chester Himes, and myself went out
and got drunk. It was a good night, perhaps the best I
remember in all the time I knew Richard. For he and
Chester were friends, they brought out the best in each
other, and the atmosphere they created brought out the
best in me. Three absolutely tense, unrelentingly egotistical, and driven people, free in Paris but far from home,
with so much to be said and so little time in which to say
it!

And time was flying. Part of the trouble between Richard and myself, after all, was that I was nearly twenty
years younger and had never seen the South. Perhaps I
can now imagine Richard's odyssey better than I could
then, but it is only imagination. I have not, in my own
flesh, traveled, and paid the price of such a journey, from
the Deep South to Chicago to New York to Paris; and the
world which produced Richard Wright has vanished and
will never be seen again. Now, it seems almost in the twin-
kling of an eye, nearly twenty years have passed since
Richard and I sat nervously over bourbon in his Brooklyn living room. These years have seen nearly all of the
props of the Western reality knocked out from under it,
all the world's capitals have changed, the Deep South
has changed, and Africa has changed.

For a long time, it seems to me, Richard was cruelly
caught in this high wind. His ears, I think, were nearly
deafened by the roar, all about him, not only of falling
idols but of falling enemies. Strange people indeed
crossed oceans, from Africa and America, to come to his
door; and he really did not know who these people were,
and they very quickly sensed this. Not until the very end

of his life, judging by some of the stories in his last book,
Eight Men, did his imagination really begin to assess the
century's new and terrible dark stranger. Well, he worked
up until the end, died, as I hope to do, in the middle of
a sentence, and his work is now an irreducible part of
the history of our swift and terrible time. Whoever He
may be, and wherever you may be, may God be with you,
Richard, and may He help me not to fail that argument
which you began in me.

III. ALAS, POOR RICHARD

And my record's clear today, the church brothers and
sisters used to sing, *for He washed my sins away, And
that old account was settled long ago!* Well, so, perhaps
it was, for them; they were under the illusion that they
could read their records right. I am far from certain that
I am able to read my own record at all, I would certainly
hesitate to say that I am able to read it right. And, as for
accounts, it is doubtful that I have ever really "settled"
an account in my life.

Not that I haven't tried. In my relations with Richard,
I was always trying to set the record "straight," to "settle" the account. This is but another way of saying that I
wanted Richard to see me, not as the youth I had been
when he met me, but as a man. I wanted to feel that he
had accepted me, had accepted my right to my own vision, my right, as his equal, to disagree with him. I nour-
ished for a long time the illusion that this day was coming. One day, Richard would turn to me, with the light
of sudden understanding on his face, and say, "Oh, *that's*
what you mean." And then, so ran the dream, a great
and invaluable dialogue would have begun. And the
great value of this dialogue would have been not only in
its power to instruct all of you, and the ages. Its great
value would have been in its power to instruct me, its

power to instruct Richard: for it would have been nothing less than that so universally desired, so rarely achieved reconciliation between spiritual father and spiritual son.

Now, of course, it is not Richard's fault that I felt this way. But there is not much point, on the other hand, in dismissing it as simply my fault, or my illusion. I had identified myself with him long before we met: in a sense by no means metaphysical, his example had helped me to survive. He was black, he was young, he had come out of the Mississippi nightmare and the Chicago slums, and he was a writer. He proved it could be done—proved it to me, and gave me an arm against all those others who assured me it could *not* be done. And I think I had expected Richard, on the day we met, somehow, miraculously, to understand this, and to rejoice in it. Perhaps that sounds foolish, but I cannot honestly say, not even now, that I really think it is foolish. Richard Wright had a tremendous effect on countless numbers of people whom he never met, multitudes whom he now will never meet. This means that his responsibilities and his hazards were great. I don't think that Richard ever thought of me as one of his responsibilities—*bien au contraire!*— but he certainly seemed, often enough, to wonder just what he had done to deserve me.

Our reconciliation, anyway, never took place. This was a great loss for me. But many of our losses have a compensating gain. In my efforts to get through to Richard, I was forced to begin to wonder exactly why he held himself so rigidly against me. I could not believe—especially if one grants *my* reading of our relationship— that it could be due only to my criticism of his work. It seemed to me then, and it seems to me now, that one really needs those few people who take oneself and one's work seriously enough to be unimpressed by the public hullabaloo surrounding the former or the uncritical solemnity which menaces the latter from the instant that, for whatever reason, it finds itself in vogue.

No, it had to be more than that—the more especially as his attitude toward me had not, it turned out, been evolved for my particular benefit. It seemed to apply, with equal rigor, against a great many others. It applied against old friends, incontestably his equals, who had offended him, always, it turned out, in the same way: by failing to take his word for all the things he imagined, or had been led to believe, his word could cover. It applied against younger American Negroes who felt that Joyce, for example, not he, was the master; and also against younger American Negroes who felt that Richard did not know anything about jazz, or who insisted that the Mississippi and the Chicago he remembered were not precisely the Mississippi and the Chicago that they knew. It applied against Africans who refused to take Richard's word for Africa, and it applied against Algerians who did not feel that Paris was all that Richard had it cracked up to be. It applied, in short, against anyone who seemed to threaten Richard's system of reality. As time went on, it seemed to me that these people became more numerous and that Richard had fewer and fewer friends. At least, most of those people whom I had known to be friends of Richard's seemed to be saddened by him, and, reluctantly, to drift away. He's been away too long, some of them said. He's cut himself off from his roots. I resisted this judgment with all my might, more for my own sake than for Richard's, for it was far too easy to find this judgment used against myself. For the same reason I defended Richard when an African told me, with a small, mocking laugh, *I believe he thinks he's white.* I did *not* think I had been away too long: but I could not fail to begin, however unwillingly, to wonder about the uses and hazards of expatriation. I did not think I was white, either, or I did not *think* I thought so. But the Africans might think I did, and who could blame them? In their eyes, and in terms of my history, I could scarcely be considered the purest or most dependable of black men.

And I think that it was at about this point that I began to watch Richard as though he were a kind of object lesson. I could not help wondering if he, when facing an African, felt the same awful tension between envy and despair, attraction and revulsion. I had always been considered very dark, both Negroes and whites had despised me for it, and I had despised myself. But the Africans were much darker than I; I was a paleface among them, and so was Richard. And the disturbance thus created caused all of my extreme ambivalence about color to come floating to the surface of my mind. The Africans seemed at once simpler and more devious, more directly erotic and at the same time more subtle, and they were proud. If they had ever despised themselves for their color, it did not show, as far as I could tell. I envied them and feared them—feared that they had good reason to despise me. What did Richard feel? And what did Richard feel about other American Negroes abroad?

For example: one of my dearest friends, a Negro writer now living in Spain, circled around me and I around him for months before we spoke. One Negro meeting another at an all-white cocktail party, or at that larger cocktail party which is the American colony in Europe, cannot but wonder how the other got there. The question is: Is he for real? or is he kissing ass? Almost all Negroes, as Richard once pointed out, are almost always acting, but before a white audience—which is quite incapable of judging their performance: and even a "bad nigger" is, inevitably, giving something of a performance, even if the entire purpose of his performance is to terrify or blackmail white people.

Negroes know about each other what can here be called family secrets, and this means that one Negro, if he wishes, can "knock" the other's "hustle"—can give his game away. It is still not possible to overstate the price a Negro pays to climb out of obscurity—for it is a *particular* price, involved with being a Negro; and the great wounds, gouges, amputations, losses, scars, endured in such a journey cannot be calculated. But even this is not the worst of it, since he is really dealing with two hierarchies, one white and one black, the latter modeled on the former. The higher he rises, the less is his journey worth, since (unless he is extremely energetic and anarchic, a genuinely "bad nigger" in the most positive sense of the term) all he can possibly find himself exposed to is the grim emptiness of the white world—which does not live by the standards it uses to victimize him—and the even more ghastly emptiness of black people who wish they were white. Therefore, one "exceptional" Negro watches another "exceptional" Negro in order to find out if he knows how vastly successful and bitterly funny the hoax has been. Alliances, in the great cocktail party of the white man's world, are formed, almost purely, on this basis, for if both of you can laugh, you have a lot to laugh about. On the other hand, if only one of you can laugh, one of you, inevitably, is laughing at the other.

In the case of my new-found friend, Andy, and I, we were able, luckily, to laugh together. We were both baffled by Richard, but still respectful and fond of him—we accepted from Richard pronouncements and attitudes which we would certainly never have accepted from each other, or from anyone else—at the time Richard returned from wherever he had been to film *Native Son*. (In which, to our horror, later abundantly justified, he himself played Bigger Thomas.) He returned with a brainstorm, which he outlined to me one bright, sunny afternoon, on the terrace of the Royal St. Germain. He wanted to do something to protect the rights of American Negroes in Paris; to form, in effect, a kind of pressure group which would force American businesses in Paris, and American government offices, to hire Negroes on a proportional basis.

This seemed unrealistic to me. How, I asked him, in the first place, could one find out how many American Negroes there were in Paris? Richard quoted an approximate, semi-official figure, which I do not remember, but I was still not satisfied. Of this number, how many were looking for jobs? Richard seemed to feel that they spent most of their time being turned down by American bigots, but this was not really my impression. I am not sure I said this, though, for Richard often made me feel that the word "frivolous" had been coined to describe me. Nevertheless, my objections made him more and more impatient with me, and I began to wonder if I were not guilty of great disloyalty and indifference concerning the lot of American Negroes abroad. (I find that there is something helplessly sardonic in my tone now, as I write this, which also handicapped me on that distant afternoon. Richard, more than anyone I have ever known, brought this tendency to the fore in me. I always wanted to kick him, and say, "Oh, come off it, baby, ain't no white folks around now, let's tell it like it *is*.")

Still, most of the Negroes I knew had *not* come to Paris to look for work. They were writers or dancers or composers, they were on the G.I. Bill, or fellowships, or more mysterious shoestrings, or they worked as jazz musicians. I did not know anyone who doubted that the American hiring system remained in Paris exactly what it had been at home—but how was one to prove this, with a handful, at best, of problematical Negroes, scattered throughout Paris? Unlike Richard, I had no reason to suppose that any of them even *wanted* to work for Americans—my evidence, in fact, suggested that this was just about the last thing they wanted to do. But, even if they did, and even if they were qualified, how could one *prove* that So-and-So had not been hired by TWA *because* he was a Negro? I had found this almost impossible to do at home. Isn't this, I suggested, the kind of thing which ought to be done from Washington? Richard, however, was not to be put off, and he had made me feel so guilty that I agreed to find out how many Negroes were then working for the ECA.

There turned out to be two or three or four, I forget how many. In any case, we were dead, there being no way on earth to prove that there should have been six or seven. But we were all in too deep to be able to turn back now, and, accordingly, there was a pilot meeting of this extraordinary organization, quite late, as I remember, one evening, in a private room over a bistro. It was in some extremely inconvenient part of town, and we all arrived separately or by twos. (There was some vague notion, I think, of defeating the ever-present agents of the CIA, who certainly ought to have had better things to do, but who, quite probably, on the other hand, didn't.) We may have defeated pursuit on our way there, but there was certainly no way of defeating detection as we arrived: slinking casually past the gaping mouths and astounded eyes of a workingman's bistro, like a disorganized parade, some thirty or forty of us, through a back door, and up the stairs. My friend and I arrived a little late, perhaps a little drunk, and certainly on a laughing jag, for we felt that we had been trapped in one of the most improbable and old-fashioned of English melodramas.

But Richard was in his glory. He was on the platform above us, I think he was alone there; there were only Negroes in the room. The results of the investigations of others had proved no more conclusive than my own— one could certainly not, on the basis of our findings, attack a policy or evolve a strategy—but this did not seem to surprise Richard or, even, to disturb him. It was decided, since we could not be a pressure group, to form a fellowship club, the purpose of which would be to get to know the French, and help the French to get to know us. Given our temperaments, neither Andy nor myself felt any need to join a club for this, we were getting along just fine on our own; but, somewhat to my surprise, we did not know many of the other people in the room, and so we listened. If it were only going to be a social club, then, obviously, the problem, as far as we were concerned, was over.

Richard's speech, that evening, made a great impact on me. It frightened me. I felt, but suppressed the feel-

ing, that he was being mightily condescending toward
the people in the room. I suppressed the feeling because
most of them did not, in fact, interest me very much; but
I was still in that stage when I felt guilty about not loving every Negro that I met. Still, perhaps for this very
reason, I could not help resenting Richard's aspect and
Richard's tone. I do not remember how his speech began,
but I will never forget how it ended. News of this get-
together, he told us, had caused a great stir in Parisian
intellectual circles. Everyone was filled with wonder (as
well they might be) concerning the future of such a
group. A great many white people had wished to be present, Sartre, de Beauvoir, Camus—"and," said Richard,
"my own wife. But I told them, before I can allow you to
come, we've got to prepare the Negroes to receive you!"

This revelation, which was uttered with a smile, produced the most strained, stunned, uneasy silence. I
looked at Andy, and Andy looked at me. There was
something terribly funny about it, and there was something not funny at all. I rather wondered what the probable response would have been had Richard dared make
such a statement in, say, a Negro barber shop; rather
wondered, in fact, what the probable response would
have been had anyone else dared make such a statement
to anyone in the room, under different circumstances.
("Nigger, I been receiving white folks all my life—prepare *who?* Who you think you going to *prepare?"*) It
seemed to me, in any case, that the preparation ought, at
least, to be conceived of as mutual: there was no reason
to suppose that Parisian intellectuals were more "prepared" to "receive" American Negroes than American
Negroes were to receive them—rather, all things considered, the contrary.

This was the extent of my connection with the Franco-
American Fellowship Club, though the club itself, rather
anemicly, seemed to drag on for some time. I do not know
what it accomplished—very little, I should imagine, but
it soon ceased to exist because it had never had any rea-

son to come into existence. To judge from complaints I heard, Richard's interest in it, once it was—roughly speaking—launched, was minimal. He told me once that it had cost him a great deal of money—this referred, I think, to some disastrous project, involving a printer's bill, which the club had undertaken. It seemed, indeed, that Richard felt that, with the establishment of this club, he had paid his dues to American Negroes abroad, and at home, and forever; had paid his dues, and was off the hook, since they had once more proved themselves incapable of following where he led. For yet one or two years to come, young Negroes would cross the ocean and come to Richard's door, wanting his sympathy, his help, his time, his money. God knows it must have been trying. And yet, they could not possibly have taken up more of his time than did the dreary sycophants by whom, as far as I could tell, he was more and more surrounded. Richard and I, of course, drifted farther and farther apart— our dialogue became too frustrating and too acrid—but, from my helplessly sardonic distance, I could only make out, looming above what seemed to be an indescribably cacophonous parade of mediocrities, and a couple of the world's most empty and pompous black writers, the tough and loyal figure of Chester Himes. There was a noticeable chill in the love affair which had been going on between Richard and the French intellectuals. He had always made American intellectuals uneasy, and now they were relieved to discover that he bored them, and even more relieved to say so. By this time he had managed to estrange himself from almost all of the younger American Negro writers in Paris. They were often to be found in the same café, Richard compulsively playing the pin-ball machine, while, they, spitefully and deliberately, refused to acknowledge his presence. Gone were the days when he had only to enter a café to be greeted with the American Negro equivalent of *"cher maître"* ("Hey, Richard, how you making it, my man? Sit down and tell me something"), to be seated at a table, while

all the bright faces turned toward him. The brightest
faces were now turned from him, and among these faces
were the faces of the Africans and the Algerians. They
did not trust him—and their distrust was venomous because they felt that he had promised them so much.
When the African said to me *I believe he thinks he's
white,* he meant that Richard cared more about his safety and comfort than he cared about the black condition.
But it was to this condition, at least in part, that he owed
his safety and comfort and power and fame. If one-tenth
of the suffering which obtained (and obtains) among
Africans and Algerians in Paris had been occurring in
Chicago, one could not help feeling that Richard would
have raised the roof. He never ceased to raise the roof, in
fact, as far as the American color problem was concerned.
But time passes quickly. The American Negroes had discovered that Richard did not really know much about
the present dimensions and complexity of the Negro
problem here, and, profoundly, did not want to know.
And one of the reasons that he did not want to know
was that his real impulse toward American Negroes, individually, was to despise them. They, therefore, dismissed his rage and his public pronouncements as an
unmanly reflex; as for the Africans, at least the younger
ones, they knew he did not know them and did not want
to know them, and they despised *him.* It must have been
extremely hard to bear, and it was certainly very frightening to watch. I could not help feeling: *Be careful.
Time is passing for you, too, and this may be happening
to you one day.*

For who has not hated his black brother? Simply *because* he is black, *because* he is brother. And who has not
dreamed of violence? That fantastical violence which
will drown in blood, wash away in blood, not only generation upon generation of horror, but which will also release one from the individual horror, carried everywhere
in the heart. Which of us has overcome his past? And
the past of a Negro is blood dripping down through

leaves, gouged-out eyeballs, the sex torn from its socket
and severed with a knife. But this past is not special to
the Negro. This horror is also the past, and the ever-
lasting potential, or temptation, of the human race. If we
do not know this, it seems to me, we know nothing about
ourselves, nothing about each other; to have accepted
this is also to have found a source of strength—source of
all our power. But one must first accept this paradox,
with joy.

The American Negro has paid a hidden, terrible price
for his slow climbing to the light; so that, for example,
Richard was able, at last, to live in Paris exactly as he
would have lived, had he been a white man, here, in
America. This may seem desirable, but I wonder if it is.
Richard paid the price such an illusion of safety demands. The price is a turning away from, an ignorance
of, all of the powers of darkness. This sounds mystical,
but it is not; it is a hidden fact. It is the failure of the
moral imagination of Europe which has created the
forces now determined to overthrow it. No European
dreamed, during Europe's heyday, that they were sowing,
in a dark continent, far away, the seeds of a whirlwind.
It was not dreamed, during the Second World War, that
Churchill's ringing words to the English were overheard
by English slaves—who, now, coming in their thousands
to the mainland, menace the English sleep. It is only
now, in America, and it may easily be too late, that any
of the anguish, to say nothing of the rage, with which
the American Negro has lived so long begins, dimly, to
trouble the public mind. The suspicion has been planted
—and the principal effect, so far, here, has been panic
—that perhaps the world is darker and therefore more
real than we have allowed ourselves to believe.

Time brought Richard, as it has brought the American
Negro, to an extraordinarily baffling and dangerous
place. An American Negro, however deep his sympathies,
or however bright his rage, ceases to be simply a black
man when he faces a black man from Africa. When I say

simply a black man, I do not mean that being a black
man is simple, anywhere. But I am suggesting that one of
the prices an American Negro pays—or can pay—for
what is called his "acceptance" is a profound, almost ineradicable self-hatred. This corrupts every aspect of his
living, he is never at peace again, he is out of touch with
himself forever. And, when he faces an African, he is
facing the unspeakably dark, guilty, erotic past which the
Protestant fathers made him bury—for their peace of
mind, and for their power—but which lives in his personality and haunts the universe yet. What an African,
facing an American Negro sees, I really do not yet know;
and it is too early to tell with what scars and complexes
the African has come up from the fire. But the war in the
breast between blackness and whiteness, which caused
Richard such pain, need not be a war. It is a war which
just as it denies both the heights and the depths of our
natures, takes, and has taken, visibly and invisibly, as
many white lives as black ones. And, as I see it, Richard
was among the most illustrious victims of this war. This
is why, it seems to me, he eventually found himself wandering in a no-man's land between the black world and
the white. It is no longer important to be white—thank
heaven—the white face is no longer invested with the
power of this world; and it is devoutly to be hoped that
it will soon no longer be important to be black. The experience of the American Negro, if it is ever faced and
assessed, makes it possible to hope for such a reconciliation. The hope and the effect of this fusion in the breast
of the American Negro is one of the few hopes we have of
surviving the wilderness which lies before us now.

13. THE BLACK BOY LOOKS
AT THE WHITE BOY

I walked and I walked
Till I wore out my shoes.
I can't walk so far, but
Yonder come the blues.
    —Ma Rainey

I first met Norman Mailer about five years ago, in Paris, at the home of Jean Malaquais. Let me bring in at once the theme that will repeat itself over and over throughout this love letter: I was then (and I have not changed much) a very tight, tense, lean, abnormally ambitious, abnormally intelligent, and hungry black cat. It is important that I admit that, at the time I met Norman, I was extremely worried about my career; and a writer who is worried about his career is also fighting for his life. I was approaching the end of a love affair, and I was not taking it very well. Norman and I are alike in this, that we both tend to suspect others of putting us down, and we strike before we're struck. Only, our styles are very different: I am a black boy from the Harlem streets, and Norman is a middle-class Jew. I am not dragging my personal history into this gratuitously, and I hope I do not need to say that no sneer is implied in the above description of Norman. But these are the facts and in my own relationship to Norman they are crucial facts.

Also, I have no right to talk about Norman without risking a distinctly chilling self-exposure. I take him very seriously, he is very dear to me. And I think I know something about his journey from my black boy's point of view because my own journey is not really so very different, and also because I have spent most of my life, after all, watching white people and outwitting them, so that I might survive. I think that I know something about the American masculinity which most men of my generation do not know because they have not been menaced by it in the way that I have been. It is still true, alas, that to be an American Negro male is also to be a kind of walking phallic symbol: which means that one pays, in one's own personality, for the sexual insecurity of others. The relationship, therefore, of a black boy to a white boy is a very complex thing.

There is a difference, though, between Norman and myself in that I think he still imagines that he has something to save, whereas I have never had anything to lose. Or, perhaps I ought to put it another way: the things that most white people imagine that they can salvage from the storm of life is really, in sum, their innocence. It was this commodity precisely which I had to get rid of at once, literally, on pain of death. I am afraid that most of the white people I have ever known impressed me as being in the grip of a weird nostalgia, dreaming of a vanished state of security and order, against which dream, unfailingly and unconsciously, they tested and very often lost their lives. It is a terrible thing to say, but I am afraid that for a very long time the troubles of white people failed to impress me as being real trouble. They put me in mind of children crying because the breast has been taken away. Time and love have modified my tough-boy lack of charity, but the attitude sketched above was my first attitude and I am sure that there is a great deal of it left.

To proceed: two lean cats, one white and one black, met in a French living room. I had heard of him, he had heard of me. And here we were, suddenly, circling around each other. We liked each other at once, but each was frightened that the other would pull rank. He could have pulled rank on me because he was more famous and had more money and also because he was white; but I could have pulled rank on him precisely because I was black and knew more about that periphery he so helplessly maligns in *The White Negro* than he could ever hope to know. Already, you see, we were trapped in our roles and our attitudes: the toughest kid on the block was meeting the toughest kid on the block. I think that both of us were pretty weary of this grueling and thankless role, I know that I am; but the roles that we construct are constructed because we feel that they will help us to survive and also, of course, because they fulfill something in our personalities; and one does not, therefore, cease playing a role simply because one has begun to understand it. All roles are dangerous. The world tends to trap and immobilize you in the role you play; and it is not always easy—in fact, it is always extremely hard—to maintain a kind of watchful, mocking distance between oneself as one appears to be and oneself as one actually is.

I think that Norman was working on *The Deer Park* at that time, or had just finished it, and Malaquais, who had translated *The Naked and the Dead* into French, did not like *The Deer Park*. I had not then read the book; if I had, I would have been astonished that Norman could have expected Malaquais to like it. What Norman was trying to do in *The Deer Park,* and quite apart, now, from whether or not he succeeded, could only—it seems to me—baffle and annoy a French intellectual who seemed to me essentially rationalistic. Norman has many qualities and faults, but I have never heard anyone accuse him of possessing this particular one. But Malaquais' opinion seemed to mean a great deal to him—this astonished me, too; and there was a running, good-natured but astringent argument between them, with Malaquais playing the role of the old lion and Norman playing the role of the powerful but clumsy cub. And, I must say, I

think that each of them got a great deal of pleasure out
of the other's performance. The night we met, we stayed
up very late, and did a great deal of drinking and shouting. But beneath all the shouting and the posing and the
mutual showing off, something very wonderful was happening. I was aware of a new and warm presence in my
life, for I had met someone I wanted to know, who wanted to know me.

Norman and his wife, Adele, along with a Negro jazz
musician friend, and myself, met fairly often during the
few weeks that found us all in the same city. I think that
Norman had come in from Spain, and he was shortly to
return to the States; and it was not long after Norman's
departure that I left Paris for Corsica. My memory of
that time is both blurred and sharp, and, oddly enough,
is principally of Norman—confident, boastful, exuber-
ant, and loving—striding through the soft Paris nights
like a gladiator. And I think, alas, that I envied him: his
success, and his youth, and his love. And this meant that
though Norman really wanted to know me, and though
I really wanted to know him, I hung back, held fire,
danced, and lied. I was not going to come crawling out
of my ruined house, all bloody, no, baby, sing no sad
songs for *me*. And the great gap between Norman's state
and my own had a terrible effect on our relationship, for
it inevitably connected, not to say collided, with that
myth of the sexuality of Negroes which Norman, like so
many others, refuses to give up. The sexual battleground,
if I may call it that, is really the same for everyone; and I,
at this point, was just about to be carried off the battleground on my shield, if anyone could find it; so how
could I play, in any way whatever, the noble savage?

At the same time, my temperament and my experience
in this country had led me to expect very little from most
American whites, especially, horribly enough, my friends:
so it did not seem worthwhile to challenge, in any real
way, Norman's views of life on the periphery, or to put
him down for them. I was weary, to tell the truth. I had

tried, in the States, to convey something of what it felt like to be a Negro and no one had been able to listen: they wanted their romance. And, anyway, the really ghastly thing about trying to convey to a white man the reality of the Negro experience has nothing whatever to do with the fact of color, but has to do with this man's relationship to his own life. He will face in your life only what he is willing to face in his. Well, this means that one finds oneself tampering with the insides of a stranger, to no purpose, which one probably has no right to do, and I chickened out. And matters were not helped at all by the fact that the Negro jazz musicians, among whom we sometimes found ourselves, who really liked Norman, did not for an instant consider him as being even remotely "hip" and Norman did not know this and I could not tell him. He never broke through to them, at least not as far I know; and they were far too "hip," if that is the word I want, even to consider breaking through to him. They thought he was a real sweet ofay cat, but a little frantic.

But we were far more cheerful than anything I've said might indicate and none of the above seemed to matter very much at the time. Other things mattered, like walking and talking and drinking and eating, and the way Adele laughed, and the way Norman argued. He argued like a young man, he argued to win: and while I found him charming, he may have found me exasperating, for I kept moving back before that short, prodding forefinger. I couldn't submit my arguments, or my real questions, for I had too much to hide. Or so it seemed to me then. I submit, though I may be wrong, that I was then at the beginning of a terrifying adventure, not too unlike the conundrum which seems to menace Norman now:

"I had done a few things and earned a few pence"; but the things I had written were behind me, could not be written again, could not be repeated. I was also realizing that all that the world could give me as an artist, it had, in effect, already given. In the years that stretched before me, all that I could look forward to, in that way, were a few more prizes, or a lot more, and a little more, or a lot more money. And my private life had failed— had failed, had failed. One of the reasons I had fought so hard, after all, was to wrest from the world fame and money and love. And here I was, at thirty-two, finding my notoriety hard to bear, since its principal effect was to make me more lonely; money, it turned out, was exactly like sex, you thought of nothing else if you didn't have it and thought of other things if you did; and love, as far as I could see, was over. Love seemed to be over not merely because an affair was ending; it would have seemed to be over under any circumstances; for it was the dream of love which was ending. I was beginning to realize, most unwillingly, all the things love could not do. It could not make me over, for example. It could not undo the journey which had made of me such a strange man and brought me to such a strange place.

But at that time it seemed only too clear that love had gone out of the world, and not, as I had thought once, because I was poor and ugly and obscure, but precisely because I was no longer any of these things. What point, then, was there in working if the best I could hope for was the Nobel Prize? And *how*, indeed, would I be able to keep on working if I could never be released from the prison of my egocentricity? By what act could I escape this horror? For horror it was, let us make no mistake about that.

And, beneath all this, which simplified nothing, was that sense, that suspicion—which is the glory and torment of every writer—that what was happening to me might be turned to good account, that I was trembling on the edge of great revelations, was being prepared for a very long journey, and might now begin, having survived my apprenticeship (but had I survived it?), a great work. I might really become a great writer. But in order to do this I would have to sit down at the typewriter again, alone—I would have to accept my despair: and I could not do it. It really does not help to be a strong-willed person or, anyway, I think it is a great error to misunderstand the nature of the will. In the most important areas of anybody's life, the will usually operates as a traitor. My own will was busily pointing out to me the most fantastically unreal alternatives to my pain, all of which I tried, all of which—luckily—failed. When, late in the evening or early in the morning, Norman and Adele returned to their hotel on the Quai Voltaire, I wandered through Paris, the underside of Paris, drinking, screwing, fighting—it's a wonder I wasn't killed. And then it was morning, I would somehow be home—usually, anyway—and the typewriter would be there, staring at me; and the manuscript of the new novel, which it seemed I would never be able to achieve, and from which clearly I was never going to be released, was scattered all over the floor.

That's the way it is. I think it is the most dangerous point in the life of any artist, his longest, most hideous turning; and especially for a man, an American man, whose principle is action and whose jewel is optimism, who must now accept what certainly then seems to be a gray passivity and an endless despair. It is the point at which many artists lose their minds, or commit suicide, or throw themselves into good works, or try to enter politics. For all of this is happening not only in the wilderness of the soul, but in the real world which accomplishes its seductions not by offering you opportunities to be wicked but by offering opportunities to be good, to be active and effective, to be admired and central and apparently loved.

Norman came on to America, and I went to Corsica. We wrote each other a few times. I confided to Norman that I was very apprehensive about the reception of *Giovanni's Room*, and he was good enough to write some very encouraging things about it when it came out. The critics had jumped on him with both their left feet when

he published *The Deer Park*—which I still had not read
—and this created a kind of bond, or strengthened the
bond already existing between us. About a year and several overflowing wastebaskets later, I, too, returned to
America, not vastly improved by having been out of it,
but not knowing where else to go; and one day, while I
was sitting dully in my house, Norman called me from
Connecticut. A few people were going to be there—for
the weekend—and he wanted me to come, too. We had
not seen each other since Paris.

Well, I wanted to go, that is, I wanted to see Norman;
but I did not want to see any people, and so the tone of
my acceptance was not very enthusiastic. I realized that
he felt this, but I did not know what to do about it. He
gave me train schedules and hung up.

Getting to Connecticut would have been no hassle if I
could have pulled myself together to get to the train.
And I was sorry, as I meandered around my house and
time flew and trains left, that I had not been more honest with Norman and told him exactly how I felt. But I
had not known how to do this, or it had not really occurred to me to do it, especially not over the phone.

So there was another phone call, I forget who called
whom, which went something like this:

N: Don't feel you have to. I'm not trying to bug you.

J: It's not that. It's just—

N: You don't really want to come, do you?

J: I don't really feel up to it.

N: I understand. I guess you just don't like the Connecticut gentry.

J: Well—don't you ever come to the city?

N: Sure. We'll see each other.

J: I hope so. I'd like to see you.

N: Okay, till then.

And he hung up. I thought, I ought to write him a
letter, but of course I did nothing of the sort. It was
around this time I went South, I think; anyway, we did
not see each other for a long time.

But I thought about him a great deal. The grapevine keeps all of us advised of the others' movements, so I knew when Norman left Connecticut for New York, heard that he had been present at this or that party and what he had said: usually something rude, often something penetrating, sometimes something so hilariously silly that it was difficult to believe he had been serious. (This was my reaction when I first heard his famous running-for-President remark. I dismissed it. I was wrong.) Or he had been seen in this or that Village spot, in which unfailingly there would be someone—out of spite, idleness, envy, exasperation, out of the bottomless, eerie, aimless hostility which characterizes almost every bar in New York, to speak only of bars—to put him down. I heard of a couple of fist-fights, and, of course, I was always encountering people who hated his guts. These people always mildly surprised me, and so did the news of his fights: it was hard for me to imagine that anyone could really dislike Norman, anyone, that is, who had encountered him personally. I knew of one fight he had had, forced on him, apparently, by a blowhard Village type whom I considered rather pathetic. I didn't blame Norman for this fight, but I couldn't help wondering why he bothered to rise to such a shapeless challenge. It seemed simpler, as I was always telling myself, just to stay out of Village bars.

And people talked about Norman with a kind of avid glee, which I found very ugly. Pleasure made their saliva flow, they sprayed and all but drooled, and their eyes shone with that blood-lust which is the only real tribute the mediocre are capable of bringing to the extraordinary. Many of the people who claimed to be seeing Norman all the time impressed me as being, to tell the truth, pitifully far beneath him. But this is also true, alas, of much of my own entourage. The people who are in one's life or merely continually in one's presence reveal a great deal about one's needs and terrors. Also, one's hopes.

I was not, however, on the scene. I was on the road—
not quite, I trust, in the sense that Kerouac's boys are;
but I presented, certainly, a moving target. And I was
reading Norman Mailer. Before I had met him, I had
only read *The Naked and The Dead, The White Negro,*
and *Barbary Shore*—I think this is right, though it may
be that I only read *The White Negro* later and confuse
my reading of that piece with some of my discussions
with Norman. Anyway, I could not, with the best will in
the world, make any sense out of *The White Negro* and,
in fact, it was hard for me to imagine that this essay had
been written by the same man who wrote the novels.
Both *The Naked and The Dead* and (for the most part)
Barbary Shore are written in a lean, spare, muscular prose
which accomplishes almost exactly what it sets out to do.
Even *Barbary Shore*, which loses itself in its last half (and
which deserves, by the way, far more serious treatment
than it has received) never becomes as downright impenetrable as *The White Negro* does.

Now, much of this, I told myself, had to do with my
resistance to the title, and with a kind of fury that so
antique a vision of the blacks should, at this late hour,
and in so many borrowed heirlooms, be stepping off the
A train. But I was also baffled by the passion with which
Norman appeared to be imitating so many people inferior
to himself, i.e., Kerouac, and all the other Suzuki rhythm
boys. From them, indeed, I expected nothing more than
their pablum-clogged cries of *Kicks!* and *Holy!* It seemed
very clear to me that their glorification of the orgasm was
but a way of avoiding all of the terrors of life and love.
But Norman knew better, had to know better. *The Naked
and The Dead, Barbary Shore,* and *The Deer Park* proved
it. In each of these novels, there is a toughness and sub-
tlety of conception, and a sense of the danger and complexity of human relationships which one will search for
in vain, not only in the work produced by the aforemen-
tioned coterie, but in most of the novels produced by

Norman's contemporaries. What in the world, then, was he doing, slumming so outrageously, in such a dreary crowd?

For, exactly because he knew better, and in exactly the same way that no one can become more lewdly vicious than an imitation libertine, Norman felt compelled to carry their *mystique* further than they had, to be more "hip," or more "beat," to dominate, in fact, their dreaming field; and since this *mystique* depended on a total rejection of life, and insisted on the fulfillment of an infantile dream of love, the *mystique* could only be extended into violence. No one is more dangerous than he who imagines himself pure in heart: for his purity, by definition, is unassailable.

But *why* should it be necessary to borrow the Depression language of deprived Negroes, which eventually evolved into jive and bop talk, in order to justify such a grim system of delusions? Why malign the sorely menaced sexuality of Negroes in order to justify the white man's own sexual panic? Especially as, in Norman's case, and as indicated by his work, he has a very real sense of sexual responsbility, and, even, odd as it may sound to some, of sexual morality, and a genuine commitment to life. None of his people, I beg you to notice, spend their lives on the road. They really become entangled with each other, and with life. They really suffer, they spill real blood, they have real lives to lose. This is no small achievement; in fact, it is absolutely rare. No matter how uneven one judges Norman's work to be, all of it is genuine work. No matter how harshly one judges it, it is the work of a genuine novelist, and an absolutely first-rate talent.

Which makes the questions I have tried to raise—or, rather, the questions which Norman Mailer irresistibly represents—all the more troubling and terrible. I certainly do not know the answers, and even if I did, this is probably not the place to state them.

But I have a few ideas. Here is Kerouac, ruminating on what I take to be the loss of the garden of Eden:

> At lilac evening I walked with every muscle aching among the lights of 27th and Welton in the Denver colored section, wishing I were a Negro, feeling that the best the white world had offered was not enough ecstasy for me, not enough life, joy, kicks, darkness, music, not enough night. I wished I were a Denver Mexican, or even a poor overworked Jap, anything but what I so drearily was, a "white man" disillusioned. All my life I'd had white ambitions. . . . I passed the dark porches of Mexican and Negro homes; soft voices were there, occasionally the dusky knee of some mysterious sensuous gal; and dark faces of the men behind rose arbors. Little children sat like sages in ancient rocking chairs.

Now, this is absolute nonsense, of course, objectively considered, and offensive nonsense at that: I would hate to be in Kerouac's shoes if he should ever be mad enough to read this aloud from the stage of Harlem's Apollo Theater.

And yet there is real pain in it, and real loss, however thin; and it *is* thin, like soup too long diluted; thin because it does not refer to reality, but to a dream. Compare it, at random, with any old blues:

> Backwater blues done caused me
> To pack my things and go.
> 'Cause my house fell down
> And I can't live there no mo'.

"Man," said a Negro musician to me once, talking about Norman, "the only trouble with that cat is that he's white." This does not mean exactly what it says— or, rather, it *does* mean exactly what it says, and not what it might be taken to mean—and it is a very shrewd observation. What my friend meant was that to become a Negro man, let alone a Negro artist, one had to make oneself up as one went along. This had to be done in the not-at-all-metaphorical teeth of the world's determination to destroy you. The world had prepared no place for you, and if the world had its way, no place would ever exist. Now, this is true for everyone, but, in the case of a Negro, this truth is absolutely naked: if he deludes himself about it, he will die. This is not the way this truth presents itself to white men, who believe the world is theirs and who, albeit unconsciously, expect the world to help them in the achievement of their identity. But the world does not do this—for anyone; the world is not interested in anyone's identity. And, therefore, the anguish which can overtake a white man comes in the middle of his life, when he must make the almost inconceivable effort to divest himself of everything he has ever expected or believed, when he must take himself apart and put himself together again, walking out of the world, into limbo, or into what certainly looks like limbo. This cannot yet happen to any Negro of Norman's age, for the reason that his delusions and defenses are either absolutely impenetrable by this time, or he has failed to survive them. "I want to know how power works," Norman once said to me, "how it really works, in detail." Well, I know how power works, it has worked on me, and if I didn't know how power worked, I would be dead. And it goes without saying, perhaps, that I have simply never been able to afford myself any illusions concerning the manipulation of that power. My revenge, I decided very early, would be to achieve a power which outlasts kingdoms.

II

When I finally saw Norman again, I was beginning to suspect daylight at the end of my long tunnel, it was a

summer day, I was on my way back to Paris, and I was
very cheerful. We were at an afternoon party, Norman
was standing in the kitchen, a drink in his hand, holding
forth for the benefit of a small group of people. There
seemed something different about him, it was the bellig-
erence of his stance, and the really rather pontifical tone
of his voice. I had only seen him, remember, in Malaquais'
living room, which Malaquais indefatigably dominates,
and on various terraces and in various dives in Paris. I
do not mean that there was anything unfriendly about
him. On the contrary, he was smiling and having a ball.
And yet—he was leaning against the refrigerator, rather
as though he had his back to the wall, ready to take on
all comers.

Norman has a trick, at least with me, of watching,
somewhat ironically, as you stand on the edge of the
crowd around him, waiting for his attention. I suppose
this ought to be exasperating, but in fact I find it rather
endearing, because it is so transparent and because he
gets such a bang out of being the center of attention. So
do I, of course, at least some of the time.

We talked, bantered, a little tensely, made the usual,
doomed effort to bring each other up to date on what
we had been doing. I did not want to talk about my novel, which was only just beginning to seem to take shape,
and, therefore, did not dare ask him if he were working
on a novel. He seemed very pleased to see me, and I was
pleased to see him, but I also had the feeling that he had
made up his mind about me, adversely, in some way. It
was as though he were saying, Okay, so now I know who
you are, baby.

I was taking a boat in a few days, and I asked him to
call me.

"Oh, no," he said, grinning, and thrusting that forefinger at me, "*you* call me."

"That's fair enough," I said, and I left the party and
went on back to Paris. While I was out of the country,

Norman published *Advertisements for Myself,* which presently crossed the ocean to the apartment of James Jones. Bill Styron was also in Paris at that time, and one evening the three of us sat in Jim's living room, reading aloud, in a kind of drunken, masochistic fascination, Norman's judgment of our personalities and our work. Actually, I came off best, I suppose; there was less about me, and it was less venomous. But the condescension infuriated me; also, to tell the truth, my feelings were hurt. I felt that if that was the way Norman felt about me, he should have told me so. He had said that I was incapable of saying "F—— you" to the reader. My first temptation was to send him a cablegram which would disabuse him of that notion, at least insofar as one reader was concerned. But then I thought, No, I would be cool about it, and fail to react as he so clearly wanted me to. Also, I must say, his judgment of myself seemed so wide of the mark and so childish that it was hard to stay angry. I wondered what in the world was going on in his mind. Did he really suppose that he had now become the builder and destroyer of reputations?

And of *my* reputation?

We met in the Actors' Studio one afternoon, after a performance of *The Deer Park*—which I deliberately arrived too late to see, since I really did not know how I was going to react to Norman, and didn't want to betray myself by clobbering his play. When the discussion ended, I stood, again on the edge of the crowd around him, waiting. Over someone's shoulder, our eyes met, and Norman smiled.

"We've got something to talk about," I told him.

"I figured that," he said, smiling.

We went to a bar, and sat opposite each other. I was relieved to discover that I was not angry, not even (as far as I could tell) at the bottom of my heart. But, "Why did you write those things about me?"

"Well, I'll tell you about that," he said—Norman has

several accents, and I think this was his Texas one—"I sort of figured you had it coming to you."

"Why?"

"Well, I think there's some truth in it."

"Well, if you felt that way, why didn't you ever say so —to me?"

"Well, I figured if this was going to break up our friendship, something else would come along to break it up just as fast."

I couldn't disagree with that.

"You're the only one I kind of regret hitting so hard," he said, with a grin. "I think I—probably—wouldn't say it quite that way now."

With this, I had to be content. We sat for perhaps an hour, talking of other things and, again, I was struck by his stance: leaning on the table, shoulders hunched, seeming, really, to roll like a boxer's, and his hands moving as though he were dealing with a sparring partner. And we were talking of physical courage, and the necessity of never letting another guy get the better of you.

I laughed. "Norman, I can't go through the world the way you do because I haven't got your shoulders."

He grinned, as though I were his pupil. "But you're a pretty tough little mother, too," he said, and referred to one of the grimmer of my Village misadventures, a misadventure which certainly proved that I had a dangerously sharp tongue, but which didn't really prove anything about my courage. Which, anyway, I had long ago given up trying to prove.

I did not see Norman again until Provincetown, just after his celebrated brush with the police there, which resulted, according to Norman, in making the climate of Provincetown as "mellow as Jello." The climate didn't seem very different to me—dull natives, dull tourists, malevolent policemen; I certainly, in any case, would never have dreamed of testing Norman's sanguine conclusion. But we had a great time, lying around the beach, and driving about, we began to be closer than we had been for a long time.

It was during this Provincetown visit that I realized, for the first time, during a long exchange Norman and I had, in a kitchen, at someone else's party, that Norman was really fascinated by the nature of political power. But, though he said so, I did not really believe that he was fascinated by it as a possibility for himself. He was then doing the great piece on the Democratic convention which was published in *Esquire,* and I put his fascination down to that. I tend not to worry about writers as long as they are working—which is not as romantic as it may sound—and he seemed quite happy with his wife, his family, himself. I declined, naturally, to rise at dawn, as he apparently often did, to go running or swimming or boxing, but Norman seemed to get a great charge out of these admirable pursuits and didn't put me down too hard for my comparative decadence.

He and Adele and the two children took me to the plane one afternoon, the tiny plane which shuttles from Provincetown to Boston. It was a great day, clear and sunny, and that was the way I felt: for it seemed to me that we had all, at last, reestablished our old connection.

And then I heard that Norman was running for mayor, which I dismissed as a joke and refused to believe until it became hideously clear that it was not a joke at all. I was furious. I thought, You son of a bitch, you're copping out. You're one of the very few writers around who might really become a great writer, who might help to excavate the buried consciousness of this country, and you want to settle for being the lousy mayor of New York. *It's not your job.* And I don't at all mean to suggest that writers are not responsible to and for—in any case, always for—the social order. I don't, for that matter, even mean to suggest that Norman would have made a particularly bad Mayor, though I confess that I simply cannot see him in this role. And there is probably some

truth in the suggestion, put forward by Norman and
others, that the shock value of having such a man in such
an office, or merely running for such an office, would
have had a salutary effect on the life of this city—particularly, I must say, as relates to our young people, who
are certainly in desperate need of adults who love them
and take them seriously, and whom they can respect.
(Serious citizens may not respect Norman, but young people do, and do not respect the serious citizens; and their
instincts are quite sound.)

But I do not feel that a writer's responsibility can be
discharged in this way. I do not think, if one is a writer,
that one escapes it by trying to become something else.
One does *not* become something else: one becomes nothing. And what is crucial here is that the writer, however
unwillingly, always, somewhere, knows this. There is no
structure he can build strong enough to keep out this
self-knowledge. What *has* happened, however, time and
time again, is that the fantasy structure the writer builds
in order to escape his central responsibility operates not
as his fortress, but his prison, and he perishes within it.
Or: the structure he has built becomes so stifling, so lonely, so false, and acquires such a violent and dangerous
life of its own, that he can break out of it only by bringing the entire structure down. With a great crash, inevitably, and on his own head, and on the heads of those
closest to him. It is like smashing the windows one second before one asphyxiates; it is like burning down the
house in order, at last, to be free of it. And this, I think,
really, to touch upon it lightly, is the key to the events
at that monstrous, baffling, and so publicized party.
Nearly everyone in the world—or nearly everyone, at
least, in this extraordinary city—was there: policemen,
Mafia types, the people whom we quaintly refer to as
"beatniks," writers, actors, editors, politicians, and gossip columnists. It must be admitted that it was a consid-
erable achievement to have brought so many unlikely

types together under one roof; and, in spite of everything, I can't help wishing that I had been there to witness the mutual bewilderment. But the point is that no
politician would have dreamed of giving such a party in
order to launch his mayoralty campaign. Such an imagi-
native route is not usually an attribute of politicians. In
addition, the price one pays for pursuing any profession,
or calling, is an intimate knowledge of its ugly side. It is
scarcely worth observing that political activity is often,
to put it mildly, pungent, and I think that Norman, perhaps for the first time, really doubted his ability to deal
with such a world, and blindly struck his way out of it.
We do not, in this country now, have much taste for, or
any real sense of, the extremes human beings can reach;
time will improve us in this regard; but in the meantime
the general fear of experience is one of the reasons that
the American writer has so peculiarly difficult and dangerous a time.

One can never really see into the heart, the mind, the
soul of another. Norman is my very good friend, but perhaps I do not really understand him at all, and perhaps
everything I have tried to suggest in the foregoing is
false. I do not think so, but it may be. One thing, however, I am certain is *not* false, and that is simply the fact
of his being a writer, and the incalculable potential he
as a writer contains. His work, after all, is all that will be
left when the newspapers are yellowed, all the gossip
columnists silenced, and all the cocktail parties over, and
when Norman and you and I are dead. I know that this
point of view is not terribly fashionable these days, but I
think we *do* have a responsibility, not only to ourselves
and to our own time, but to those who are coming after
us. (I refuse to believe that no one is coming after us.)
And I suppose that this responsibility can only be discharged by dealing as truthfully as we know how with
our present fortunes, these present days. So that my concern with Norman, finally, has to do with how deeply he

has understood these last sad and stormy events. If he
has understood them, then he is richer and we are richer,
too; if he has not understood them, we are all much
poorer. For, though it clearly needs to be brought into
focus, he has a real vision of ourselves as we are, and it
cannot be too often repeated in this country now, that,
where there is no vision, the people perish.